THE GENESIS INQUIRY

THE GENESIS INQUIRY

OLLY JARVIS

This edition produced in Great Britain in 2021

by Hobeck Books Limited, Unit 14, Sugnall Business Centre, Sugnall, Stafford, Staffordshire, ST21 6NF

www.hobeck.net

A CIP catalogue for this book is available from the British Library.

ISBN 978-1-913-793-41-8

Cover design by Jem Butcher

www.jembutcherdesign.co.uk

Printed and bound in Great Britain by Clays Ltd, Elcograf S.p.A.

❦ Created with Vellum

For all of us

A people without the knowledge of their past history, origin and culture is like a tree without roots.

Marcus Garvey

Chapter One

Northumberland, northeast coast of England

Ella knew how the wind played tricks, but she was sure she could hear a car approaching. She pulled back the curtain on the van's side window and peered out into the darkness. She couldn't see anything in the field. No one else was fool enough to camp in March a couple of miles from the swirling winter gales of the northeast coast.

Tyres crunching on gravel. The sound grew louder and she watched as twin beams illuminated the dry-stone wall that snaked down the path onto the site.

The car stopped briefly at the end of the lane, then crossed the field, pulling up alongside her van. The headlights were switched off. A man got out. Ella could tell he was in a suit but couldn't make out his features in the darkness.

She watched him take his coat off the headrest and thrust his arms through the sleeves, battling with the buttons as the back and sides flapped and whooshed around him in the wind.

He squelched through the sodden ground towards the

van, doing a kind of jig as if in a hopeless attempt to keep his shoes dry.

Ella moved away from the window, anxiety engulfing her.

There was a tap on the door.

She didn't move.

'Miss Blake?' The voice was cockney. It sounded familiar. 'Miss Blake, it's me.'

'Jim?' The tension left her body. Why hadn't she recognised her clerk? But then in all the years she'd know him, she'd never seen him hop over a waterlogged field in the dark.

'Yes, ma'am, Jim Hodges.'

She slid open the door. 'Jim, what the hell are you doing here?'

Jim opened his mouth as if to explain, then shut it again. 'Can I come in, ma'am? It's blowing a gale out here.'

'Yes, of course, sorry, climb in.'

Jim stepped up into the van, falling sideways onto a leather seat. Ella pulled the sliding side door back into place then sat down on the other side of the pull-out table. 'Have you just driven up from London?'

'Yeah, took hours, bloody A1,' he said, inspecting the muck on his shoes. 'It was one lane half the time.'

The wind yawed around the van, pummelling the windows.

Ella opened a cupboard and pulled out a tumbler to accompany the one already on the table next to a half empty bottle of Courvoisier. She could feel Jim looking at the mud on her fleece.

'Just a small one, got to drive back in a bit.'

Ella had already guessed why he'd come, but she wasn't going to disappoint him before he'd even made himself comfortable.

'It's nice, cosy,' said Jim, patting the seat. 'But why...' he paused. 'If you don't mind me asking, ma'am, why would a

2

woman want to live alone in a van in the middle of nowhere when she's got a house in Belgravia?'

Ella sipped at her brandy and shrugged. 'Too many memories.'

He gave an awkward grimace. 'Ah, of course, sorry.'

'Nothing to apologise for.' In a way, she was pleased people were starting to forget.

'But what do you do all day?' he asked, looking around at the books lined up on shelves behind an elastic strip.

'Go for walks. Read. Think. Try and clear my head.'

'Has it worked?'

Ella glanced away. 'Not yet.'

Jim sat up straight. 'Look, ma'am, I've known you for over twenty years. I'd like to think…'

She watched him struggle to maintain eye contact.

'…we've become more than just a barrister and her clerk.'

'Then stop calling me ma'am,' Ella teased, remembering how he'd always stood by her, helped her become a QC, and had her back after it all happened.

'Force of habit, ma'am. Er… I mean Ella.' He blushed. 'I know the young clerks use first names now.'

Ella reached across and gave him a reassuring pat on the wrist. 'What is it, Jim? You've come a long way, let's have it.'

He took a deep breath. 'OK, here goes…'

Ella felt a wave of empathy for her old friend. He'd obviously been rehearsing his pitch all the way from London.

'Ma'am, it's been three years. It's time to stop beating yourself up.' He paused, then blurted, 'Is this whole retirement thing because of the complaint?'

'No.' She took a swig. 'Partly, I should never have come back so soon after—'

'But you didn't do anything wrong. You lost a case, so what?'

'A case I should've won. I should never have been back at work.' She stared him down. 'I wasn't in any fit state after…'

An awkward silence.

'But you must be ready now? You need your work, ma'am.'

Ella scoffed. 'I can't.'

'Why? You're the best silk in England.'

'Was,' corrected Ella.

'Why throw all that away? You're not even fifty, it's not too late to come back.'

Ella refilled her glass. 'I just don't give a shit anymore. That's the problem.' She took a large gulp of her drink. 'You have to live and breathe the courtroom if you're going to survive.'

'But—'

'No buts, Jim.' She could tell by the look on his face that a barrister and clerk impasse had been reached. 'Anyway, how did you know where to find me?' asked Ella.

'I didn't. Lizzie guessed.' He frowned. 'Why don't you ever answer your phone?'

'No reception.'

'Yeah, right,' Jim's voice was full of sarcasm. 'Look…' He took another deep breath. 'I've got a job for you.'

'I've just told you, I—'

'Hear me out,' Jim replied. 'It's not in the courtroom as such, it's an inquiry.'

Ella felt stressed even talking about work. 'What, like a government inquiry?'

'Nothing so grand, I'm afraid, internal, in a university, some sort of discipline issue, I think. Pays well.'

'Employment law?' Ella let out a hollow laugh. 'Haven't done that since I was a junior. And you took the trouble to come all the way up here for that? I thought you'd at least try me with a public inquiry, or a murder, or even a celebrity libel job. Something a bit sexier.'

'It's easy money.' Jim's back stiffened as if readying to play his ace. 'It's in Cambridge.'

Ella fell silent.

'Accommodation's paid for.' Then, in a hushed tone, he added, 'It means you could spend—'

'I know what it means.' Ella bit her lip. 'Sorry, I didn't mean to snap.' She took a sip. 'You're a good friend,' she said with a faint slur. 'I appreciate you coming all this way.'

'Does that mean you'll at least think about it?'

Ella managed a faraway smile. 'Sure, I will. Now come outside while I have a smoke.' She slid the door open and pulled a cigarette out of her pocket. 'Wind's eased off a bit.'

Once they were in the blackness, sheltering in the lee of the caravan from the biting coastal wind, she cupped the lighter and, after repeated attempts, sparked up.

'Seeing you dressed like this takes some getting used to,' said Jim, shivering beside her.

'Don't worry, got a two-piece and heels in the back of the van,' she replied. 'The old uniform.' She took a drag then exhaled. 'Look at that, constellation after constellation,' she said, staring up at the night sky. 'You won't see anything like that in London.'

'Jesus,' said Jim. 'Why are there so many?'

'No light pollution around here.'

'What the hell must people have thought, looking up at this thousands of years ago?'

'That the sky held all the secrets? Yeah, makes you feel pretty insignificant,' she replied.

They stood in silence, marvelling at the stars.

Chapter Two

The next day, Ella slid open the door and bathed her face in the morning sun. The wind blustered, delivering a crisp, farm-fresh fragrance.

Hiking and its solitude were the nearest Ella Blake came to a respite from her jagged memories. In the early days she'd tried to analyse what had happened from a lawyer's perspective, objectively. But it had all become too much.

Now it was easier just to block everything out.

Thoughts of Jim's visit swirled in her head as she sat on the metal step and pulled on her boots. It had been an uncomfortable reminder that she was going to have to face the world at some point. Weeks had turned into months and then years. She was already worried that her estrangement from the world she knew had reached the point of no return. She wasn't just ring-rusty, the law had moved on. How could she navigate her way through the confrontations and subtleties of a crown court trial when she couldn't even conduct a basic conversation with a stranger without feeling anxious?

She locked the van and set off along the footpath towards

the sea. The campsite was only a few miles from the coast. She looked forward to the simple routine of her morning walk. The rain had stopped, but angry clouds still threatened. The wind was making her nose run and her ears sting. She pulled her woolly hat further down and strode up towards the brow of the hill. As she neared the top, the glorious view down to the coast and the island of Lindisfarne opened up before her.

The clouds began to break up, allowing light to glisten off the morning dew, lifting her melancholy mood on the walk down to the causeway. Ella knew the tide tables backwards, arriving by 10 a.m., just in time to watch her favourite spectacle – the sea receding and magically revealing the road to Holy Island. She crossed on the pedestrian path, marked out by poles spaced along the sand. Once she was on the other side, she followed the road along the shoreline past the signs for tourists showing pictures of four-by-fours that left it too late to go back across, sitting marooned on the causeway, seawater up to the windows. She cut across the dunes and Lindisfarne Castle came into view, perched on a twirling, grassy rock.

After she'd climbed the steps to the top of the castle, to a backing track of squawking gulls, she rested. She found the rhythm of the gulls' unyielding wails soothing. From the top she could see for miles in every direction.

Looking out over the battlements, Ella could make out the distant shape of Bamburgh Castle on the mainland. She preferred the view below, of the island itself. She could see the remains of the ancient Priory in the village, a few hundred metres off. A surviving stone arch rose out of the remnants, framing the sky. This was a place that had always mattered to her, ever since childhood. She leaned over the battlements and stared out to sea, remembering her mother's mystical history lessons about the first Viking raid on the British Isles, a clash of two cultures. Ella wondered what those priests had thought in AD 793 when they saw a fleet of strange ships on the horizon. A portent for centuries of conflict.

Heading back down, she spotted Rob, the young hippie tour guide, doing his speech to a couple of off-season tourists at the castle entrance. 'Simeon of Durham recorded the terrible events,' he announced with a pompous puffing out of his chest and what Ella suspected was a hamming up of his Geordie accent. '*And they came to the church of Lindisfarne, laid everything waste with grievous plundering.*' He checked his notes, then continued his oration. '*They killed some of the brothers, took some away with them in fetters… some they drowned in the sea…*'

Ella made her way back towards the narrow stone staircase and along the shore past a couple of upturned rowing boats dragged high onto the beach into the marram grass. She breathed in the salty air and kicked a few stones off the path as she walked around the curved inlet. A couple of fishing boats sat listed and marooned by the tide on the wet sand, their chains draped in seaweed.

Try as she might, she couldn't seem to get Jim's words out of her head. Images of the Cambridge colleges in her mind's eye. She remembered her daughter's excited phone call about getting in. A rare moment of connection. And deep down, part of her knew she needed a new challenge.

She ambled past the cluster of houses that surrounded the ruins of the Priory to the Inn with its low, beamed ceiling and exposed, stone walls. Inside a fire was already roaring in the huge hearth, ready for the first customer of the day.

'Rum and coke, pet?' asked the old man behind the bar. She realised for the first time that she'd never bothered to ask his name.

'Double,' she replied. She slid onto a stool, reached into the pocket of her tatty Barbour and took out her phone. Two bars. She pressed contacts and scrolled down to "Lizzie". Her finger hovered over the screen for a moment, then pulled away. She pursed her lips.

Rob the tour guide came in and slid onto the stool next to her.

The barman poured a Guinness without speaking.

'Nice little tip from those Yanks, like,' said Rob with a satisfied sniff. Then he swivelled towards Ella. 'I googled you last night, lass.'

Eyes staring firmly ahead, Ella didn't respond.

He flicked his head up. 'Don't you want to know how I got your name – Ella Blake?'

She downed the rum. 'Same again.'

Rob smirked. 'Found this on the floor a couple of days ago,' he said, waving her credit card in front of her face. 'Must've dropped it after one of your sessions.' He was laughing now. 'Bit of a lush, aren't you?'

She bristled. Deep down she knew her drinking had made her vulnerable, weak. She hated who she'd become. She reached out to take back her card, but he pulled it away, then stopped, letting her snatch it from his hand.

'Seems you were a right ball-crusher back in the day, won some big cases?'

She didn't engage, hoping he would back off.

'What happened?' he goaded. 'How does a top QC end up getting pissed every day in an empty pub on a remote island?'

Ella continued to stare straight ahead, sipping at her drink.

Rob looked her up and down. 'You not going to thank me for the card?'

She ignored him.

'Arrogant bitch.'

'That's enough, Rob,' said the barman, who had been hovering within earshot.

Ella put down her glass and turned to face the young man, putting a hand on the bar. 'How come a bloke who comes in here every day banging on about his masters in early medieval history ends up working as a tour guide?' She gave a contemptuous shake of the head. 'Every day you recite your little quote from Simeon of Durham.' Her voice was getting louder. 'That was written hundreds of years after the invasion.' She stood up, her face inches from his. 'Why don't you quote from something written nearer the actual fucking time?'

The barman glanced at the startled guide.

Ella waited for a reaction.

Nothing.

'I bet you haven't even got a degree,' she said with a sneer.

Rob sneered. 'Who the fuck do you think you—'

'Save it,' she snapped, turning back to the bar. She downed the rest of her drink and slammed the glass down.

She felt Rob watching her every move, trying to regroup for a new attack.

Ella took a twenty out of her pocket and left it on the bar, heading purposefully towards the door.

Behind her she heard Rob get off his perch and follow her out. From the doorway, he called after her, 'Yeah, away, piss off. You're not welcome here.'

She walked off up the lane, a tirade of abuse piercing her back like an arrow.

'No one wants a dried-up old prune, anyway.'

Despite herself a tear fell, then more.

She trudged back towards the causeway. She hated that she couldn't control her emotions anymore. She'd never been like this before. People used to say she was a closed book; some even called her the ice queen.

She kept on walking, increasing her pace with every step as she crossed over to the mainland. She strode on over the top of the hill that overlooked the campsite and down the rocky path. Her foot slipped into a pothole causing her body to rocket forward; her outstretched arms did little to break her fall. There was a thud as she hit the uneven ground.

She lay sprawled out on the track, her eyes closed, despair sweeping through her like the tide. This was it, rock bottom. If that was where she'd wanted to go, she'd made it. Dark memories she'd kept at bay came flooding back. She lifted her head, her cheek studded with grit, and gave a deep guttural groan, then sobbed. She let her head drop back down. What reason did she have to get up? Lizzie danced across her mind in the pink fairy dress she'd worn to her seventh birthday party, waving the wand she'd loved so much. She got slowly to her feet and brushed the mud and stones off her clothes. Straightening up, she took in the patchwork quilt of undulating fields around her.

She couldn't stand another day of feeling numb.

It was now or never.

Chapter Three

Ella manoeuvred the campervan into a space at the front of the Gonville Hotel. It took a few attempts to straighten it up. She turned off the ignition and puffed out her cheeks, relieved the long drive was over. A few raindrops settled on the windscreen.

She made a half-hearted attempt to brush some specks of mud off her fleece, then leaned forward, studying her face in the rear-view mirror. As expected, the verdict wasn't good; she looked tired, dark circles under her eyes, her cheeks ruddy from a cocktail of whisky and weather. She turned her head slightly and touched the grey roots sprouting from her temple, making a mental note that she needed to sort out her colour. She wondered if she was too old to have long hair. She took a bobble out of the cup holder and pulled her hair back into a ponytail. She'd been letting things slide for too long, needed a complete overhaul.

There was a knock on the driver's window.

Ella jumped.

'You can't leave that here,' said an officious teenager in a doorman's livery.

It took a moment to get her bearings. 'I'm a guest,' she said, opening the door and climbing out. It was still spitting. 'I'm sure parking is included?' She slid open the side door and reached in for her bag and suit carrier.

The young man peered in at the rows of books.

'Maybe you could take this?' she asked, thrusting her luggage at him.

After an inspection of the outside of the van, then of her, he complied. He hunched his shoulders, as if in protection from the spots of rain that nestled onto his crisp white shirt, and waited for her to follow.

Ignoring the drizzle, she took in the view across the road towards Parker's Piece, a spacious flat green with groups of students milling around, chatting under their umbrellas. Others criss-crossed the paths with small knapsacks on their backs. She remembered the warm spring days when she'd been one of them, sitting cross-legged with friends, drinking Spumante. Another lifetime.

'That's the birthplace of Association football,' the young man offered.

'I know,' Ella replied, fully aware she was getting the standard patter. '1863.'

He gave her a double-take. 'You're a historian?'

'Sadly not,' she replied, staring wistfully across the open space at Hobbs' Cricket Pavilion. 'Just good with dates.'

She followed him across the forecourt and through the contemporary glass portico of the Georgian hotel.

'Thought you might be a professor or something?' he asked. 'With all those books?'

'No.' She was only half-listening. 'I'm a lawyer.'

The young man put the luggage down in reception and lingered for a tip.

'Ella Blake,' she said, turning her attention to a receptionist with hair up like a cottage loaf and a name tag on her blouse. 'I have a reservation.'

'Ah yes,' her eyes widened in awe. 'The QC?'

Ella gave her a plastic smile. She noticed the luggage kid blushing, so she took her wallet out of her back pocket and handed him a fiver.

He accepted the note without his former swagger.

'Here we are,' the receptionist said, reading off the computer. 'De Jure College are taking care of everything.' She handed Ella a key-card and gave an obsequious smile. 'Welcome to Cambridge, Miss Blake.'

Chapter Four

Ella paced her hotel room, took a deep breath then touched the contact name on her phone. Her stomach tightened as she heard the call being answered.

'Hi Mum, what's wrong?'

Ella had already forgotten her opening line. 'Why do you assume... never mind. How are you?'

'Good,' came the flat response. Then a reluctant sounding, 'You?'

'I'm good, thanks,' Ella replied with exaggerated enthusiasm.

Silence. Ella bit her lip. Their conversation was already out of steam. She stood at her window and closed her eyes, concentrating, readying herself to go again. 'Lizzie,' she said, trying her best to sound unrehearsed, 'I'm in Cambridge actually – for work.'

'Obviously,' Lizzie replied sharply. 'It wouldn't be to see me.'

The missile landed in Ella's gut, ripping it apart. 'No, Lizzie... I...' She floundered, eyes tightly shut, admonishing herself. 'I didn't mean—'

'Forget it,' Lizzie replied. 'I thought you'd retired?'

Ella fixed on the traffic beyond the car park but saw nothing. 'I have… I had.' More silence. 'I thought we could have dinner?'

No reply.

'I used to know a great Italian in Market Square.'

Eventually Lizzie spoke. 'Don Pasquale?'

'That's it,' Ella replied, realising she sounded more like an over-excited child than a mother.

'Yeah, it's still there.'

Ella convinced herself there was a microscopic hint of interest in Lizzie's nonchalant response. 'Tonight, say eight, I'll book a table?'

'Sure. That's doable.'

'Doable? You make it sound like a business meeting,' Ella said, then winced, wishing she could take it back.

'Ok, Mum, whatever.'

Ella felt herself sinking further. 'Sorry, ignore me,' she said, as if releasing an air bubble, fighting its way back to the surface. 'See you later.' She pressed "end call".

'You total idiot,' she shouted, covering her face with her hands and crumpling onto the bed.

Chapter Five

Ella saw Lizzie first, already sitting at the table, centre stage under a white, vaulted ceiling. The place was full and a term-time buzz hummed from lecturers and students leaning into their conversations.

A wave of regret washed over Ella seeing the apprehension on her daughter's face, her hands fiddling with a napkin. Ella weaved her way around the other diners, keeping a smile firmly fixed in place. 'Hi Lizzie,' she called out, using her best advocacy to hide her trepidation.

Lizzie didn't get up.

Ella bent down to administer a mumsy hug, but her shawl got in the way, making her feel like a squid enveloping its prey. She took a seat opposite her daughter. 'Place hasn't changed at all,' she observed, the tension now obvious. 'Still got the same tablecloths.'

Two faux smiles.

A waiter came over with a couple of menus and lit a red candle sticking out of a Chianti bottle.

An awkward wait for him to retreat.

Lizzie went first: 'I'm sure they've washed them since you were last here.'

Ella laughed, grateful for the connection. She took a deep breath. 'So, how are you, really?' The flame danced to the tune of her breath.

It drew Lizzie's focus. 'Happy.' She picked at the bottle, snapping off some wax.

'That's great,' Ella replied, studying her daughter's face for other clues.

Lizzie gave her mother a prickly stare. 'Where you staying?'

'The Gonville,' she announced in triumph. 'It seemed fitting with my brilliant daughter being at Gonville and Caius.'

Lizzie ignored the compliment. 'And what's the job?'

Ella put her elbows on the table, beginning to relax now that the exchange had gained some rhythm. 'Believe it or not, I don't really know much yet. An internal issue at one of the colleges, De Jure.'

One side of Lizzie's mouth curled upwards. 'You took your first job in three years and that's it?' Realisation spread across her face. 'Oh, I get it, because it's in Cambridge?'

Ella leaned in. 'I thought we could catch up… *properly*.'

Lizzie looked down and straightened her cutlery. 'It's a bit late, Mum.'

'It's never too late,' Ella almost shouted. Then, in a loud whisper: 'There's always a way back.'

'A way back?' Lizzie repeated. 'Interesting word choice.'

'It's not like you to be so cold,' Ella replied, locking into their familiar pattern.

Lizzie's eyes did a room scan. She said, in a louder voice, 'I learned from the master.'

Ella felt crushed. 'Please Lizzie, let's not do this?'

Lizzie pursed her lips then closed her eyes for a moment and exhaled.

The waiter saved them.

'Two diet cokes?' Ella suggested.

Lizzie shrugged her shoulders. 'Have what you want, Mum, I'm not your keeper?'

'OK,' Ella replied, fiddling with the tassels on her shawl. 'One diet coke and a large glass of Sauvignon Blanc.'

The waiter gave a slight bow and left.

Lizzie made an obvious inspection of her mother's face. 'You look different.'

'Really?' Ella replied, self-consciously brushing away a few strands of hair. 'I'm off the fags again, only been a couple of days.'

'No, it's your clothes, and—'

'I know,' Ella cut in, unable to stand more. 'I came straight from Lindisfarne in the van.'

Lizzie frowned. 'Why didn't you go home first?'

Ella felt her body shrink. As always, her daughter had got the better of her.

'If you hate the house that much,' said Lizzie, 'why don't you sell it, move somewhere else?'

Ella's thoughts lurched backwards and forwards. 'But, don't you want the memories?'

Lizzie looked bemused. 'It's your house, Mum.'

The waiter arrived with the drinks.

'Cheers!' Ella clinked Lizzie's glass, frantically trying to move the conversation on. 'So, met any nice men since you've been here?'

'Are you for real?' said Lizzie, throwing her head back. 'Is that really going to be your first foray about my time at Cambridge?'

Ella's shoulders dropped. 'I'm sorry, you're right, trying too hard.'

Lizzie gave an affirming nod.

The flame stopped dancing.

Ella dropped her shawl onto the back of her chair and started again. 'Tell me about the course?' Encouraged by the twitch of excitement around Lizzie's mouth, she said, 'Three years of history, you're so lucky.'

'It's incredible,' Lizzie replied, suddenly animated. 'I'm learning so much – trying to answer the big questions – I'm loving it.'

Ella's eyes moistened. 'The big questions?'

'Come on, you know that's what Cambridge is all about, Mum,' she gushed, seeming relieved to be free of their normally guarded interaction.

Moved, Ella reached out to touch Lizzie's hand. 'I'm so proud of you.'

For a moment there was peace, at ease with their shared history.

There was always a way back.

Chapter Six

Ella had bought a new pin–striped trouser suit and some flats for her meeting at De Jure. Even without wearing stilettos it felt odd to be dressing for work after so long.

King's Parade hadn't changed at all. The sight still took her breath away. The white, limestone spires and gothic detail made the colleges seem unreal, like a movie set. She crossed the street to get a better look at the immaculate lawns of King's College until someone shouting 'move' made her jump onto the pavement. A line of bicycles flew past, prompting a flurry of memories. She'd been so happy when she'd been a student here, not a care in the world.

She dodged her way back across the road and into the cobbled entrance to De Jure. Her eyes were immediately drawn to the view of the huge courtyard with its bedded rose bushes bordering a grass square.

'Miss Blake?' A little, balding man poked his head out of a tiny archway leading to a small office. His round belly pushed at his shirt, revealing slits of white skin between the buttons. He brushed a few flakes of pastry from around his mouth.

'Yes, that's me.' She could see a Gregg's paper bag poking out of his trouser pocket.

'I'm Bartlett, one of the porters,' he said. 'Follow me, please.'

She waited for him to shuffle past and fell in behind. They crossed the courtyard then under a low, medieval arch built at a time when men were shorter, and into another, smaller courtyard. A few bleary-eyed students trudged across the open space in dressing gowns.

'No en suites here,' he said by way of explanation. 'That's the price you pay if you want to be in fourteenth-century accommodation.'

Ella laughed, hurrying to keep up.

After a few more turns and a climb up a stone staircase, they were at the Master's office. The porter knocked at the door.

A voice from inside said, 'Come.'

'Miss Blake, sir.'

'Thank you, come in Miss Blake, welcome.' A middle-aged man, impeccably dressed in a charcoal grey suit, held out his hand. 'John Desmond, Master of De Jure.'

Ella was pleasantly surprised by his firm handshake. He wasn't the stereotypical academic Ella remembered. The days of scruffy professors seemed to have gone. She scanned the room, taking in the framed certificates on the walls, amongst them a photo of John Desmond in a gown and mortar board. There was an ornate, Victorian fireplace and bookshelves either side of an oval window looking onto the main courtyard.

'Please,' he said, pointing to an antique chair in front of a tidy, mahogany desk.

'Thank you,' She sat down and crossed her legs – an automatic posture from the days when confidence at meetings was everything.

'Miss Blake,' he began. 'Or should I call you *Mrs* Blake?'

She flinched. Did he know? 'Ella's fine.'

'Ok, Ella,' he said deliberately, seemingly uncomfortable digressing from the usual etiquette. 'We are hugely honoured that you have agreed to take this... brief.'

'Not at all, the honour is all mine.'

Desmond gave a grateful smile. He leaned forward on his elbows. 'Your alma mater was Newnham College, I believe?'

'It was,' she replied, wondering what else he knew. 'So, you've done your homework?'

'Homework is our business,' he said, arching back in a superior pose.

They both laughed without sincerity in their voices.

'I must apologise for all the cloak and dagger,' he said, his hand movements losing a little of their finesse. 'I'm sure you're not used to taking a job where you've been told so little?'

'It's fine,' she replied. 'You can fill me in now, unless there is a written brief to counsel?'

He tapped a finger on the flimsy file on his desk. 'Perhaps I should begin by saying that this is very sensitive.' He lowered his voice: 'The reputation of the college and the wider university is of the greatest importance to our continued success.'

'Understood.' She'd lost count of the number of times new instructions had begun with that speech.

'We had – have,' he corrected, 'an academic at De Jure called Matthew Shepherd.' Desmond adjusted his posture. 'He left a few weeks ago.'

'Left?'

'Well actually, that's the issue here.' He cleared his throat. 'He disappeared.'

'I see.' She decided to let him tell her more before pressing him on her role. She deduced by his worried expression that this disappearance wasn't a case of going on holiday and not telling anyone.

He continued, 'There was a police enquiry, obviously very thorough, and they concluded that he left of his own accord.'

'That there was nothing untoward?'

'Exactly. Apparently, he just packed a bag and went.'

'I see,' Ella replied. 'What's his discipline?'

Desmond took his time formulating a reply. 'He doesn't really have one, not in the traditional sense.'

'Really?' Ella said, being drawn in for the first time.

'He had degrees in European history, astrophysics and numerous languages, and all before he was eighteen.' He took a breath, then said more slowly: 'Matthew was a true polymath, he transcended the concept of subject headings – thought outside the box.'

'Wow.' Ella didn't know what else to say.

'Wow indeed,' he replied. 'He is, in my opinion,' he said, lowering his head and raising a finger for emphasis, 'and that of many others, the greatest polymath since da Vinci.'

'Really?'

'Well, maybe not Da Vinci,' Desmond corrected. 'Certainly, since Newton.'

Ella shot him a quizzical glance. 'Why haven't I heard of him?'

'He shuns publicity and he's not published anything for some time,' he said. 'Not his thing.' His expression was one of resigned pragmatism. 'He's been with us for almost ten years, on one of our special bursaries. We just let him get on with it.' He stopped as if to consider the policy for the first time. 'Attracting someone like Matthew under our umbrella was of huge importance to us. You have to understand, these people come along once or twice in a millennium.' He was in full lecture mode now. 'Having him here reminds us what Cambridge is all about.'

'You've no idea what he was working on in all that time?'

Desmond rubbed his chin. 'Like all polymaths, he was trying to answer the big questions.'

She raised her eyebrows. 'The big questions?' She remembered Lizzie's use of the phrase. 'What does that mean?'

He smiled, as if about to explain something to a child. 'How and why?'

'How and why?'

'Yes,' he replied as if these were the questions that everyone was asking.

It took Ella a moment to refocus on controlling the meeting. 'Have you got any of his devices, laptops?'

'We think he had one phone and one laptop; he took them with him.' Desmond was back in business mode now.

'The police report?'

'They won't part with it – legal reasons apparently.'

Considering this, she glanced over at an eighteenth-century portrait on the wall of some noble gent in a red hunting jacket with a riding crop by his thigh, standing proud and looking off into the middle distance. She fixed her gaze on the Master again. 'So, where do I come in?'

He sat back, clearly a man comfortable giving orders. 'We would like you to chair an internal inquiry, on behalf of the university – to find out what happened to Matthew – and write a report.' Leaning forward he said, 'We're very worried about him.'

Ella decided to go through the motions of subservient lawyer. 'The police don't know where he is?'

'No.'

'Has anyone heard from him?'

'No, nothing, the trail went cold on the day he disappeared.'

'I'm confused.' Her brow furrowed. 'Why me, why not hire an investigator?'

'There are other matters to consider.'

'As his employer?'

'Yes.' He sighed. 'This is new ground for us. There are legal issues: do we stop paying his wages? Was he having some kind of breakdown? What are our obligations?'

Something didn't feel right. 'So, what is the exact remit of this inquiry?'

Desmond opened a folder in front of him and slid the top page across the desk.

Ella picked it up and read aloud: 'One, where is Matthew Shepherd? Two, why did he leave?' She paused. 'Why number three?'

'What was he working on when he disappeared? We'd like to know because strictly speaking, that's the property of the university.'

Ella got up and began to pace the room while she decided on her next step. 'Can I speak plainly?'

'Of course.'

'You already have a police report saying there was no foul play,' she said, vocalising her thoughts as she worked them through. 'Your obligations to this man finished the moment he abandoned his post.'

Desmond's eyes followed her around the room, but he didn't comment on her observations.

'There's no real need for an inquiry,' she said, watching Desmond carefully. 'Certainly not chaired by someone from outside the college.'

Still no comment.

She frowned. 'An inquiry is the last thing you'd want. All that publicity…?' Although rusty, her analytical mind was beginning to get into gear. 'Unless someone was putting pressure on De Jure?'

Desmond's eyes flickered.

'Someone who was unhappy with the police findings?'

26

Desmond nodded. 'Impressive. His brother, Cameron, he's in Arizona. Non-profit lawyer and a politician, the worst combination.' He looked at Ella. 'No offence.'

'None taken,' she replied without emotion.

'Been making a lot of noise. He will want to speak to the inquiry. Quite a big wig apparently. I'm told he could be the next state governor.'

She was still thinking it through. 'So, you instructed me because of my reputation as a barrister?'

'In part,' he replied,

'You thought that would calm the waters and placate any conspiracy theorists?'

He picked up a fountain pen and began to rotate it with his fingers. 'You understand university politics, Miss Blake.'

'And his brother thinks whatever he was working on is connected to his disappearance?'

Desmond carefully placed the pen back on the desk. 'He does,' he replied, sighing.

Ella stopped pacing and fixed Desmond with one of her adversarial stares. 'Do you?'

He didn't return the eye contact. 'I really don't know.' He held out his palms. 'Matthew was unique, possibly mildly autistic or aspergic, some would say lacking in empathy, or at least social skills. Going off without telling anyone couldn't be said to be entirely out of character.' He returned her gaze now. 'That may be difficult for his brother to hear.'

Ella could see how troubled he was by it all. She dreaded the answer to her next question. 'But why me? You must be aware that I haven't accepted any work for three years? You'd never request someone who'd been out of the game for so long, unless…' She stopped. 'Unless I had some special skill?'

Desmond stood up and walked around the desk to face her. 'You came highly recommended. And you have a PhD in history,' he replied, as if the answer was obvious.

She looked at him, surprised. 'That was over twenty years ago.'

Desmond was unruffled by her derision. 'I'm told you read everything.' He rested an elbow on the mantelpiece. 'We think whatever Matthew was working on had some connection with world history.'

'Which period?' she asked, finding herself becoming intrigued.

Desmond shrugged. 'All of it.'

Ella scoffed. 'How do you know?'

'Many of the books he was borrowing from the libraries are still in his room.'

Ella fell silent, trying to take it all in. This brief was definitely a first. 'So, who recommended me?'

'Oh,' he replied, sounding matter-of-fact. 'One of our professors, he's on the committee, Simon Carter.'

She smiled. It had been a while since she'd heard that name. 'I should've guessed.' She stared through the oval window at the cotton wool clouds.

Desmond put a hand on a binder on the desk. 'The police contact is in this file, a young detective called McDonald.'

Ella glanced at the folder. 'Do you have a photo of Matthew?'

He opened it and handed her his picture.

She studied the mugshot, taken in some passport booth. 'He's young?'

'Yes, thirty-two, a US national, from Arizona. Father was African American. Both parents are dead.' He got up and walked around the desk. 'Any questions, my details are in there,' he said, handing her the file.

'Thanks,' she replied, still thinking about Simon. 'Is the inquiry confidential?'

'We've discussed that in committee. Not the fact of the inquiry...' he said, wagging a finger a little too close to her face. 'That would go against our policy of transparency at De Jure, but for now, your findings should be.'

'Makes sense,' she replied, putting more space between her and his finger.

'Of course, you know what De Jure means, Miss Blake?'

'Yes, it's Latin – *according to law*,' she replied.

Desmond seemed reassured. 'That's how we do things here.'

She blinked. 'Of course.'

'Right,' he said, moving back around the desk and opening one of the drawers. 'Here are the keys to Matthew's rooms, Bartlett will show you there,' he said, ushering her towards the door. 'We're hoping you'll have this wrapped up very quickly, I know how you barristers work.' He opened the door and signalled to the porter who was waiting down the narrow corridor.

'Hang on,' Ella protested as she took the keys and dropped them in her tote. 'Can you tell me a little more. I don't know anything about him.'

'No one does, I'm afraid, he was a very private man.'

'At least tell me if he had any particular interests, apart from *history*?' she asked, pausing in the doorway.

Desmond was silent for a moment, tapping his chin. 'The ancient Greeks, Aristotle, for one. It's no exaggeration to say Matthew was obsessed with him, and Plato.' He looked down the corridor. 'Mr Bartlett, would you mind taking Miss Blake to Mr Shepherd's rooms?'

Bartlett gave an almost imperceptible bow. 'This way, ma'am.'

'Oh, and don't forget this,' Desmond called after her. 'It's a pass, access all areas, in case you need the college libraries, many are open around the clock.'

Chapter Seven

Lizzie Blake had one of the best rooms in her halls of residence, but it was the terrace leading onto the gardens of the Stephen Hawking Building that she loved the most. And she had her favourite seat. It was the perfect place to read, although today reading was proving challenging.

A few spots of rain landed on her copy of Homer's *Iliad* and soaked into the page. Holding it closed with her finger as a bookmark, she let it drop into her lap and peered over the top of her reading glasses. The gardener, Jay, in brown dungarees and heavy boots, was messing with an upturned mower, preparing for the first cut of the year. He was tall and lithe. His thick, straight black hair and faintly dusky skin tone made his ethnicity hard to place.

She liked to watch him nurturing his surroundings, totally immersed in his work. Something made him look up. He gave a bashful smile.

Lizzie blushed.

He raised an arm and waved.

In panic, she held her book up and opened it as a screen, pulse racing. With so many available undergrads, their tongues hanging out like hungry puppies, she couldn't understand why she fancied the college gardener. There was just something about him. A force pulling her to him, even though they'd hardly spoken.

She watched him saunter across the lawn towards the shed, her mind lurching from him to her latest essay and finally, inevitably, to her mother. Lizzie didn't want her here, pulling her back into the abyss. Was she being selfish? She felt guilty. She got up, put the book in her backpack and set off towards the rows of bicycles on the stand outside the halls, fiddling anxiously with the straps of her bag. She unlocked her bike and wrapped the chain around the bar underneath the saddle.

'Morning, Lizzie.'

She looked up.

Jay was pushing a green wheelie bin in her direction.

'Morning, Jay,' she replied. She stole a lingering look at his face. He was young, like her – twenty at most.

He gave her a shy half-smile as he passed.

'Nice and sunny,' she spluttered, determined this time to make their conversation last more than a few words.

He stopped. 'Yes,' he replied with a fuller smile. 'Makes my job easier. Off to a lecture?'

'To see my tutor.' She found herself pointing in the direction of Cambridge town centre.

'I know where the college is,' he replied. 'I do some work there too, you know, maintaining the courtyards.'

'Oh, right of course.' She felt a fool. 'Such beautiful surroundings.'

He put his hands in his pockets then took them out again. 'Yes, we're very lucky.'

She couldn't tell if he was being ironic. 'Well, better get on,' she said, chastising herself for being unable to cope with the intensity of the encounter. She got on her bike and cycled off down the road, then slowed, falling into line behind the rows of cyclists waiting at the lights.

She could feel her heart beating. She looked over her shoulder but Jay was gone. The lights changed and she pedalled hard across the Backs, crossing over one of the bridges spanning the Cam. Her bike chain's clanking grind was getting worse. Distracted by the noise she came out onto Trinity Street, then there was an almighty crash.

She found herself on the ground.

'Oh my God, are you OK?' A young man was lying beside her, tangled up in his own bicycle. 'I'm sorry, you came out of nowhere.'

Lizzie sat up and touched her forehead, then checked her hand for blood. 'I'm all right.'

'Thank God, I'm so sorry,' he said, untangling himself and getting to his feet.

'It's my fault,' she replied, still dazed. 'I wasn't looking.' Across the road, a group of Chinese students stopped and watched them, whispering excitedly to one another.

The man crouched down and gently pulled her up. 'OK?'

She nodded, looking nervously around at the gathering crowd.

With an appealing self-assurance he lightly brushed some dirt off the front of her jeans, picked up her bike, then stood astride the front wheel and began straightening the handlebars. 'Nothing to see here,' he said, laughing at the spectators who began to disperse. 'At least let me take you for elevenses?' he asked, followed by a carefree grin.

She giggled. 'Haven't heard that phrase for years.'

He laughed.

She looked at her shoes. 'I haven't really got time.'

He bent his knees to make eye contact. 'Not even ten minutes, just to make sure you haven't got concussion?'

She looked up and gave a nervous smile. 'OK,' she replied. 'Why not.'

He grinned again and picked up her bike. 'That should do it,' he said, showing her that the bars were aligned.

They wheeled the cycles to a stand and went into the nearest coffee shop. He helped her to a table by the window. 'Coke or tea?' he offered. 'You need sugar for the shock.'

'Tea, please.' She watched him order from the waitress with an easy confidence. It felt refreshing to be with a stranger, someone who didn't know what a loner she was, that she hadn't even been on a date in the two terms she'd been at Cambridge. Perhaps this could be a chance to reinvent herself. Become someone that goes to parties and plays drinking games. Be one of those people that clamber back through the gardens at 3 a.m. laughing like a hyena.

'I'm Greg by the way, Greg Brooks.' He reached across the table to shake her hand.

She did the same. 'Lizzie Blake.'

'Undergrad?'

'Yeah, history at Gonville and Caius,' she replied. 'You?'

'Postgrad, international politics at Wolfson.'

'Ah,' she said, half-closing one eye. 'Then I know you must be over twenty-one.'

'Twenty-five, the eternal student, I'm afraid.'

She studied his face, strong but kind. 'There're worse crimes.'

Chapter Eight

E lla reflected on the briefing as she tried to keep pace with Bartlett, feeling unnerved. It felt strange to be working again, but she tried to dismiss her anxieties. She caught up with the porter. 'Did you know Mr Shepherd?'

'Not to talk to, ma'am,' he replied, without altering his pace. 'I'd see him out and about.' They turned onto another corridor connecting two buildings which had tall, stained glass windows on either side. 'Not one for eye-contact, like all the brainy ones, if you know what I mean?'

'Bit of a loner, was he?'

They moved to the side of the corridor to let a group of cleaners with mops and buckets pass by. 'Verging on creepy if you ask me, but then you don't get here by being a party animal, do you?'

Ella laughed. 'I suppose not.'

They walked on and then he stopped. 'This is it,' he said, touching the highest lock on the door. 'The two silver ones at the top, brown at the bottom.'

'Bit over the top, isn't it?' she said, getting the keys out of her bag. 'He was paranoid, wasn't he?' She went through the locks, finally managing to open the door. A damp, unlived-in smell filled her nostrils. She instinctively put a hand over her nose.

'It's been left pretty much as it was,' Bartlett explained, seeming unaffected by the musty smell. 'Maybe once you're done, we can tidy up, move his stuff.' He scratched his head. 'God knows where to though.'

The main room was full of books, on floor-to-ceiling shelves and piled around the floor. The wallpaper had a seventies pattern of dots and lines. A huge desk and chair dominated the room, and there were a couple of gas rings on a trunk in the corner. She could see through an open door on the other side of the room that there was a tiny, sparse bedroom off the main area and small bathroom with shower and toilet. 'He lived like an undergrad,' she said, taking photos with her phone.

'It was all about his work, wasn't it? No need for anything else. We'd see his light on from the courtyard. Stayed on for days at a time.' He gave the room a cursory glance. 'For years he lived here. Years and years, but he was only young.'

She opened the file. 'Thirty-two.'

'Young to me,' he scoffed.

'And me.'

'Well, I'll leave you to it, ma'am,' he said on his way out of the door.

'Thanks for all your help, Mr Bartlett, appreciate it.'

He touched his forehead.

Ella shut the door behind him, then, beginning to acclimatise, stood, hands on hips, taking in her task. On impulse, she opened the mini-fridge and was greeted by another stench, forcing her backwards, more powerful than the last. She slammed it shut as she caught sight of a carton of milk and some green cheese. She moved a stack of books off a three-legged stool in the corner of the room and sat down to recover.

There was something curiously familiar about her surroundings. She couldn't quite put her finger on it. Who was this man? Had he been as unhappy as her? Maybe it was suicide. An involuntary tear caught her by surprise. She chastised herself and stood up, instinctively dusting herself down before beginning a systematic scouring of the shelves and piles of reading material stacked up like some bizarre rock formation. No order to anything. Books on every subject: all aspects of science, the natural world, history, religion, and countless biographies on the life and works of all the greats – Newton, Einstein, Plato, Confucius and many others.

In one corner, piled on the floor, one particular stack caught her eye. Desmond had been right – all were about the ancient Greeks. She picked one up. It was a translation of Aristotle's *On The Heavens*. She flicked through, marvelling that his thoughts had travelled across several millennia. She put the book in her handbag.

After the laborious process of locking up, Ella headed back down through the courtyards, weaving her way around groups of students laughing and chatting or staring at their phones. She waved at Bartlett as she passed the porter's lodge then went out onto Trumpington Street.

She walked down to King's Parade, wondering whether it was too early for a drink, but, stiffening her resolve, decided to get back to the Gonville so she could study the file and formulate a plan of action.

Bikes streamed up and down King's Parade with bells ringing as pedestrians shimmied across the road. Ella loitered outside a newsagent for a few minutes, then finally succumbed to her craving, going in to buy a pack of B & H Silver and a lighter. She stuck her card on the contactless terminal, distracted momentarily by a muffled radio broadcast from behind the counter.

Another American Navy frigate has been sent to the Gulf as tensions esca-late between Iran and the USA.

She raced for the exit and sparked up. A long drag was followed by a rare moment of calm, then, furious with herself, she flicked the cigarette in the gutter and used a foot to stub it. She scrunched up the packet and tossed it in the bin, then went on her way, gazing into the windows of the coffee shops, captivated by the enthusiastic young faces, bursting with chatter.

Then something, someone, caught her eye – it made her jolt – Lizzie, deep in conversation with a man. Transfixed by the sight of this young woman, her only child, Ella began to well up. She moved towards the door, then stopped, impulse overruled.

'Ella?' A voice from behind interrupted her thoughts.

She spun around. 'Simon!'

She stood motionless for a split second, a thousand memo-ries flooding back, followed by an awkward embrace.

'I'm so pleased I caught you,' he said. 'I wanted to come to the meeting, but you know how it is?'

'Don't worry about it,' she said, recovering from the momentary intimacy. 'I should thank you for getting me the gig.'

He gave a nonchalant wave. 'I know it's way beneath your usual—'

She cut him off, suddenly realising the motive. 'But it gives me a chance to catch up with Lizzie.' She felt a tenderness for him.

He raised his arms in surrender. 'Guilty.'

She laughed. 'I'm glad, thank you. I saw her last night.'

He looked surprised. 'That's great.'

Preliminaries over, there was an embarrassing silence. Too much had gone unsaid.

'Simon, I'm sorry about not being in touch, I—'

'It's fine.' He touched her arm. 'You've had a lot to deal with, and anyway, I get it, I was more Tom's friend, you didn't need reminding.'

She was glad he understood. Any remaining tension dissipated. 'Thank you,' she said.

'I suppose it's far too early for a drink?' he asked. 'I'd love to hear what you make of the assignment?'

'I won't tell if you won't,' she replied, putting an arm through his. 'I'm hooked! Did you know Matthew Shepherd?'

'Drink first.' He guided her towards The Eagle on Bene't Street. 'Still on the Sauvignon?'

She chuckled. 'You've got a good memory.'

The stone slabs in the entrance had been smoothed over time by a million feet, including Ella's. She found a table and watched Simon order at the bar. The walls were dark, wood panelled to shoulder height with old brick above. She gazed up at the old wooden oar on a dado rail, a trophy from some long-forgotten race.

'You always did like this spot,' he said, arriving with the drinks. 'Bet you haven't been here for a while?'

'At least twenty years,' she replied, still taking it all in. 'Hasn't changed a bit.'

'Cambridge doesn't,' he said, having to raise his voice above the chatter. 'It's timeless. Only the ideas move on.'

She could see how much he loved the place. She envied him his life of stress-free academia.

He sat down and swigged at his pint, leaving a white moustache which he wiped off. 'In answer to your question, yes, I met Matthew a few times. Seems ridiculous when he'd been here years, but he was a recluse, living in that little room, never spoke to anyone.'

She took a sip, careful not to glug, then put the glass on the table, using her forefinger and thumb to rotate the stem. 'Is he really a genius?'

Simon shrugged. 'That's what they say. I really don't know anything about him. I have a couple of friends who knew him vaguely at Yale, when he was a bit more forthcoming.'

'And?' She took another sip.

'They said he believed the answers were already out there, in history.'

Her nose creased up. 'Answers to what? What does that mean?'

'I don't know.' He shrugged. 'He was a theorist,' Simon explained. 'Big concepts. It's a different way of thinking.'

She watched him down his pint. 'This is all too wishy-washy for me. I'm a good old-fashioned lawyer, I like straight-forward facts.'

'Nonsense,' he replied. 'You always loved history. I never understood why you switched to law, that was always my thing.'

She sighed. 'I often think about that.'

'Nobody knew more about the Anglo-Saxons than you.'

'Yeah well, I needed to earn a living and it quickly became clear Tom wasn't going to.'

'Yeah, he was a real one-off,' he replied, without humour. 'And how we loved him.'

Their eyes met.

Chapter Nine

Lizzie cycled back after her tutorial and padlocked her bike outside the Stephen Hawking Building, engrossed in thoughts of what to wear for her date with Greg. He'd suggested they meet up again that evening and, though she was determined not to try too hard, she couldn't wait.

'How was your day?' It was Jay, pushing a wheelbarrow full of leaves. Was it coincidence that he was always there?

'Good thanks,' she replied, without stopping.

'Lizzie?' He put down the barrow and called after her. 'I was wondering if...' he shifted nervously from one foot to the other, '...could I ask a favour?'

'In a bit of a rush,' she replied. 'Can we talk tomorrow?' The question didn't require a response.

Jay picked up the handles and walked on.

By the time Lizzie got to her room, the tiny pang of guilt about snubbing him had grown. It was an emotion she knew well. She shook it off and started to go through her wardrobe, taking out a blouse and holding it against herself in front of the mirror. She turned and gazed out of the window, scanning the gardens for Jay. She couldn't see him.

Chapter Ten

Ella tapped in the number she'd found in the file, then paced up and down her hotel room.

'Hello?'

'Hi, is that Cameron Shepherd?'

'Yeah, who's this?'

'It's Ella Blake, I'm chairing the De Jure College Inquiry into your brother's disappearance.' She gave him a few seconds to digest. 'I'd like to ask you some questions about Matthew?' She waited.

'I guess they hired you to shut me up?'

She could hear his Arizona accent. 'You guessed right, but it won't work. I'm going to find out what happened to him.'

There was no response. Ella waited.

'Not on the phone. I'll come as soon as I can get a flight.'

'From Arizona?' Her heart sank. Desmond had been right; this man was going to make a nuisance of himself.

'There's a red-eye from Phoenix – it gets into Heathrow Friday morning. I'll get a train from there.'

'Great,' Ella replied with fake enthusiasm.

'But let's not meet at the university.'

'OK…' she replied. 'Come to the Gonville Hotel.'

'Sounds good. I'm googling you right now, a hot shot lawyer, I like it.'

Ella began to relax. 'It's a while since I've been called that.'

'You got anything yet?'

'No, but I've only just started. I'd appreciate any input, from one lawyer to another?'

'Plenty. Find out who kept breaking into his room?'

She sat down on the bed. 'When? That's not in anything I've seen.'

'There was no evidence, no forced locks, real pros. He knew he couldn't stop it; he was scared. I told that guy Desmond – after Matthew went missing.' She could hear his frustration. 'They think he was paranoid, nuts.'

'I've heard phrases like aspergic and autistic,' Ella recalled. 'Lacking empathy.'

Cameron huffed. 'Bullshit. Labels don't work with a guy like Matthew, he's different because he is an outstanding mind, that's hard to live with.' A pause. 'To me he's just my little bro.'

Before she had a chance to ask, he answered. 'He wouldn't just vanish for this long without making contact. I know my brother.'

'Do you have any idea what he was working on?'

A slight pause. 'No. All I know is that it was important. There was this one time he phoned me, few months ago, all fired up. Said he'd found a new way of looking at it.'

'At what?'

'I don't know. He said he got the idea from the case of some British serial killer from the eighties.'

Ella thought for a moment. 'Peter Sutcliffe?'

'Yeah, that's it… The Yorkshire Ripper?'

'That's right,' she replied.

'He kept saying, elementary my dear Watson, repeating it over and over.'

Ella made a note.

'I said to him, sounds like you got it, Sherlock. He found that real funny.' Cameron laughed, but it quickly began to sound more like a sob.

'Let's save the rest for Friday,' Ella said. Her heart went out to him. She knew all about loss. 'Oh, one last thing, if you've got any video recordings of Matthew, I'd love to see them. I have no real sense of who he was.'

'See what I can find,' he replied, sounding more composed. 'And Miss Blake, be careful.' He ended the call.

Cameron Shepherd puffed out his cheeks and leaned back in his chair. The Arizona sun sliced through the slats on the blind, making yellow lines across his office. He had a view of the rest of the firm through the glass walls that sectioned off his workspace. His desk was covered in papers. He hadn't been able to concentrate for some time, or sleep. It would all just have to wait.

He watched the other lawyers and their staff bustling around to a background noise of ringing phones. He tapped his fingers on the desk and looked down at the drawer. Maybe he should've actually told her about the letter? Maybe he should've given it to Desmond or that English policeman weeks ago, but his instincts said not to. It wasn't like he understood it.

He slid the key out of his pocket, unlocked the drawer and took out the envelope, date stamped three weeks ago. The paper was creased from handling it so much. He opened it and read the contents for the hundredth time.

Bro, if anything happens, trust your instincts — you'll know when and who to give this to. He and I are the inverse of here and there.

It still made no sense to him.

He and I are the inverse of here and there?

He was oblivious to the phone on his desk ringing out.

'Sir?' His secretary was leaning through the half open door. 'Sir?'

Still miles away he looked up. 'Sorry, what is it?'

'Your meeting's here, the Stupskis?' She leaned her head forward. 'You OK?'

'Yeah,' he replied, gathering himself. 'Rough night.'

He put the letter back in the drawer and waited for her to leave before locking it.

Chapter Eleven

Lizzie rolled over onto her front and rested on her elbows, playing with the hairs on Greg's chest. 'You do realise…?' She gazed into his eyes daring to wonder if they were on the same wavelength.

He played with her hair. 'That we only met today?'

She gave a coy smile. 'How did you know I was going to say that?'

He rolled onto his side and kissed her nose. 'Great minds.'

She kissed him back. 'You don't think it's happening too quickly.'

He ran his hand down her bare back and rested it on her bottom. 'When you know, you know.'

She felt her body flush.

'Does that scare you?' he asked.

'No,' she replied, wanting to reassure him. 'There's just so much going on at the moment.'

The faint lines on his forehead formed into ridges. 'Like what?'

For a split second Jay passed through the back of her mind. 'My mum's in town.'

'I sense that's a bad thing?' he asked, sitting up against the headboard.

She did the same and pulled the sheet up over their naked bodies. 'No… yes, maybe. It's complicated.'

He picked up the wine glasses on the bedside table and handed her one. 'You're not close?'

She took a sip. 'We were, once.'

'Families, it's never easy.'

She leaned across and kissed his lips, then pulled back and examined his face, the contours, his easy smile.

He returned her gaze. 'What?'

She had to look away. 'I've got to have dinner with her tomorrow night.'

'Do you want me to come?'

She looked at him again. 'I don't want to freak you out.' She slapped her forehead. 'Forget I said anything, it's too soon.' She covered her eyes.

He pulled her hand away. 'I'd love to.'

'Really?' She beamed.

'Course. I could just come as your friend, right? Not your *special* friend.' He winked.

She giggled.

'What does she do, anyway?'

'Not much.' She leaned back against the headboard. 'Used to be a top barrister.'

His eyes widened. 'Not Ella Blake?'

She looked at him again. 'You've heard of her?'

'Of course. Wait a minute, she's not here about that poly-math from De Jure?'

'I don't know, what do you mean?'

'Everyone's talking about it. Some super-secret academic went missing. They've hired a QC to chair some sort of inquiry about it. It's got to be her.'

She found herself resenting his interest in her mother. Always second fiddle. 'Sounds like it, I know it's at De Jure.'

'That's a big job,' he said, stroking her leg under the duvet. 'You know what that means?'

'What?'

'Your mum's going to be here for a while.'

She had a feeling of dread.

Chapter Twelve

The bar in the Gonville was empty. She chose an armchair by the window while she waited for her four o'clock to arrive and opened up the book she'd bought on the Yorkshire Ripper. She remembered the case well, as a child, how the whole of the North of England had lived in fear. The case had become infamous, not just because of Sutcliffe's thirteen victims, but because it had taken the police six years to catch him.

Reading the details of his crimes was chilling, but she couldn't see how there was any link to Aristotle, or any other polymath.

'Miss Blake?'

'Yes?'

A smartly dressed man with short hair, parted neatly at the side, stood before her. He wore a serious, business-like expression. 'DC McDonald, Cambridgeshire Police.'

Ella got up. Her first thought was that he was too young to be out of uniform, or maybe she was getting old? 'Thanks for agreeing to meet me, officer.'

'It's no problem. I'm based at Parkside, just across the

Piece.'

'Oh, right. Tea?'

'Thank you,' he replied, eyeing up the cake stand.

They sat down and she poured him a cup.

'I should say I'm big fan,' he said in a looser voice. 'Although I bet you've got a few murderers off in your time?'

She decided to ignore the barbed compliment and put it down to youthful idealism. 'I've been briefed on the case but I just want to go over a couple of things, if that's OK?'

'Sure, fire away,' he replied, putting a finger sandwich onto his plate.

'Laptop, phone, suitcase and personal items missing?'

'Yeah, unless he didn't brush his teeth.'

Outwardly, she laughed along with him. 'Any CCTV?'

'No.' He picked up the sandwich and took a bite.

'How come?' She waited for him to swallow.

'We don't actually know when he left. We weren't notified for a while, so there would've been hundreds of hours to check, not that we would've necessarily been able to identify him.' He put the rest of his sandwich in his mouth and poured some milk into his cup.

Ella watched him take a sip. 'So where are the cameras?'

'From his room there's nothing until the street, just above the archway leading out. People coming and going all the time, often with bags. You can't see much of them.'

'Did you seize any footage?'

McDonald's affable demeanour vanished. 'Oh, I see where this is going,' he said, putting his cup back on the saucer. 'Where do you people think we get the time and money for hundreds of man hours on a missing person?'

She sat back to let him finish his rant.

'We've got stabbings, robberies and drug dealers taking up all our bloody time.'

'No one's criticising your investigation,' Ella soothed. 'I totally understand what pressures you're under.'

She could feel him studying her.

'Officer, I've just got some boxes to tick, that's all.'

Clearly recognising that language, McDonald calmed down and replied: 'OK.'

'Anyone been spoken to, friends, people he worked with?'

McDonald hesitated, then with an exaggerated nonchalance: 'He didn't have any, just his brother and we spoke to him of course.' He gave her a knowing look, one that people on the same side share. 'An arrogant sod, if you ask me.'

Ella didn't reciprocate. 'Has there been any proof of life since his disappearance? I'm assuming you've accessed his phone number and email account?'

His agitation returned. 'You know we can't disclose any communications, save to say, if there was any proof of life, I'd tell you.'

'Thanks, I appreciate that,' she said, resolving to tread far more carefully. 'You're the expert, but that's odd isn't it? Usually something pops up eventually, right? Credit card use, travel arrangements?'

'You'd be surprised,' McDonald replied, reaching for a scone. 'Sometimes it's a total flatline and then ten years later they turn up living in a cardboard box under Waterloo Bridge.'

'And is there a reason why they leave their life behind?'

'Life isn't easy,' he said, using a teaspoon to scoop up a blob of jam. 'There's usually a mental health issue in the background somewhere, tends to make coping harder.'

Ella went to pour him another cup.

'Not for me thanks,' he said, getting up, still holding the scone. 'Got to get back for a meeting.' He rolled his eyes.

She stood up. 'Well, thanks again for coming, and I'll let you know if I turn up anything.'

'I won't hold my breath,' he replied, taking a huge bite, then discarding what was left on his plate.

She watched him leave, then followed him out into the lobby. 'Officer, just one more thing.'

He swivelled around. 'Sure.'

'Who decided to sign it off as a non-crime?'

His mouth didn't move.

'I mean, who decided the case was closed. Was it you?'

'Well, we have our internal protocols.'

'So, a senior officer signed it off?'

'Like I said,' came the emphasised reply. 'We have our protocols.'

Chapter Thirteen

Ella woke with a start. She was sweating. It had been the same dream, the same image, crystal clear. She checked her phone: 12.15 a.m. She could forget getting back to sleep. She put on some jeans and a fleece and went downstairs. There was no one around. She walked out into the car park and reached into her pocket for her cigarettes, then remembered she'd given up again. She watched the traffic for a while, thinking through the route to her old college. She smiled to herself, then set off along the Fen Causeway to Newnham. The breeze whistled through the grass.

The solitude of the walk at that time of night helped clear her head. The sky was flawless, revealing a brilliant, full moon.

Newnham Women's College was an imposing Victorian building just beyond the main Sedgwick Campus. After showing her pass to the night porter and some discussion, she was allowed through to the library. Two students in pyjamas and fluffy slippers who were walking out held the door for her. Seeing the old wooden beams and the high, glass-panelled windows gave her a feeling of sanctuary. Ella remembered coming down from her room at all hours as an undergraduate, working late into the night in some hidden alcove.

It didn't take her long to find what she was looking for – the Greek philosophers, and in particular a book about the life of Aristotle. She was soon engrossed. There was so much about him – the breadth of knowledge and the scale of his influence – that she hadn't known. She picked out a selection of books before setting off back to the Gonville.

Crossing the Fen, she had a strange sensation that someone was behind her. She stopped and turned. Just shadows fidgeting in the wind. Then something caught her eye. A figure, ducking down in the long grass. No, she was imagining it. Unsettled, she quickened her pace, then, telling herself it was just a symptom of her anxiety, she slowed. She had to try and find the old, confident Ella.

She got back to the car park and stood for a moment, staring at the entrance to the Gonville. She thought about how much of her adult life had been spent in hotel rooms, away on cases. As she was about to go inside, she changed her mind and walked over to the van. She clicked the fob, slid open the side door and climbed in, turning on the battery light. She kicked off her shoes, pulled out the bed and lay down under the duvet. She let out a yawn.

It was the closest thing she had to home.

Chapter Fourteen

Cameron Shepherd took a last spoonful, then sat back and pushed the bowl away. Nobody could make hopi corn stew like him but this batch didn't taste good. Maybe he was just too anxious about the trip to eat a proper meal. The break-in at the office hadn't helped.

He got up, loosened his tie and took a beer out of the fridge. He pulled the ring, went out onto the front porch and breathed in the Arizona air – his nightly ritual. Priceless downtime after all the craziness of work in Phoenix.

An orchestra of bugs tapped out a familiar tune on the bulb above his head as he drank from the can. The Milky Way was so thick with stars it looked like a huge sequined scarf wrapped around the world. It always made him draw breath, made it worth the daily commute from the Sonoran desert ranch he'd grown up on. It would always be home, even with Matthew so far away.

A coyote let out a high-pitched wail from some distant ridge as if calling to the constellations. Cameron let out his own bark which caused a cacophony of replies. He chuckled to himself. 'Going to miss you guys,' he said, before heading back in to finish packing.

He put a foot on the pedal and threw the empty tin in the trash. Suddenly feeling giddy, he rubbed his forehead, then staggered sideways, putting a hand on the table to steady himself. He'd been overdoing it at work and all the worry about Matthew had only added to it. But now his vision began to lose focus. He had an overwhelming desire to sleep. In front of him were blurred images – people, moving around the kitchen. Was he dreaming? Hallucinating?

A gloved hand came over his mouth, and he felt himself being lifted and carried off. He tried to struggle but his body was too weak. In and out of consciousness, now he was somewhere else, sitting in his car. He could make out the sound of the engine running. He had no strength, unable to move.

Muffled voices came from outside the vehicle. 'Look everywhere, but don't leave anything out of place.'

He could smell the exhaust. The fumes seemed to envelop him. They were somehow inside the car. He gave an involuntary cough, then another. The full horror of what was happening dawned on his groggy consciousness.

He felt his throat tighten, choking.

He had just enough presence of mind to realise his future was lost.

So much more to do…

Chapter Fifteen

Lizzie scanned the gardens under an angry sky and unpadlocked her bicycle. Still no Jay. She spotted Bob, the head gardener, pottering about outside the shed. 'Sod it,' she said to herself, and wheeled her bike around the lawn.

She could see Bob through the open door, pouring water from a kettle into a mug, surrounded by tools and bags of compost. Boot marks had branded loose soil onto the wooden floor.

She knocked nervously on the timber frame, still holding her cycle.

'Looks like it's going to rain,' he said, stirring his tea.

'Yes,' she replied, glancing heavenwards. 'Have you seen Jay?'

'Brew?' he asked, pointing to the cup.

'No, thanks.'

He turned to face her properly with an expression of mild curiosity. 'He's not here love.'

'Oh. Do you know when he's back?' she asked, trying to sound blasé.

Bob didn't reply immediately. 'You a friend of his?'

'No… yes.' She could tell he was sizing her up now, deciding whether to confide in her.

He used a spoon to fish the tea bag out of his mug and dump it in an orange bucket, then poured in some milk from a carton. He sat down on some sacks of mulch and blew onto his drink. 'It was his last day yesterday. He's left.'

'Left? Why?' She leaned her bike up against the shed.

'Well, he's going away for a while.'

She went in and sat down on an upturned crate. 'Where?'

'It's not really my place, love.' He stirred his tea.

She was going to have to say more. 'He asked me for a favour, but I was in a rush, and…'

'All right, all right,' he replied, sparing her anymore of the gushing confession. He looked at her as if he was studying her face for the first time. He put down the mug and reached for a plastic tub. 'Biscuit?'

'No thanks,' she replied, trying not to sound impatient.

He put down the tub and puffed out his cheeks. 'He's up in Court today.'

'Court?' Her brow furrowed. 'What for?'

He swigged at his tea then used the back of his hand to wipe his mouth. 'I don't know the details, but anyway, that's for him to say, isn't it?'

Still processing the information: 'Has he got anyone with him?'

'No. He ain't got no family. Nice kid.'

Lizzie's mind was racing. 'Magistrates' Court?'

'Err, no,' Bob replied, scratching his head. 'Crown, I think.'

She got up. 'So, it's serious?'

Bob didn't comment.

'Thanks,' she said, going back outside and retrieving her bike. She wheeled it back to the road. She was in two minds. She knew Cambridge Crown Court was on East Road, a modern non-descript building not far from Parker's Piece. She checked her Rolex, an eighteenth birthday present from her mother. She could be there in minutes and still make the lecture. She got on her bike, stood up in the saddle, then, head down, pedalled off at full pelt.

Ten minutes later she was through security and scanning the faces on the landing outside the courtrooms. A muscular man in a tight t-shirt with a roll-up behind his ear was arguing with a scrawny woman in stone-wash jeans. Her free hand jabbed at his chest as the other rocked a pushchair in short jerks, perfectly in time with her oratory. The toddler in the pushchair sucked intently on a sweet, transfixed by the defendants milling about and seemingly oblivious to his parents' discord.

Lizzie saw Jay sitting on a metal bench outside Court One, a folder and a MacBook on his lap. She almost didn't recognise him – in a suit that was too small and showed off a pair of mismatched socks. Even the shirt was too short, cuffs finishing halfway up his wrists. The white collar had a subtle, pink hue from being through a coloured wash. The fear on his face was obvious.

He looked up as she approached. 'Lizzie?'

'Hi,' she said, knowing instinctively that she'd made the right decision.

His hands twitched as if lost for something to do, so different from his easy manner around the gardens. 'What are you doing here?'

She sat down next to him. 'Bob told me where I could find you. You needed a favour?'

'Oh, of course.' He managed a bashful smile. 'I'm sorry, I get it that we don't really know each other, but—'

'You didn't know who else to ask,' she said, taking control of the situation in the way she'd seen her mother do a thousand times.

'Yes.' He sighed. 'And I know I can trust you.'

For the first time their eyes met, then they looked away.

He took a key out of his pocket. 'It's for my front door. I was hoping you could check on the place from time to time.'

She went to take it, then changed her mind, folding his hand around it. She could feel it shaking. 'Let's see if I'm going to need to first.'

He nodded. 'OK.'

Suddenly unsure, she frowned. 'It's not a sexual offence, is it?'

'No,' he replied, with a wince.

'Violence?'

'No, nothing like that.' He took a deep breath, then exhaled. 'When I was a kid, I got into environmental hacktivism.'

It took a moment for the phrase to sink in. 'What, you mean like computer hacking?'

'Yeah, exposing huge corporations for the way they deal with waste.' There was passion behind his eyes. 'You know, polluting the environment.'

She didn't reply immediately. 'That wasn't what I expected.'

He looked down at his hands. 'I didn't have a lot of guidance.' He began to fiddle with a corner of the file. 'My mum had issues, well, she was a junkie actually. I suppose it gave me another focus.'

Lizzie tried to look like she was taking it all in her stride. 'So that's what you're up for today?'

He swivelled ninety degrees to face her full on. 'No, they never report any hacks, don't want to draw any attention to what they're up to.' His fingers tensed up. 'They're breaking the law and no one gives a shit.'

Lizzie realised she knew virtually nothing about the man, yet despite his disclosure, she felt a connection. She wondered if it was her own need to always have a project, to fix something or someone that was broken. 'OK, you stopped doing that, so what are the charges?'

His eyes contracted, then in a hushed tone: 'I hacked into MI6.'

'What the fuck?' She looked at him anew.

He blinked. 'I know, I was an idiot.'

'That's jail,' said Lizzie.

He looked at his hands again. 'I know.'

She wanted to say something reassuring but nothing sprang to mind. 'What does your lawyer say?'

He had a sheepish expression. 'I'm representing myself.'

Lizzie gasped. 'Are you mad? You could have one for free on legal aid.'

'I did. I sacked him,' Jay explained. 'He said I had to plead guilty.'

She frowned, confused. 'But you did it, right?'

'Yeah, but I got played,' he replied, sounding exasperated. 'I thought I was working for the government.'

'What?' she said, failing to hide her cynicism.

Before she could ask anything else a female voice called out, 'Jason Pitois?'

He stood up. 'That's me.'

The usher, an elderly lady in a black gown, came over holding a clip board. 'Just checking you're here. The judge has got a couple of sentences and then we will start your trial.'

'How long has he got?' asked Lizzie, getting up.

'Shouldn't be more than an hour,' she replied, adjusting her gown before going back into the courtroom.

An addict on autopilot, skin tightly drawn around his skeleton, meandered over in a pleading pose, an upturned hand already outstretched. They greeted him with icy stares causing him to do an about-turn before he could open his mouth.

Lizzie refocused on Jay, still trying to work out if he was all there. 'So how are you going to defend yourself?'

He shrugged. 'Just tell the truth.'

Lizzie put a hand to her forehead and rubbed it. 'To be honest I can't take all this in, but I know you need help.' She took out her phone and made a call. It went straight to voice-mail. 'Wait there.'

'Where are you going?' he asked, sounding panicked.

She was already running down the stairs.

Chapter Sixteen

Ella looked up from her book, unable to distract herself any longer. He was over an hour late and the online arrival page had showed no delays.

She walked through to the lobby trying to recall the receptionist's name. Blank. She used to remember everything, even tiny details. That was what made her the best. Reading off the tag, she said, 'Karen, has anyone left any messages for Ella Blake?'

After a check on the computer, the answer from the receptionist came back negative.

Cameron Shepherd had her mobile number anyway, but why hadn't he called? She walked out onto the car park and phoned him again.

This time someone answered.

'Mr Shepherd, everything OK?' It felt like an age, waiting for a response.

'Who is this?'

'It's Ella Blake.'

'You've called this number a few times.' The accent was

West Coast or maybe Arizonan, but the voice sounded different.

'Yes, I was just making sure you were on your way?'

'On the way where?'

Ella was confused. 'Who is this, please?'

Another pause. 'Detective Hank Broady, Phoenix Police Department.'

'Sorry, who?' She walked back inside. 'Is this a joke?'

'No, ma'am, why were you calling Mr Shepherd?'

It was getting too weird. 'I was supposed to be meeting him in Cambridge.'

'Cambridge, England?' The voice sounded as confused as Ella.

'Yes, he was assisting me with an inquiry.'

'You police?' he asked.

It felt like she was being cross-examined. 'No, I'm a barrister.'

'What, like a lawyer?'

'Yes.'

'What kind of inquiry?'

She'd had enough. 'I don't want to be unhelpful but that's confidential and I should have some kind of confirmation as to your identity.'

Another pause. 'I see.'

'Is Mr Shepherd OK?' Ella walked back and forth inside the lobby.

Silence. Then: 'No, I'm sorry to tell you, he's dead.'

'Dead?' Ella's mouth went dry. 'How?'

'Car accident.'

She couldn't quite take it in. 'I only spoke to him the other day.'

'Where can I reach you if I need to contact you?'

The question hardly registered. 'On this number.'

'No, I need an address?'

'Oh, I see.' She thought about it. 'The Gonville Hotel.'

'You live in a hotel?'

'No, just while I'm on this inquiry.'

'Got it, thanks.'

The line went dead.

Ella walked back outside and began to pace up and down the car park. She wished she hadn't given him her address but wasn't sure why.

'Mum!' Lizzie's brakes squealed as she skidded onto the forecourt. 'I need a favour.' As she dismounted, she saw her mother properly. 'Are you all right?'

'Yeah,' Ella replied, wiping the moisture from her eyes. 'Just heard someone died.'

'Oh my God, I'm so sorry.'

'It's OK,' she replied. 'I didn't really know him, it's just—'

'Brings back memories?'

She touched Lizzie's shoulder. 'Maybe. What's the favour?'

Lizzie's expression became intense. 'I need you to come to court and defend someone.'

'What do you mean?' Ella asked, still distracted by the phone call. 'Who?'

'Jay Pitois, he's the college gardener. He's on trial today at Cambridge Crown and he hasn't got a lawyer.'

'Hang on a minute,' Ella replied, wiping her eyes. 'I can't just turn up and defend someone just like that.'

'Why not?'

'I'm in the middle of a job, I can't just bugger off and do a trial, and I'd have to read the brief, get instructed by a solicitor.'

Lizzie's eyes narrowed. 'You can take it *direct access* from the client, can't you?'

Even the mere thought of court filled Ella with dread. 'I'd need to prepare; I haven't been inside a courtroom for three years. It's impossible. Who is this guy to you anyway, not the one you're bringing tonight?'

'No, he's just a friend.' Speaking more deliberately she said, 'I need your help, Mum. Isn't that enough?'

Lizzie's pleading eyes reminded Ella of Christmas morning, begging to open her presents. She knew what a no would mean for their almost non-existent relationship. She took a moment, then, despite feeling nauseous at the thought, she replied, 'OK.'

She expected Lizzie to throw her arms around her, but all she got was a pointed, 'Thank you. Let's go, it's only a couple of minutes up the road.'

Still reeling from the news of Cameron Shepherd's death, Ella opened the boot of the van and rummaged around for her wig bag.

'Take one of the hotel's bikes,' Lizzie bossed, pointing at the rack.

'What? I haven't been on one of them for years.'

'Come on, Mum, hurry.'

'OK, OK.' The whole thing felt like a huge mistake.

Chapter Seventeen

'That's him,' said Lizzie, pointing out the young man sitting on a bench, playing with his phone.

Ella strode over and stretched out an arm. 'Hi, I'm Ella Blake, Lizzie's mum. I'm also a barrister.'

'She's a top QC,' added Lizzie.

Jay looked like a rabbit caught in headlights.

Before he had time to respond, Ella said, 'Let's go into a conference room and have a chat.' Old instincts kicking in, she held the door open and shot the client a look of supreme confidence.

'Miss Blake?' came a familiar voice from behind her. She swung around to see a young man in a suit. She couldn't quite place him.

He seemed to be waiting for an acknowledgement, then said, with a hint of indignation, 'Officer *McDonald*... we met at The Gonville.'

'Yes, of course.' She shook his hand.

'How's the inquiry going?' he asked, checking out the two people with her.

She knew she should tell him about Cameron's death. For some reason her gut said not to. 'Slowly. Here for a case?'

'Yes, a cybercrime, that young man,' he said flicking his head towards Jay. 'Just here as the officer in charge to keep an eye, you?'

Just her luck. 'Likewise.'

His genial persona closed down. 'Really? You're for him – Pitois?'

''Fraid so,' she replied, as if in apology.

Lizzie pulled Jay into the room and the door closed behind them.

McDonald glared at Jay through the glass panel in the door. 'Surprised he has the financial backing?'

'Pro bono,' Ella replied. 'Better get on. I suppose I'll see you later.'

He stared at her, but said nothing. She turned, but could still feel his eyes in the back of her head as she went into the conference. She sat down in front of the client and spotted the file on the table. 'Is that the prosecution papers?'

'Err, yes,' Jay replied, sliding it across. 'It's all they've given me.'

Ella saw Lizzie give Jay a reassuring smile.

They sat in silence while she speed-read the documents.

After a few minutes, still immersed in the statements, Ella said, 'You raised your defence in interview – that's good.'

Jay glanced at Lizzie. 'Is it?'

'It put the onus on them to check it out,' Ella replied, without taking her eyes off the papers. 'So, born in Brixton to a Mauritian mother, moved to a council flat in Cambridge with your mum when you were twelve?'

'Yes.'

'She was an addict,' Ella said with no sensitivity. 'Died of a heroin overdose when you were sixteen?'

'Mum!' exclaimed Lizzie. 'Do you have to be so blunt?'

'I need to get the facts right – we can use that to soften up the jury.' She looked at Jay properly for the first time. 'Caution for a Section 5 Public Order?'

'Yeah, a climate change rally.' He looked even more concerned now. 'Does it matter?'

She ignored the question. 'You got a scholarship to Cambridge to read computer science?'

Lizzie stared at Jay, open-mouthed.

'Yeah, I had to defer it,' he replied, giving Ella a furtive glance in the way shy people do.

'If you get off this, the place is still open?'

'Think so.'

She pushed back her chair. 'Wait there while I go and find the prosecutor.'

Lizzie jumped up. 'I'm coming.'

Head down and focused, Ella marched off to the robing room with Lizzie a step behind.

Everyone looked up when the off-circuit barrister walked in. A few mis-matched tables were covered with a jumble of bags, small suitcases on wheels and open wig tins with the names of counsel written on them in gold leaf. A couple of junior barristers were putting on their wing collars and bands. Ella was aware of them watching as she unpacked her bag.

She faced them down. 'Anyone prosecuting Jason Pitois?'

'Ah yes, the black hat,' said a man in his fifties, taking his wig out of the tin.

'He says he's a white hat,' Ella replied without any of the customary warmth for a first encounter with opposing counsel.

'He would say that, wouldn't he?' he replied, taking off his day collar and putting his wing on the stud. 'Jim Stubbs, CPS.'

'Ella Blake.'

Stubbs' face lost some of its colour. 'Queen's Counsel? I was told he was defending himself?'

'Change of plan,' she replied. 'Why hasn't he got the schedule of unused material?'

Stubbs glanced at the other barristers, seemingly thrown off by the direct assault. 'I assumed it was a guilty plea? He hasn't even served a defence statement.'

'He made it clear in his interview,' she replied, opening her wig tin. 'The police must've investigated his defence – where's the *evidence* of that?'

The other advocates stopped what they were doing and watched.

'As you can imagine, I'm sure it's all very sensitive, he did hack MI6.'

She put on her bands, watching Stubbs in the mirror, and continued the bombardment, 'Then you've seen a sensitive schedule?'

'Well, err, I—'

She turned around and faced him. 'Mr Stubbs, he gave a full account in interview and provided an email string with the people that set him up, all that must have been looked into?'

'It was obviously part of his cover,' Stubbs replied. 'In case he got caught.'

'Come off it,' she scoffed. 'It's the oldest scam in the book. Cyber criminals target an impressionable kid who is great with computers, they tell him the government are interested in employing him for top secret work and they ask him to hack into a site making out it's to test his ability.'

Stubbs let out a cynical laugh but the atmosphere was deteriorating fast.

'I'm going to need chapter and verse on whether the police investigation has complied with its duties under code 3.4 of the Criminal Procedure and Investigation Act – *to pursue all reasonable lines of inquiry that point away from the defendant.*' She put on her gown and turned back to the mirror. 'If they've sat on this, I'll be arguing abuse of process.'

Stubbs talked to her back: 'It would've been nice if I'd had these disclosure requests before the day of trial.'

She placed her wig carefully on her head. She'd forgotten how well it suited her. 'You'd better tell the officer in the case that he's got to go in the box. It's a central issue what he has and hasn't done on the case.'

'A smoke screen – attacking the investigation?'

Ella knew he was losing his cool. She gave him time to consider the implications.

He fiddled anxiously with his bands. 'All right, all right, I'll go and find him.'

'McDonald? He's outside,' Ella replied, pushing a few loose strands of hair under her wig.

Stubbs did a double take then left the room.

The other advocates in the room stared at Ella as she continued getting ready.

Once Ella had applied the war paint, Lizzie followed her out onto the landing.

'All parties in Jason Pitois to Court One,' came through the tannoy.

Ella could feel the prickly heat on the back of her neck. She had to keep it together for Lizzie, for Lizzie's friend. She gritted her teeth, determined to brazen it out.

Beads of sweat formed on her forehead.

'You OK, Mum?' asked Lizzie, sounding more surprised than concerned.

'Yeah,' she replied, wiping her hands on her gown.

The usher held open the door as the parties filed into court.

The layout was contemporary; light wood panelling without frills and with fold down seats for counsel. A tattooed prison officer stood in the dock with a chain looped from his belt to a bunch of keys bulging in his pocket.

The judge was still on the bench, elbows in front and hands cupping his face. His eyes tracked her as she took her place in counsels' row and placed her papers on a lectern. He had the judicial default expression of a mix of boredom and mild amusement.

Ella could tell from the fading colour of his purple robes that he was an old hand. She knew her own silk gown gave away her status.

'Are you Jason Pitois?' asked the clerk of the court from below the bench.

Jay stood up in the dock and replied in a shaky voice, 'Yes.'

The dock officer put a hand on his shoulder and pushed him back down into the seat.

The prosecutor got up to address the court.

The judge gave him his attention. 'Yes, Mr Stubbs?'

'May it please Your Honour, I prosecute, and my learned friend, Miss Blake, Queen's Counsel, defends.'

The judge dipped his head to acknowledge her. 'Miss Blake, although I am delighted to have such eminent counsel before me, the court understood Mr Pitois was unrepresented?'

'Yes, apologies, Your Honour, a late instruction.'

'Not at all, much the preferred course and very pleased for Mr Pitois, if not a little surprised that he can afford someone of your calibre. I'm quite sure the legal aid would not fund the services of Queen's Counsel?'

'I'm acting pro bono, Your Honour.'

'Ah,' he replied, eyebrows slightly raised. 'A laudable endeavour.'

She bowed.

He took out a handkerchief and blew his nose. 'Are we

ready to swear a jury?'

Stubbs got up again. 'We've had rather a lot of disclosure requests this morning, Your Honour.' He made his play: 'Which is going to take some time, I'm afraid.'

The judge rolled his eyes. 'How long?'

'Impossible to say at this stage.' Stubbs clasped his hands behind his back in full adversarial mode and lowered his tone. 'It may be Your Honour feels the trial ought to be adjourned?'

The judge raised an eyebrow and turned to defence counsel. 'Miss Blake?'

Ella took her time getting up. She knew this had to be good to avoid the case being kicked into the long grass and eventually re-fixed for a new trial date when she would be long gone. It wasn't fair on the kid to have to wait, whatever he had or hadn't done. 'Your Honour, this young man has no previous convictions. He was arrested and interviewed nine months ago—'

'Just a minute,' interrupted the judge. He opened up his laptop and tapped a couple of buttons. 'I'm sure I read somewhere that he's got a public order offence on his record.'

'Caution, Your Honour, not a conviction. A climate change protest that got out of hand. He wanted to save the planet.'

'Don't we all, Miss Blake,' he replied, seemingly placated. 'Don't we all.' An imperceptible nod indicated that she could continue with her submission.

'He has a place at Cambridge awaiting the outcome of this matter, Your Honour. His defence has been clear from the outset of these proceedings – that he was manipulated by sophisticated criminals via email – all of which he disclosed to the police. He believed he was working for a government agency and therefore did not believe he was committing a crime.'

'I've read the interview, Miss Blake,' he interrupted, almost in a growl. 'But what do you say about an adjournment?'

She took a breath. 'They've had nine months to investigate this case. That's long enough. My learned friend says he had these requests today but we are talking about enquiries that should have been made months ago. If they can't satisfy this court that the proper disclosure obligations have been complied with then—'

'Thank you, Miss Blake,' the judge cut in. 'I get the picture.' He mulled it over then looked across at her opponent. 'I tend to agree with her, Mr Stubbs. Justice delayed is justice denied. I'll give the prosecution twenty minutes to provide the unused schedule and then I will hear further argument.'

Clearly struggling to keep up, Stubbs didn't have a counter.

'All rise,' said the usher.

Both counsel bowed as the judge shuffled out.

'I can see what you're doing,' Stubbs hissed across the row.

As Ella walked past him, she replied, 'Good.' She looked at Lizzie who had been watching the hearing from the public gallery. 'Take him back in that conference room, I'll meet you there.'

Ella went straight into the ladies, shut herself in a cubicle and gulped for air. Once she'd caught her breath, she put the lid down and sat on it, head in hands. Her reaction to the hearing scared her. She wondered whether it was actually about being back in court, or more about all this interaction with people over the last few days. That was a price she'd have to pay if she was going to salvage something with Lizzie. Otherwise, what was the point of anything?

Chapter Eighteen

The midday sun shone through the glass atrium at the end of the landing, lighting up the mezzanine outside the courtrooms.

'So, what happens now?' asked Lizzie as soon as Ella came in.

'We wait,' Ella replied, sitting down and rereading the file.

Jay put his weight on one foot then the other. 'Would you mind explaining the strategy?'

Ella didn't look up.

Nervously interrupting the silence again, Jay asked: 'Asking all these disclosure questions, isn't there a risk of them just getting more evidence together to convict me?'

'Yes, it's a gamble,' she replied, turning over a page.

'Explain,' ordered Lizzie.

Ella stopped reading and looked at her client. 'The Criminal Justice System is on its knees. There's no funding for the police or the CPS. They're all doing the job of ten people. The officer in charge is snowed under and the prosecutor works in-house at the CPS, he's not from the independent

Bar, so he's got people to answer to back at the office if this goes pear-shaped.'

'I don't get it?' said Jay.

Irritated by the question, Ella replied, 'I'm guessing they thought you would plead guilty or defend yourself and so did nothing on the case. They didn't investigate your defence and didn't even put together a schedule of unused evidence – listing all the pieces of evidence that they've obtained but aren't relying on.' She gave him a lawyer's look. 'If I'm right they might think twice about exposing their failures in a public courtroom, in front of the press, during a five-day trial.'

Jay sat down across from her. 'You mean they might choose...'

She nodded. 'To drop the case, yes.'

Lizzie sat down next to him. 'But what's any of that got to do with Jay?'

'Arguably, not much,' Ella replied. 'But who cares?' She turned her attention back to the papers.

'Yeah, who cares,' echoed Jay.

'Obviously,' agreed Lizzie after some hesitation. 'It just all seems so cold and calculating.'

'Miss Blake?' Jay's hands started fidgeting again. 'You do believe I'm innocent, though?'

Of course,' she replied, without even looking up.

'Why do you believe me?' he asked

Realising her previous answer hadn't been enough, gave him her attention now. She pointed to his MacBo the table. 'You've got stickers on your laptop, you're a ki

Jay looked even more disconcerted.

Stubbs knocked on the door. 'Can I have a word?'

Ella got up and went out onto the landing wh was waiting with an agitated McDonald just behin

Stubbs was breathing hard. 'We're dropping

McDonald's expression made clear his resentment at what was unfolding.

'How come?' Ella asked, trying to sound surprised.

Stubbs took off his wig and rubbed his head. 'We've carefully reviewed the papers, and—'

'Actually,' she said, losing interest, 'save it for the judge.'

'Is this how you win cases?' asked McDonald, jutting out his chin. 'Trying to call out the prosecution, blame everyone else?'

Ella stared him down. 'If it's legal. I do what it takes, it's nothing personal.'

'It is to me.' McDonald moved a little further into her space.

Ella was no stranger to this kind of intimidation, especially from men. She continued to hold his gaze. 'Then try and be a bit more professional.'

'You cheeky cow,' stammered McDonald, raising a finger to her face. 'You know how overworked we are.'

'Come on,' said Stubbs, pulling the officer away. 'A total pleasure, Miss Blake.' This time there was no awe in his voice, only contempt.

Chapter Nineteen

The remnants of the case played out in court in a matter of seconds.

Even though the judge told Jay that he was not guilty and free to go, it seemed to take a while to sink in. He remained in the dock for a few seconds, unsure of what to do until the Dock Officer gave him a gentle push. When Ella had got changed out of her robes, she found him still waiting on the landing with Lizzie.

'So that's really it?' he asked Ella. 'Completely finished?'

'Yes,' she said, relieved as much for herself as for him. 'You can go to uni and have a great life.'

He ran his fingers through his thick, black, hair. 'It's all a bit of a shock. Just wasn't expecting it to end like this, and so quickly.'

'Don't knock it,' Ella replied.

'No, of course not, it's...' His voice cracked. 'I don't know how to thank you.'

'Thank Lizzie,' she replied, unmoved. 'I've really got to be somewhere.'

'Miss Blake, Ella, err...' he said, struggling to open up. 'If there's anything I could ever do in return? Anything, to say thank you?'

She managed to raise a smile. 'If I ever need a gardener who is great with computers, I know where to come.'

A grin gave his uptight face a break. 'Deal.'

They shook hands.

'See you tonight Lizzie,' Ella shouted back as she headed for the stairs. 'Really looking forward to it.'

Jay and Lizzie followed her then hovered outside the entrance. 'She's one hell of a barrister,' said Jay. 'She... you both have saved my life.'

Lizzie patted his arm. 'What will you do now?'

He was still choked. 'Get a job until September.'

'Can't you go back to the gardening?'

'Handed my notice in, they've already filled it.' He rolled his eyes. 'I was so sure I was going down. I'll find something, it's only for a few months.'

She gave him an encouraging smile. 'I'm sure you will.'

'Do you want to get a coffee or something?' he blurted. 'Some lunch?'

She half grimaced. 'I can't.'

His head dropped. 'No problem.'

'I've got lectures,' she said, touching his arm again.

Still looking down, he replied, 'Of course.'

She needed to explain. 'Jay, I've just started seeing someone.'

He looked at her intensely – but said nothing. It made her feel she had to say more. 'It just wouldn't feel right.'

He glanced off. 'You don't have to explain.'

She stood on tiptoes and kissed him on the cheek. 'Bye Jay.'

Chapter Twenty

'Thanks for seeing me at such short notice,' said Ella.

'No problem,' Master Desmond replied, walking back to his desk. 'I want to hear how it's all going?'

'For a start,' she said, sitting down in her usual seat. 'Cameron Shepherd is dead.'

'What?' Desmond's mouth fell open as he flopped onto his chair.

'Car accident, apparently.'

Shaking his head, he said, 'Where did you learn this?'

'Phoenix Police. He was supposed to meet me in Cambridge but didn't show.' Ella gave Desmond time to process the information.

He leaned forward on his elbows and clasped his hands together. 'You don't think…?'

She let him be the one to say it.

'It *was* an accident? Nothing linked to this inquiry?'

She shrugged. 'That's all I know. The timing is very worrying.'

She could feel Desmond studying her.

'Are you all right?' he asked.

'Yes,' she replied, feeling self-conscious. 'It's unsettling, obviously.'

'Of course. Have you told Officer McDonald?' he asked, giving her face even more scrutiny.

'No,' she replied, trying to sound as if the thought had never occurred to her. 'Why?'

'So he's got the full picture, if nothing else. I don't know... he could liaise with Arizona?'

'McDonald's not interested,' she said, then pretended to think it through. 'But you're right, he should know.'

'Surprised you didn't tell him this morning?' Desmond raised his eyebrows.

Ella dropped her shoulders. 'I see. He's been in touch?'

'Yes,' Desmond replied, his irritation obvious. 'He says he tried to be helpful at your first meeting and that you were critical of his investigation.'

Ella moved her head back. 'That's not quite right.'

Desmond leaned forward. 'And that you were defending one of the university gardeners at court today and, to use McDonalds's words, stitched up the prosecution?'

'No,' she protested. 'I was just doing my job and—'

'Miss Blake,' he cut in. 'With respect, I think you're missing the point. I hired you for this inquiry, then I hear you are taking cases, on our time, banging heads with the very people whose cooperation you should be gaining.'

Ella sat up straight. 'Master Desmond, I was asked this morning to do the case, it was a friend of my daughter, he didn't have a lawyer.'

Desmond scoffed. 'I heard it was a trial that could've gone on for days.'

'I didn't know that when—' She stopped, took a breath and slumped back in her chair. 'You're right.' She closed her eyes for a couple of seconds. 'I'm sorry, it was unprofessional.'

Desmond's tone softened: 'Do you want this job? Are you up to it?'

She sat up again. 'Of course.'

Desmond put a hand on the desk. 'No, I mean do you really want it? Not just as a cover for seeing your daughter?'

She winced. 'Who told you that?'

He held her gaze. 'I'm a father.'

She felt embarrassed. 'I'm sorry, this is isn't who I am normally.'

'I know from Simon you've had a lot to deal with in recent times,' he said with a sideways tilt of the head. 'But—'

Ella interrupted, 'You need one hundred percent focus, discretion, and someone who is totally committed to this very difficult assignment?'

He slammed his hand down on the mahogany. 'Exactly.'

'I am that person and I will make things right with McDonald.'

Desmond sighed, eventually replying, 'Thank you.'

Ella got up to leave. She decided it was not a good time to share how little progress she'd actually made. 'I've read a lot about Aristotle, an extraordinary man.'

'A true genius,' Desmond replied, blowing a speck of dust off the mantelpiece.

'Who would you say was the greatest English polymath?'

His face lit up. 'Sir Isaac Newton. He was a fellow here at Cambridge, at Trinity. So much of his greatest work wasn't published until after his death, you know.' Then he added, 'I do hope Matthew doesn't suffer the same fate.'

'We have to find his work first,' Ella responded gloomily.

Desmond gave a solemn nod.

'I'll have to do some homework on Newton, I don't know much more about him other than the law of gravity – the apple hitting him on the head.'

'Ah, yes, and he was sitting under a tree on this very

street.' Desmond laughed, then his expression turned serious. 'The breadth of his work was extraordinary, a true cosmic polymath.'

'Cosmic?'

'Yes,' Desmond replied, racing on. 'He drew everything together, from the planets to the natural world below. He saw the links – tides, orbits, and yes, why an apple falls.'

'He saw the bigger picture?'

'Exactly!'

Ella warmed to Desmond, seeing him begin to enjoy the conversation.

'It's all about joining the dots, Miss Blake.'

'Of course,' she muttered, distracted about how she was going to handle McDonald.

Chapter Twenty-One

Ella decided to stop off at the Gonville to psych herself up before giving McDonald the grovelling apology. She walked through the lobby, debating whether to have a glass of wine in the bar before going up. She felt so wired.

'Miss Blake?'

'Yes?'

The receptionist was holding up a parcel. 'This came for you, special delivery.'

'Thanks.' Something made her scan the area for prying eyes before taking the package. She could see it was from the States. She went straight to her room and locked the door before ripping it open. Inside was a CD in a case, nothing else.

Ella tossed the remains of the padded envelope on the bed and stuck the disc into her laptop. She waited. Eventually it sprang to life – footage from a home video, some kids messing about in a paddling pool. She identified Matthew immediately. He was involved in the fun, but also, somehow removed. Not quite connected. It was how she remembered her own childhood. She often wondered if her brilliance at tearing witnesses to pieces in the box was some sort of revenge for the bullying she'd suffered at school.

The clip finished playing, over in seconds. She picked up the envelope again and scrutinised it more carefully. No note. She looked at the CD case again and saw a piece of paper sticking out from behind the cardboard cover. She pulled it out and unfolded it.

Bro, if anything happens, trust your instincts — you'll know when and who to give this to. "He and I are the inverse of here and there.

Underneath, in a different hand, it read:

Just in case,
Cam

Just in case? In case he didn't make it? It sent a shiver down Ella's spine. She remembered how Cameron had ended the call — *be careful* — how she hadn't given it a second thought. And what did the words mean? She read them again.

He and I are the inverse of here and there.

Was it a quote from something? Were they Matthew's own words? What was he trying to say?

Chapter Twenty-Two

Lizzie and Greg ambled down King's Parade holding hands. She'd thought she loved Cambridge, but now, the buzz, the excitement, everything seemed more intense.

Greg gave her shoulder a playful nudge as they weaved their way along the street, dodging walkers coming their way.

Lizzie noticed a stream of young people funnelling from both directions into an alley. Keeping a firm grip, she steered Greg across the street for a better look.

'David Kline!' she said, reading the poster. 'I've heard he's amazing,' she added, pouring enthusiasm onto her new boyfriend. 'It's free.' She pointed towards some assembly rooms further up. 'Come on.'

Greg gently pulled away. 'Wouldn't you prefer a nice cold pint?'

She threw her head back and laughed. 'Where's your social conscience?'

She cajoled him towards the entrance. A group of students in the foyer were holding buckets, each with a letter in large print written on the side. 'Phones in here please,' said one marshal wearing a back to front baseball cap. A couple of others shouted the same mantra, followed by, 'Remember the letter and you can collect them when you leave.'

'This is all a bit new age, isn't it?' said Greg as they put their mobiles into the nearest container.

Lizzie wasn't listening, fascinated by the different faces, students from all corners of the world, filing into the auditorium. She had an immediate sense of belonging, of being part of some higher purpose. This was why she'd come to Cambridge.

The place was full, rows of chairs on either side of a central aisle, every seat taken. The hall was Victorian with a high ceiling. At the front was a make-shift stage with an unattended oak lectern in the centre.

Greg had spotted a couple of chairs at the side near the back and led Lizzie along a line of people already in situ, accidentally bumping into knees as they scrambled their way past.

'Sorry!' Lizzie said, falling into a pretty young blonde woman deep in conversation with a grim-faced, burly man who reached out in a flash to block the contact and push Lizzie back to her feet. She noticed a scar on his neck, just above the collar. The woman gave her a lost smile. Lizzie reciprocated, noticing her lonely eyes. Lizzie felt an instant connection, maybe they were both shy, she thought, both searching for something, for some kind of meaning to their lives. She seemed familiar, and it niggled her but she couldn't think where she'd seen her before. Maybe a lecture? As Lizzie moved along, she could see the man giving her the once-over, then shifting his attention elsewhere. They seemed such an unlikely pair.

'Are you ready everybody?' boomed a voice from the wings.

'Yes,' the audience replied. It reminded Lizzie of the pantomimes her mother would take her to at Christmas, but more exciting, almost like the born-again religious stuff she sometimes saw on TV.

'Then put your hands together for the great academic and thinker, Dr... David Kline.'

The audience broke into rapturous applause, some even getting to their feet.

Lizzie and Greg exchanged amused glances.

A man of undeniable beauty bounded up the steps from the side of the stage and skipped over to the podium. His brown shoulder-length hair and beard made him resemble movie depictions of Jesus Christ. Everything about him exuded youth and energy. He had a mic at the side of his mouth on a static wire. His aura was palpable, reaching out across the sea of people.

Lizzie's supercilious expression was completely wiped off her face, replaced by one of unreserved fascination.

Kline patted the air to stop the clapping which eventually petered out. 'Can we lose the stand?' he shouted over to the wings in a seemingly unrehearsed intro. His accent was unmistakably English, but with no edge that could place his upbringing. It had a cool kind of bounce to it. 'We've got enough barriers already.'

A couple of young lackeys ran on to the stage, picked up the stand and carried it off.

The audience cheered.

Kline kicked the air then started striding up and down the stage, generating more electricity in the crowd. 'When are we going to start thinking in a different way?' he shouted.

A hush descended over the auditorium, each soul hanging on his every word.

Kline held his arms up to the heavens. 'Governments will never see it. Emission targets by 2050, blah, blah blah.' Another head shake. 'Haven't they read the data?' He moved forward to the edge of the stage. 'That's too late.' He put a hand to his forehead. 'Don't they want to keep the Arctic?'

There was an unsettled murmur of agreement from the multitude.

'You are the ones who can save this planet.' He pointed out at the audience, eyes blazing, moving his finger from one to the other. 'Because you can be damn sure no one else will.'

Lizzie felt like he was staring straight at her, his eyes boring in – just at her. It made her breathless.

'Our world is warming faster than anyone predicted.' He paused, with an expression of deepest sorrow. 'Our oceans are choking with plastic… we've even turned the orbit around our planet into a garbage dump of broken satellites.'

A kid with a Chinese accent jumped up and pulled down his mouth cover. 'What can we do, Dr Kline?'

'The capitalist model cannot, does not, and never will address climate change.'

There were more shouts from the audience, a myriad of accents discernible in the throng.

Kline held out his arms. 'Because there's no quick buck to be made in saving our world.'

'So, what do we do?' people called out again. 'Tell us?'

Kline made a theatrical about-turn and walked back across the stage. 'We retrace our steps.'

The crowd fell silent, in communal confusion.

He lowered his voice to a whisper as if about to reveal some great secret. 'We go back to the beginning and we start again.' The endearing whirr of his undertone carried into the mic and out through the sound system. 'Back to our genesis.' The word Genesis reverberated around the auditorium. Kline crouched down like a father talking to a child. He put a hand on one knee. 'Only I know the way, but if you are as committed as me, I will show you.' He nodded. His voice was soft and kindly. 'I promise I will show you.'

There was a delay while the congregation tried to decipher his meaning but then, gradually, one by one, people got to their feet. It wasn't long before everyone was clapping and cheering, and even Lizzie and Greg were swept along.

Kline stood back up, in total control of the room. 'Socrates knew the secret. He taught it to his greatest student, Plato. Plato told his best student, Aristotle. It's all there in the history books.' He padded up and down. 'And who was Aristotle's best student?' he shouted, punching an arm in the air.

'Alexander?' someone called.

He immediately gestured in the direction of the voice. 'Yes. Alexander the Great.'

The hum of the crowd was growing with every revelation, reminding Lizzie of the sound of a beehive when her mum had taught her how to reach in and take the honeycomb.

'Is that right?' Greg shouted towards Lizzie's ear.

'Yes,' she hollered back in wonder. 'They did teach each other. I just never really thought about it!'

Kline leaned forward again, a signal that he had more to share. 'Alexander used that knowledge to conquer the whole of Europe.' He scanned the room with a finger. 'The greatest conqueror that ever lived. He was dead by the age of thirty-two, the same age as me now… and the secret died with him.' He looked out at the sea of faces with complete authority. 'Until now.'

The meeting carried on for an hour. Lizzie watched enrapt as Kline whipped them all into a frenzy, followed by moments of calm, then coming back again and again to his unique angle on history and his promise to teach information-hungry minds something those in power could never understand. A doctrine for the educational elite of the future.

By the time the meeting was over, Lizzie felt totally energised, like there was still a chance her lifetime might not just be about witnessing extinctions and the final death knell of an ecosystem previous generations had taken for granted. Kline had made her feel anything was possible.

She rummaged around in the bucket and took out her phone, then hung back to wait for Greg in the foyer while he went to the gents. She watched the other excited students collect their phones, full of chatter about what they'd heard. She noticed the burly man again, this time without the young blonde. He appeared to be almost running up and down the entrance hall, manically checking faces. His panicked expression was incongruous with his physical stature.

By the time Greg returned they were one of the last out into the alley. As they turned right towards the Parade, Lizzie glanced to her left just in time to see Kline being ushered out of the stage door by some dutiful flunkies. The blonde girl was amongst the entourage.

At the same moment, Kline looked to his right and acknowledged Lizzie with a nod, one comrade to another. It went through her like a bullet. She watched him climb into the back of a Range Rover with blacked-out windows. She felt exhilarated but at the same time a tiny qualm tickled the back of her mind. A paradox between the message and the mode of transport.

She dismissed it.

Chapter Twenty-Three

Ella checked her watch again. She'd been waiting at the police station for half an hour and there was no one else in the queue. Even some mad woman with a grouchy Shih Tzu who had come in after her had been allowed to rant on at the sergeant about her neighbour. It had to be McDonald's way of getting back at her. She got up and walked back over to the uniformed officer behind the glass. His shirt-sleeves were rolled up to the elbows. 'How much longer is he going to be?'

He looked up momentarily, then back at whatever he was reading. 'I said he'll be out when he gets a moment,' he said in a patronising tone. 'We're very busy.'

She couldn't help but laugh. 'Touché,' she muttered to herself. It occurred to her that he was probably watching her on a monitor inside the station, laughing with his colleagues. She walked back to her seat and carried on trying to make sense of Cameron's note. She'd got nowhere other than deduce that it was some kind of riddle. She'd even rewritten each letter as a number in the alphabet, wondering whether it was some kind of code.

A buzzer sounded and a door opened. McDonald strutted into reception with a haughty expression. 'Sorry to keep you waiting, Miss Blake,' he said with a dash of sarcasm.

She refused to rise to it. There was no escaping the fact she needed him on side so she followed him obsequiously into a side-room with a glass door. It had a table but no chairs. 'What can I do for you?' he asked, peering out at inconsequential goings on at the front desk.

Ella took a deep breath. 'Well, firstly I want to apologise for a few things I said, you know, in the heat of battle.' She waited for an olive branch, but he remained tight-lipped. 'I know how professional you are and what a great officer you are, Stubbs told me how much work you'd put in.'

He unfolded his arms.

She put her bag on the table. 'If it had been me prosecuting, I'd have been as angry as you were.'

He shrugged, still more interested in the desk sergeant outside. 'All's fair in love and war, I suppose.'

'Thank you, that's very generous. I'm sure I don't deserve it.'

He didn't disagree. 'Was there anything else?'

She had wondered whether he was going to admit to snitching on her to Desmond but decided against bringing it up herself. 'Yes, just this – on the Matthew Shepherd Inquiry.'

He refolded his arms. 'What about it?'

'I was informed by the Phoenix Police Department that his brother Cameron has been killed in a car crash. He was due to come and see me – to speak to the inquiry.'

McDonald didn't bat an eyelid. 'And your point is?'

'I don't really know, I just thought because there was a death, I should tell you right away even though, on the face of it, it doesn't seem to have any bearing on Matthew's disappearance.'

'You were right to come to me,' McDonald replied,

puffing out his chest slightly. 'But as you say, there's no evidence it has any relevance to either my or your investigation.'

Ella was about to mention the letter but something stopped her. She picked up her bag. 'I suppose you'll make contact with the Americans and tell them about Matthew, just in case?'

He gave her a condescending smile. 'It's on my list.'

'Great,' she said, reaching out to shake his hand. 'Shall we agree to keep each other in the loop?'

He stared at her hand as if it was infected. 'My investigation is closed, remember?'

'Of course, understood. Yes, well, thank you again, officer.'

Finally, a limp shake. 'My pleasure, mind how you go,' he said, in a voice she recognised as reserved for decrepit old ladies.

Ella made her way outside, relieved that her sycophantic apology was done.

Parker's Piece was filling up with groups of students sitting cross-legged in circles, surrounded by bikes lying on their sides. Ella watched a huddle passing bottles of cheap cider around and enjoying the spring evening. She got on the bike she'd borrowed from the hotel and cycled across the space towards the centre.

Chapter Twenty-Four

S imon Carter was waiting for her in the Eagle, sitting at a table with a bottle of wine and four glasses at the ready. The log burner inside the old brick fireplace was glowing. Simon's dress sense of jeans, jumper, tweed jacket and a scarf made her smile. 'I'm sure these are the same clothes you wore thirty years ago,' she said, kissing him on the cheek.

'But they have been washed, once,' he replied, brushing some imaginary dirt off his collar.

'How's the inquiry?' he asked, pouring the wine.

She rolled her eyes. 'Don't ask.'

He laughed. 'Like that, is it?'

'I suppose I shouldn't say anything,' she teased. 'With you being on some committee or other.'

'Don't worry,' he said, winking. 'I've got your back.'

She rested a hand on his arm. 'You always did.' She felt a surge of affection for her old friend.

He suddenly looked grave. 'They're going to need something soon.'

'I know, I know. Trouble is, I haven't really had a chance to get going.'

'I guess it takes a while?'

'Yeah, like a case. Lots of dead ends and then a break-through opens it all up – that's what I need.' She thought about running the note by Simon but it felt unprofessional somehow. Desperate.

'Anyway, cheers,' he said, raising his glass. 'It's good to see you working again.'

'Cheers,' she replied, deciding against it.

'So,' he said, after taking a sip. 'Do you want to tell me what happened?'

She had dreaded him asking. 'Nothing to tell,' she replied, giving his arm a reassuring rub.

He touched her hand. 'I doubt that.'

She started to relax for the first time in ages. 'I suppose I went back to work too quickly, afterwards, you know. My head was all over the place. I lost a murder I should've won. Client got off on appeal, blamed me.' She took a slurp.

'Bar Standards Board?'

'Yeah, they cleared me, but the whole process took ages. I wasn't fit for anything by the end of it, so I took some time out. A year turned into two and...'

'It's scary when you lose your balance like that.'

It felt good to talk about it. 'Totally, I was always so strong, then suddenly, I was a mess. Couldn't trust myself.'

'To keep it together?'

'Yeah.' She'd forgotten how well he knew her.

'Hello,' said Lizzie, arriving at the table with a chiselled young man in tow. 'Are we late?'

'Not at all,' said Ella. 'You remember Simon Carter, don't you? Dad's friend?'

'Of course,' she replied, leaning over the table to hug him. 'We had dinner last week.'

Ella was thrown. 'Oh, I didn't realise you guys...'

'She is my god-daughter,' said Simon.

'Of course she is.' Ella watched his mouth form into a sheepish smile. She couldn't work out why she was so bothered, whether she was just jealous, or whether it was the realisation that she knew so little about her daughter's life.

'This is my friend, Greg,' said Lizzie, grasping Greg's arm with both hands.

'Pleased to meet you,' said Simon.

Still knocked out of kilter, Ella struggled to connect as the three others exchanged pleasantries.

'Mum? You going to say hi to Greg?'

'Of course, sorry, miles away, great to meet you,' she gushed, trying to compensate for her detachment.

'It's an honour to meet you, Ella,' he said, piercing her with his blue eyes. 'Heard so much about you.'

She could already tell he was a heartbreaker. He had the calm self-assurance of a much older man. 'Are you a student too, Greg?'

'Yeah, politics, I'm doing a PhD in international politics.' He ran his fingers through his blond mane.

'Sounds fascinating,' she said, realising she'd been gulping down the wine.

'Not as fascinating as why you're in Cambridge.' He gave a conspiratorial grin. 'Everyone's talking about it. Is he the genius everyone says?'

The question caught her off guard. 'So I'm told.' She wasn't comfortable saying more to a stranger.

Lizzie shot her a look.

Ella changed her mind. 'People tell me he thinks the answers are already out there.'

'What does that mean?' asked Lizzie.

'You know why this was your mum's favourite pub?' asked Simon, coming to the rescue.

'The Sauvignon Blanc?' suggested Lizzie.

Ella laughed along, though she knew it was a dig.

Simon gave Lizzie an impish nudge. 'Your mum could never get over the fact that this was where Watson and Crick announced over lunch that they'd found...' He leaned into Ella as they said in unison: 'The secret of life.'

Even Lizzie laughed. 'DNA?'

Simon nodded. 'Just imagine what it must be like to make a discovery like that.'

'I guess they were a bit like your genius, Ella,' said Greg.

Taken aback, she inclined her head towards Lizzie's companion. 'What do you mean?'

He ran his fingers through his hair again. 'They didn't invent anything,' he replied, as if it was obvious. 'The double helix was always there, in all of us, that beautiful shape. They found a way for the world to see it – the answer was already out there.'

'Yes, I suppose you're right.' Even Lizzie's date had a better understanding of her task than she did.

Lizzie rested her head on his shoulder.

Chapter Twenty-Five

E lla set off on her bike towards the Gonville. She was annoyed with herself for being so distracted during the meal. Cameron's letter was like an itch she couldn't scratch. She'd noticed Lizzie pick up on it. Ella's obsession with her cases had always hung over the family like a dark cloud. She knew only too well how Tom had been affected by it.

Almost without thinking, she stopped outside De Jure, put the cycle on the stand under the arch and headed up to Matthew's rooms. Perhaps she would have a moment of inspiration. Going to the scene of the crime when she prosecuted murders always helped her get inside the killer's head, gave her the edge over her opponents.

She went through the locks and opened up, turning on the light. Being there after dark made her feel more connected to Matthew. She imagined him beavering away, night after night. She stood in the middle of the room and tried to look at it afresh.

He and I are the inverse of here and there she repeated to herself over and over. The phrase hadn't come up on google. She was convinced *he* was the key. *I* must be Matthew she told herself.

She kept coming back to the idea that it was about polymaths. If he was the last polymath, maybe the inverse was the first. She racked her brain. Socrates. Even if she was right, what was Matthew trying to tell her? She scoured the room until she found a book on Socrates. She flicked through looking for annotations. Nothing. It occurred to her that Pythagoras might have been earlier and then went through the same process. After flicking through another book, she discarded it on the desk and sat down.

'Think, think,' she said out loud. 'What did Matthew expect me to know?' She thought it through again. '*Here* must be Cambridge,' she said, getting up again because as a barrister, she always thought better on her feet. 'He would probably expect me to assume *there* is Arizona. The last scholar to come from Arizona to Cambridge.'

Still muttering to herself she scanned the shelves again looking at all the great works and biographies, hoping something would stand out. 'Matthew came from *there*, so the inverse would be Cambridge to Arizona.' She tapped her chin as she read the spines. 'Who was the first man from Cambridge to go to—' She stopped, racking her brain. 'Lord Darrell Duppa!' she shouted, remembering the Cambridge classicist who had arrived in Arizona in the nineteenth century and gave Phoenix its name. Ella was sure she'd seen his name somewhere in the room.

Frantically pushing over piles of books, she searched the shelves again until, out of the corner of her eye, Ella saw the word Duppa on a spine on one of the shelves. A long since out-of-print biography of the man.

She carefully pulled the book off the shelf wondering whether she was even on the right lines. With a sense of trepidation, she opened up the hardback cover.

A surge of excitement rose up. A small rectangle in the centre of the pages had been cut away and tucked into the space was a memory stick. She took it out and held it between two fingers, rotating it for a better look.

Ella gulped. Why send a coded message directed at someone with an academic background, a knowledge of history? She suddenly felt humbled by a deep personal connection with Matthew. She said out loud, 'Thank you.'

Triumphantly, she took her laptop out of her bag just as her phone bleeped with a text from Lizzie.

Thanks for today, meant a lot. Hope Greg was a hit? X

Ella felt a lump in her throat. Things were looking up. She texted back.

Definitely!

She pushed the flash drive into a USB port on the side of the Mac. A folder appeared onscreen – password protected. She groaned. There had to be a catch. It was just like getting evidence discs from the CPS, they always forgot to send the password.

She tried numerous combinations; Cameron Shepherd, Matthew, even polymath. Nothing worked. She got into a routine of pacing the room, entering a new word, getting more frustrated as each attempt failed.

She looked at her phone again, taking solace from Lizzie's message. Then she had an idea. She typed in another reply.

Have you got Jay's number – need to call in that debt!

Already!? 'Fraid not, didn't really know him that well x

Now you tell me! X

Ha ha x

But how could she get hold of Jay? She was sure he'd know how to override the password. Then she remembered his folder, still in her bag. She'd seen his address somewhere in there. She pulled it out and thumbed through. There it was, a flat in King's Hedges, just north of the city centre. She tapped the address into google maps on her phone. She could get there on the bike in no time.

Chapter Twenty-Six

Agent Harris came out of the cubicle and washed her hands at the sink, then dried them carefully with a paper towel. Rather than screw it up she folded it neatly and dropped it in the bin. She made a few minor adjustments to her hair in the mirror then stood back to assess her trouser suit. She flicked a piece of fluff off the lapel, leaned in, studying her complexion. It had to be important to be summoned at this time of night.

Ready as she'd ever be, she walked out into the corridor and sat down on one of the antique wooden chairs with worn, red leather upholstery. Old portraits of men in gilt frames lined the walls. Each one with its own lamp above and an engraved inscription below.

The imposing double doors at the end of the corridor opened and a man came out dressed in a Savile Row three-piece. 'You ready, Ginger?' he said in a public school accent.

Harris stood up and pulled down her jacket. 'Told you not to call me that,' she replied.

He smirked. 'Don't fuck this up, Harris. It's a last chance.'

She ignored the comment and double-checked her phone was on silent.

'Remember, this is why you never got a life?' His mouth formed into a leer. 'No husband, no kids.' He led her to the door and held it open for her.

As she passed, Harris gave him the finger.

The long narrow room had no windows and was dominated by a rectangular table, all but two empty chairs occupied by middle-aged men, a couple of whom were in military uniform, medals sewn on to the breast.

The colleague retook his place.

'Sit down, Harris,' said a portly man with a round face and spectacles, dressed in civvies. His hair was in a combover that wouldn't fool anyone.

Harris obeyed.

'So, what can you tell us?' he asked, without making any introductions.

Harris sat up straight. 'A QC called Ella Blake is chairing the inquiry. She's staying at the Gonville Hotel.'

'What does she know?'

She cleared her throat. 'Very little, less than us, anyway.' She waited obediently for the next question.

'That's not saying much,' derided a man in uniform. 'Where are you getting your information?'

She kept her back straight. 'A local DC called McDonald. Completely in the dark but he's eager to help, very ambitious but not bright.'

The main guy seemed appeased. 'Should we be concerned about her?'

She took her time. 'Not at this stage, but I wouldn't underestimate her.'

'I've heard she's a washed up drunk?' another man piped up from the other end of the room.

Harris gave him her attention. 'She does have issues.'

The chairman scoffed, making his jowls quiver. 'Issues? You can forget all that politically correct codswallop in here, Agent Harris.'

Harris touched her neck. She could feel her skin going red. 'I think she's primarily focused on building bridges with her daughter, sir. She's an undergraduate.' She placed her hands symmetrically on the table.

'More to the point, Harris, have you found your CHIS yet?' He looked at her disdainfully over the top of his glasses.

'No sir, not yet,' she replied looking down at her hands. 'But as you know sir, he wouldn't sign up, so strictly speaking, he's not an informant.'

'All right, all right,' he said, swatting her words away with the back of his hand. 'Anyway, bloody well find him,' he snarled. 'Had the embassy on four times today. You do understand how important this is?'

She looked him straight in the eye. 'Of course, sir.'

He moved his head to the side and stared at her, as if weighing her up.

She didn't flinch.

He sighed. 'All, right, that'll be all.'

'Yes, sir,' she replied, rushing to get up. 'Thank you, sir.'

The same escort showed her out. Once they were out of ear-shot, he said in a whining voice, 'She's got *issues*.' He tutted. 'You're a fucking idiot, Ginger.'

Harris kept walking.

Chapter Twenty-Seven

J ay's apartment was in a non-descript four-storey block on Topper Street.

Ella ran her finger down the numbers at the entrance. Pitois, number 22. She pressed the buzzer.

After a minute: 'Hello?'

'Hi Jay? It's Ella Blake?'

'Ella? Is everything OK?'

'Yes,' she replied, looking at her watch and realising it was after midnight. 'Sorry to come so late but I was hoping to call in that favour?'

'Sure, come up. Second floor, the lift's broken.' He buzzed her in.

The drab walls were covered in graffiti and the hallway smelt of urine. She was glad Lizzie didn't have to live in a place like this. She walked up the stairs and found Jay standing in his doorway, in a t-shirt and boxers.

'I wasn't expecting this?' he said.

'Nor was I,' she replied, jokily averting her eyes. 'Thought you'd be out celebrating your acquittal?'

He almost blushed as he looked down at his state of

undress. 'No one to do it with. Pathetic I know.' He walked back inside and picked up a pair of jogging bottoms off the sofa.

She followed him into the tiny space, surveying the kitchen-diner. The walls were covered with framed photos and posters of animals, plants – the living. The worktop and floor were in need of urgent attention, rubbish and unwashed crockery scattered about. 'Jesus, I thought you were against pollution?'

Hopping, he got one leg through, then the other. 'Sorry, I know it's a bit of a mess.' Then, finally seeming to get the joke he said, 'I suppose living alone so long, you let things slide.' Now that he was dressed, he seemed to relax a little.

'I can totally relate to that.' Her heart went out to him. 'But you'll never get a girl back here with it looking like this.'

'I thought I just did?' He winked.

Ella smiled. 'My God, you've got a sense of humour.'

Jay laughed.

Ella felt a rush of maternal affection. She started picking up some broken prawn crackers off the floor. 'How about I help you clean this place up, and then you help me?'

His eyes widened. 'Sure.'

'Got any bin liners?'

He got a roll from under the sink, ripped one off and pulled it open. 'I hear Lizzie's got a new bloke?'

Ella dropped a few empty beer cans into the bag. 'Looks like it.' She eyed him with a newfound tenderness. 'Did you think you were in the running?'

'No,' he snapped, making a mess of trying to sound matter-of-fact. 'Of course not.'

Ella stopped and gave him her full attention. 'Why *of course?*'

'Well,' he said, eyes everywhere except on Ella. 'You know.'

'No, actually I don't.' She went back to her work. Even without looking at him, she could sense Jay's surprise at her observation. 'You got a J cloth or something for this table?'

'Yeah.' He ran a dirty rag under the tap. 'So, what's he like?'

'Clever, a bit like you, just smoother.'

He seemed to mull it over. 'Nobody likes a smoothie.'

They both giggled. They worked together in companionable silence until the room was tidy.

'Right, that'll do,' Ella said, wiping the desk around a large PC.

Jay stood, hands on hips, admiring the place. 'It looks great, thank you.'

'No problem,' she said, throwing the cloth at the sink.

'So,' he said, his voice full of anticipation. 'What's the favour?'

She reached into her jeans and pulled out the flash drive. 'This.' She handed it to him. 'I can't get in.'

He turned it over in his hand. 'OK.' He sat down at the PC and inserted the stick. The same notification came up. He typed in *password*, which didn't work. 'Sorry, force of habit. You've got no idea what it could be?'

She looked over his shoulder at the screen. 'No.'

He swivelled around in the chair to face her. 'Can you tell me anything about who gave this to you?'

She grimaced. 'Sorry, confidential.'

'Then it's going to have to be brute force.'

'What?' she replied with a furrowed brow. 'You mean take it apart?'

Jay chuckled. 'No, I mean I've got software that runs millions of combinations to hack in.'

'Oh right,' she replied, embarrassed that she wasn't up on all the jargon. 'How long would it take?'

He lifted his hands, palms up. 'There's no way of knowing, hours, days, sometimes even weeks. It might not work at all.'

Ella scratched her head.

'But you'd have to let me try and download the folder.'

'You mean let you copy it?' Alarm bells began to ring.

'Yes, or leave the stick here.'

She made a face. 'I can't do that.'

He looked down at his feet, then said, softly, 'You can trust me, you know.'

She put a hand on his shoulder. 'I don't doubt it, I just can't.'

He didn't look up. 'I understand.'

'Sorry.'

Chapter Twenty-Eight

Ella was sitting under the atrium in the breakfast room, already tucking into a full English, when Lizzie arrived. 'Steady on, Mum, cholesterol levels?'

'I'm starving, it's all this cycling.' She pointed her fork at Lizzie. 'That's your fault. Anyway, it's lovely that you wanted to join me.'

'Well, to be honest Greg gave me a bit of a talking to.'

'Really?' Ella poured the coffee into Lizzie's cup.

'Yeah, about you defending Jay yesterday, taking this job to spend more time with me. He reckons I should cut you some slack.'

'Well, that's very nice of him,' she replied, wondering if Lizzie would spot the irony.

'He thinks you're really cool.'

Ella could see the difference he was making. Lizzie's cheeks had a dash of colour. 'You like him a lot, don't you?'

She gave her mum a coy smile. 'So, do you still need to get hold of Jay?'

'No, I had his address in the brief, I went round there.'

She craned her neck forward and said in a loud whisper, 'Think I woke him up.'

'Jesus, Mum,' Lizzie replied, starting to giggle. 'What was so urgent?'

'Computer problem,' she said, pushing a piece of fried egg onto her fork. 'I'm under pressure of time.' She put the food in her mouth.

'Is there anything I can help with?'

Ella reached across the table and touched Lizzie's hand. 'Just you saying that means so much, darling.'

Lizzie's gaze settled on Ella's book. '*On The Heavens*? Aristotle?'

'Yes, I'm trying to find out what this academic who went missing was working on, he's a big fan apparently.'

Lizzie's eyes seemed to sparkle. 'Me too. Until I read about him, I just thought of him as a philosopher.'

'Me too,' said Ella. 'I had no idea he was saying the earth was a sphere in 340 BC. I'd always thought that was Copernicus or Galileo.'

'Mum, he was incredible,' Lizzie gushed. 'Physics, geography, astronomy, medicine. But you could say that his greatest achievement was as a teacher.'

'How so?' Ella asked, gripped by her daughter's enthusiasm.

Lizzie held open her arms as if about to make a big reveal. 'His pupil was Alexander the Great.'

'I know.'

Lizzie leaned forward. 'Arguably the greatest leader of all time.' She lifted her arms. 'Never lost a battle. He built the biggest empire the world has ever seen, out of nothing, all in a life that ended at thirty-two.'

Ella smiled. 'Superhuman.'

'Totally,' she said waving an arm. 'Whatever Aristotle

taught him...' She picked up the salt cellar and tapped it on the tablecloth. 'It worked.'

Ella loved seeing her daughter so impassioned. 'So, do you know who taught Aristotle?'

Lizzie gave a few blinks in quick succession. 'Plato.'

Ella's head tilted left. 'Impressive.' She leaned back in her chair. 'Well, I'm glad to see they're teaching you something.' She picked up the book and tossed it across the table. 'If you want to help, read everything you can about the Ancient Greeks.'

'No problem,' Lizzie replied.

Ella was touched that she seemed so delighted to be involved. 'And, if you've got time, Isaac Newton.'

'Great,' Lizzie was like a different person. 'I'm on it.' She put the book into her rucksack.

'And Lizzie,' Ella said, more seriously. 'It's for your ears only.'

Lizzie reciprocated with a sombre nod of the head. 'Understood.' She snatched a triangle of toast from the rack. 'Got to go, Greg's taking me out for the day.'

'Don't you want some butter on that?'

She was already getting up. 'No time.'

'Oh, and take this.' Ella handed her a piece of paper.

Lizzie took it. 'What is it?'

'Jay's details. He didn't have anyone to celebrate with.' She made a sad face.

'Thanks,' Lizzie replied, remaining straight-faced. 'He's a nice guy.'

Ella smiled at her daughter. 'You've got good taste in friends.'

Lizzie folded up the paper and put it in her pocket.

Having second thoughts about the research, Ella added, 'Don't let the reading interfere with your studies.'

'Don't worry. I've pretty much broken up for Easter.'

'Of course.' Ella realised she had lost track of time.

'I was thinking,' Lizzie said, sounding self-conscious. 'With you being here and everything, I might stay up over the holidays.'

'That would be great.' Ella's mouth broke into a wide smile. 'Nothing to do with a certain person called Greg?'

Lizzie threw her head back and chuckled.

Ella watched her bite into the toast, turn on her heels and leave. 'Love you, Lizzie,' she blurted.

Lizzie didn't seem to hear.

Chapter Twenty-Nine

The drive out to Thetford Forest was just what Lizzie needed. The rain had stopped and so had the squeaking wipers on the rusty Polo Greg had managed to borrow for the day. The seat trim was a pseudo tartan, punctuated with cigarette burns that had got bigger over time so that the foam underneath had been gouged out. She'd asked him whether he was insured to drive it and he'd answered with a wink. To her surprise, she hadn't minded. Perhaps she was actually starting to loosen up. The thought made her smile. She leaned over and craned her neck so that she could plant a kiss on his cheek. Everything was well with the world.

Houses began to disappear as they approached the edge of the forest, the route now carving out a channel through the vast expanse of pine trees. The clouds moved off as if by magic, allowing the sun to splash the road with light. The breeze shook the last raindrops off the trees, sparkling in the light as they cascaded down.

Lizzie wound her window down a few inches, letting her hair fly around her head. She breathed in the overpowering smell of pine, infusing the moist air.

'Did you know,' said Greg, nodding to the view on either side. 'None of these trees are indigenous. They were planted because they grow quickly.'

'Really?' Lizzie replied. 'But there are forests like this all over the UK?'

'Same reason,' said Greg. 'This is one of the biggest pine forests in the country. It was only planted after the First World War.'

Lizzie liked watching him talk. She put a hand against his cheek so she could feel his words.

He kissed her hand. 'All the slow growing oaks were cut down in the war effort. Even conflict can bring new life.' He stared ahead as if deep in contemplation.

They drove on in silence. Lizzie had never seen him so pensive. Maybe there was a deeper side to him, she thought. She closed the window. 'Hello? Earth to Greg?'

Brought back from his reverie, he took his hand off the wheel and squeezed Lizzie's knee, then tickled the skin visible through the designer hole in her jeans. 'You ready for the surprise?'

She giggled then did a drum roll with her fingers on the dash. 'It has been nearly an hour, and I've been good.' She gave him doe-eyes then laughed again. 'I'm guessing it's a picnic?'

'Not even close.' He slowed as they neared a turning. 'This could be it. Look out for an old wooden sign saying "farm".'

'There it is!' She pointed it out. She stuck out her bottom lip and giggled. 'Which farm?'

He switched on the indicator and took a left down a muddy track. The car rocked from side to side, splashing its way through the potholes. 'The guy that lent me this car also sorted it for us to go to David Kline's retreat.'

She stared at him, dumbstruck. 'What?'

'Yeah, he's having some kind of brainstorming day, apparently.'

She felt rudderless. 'But I thought you didn't like that sort of thing?' She was so shocked, she felt herself retreating.

'*You* do,' he replied.

'Do I?'

'Course you do, and if the person you lo… like…' He blushed. 'You do what makes them happy.'

'But I don't know this guy. We don't know him…' Her protests petered out as they turned into a cobbled farmyard surrounded by old stone outbuildings. There were young people everywhere, in groups of two or three, talking intently. She'd expected new age traveller types with dreads and nose piercings but most of them had gleaming white trainers and trendy jackets – totally out of place in the English countryside.

A couple of ducks flapped their wings and jumped out of the car's path as Greg followed the muddy tyre tracks around to where a line of cars was already parked up.

'So many people,' said Lizzie, reassured by their anonymity. They got out of the car and stood for a moment, taking in the view across a fallow field towards the woods. Lizzie shivered. There was a nip in the air now that the sun had moved back behind the clouds.

'Long barn in ten minutes for David's talk,' shouted a woman in a straw hat and Wellington boots standing on an upturned metal bucket.

'Greg Brooks!'

They turned to see a twenty-something man striding towards Greg, arms out ready for a rugby player's hug. 'What are you doing here?' the guy asked, with a belly laugh that betrayed a history of student high jinks.

'John!' Greg replied, banging his pecs into his friend's chest, then a hearty back pat. 'How long's it been?'

Lizzie waited anxiously for the moment of her introduction and the requirement to mix with the others.

'Come on, Lizzie,' Greg shouted over his shoulder, as the old friend pulled him towards a group of people.

She let him go, mouthing something at her she couldn't hear, until his attention was forced elsewhere as he was inducted into the new circle.

Opting for the lesser of two evils she wandered back towards the farmyard, hoping that safety in numbers might disguise her timidity. She could hear the distinctive oinks and grunts of pigs coming from what looked like a converted stable. A couple of people in work clothes carried in a bucket brimming with vegetable peelings. She secreted herself between a few groups milling about, picking up odd words in languages she didn't recognise.

Aware that Greg was now in full flow, she sidled further in the opposite direction, towards the farmhouse. An inviting glow from a wooden door drew her closer, and she could smell the sweet fragrance of burning firewood. She caught a glimpse of the flames in an open fireplace. As she got closer to the doorway, she saw a dozen people sitting around the room, some on cushions, some on patched-up sofas. The floor was stone, concave slabs ground out over time. She recognised the blonde girl from the meeting at the assembly rooms sitting on a bean bag, legs pulled up to her chest and a coffee mug cupped in both hands. She was staring hypnotically into the open hearth.

A young Italian-looking man, certainly a Latin complexion, got up to put on another log and saw Lizzie peering in. 'Hey, you're not allowed in here.' He scowled at her.

Lizzie jumped, remembering she wasn't invisible.

'It's OK,' said a voice from a position she couldn't see. 'Who is it?'

'She's new,' said the Italian, glowering at her.

Lizzie stood frozen by indecision and embarrassment. The blonde had woken from her trance and was now looking towards the entrance. Her warm smile saved Lizzie, pulled her in. She took two steps forward. She could see the source of the voice now. It was Kline, sitting skewwhiff in an easy chair with one leg draped lazily over the arm.

She averted her eyes, intimidated by his pose.

'What's your name?' he asked, putting down his leg and leaning forward in the chair. 'Everyone is welcome.'

'Lizzie,' she replied. 'My friend Greg brought me.' She half-turned towards the yard as if that would support her claim.

Kline got up, stretched upwards and held onto a ceiling beam. His sweat-shirt rose up exposing the definition on his torso. He resumed where he had left off when she'd interrupted. 'Everything is about cycles,' he said, continuing with his lesson, seemingly unconcerned by Lizzie's presence. He moved his hands in circles. 'Everything is connected.'

He took his hands off the oak and stared intensely at Lizzie, catching her by surprise. 'Don't blind yourself to the truth.' He persisted in glaring at her. 'Will you open your eyes?' he asked her directly.

She went red, unsure how to answer.

Come,' he said, skipping out of the door and grabbing Lizzie's hand as he passed. The others followed. He pulled her playfully across the cobbles and into the barn with the pigs. It reminded her of trips to the petting zoo with her mother. A crowd from outside gathered inside the barn to get a view.

'Life, a new cycle,' said Kline leaning on the low fence that penned in a large sow. She was lying on her side, nestled on a bed of straw whilst a row of eight piglets sucked frantically at her teats, tails wagging like coiled springs.

Lizzie crooked her head and made a mock sad face. 'So cute.' She forgot herself for a moment, that she was the focus of attention, a position she usually hated.

Kline opened a creaky wooden gate panelled with chicken wire and entered the pen. He bent over the suckling babes and scooped one up, so small he could hold it in his palm. Its instinct to squeal was stemmed by Kline's expert soothing with his free hand. He walked back out to where his audience were crowding round for the lesson. He moved closer to Lizzie, and she reached out to run a hand over the downy hairs on piglet's little back. She could feel the warmth that comes with life.

'This is what you buy in the supermarket every day without a second thought,' said Kline, his voice raised slightly, causing the animal to let out a snort.

Lizzie was only half-listening, entranced by the piglet.

'Few are allowed to live beyond six months.' Kline reached up to a shelf on the wall of the barn and seized a stout sticking knife.

Lizzie didn't see it until Kline was holding it against the hog's throat.

She gasped.

'Don't let people gift-wrap the truth.' He lifted his arm so everyone could see and slit the piglet's throat in one motion, like a cellist drawing his bow. There was a shrill squeal as blood spattered across Lizzie's face. She couldn't move, shaking and frozen in shock.

Kline tossed the carcass over at one of his underlings who caught it. 'Put it on the spit.'

There were a few cheers from the crowd.

Kline looked intently at Lizzie as he used his sleeve to wipe the blood from her face with all the tenderness of a mother nursing a sick child. 'I will never lie to you.' He used a finger to wipe around her mouth causing a few drops to smear her lip.

Lizzie could see Greg standing at the back, his face blazing with jealousy.

Kline cupped her face, eyes drilling deep inside her soul, stirring up the basest of emotions.

Chapter Thirty

It was evening. Ella had spent the day in Matthew's rooms. She'd decided to go right back to basics and document everything that was there, which was pretty much just books. He didn't live like other people.

She logged every title and author, hoping she might stumble on some kind of clue for the password. Most of the books were Matthew's, but some were borrowed from the hundred or so libraries around Cambridge. She was able to build up some sort of picture of the order in which he'd taken them out. Shortly before his disappearance he'd been focussing on ancient religious texts from around the world. There were many publications on tribal beliefs from groups in South America, the Middle East and Africa.

Her phone rang. She didn't recognise the number. 'Hello?'

'Hey, is that Ella?'

She recognised the accent. 'Yes.'

'It's Detective Broady, Phoenix Police. We spoke before?'

'Oh, yes. How can I help?'

'I'm here, at your hotel, to ask you about Cameron Shepherd.'

She was completely thrown. 'But I probably know less than you.'

'That's OK, then it won't take long. I'm in room 205.'

Ella stared out of the window at the courtyard below, deliberating on a response. 'All right, give me twenty minutes.'

'Great.' The phone went dead.

Struggling to take in what had just happened, Ella put the book back and went to lock up Matthew's fortress. She made her way back down to the porter's lodge, and waved to Bartlett, who was too engrossed in his crossword to notice. She got on her bike and cycled back through town to The Gonville.

The phone call bothered her. Something wasn't right. Why would he come all this way for an R.T.A?

She stopped at reception. 'Hi, can I just check, is Detective Broady in 205? I have a meeting with him.'

The woman behind the desk looked at her computer. 'Yes, Mr Broady.'

'Mr? Did he ask if I was staying here, what room I'm in?'

She looked baffled. The phone on reception rang out. She picked up but put the handset against her shoulder. 'Not as far as I'm aware.'

'Thanks.' Against her better instincts, she went up to the room. As she was about to knock, she stopped, her fist suspended in mid-air for a moment. She inhaled, then gave three deliberate taps.

'Give me a second,' called out a voice from inside. 'Be right with you.' Finally, the door opened. 'Hey there, Ella?' A tall, naturally strong looking man. He was about her age, somewhere between scruffy and casual, definitely someone who didn't worry about such things. A swarthy complexion and a handsome, lived-in face.

She was sure he was eyeing her up. She regretted choosing tight jeans that morning. 'Yes, Detective Broady?'

'That's me, come right in.' He swept an arm in a humorous, exaggerated movement, to usher her in.

It immediately put her at her ease. 'Warm enough?' she asked, noticing the thick woollen jumper.

'Huh? Oh this.' He laughed 'Lady, I'm from the desert. This might as well be the North Pole.'

'Lucky you came in spring, then.' Her eyes scanned the room then back at him. One side of his shirt was untucked.

He looked amused. 'You got that right.'

'You didn't tell them downstairs that you're a cop?' She eyed the half-emptied suitcase, open on the bed.

His expression became serious. 'No, should I have?'

She looked at his face more carefully now. 'Would you mind showing me your ID.'

'Sure.' He took it out of his back pocket and handed it over.

She studied it, then his face again. The photo was right but she wouldn't have known if it was fake. 'I'm sorry to be so sceptical, but it's a long way to come for an investigation, even though someone died.'

He shrugged. 'I guess you got reason to be jumpy?'

Something didn't feel right. Her eyes moved across to the wardrobe. The sliding door was slightly open. She could just make out a large object through the gap. It took a moment to figure out – an odd-shaped case, for something long – it had to be a rifle

His eyes followed hers. 'OK, you got me.' He moved over to the wardrobe.

Ella's heart was beating hard against her chest. 'Stop right there.'

'What's wrong?' he asked, picking up the case.

She pointed to it and instinctively took a step back. 'What is that?'

He undid the zip revealing the barrel. 'It's my baby,' he announced with pride. 'The Celestron.'

Ella froze. 'A gun?'

'Gun?' Broady replied, sounding surprised. 'No, it's a tele-scope, for looking at the stars.' He held it up.

Ella's face relaxed into a smile, then she gave an all-out laugh.

Broady pulled the telescope out of its case. 'You thought…?'

She nodded.

He moved closer. 'You really are jumpy. Where I come from there ain't much on the ground, but if you look up at night, it sure will take your breath away.'

She began to relax. 'The desert. No light pollution?'

'That's right.'

She pointed towards the window. 'You won't see much around here, I'm afraid.'

'I know,' he replied patting his baby with a mischievous grin. 'But she goes everywhere with me. Don't tell my boss, but the real reason I'm here,' he said, lowering the volume, 'is to see the Astro Library.'

'In the Old Observatory?'

'Yeah,' he replied with another infectious grin. 'Been on my bucket list, if you know what I mean?'

Her eyes narrowed in mock outrage. 'You justified a trip to the UK so that you could go to a library?'

'When you put it like that it makes me sound like a nut.'

'You said it.'

He chuckled. 'You never done anything like that?'

Remembering why she'd taken this job, she smiled. 'Maybe.'

'So?' he asked, putting the apparatus back in the cupboard. 'What's your inquiry all about?

Ella remembered Desmond's insistence on cooperation

with McDonald. 'Will you share what you've got on Cameron?'

He walked over to her. 'OK.' He held out a hand. 'I won't spit on it.'

'Most considerate,' she replied, shaking it.

'We got ourselves a deal,' he said, holding on for a few seconds. 'How about we go down to the bar, seal it with a couple of Jack Daniels and you can tell me why you're so spooked?'

Ella smiled. 'Sounds like a plan.'

Chapter Thirty-One

Lizzie's head was a cauldron of emotions. Greg had been so attentive since the pig thing, saying he felt so bad for leaving her, but she was unsettled, way out of her depth.

They stood at the back of one of the empty outbuildings listening to Kline dispensing his radical ideas and outlining his plans for direct action to make the zombies, as he called them, sit up and pay attention to what was happening in the world. Kline's references to Genesis were what really intrigued Lizzie. He seemed to have some kind of central doctrine but only those closest to him were bestowed with any of this learning.

Greg, who was standing behind her, nestled his face into her neck and pulled her into him.

She could smell burning fat – the hog roast. She felt nauseous, but then stiffened, trying to focus on Kline's message, how she'd blinded herself to the truth. She was sure he kept looking at her as he spoke.

Greg squeezed her tighter, his crotch against her bottom.

Out of nowhere she remembered Jay, and the piece of

paper Ella had given her. Suddenly the farm wasn't where she wanted to be. She turned her face upwards. 'Can we go now?'

Greg frowned. 'What, now? We've only just got here?'

'Yes, now,' she replied, pulling away. She walked, arms folded, across the yard towards the car. Dreading the possibility of a scene, she was relieved to hear Greg's footsteps behind her. 'Sorry,' she said once he'd caught up. 'There's stuff I need to do.'

As the car reversed out, she could see two men from the farmhouse tending to the spit. She felt like an imposter.

Greg navigated back down the lane in silence, weaving around the potholes, a brooding expression on his face. Lizzie decided to let him sulk.

There was a car parked up at the end of the lane, two wheels up on a patch of grass, not even in a layby. She looked at the driver as they passed. She recognised him from somewhere, then it came back. He was the burly man who'd been looking for the blonde girl at the assembly rooms. She wondered if he was her dad. 'Why is he waiting there?' she commented to Greg, but he was still sulking and didn't answer.

Chapter Thirty-Two

'This is a nice surprise,' said Jay, leading Lizzie into the flat.

She handed him a bottle of red she'd bought from the Tesco Express. 'A delayed celebration.'

'I'm honoured,' he said, reading the label. 'Quality.'

She laughed. 'Nice place, very tidy,' she said as they went into the sitting room. She looked around and noticed a picture of a humpback being harpooned by a whaling ship. A slogan across the top said: "WHY?"

'Thanks,' he replied, walking over to the kitchenette.

She followed. 'What's that smell?'

'Rougaille.' He picked up a wooden spoon and stirred a saucepan on the hob. 'It's a Mauritian dish. You hungry?'

'Sure.' She leaned over the pan and breathed in the blended aroma of tomatoes and fish. 'Smells lovely. You cook a lot?'

He opened a cupboard and took out some plates. 'Not really.' He looked serious. 'Thought I'd have a fresh start.' He turned off the hob. 'I remember a few dishes, you know, from my mum.' He fished out some cutlery, loose in an undivided drawer.

She decided not to probe further. 'Glasses?'

'Cupboard above the sink.'

She took out two and went over to the settee as he unscrewed the bottle. 'Here,' he said, after pouring her a glass. 'What made you change your mind?'

'Just felt a bit tight,' she replied. 'After what you'd been through.'

He went over to the microwave and came back with a bag of rice, held in the corner with two fingers. He used a knife to stab it and unloaded the contents in two mounds on the plates. The steam made their faces sweat. 'What about your new fella?'

She used a fork to break up the rice. 'I explained, he's fine about it.'

'That's good,' he replied without eye-contact: 'You don't have to feel sorry for me, you know.' He went and got the saucepan and spooned some rougaille onto the rice.

'I don't.' She used a finger to lift his chin. 'Jay, I don't.'

He didn't speak.

She watched his face. 'Actually, I'm fascinated by you.'

His brow lifted. 'Really?'

'Yes,' she said. 'For starters, I want to know how you coped, how you got into Cambridge without any help? You were on your own at sixteen…'

He got up and went over to the kitchenette to put the pan back on the hob. 'It was hard.'

She watched him come back and sit down. 'I bet it was.'

He picked up a spoon and waited for her to dig in. 'Not fitting in at school didn't help. Always being an oddball.'

Lizzie noticed that his body language was at ease now. 'You won't feel like that when you start uni, we're all like that.' She got some rougaille onto her fork.

'I've noticed,' he said.

She laughed, so did he.

'Tastes amazing.' She scooped up another mouthful. 'You are full of surprises.'

'I've got a jar of lime pickle,' he said, with his first uncomplicated smile. 'But it's starting to look a bit furry.'

'Think I'll pass,' she said with a shake of the head.

As they ate and chatted in the little flat, Lizzie lost track of time. She was glad her mother had given her his number. Maybe she knew her better than she thought. Her phone pinged. A text. 'Oh shit, I've got to go, it's Greg, I was supposed to meet him ten minutes ago.'

'Oh, right,' Jay replied, getting up and hovering awkwardly.

Lizzie did the same then typed out a message.

5 mins away

She turned her attention back to Jay. 'I've had a lovely time.' She tilted her head. 'Thank you.'

'Me too,' he replied.

'Can I just use your loo?'

'Sure,' he said, signalling with his head. 'In there.'

It wasn't until she'd pushed the bolt across and sat down that she noticed all the photos on the wall of a much younger Jay and his mum in happier times. She felt choked.

Suddenly there was an almighty bang. She flinched. It sounded like the front door coming off its hinges.

There was shouting, coming from the lounge. Voices, not Jay's.

The sound of things being smashed.

She could hear Jay. He was protesting, pleading.

She stood up, trembling. Slowly, she undid the bolt.

She opened the door slightly, enough to see three figures,

all in black, wearing balaclavas. She pulled it shut, then summoned up the courage to open it again. One man had Jay pinned to the sofa, a gloved hand on his neck. He held a knife in the other which he drew back. She heard him say, 'I'm going to cut you up, motherfucker.'

Instinct took over. 'No!' Lizzie pushed the door wide open and ran in.

Chapter Thirty-Three

'Two Jack Daniels, neat,' said Broady, as they strolled past the bar.

'Coming up,' the barman replied.

They took a couple of armchairs by the window, either side of a round, ornate, low table with lions' feet on the legs. The evening sun had all but disappeared.

'Can't wait to see the place properly,' said Broady, staring out across the forecourt and onto Parker's Piece. 'Tell me about Matthew Shepherd?'

'Unfortunately, I don't know much about him,' Ella replied, crossing her legs. 'He's a recluse, an eccentric academic, a genius by all accounts. He disappeared a few weeks ago without a trace. Nobody knows what he was working on, if anything. His room at the college is like Fort Knox. He was either paranoid or afraid of something.'

A couple of business types entered the room and nodded politely at the other guests before getting into a discussion at the bar about which brand of beer they could have on draught.

Broady dug his fingers into the bowl of nuts on the table. 'What do the cops say?' He put a couple in his mouth.

'There's a young officer in charge called McDonald. He's not been very helpful. He just says there's no proof of life after his disappearance and he won't tell me if they've been into his phone records or email account.' She stopped as the barman set their drinks on the table.

Broady gave the man an appreciative wink and waited for him to leave. 'You want to know what he was doing just before he vanished?'

'Exactly.' Ella uncrossed her legs and leaned in. 'I can't help but feel this case is really important, but I don't know why.'

Broady downed his JD then put the glass firmly back on the table. 'Maybe I should see this McDonald guy. Give him the old-brother-from-another-mother routine.'

'Worth a try,' she agreed. 'So, what about Cameron?'

'Two more of these,' he called over to the barman, holding up his tumbler. 'He was a bigshot lawyer and politico. Big-hearted democrat, tipped for the very top. 'Lived alone on a desert ranch.'

She looked at her drink but didn't take a sip.

'Their folks died young in a car accident. They told me in the town that Cameron was like a father to Matthew even though they were twins. Cameron was a minute older. Matthew was the thinker, Cameron more practical. He farmed his parents' land. Paid his own way through law school.'

Ella inclined her head. 'You said that's how Cameron died too? In a car crash?'

'No, the car was in the garage,' he replied, fixing her with his gaze. 'Hosepipe in the exhaust.'

Ella winced. 'Suicide?'

'That's what they're saying. Didn't feel right to tell a stranger over the phone.' She nodded. 'Of course.'

The waiter brought the round and placed the glasses on paper mats.

Broady nodded his thanks. 'Besides, I don't buy it.'

Ella waited for the waiter to be fully out of earshot. 'What do you mean?'

'He'd just bought himself a plane ticket to London.'

Ella took a sip of her drink and leaned forward again. 'You're saying someone made it look like suicide?'

Broady shrugged. 'Just a hunch.'

She checked no one was listening 'Wouldn't he have defensive injuries, signs of a struggle?'

'There were sleeping pills in his system. A lot.'

She frowned. 'Were they his?'

'Yeah, he'd been using them for a while.'

'So, he could've taken them himself?'

'Or someone stuck them in his food or drink. Someone who wanted to knock him out so they could put him in the car without a struggle.'

'And leave no marks. Any prints on the car?'

'Only his.' Broady took a sip. 'I could be wrong, I know I'll never prove it, but I figure I owe it to him to come and ask some questions.'

Ella found his analysis unsettling. 'Motive?'

Broady sat up straight and looked Ella in the eye. 'To stop him before he told you something?'

She was thinking the same thing, but it still made her shiver, hearing someone say it out loud.

He maintained eye-contact. 'Do you know what that could be?'

'No, I wish I did. So, this trip, it's not just about the bucket list?'

Broady sighed. 'This guy really gave a shit, you know what I mean.'

Ella nodded.

He moved forward in his chair. 'No clues at all?'

She hesitated. Her phone pinged. She took it out of her bag and saw a text from Lizzie, some calls she must have missed earlier. 'Something's happened. It's my daughter.' She began reading Lizzie's text.

'What is it?'

She stood up. 'She's at the police station, I've got to go.'

He downed the rest of his drink. 'I'll come with you.'

Ella ran out of the hotel and across the road onto Parker's Piece. A car screeched to a stop and hooted. The driver shouted abuse out of the window.

She raced across the green, Broady in her wake.

Just as she arrived in the reception, Lizzie and Jay were being brought back through to the front desk by McDonald.

'Mum!' Lizzie stopped short of running into her mother's arms.

Forgetting their protocol, Ella threw hers around her daughter. 'What happened?' She pulled her tight.

Broady panted in behind her.

'Looks like a nasty robbery,' explained McDonald. He shot Jay a disapproving look. 'Probably by some of Mr Pitois' associates.'

Putting a sports bag over his shoulder, Jay said nothing. Ella could see how shaken he was.

'We'll take statements in the morning.' McDonald came closer to Ella and said, *sotto voce*, 'Not the best choice of companion for your daughter.' Turning to Jay, and in a louder voice he said, 'You know what they say, if you live by the sword…'

'…you die by the sword,' interrupted Broady.

McDonald raised an eyebrow at the stranger.

'Detective Hank Broady, Phoenix Police Department,' he said, flashing his badge. 'Great to meet you, officer.'

'DC McDonald,' he replied tentatively. 'Are you with her?'

'I'll leave you to explain, Detective Broady,' said Ella. 'I need to get them back.' She ushered the two young people towards the door. 'Thank you, detective.'

As soon as they were across the road and on the Piece, Lizzie stuttered, 'Mum, they had weapons.'

They huddled together in the moonlight. Ella looked from one to the other.

Lizzie was angry now. 'They kicked the fucking door in,' she sobbed. 'I thought they were going to kill him.'

Ella put an arm around her. 'Are you hurt, either of you?'

'No,' they replied in unison.

Lizzie pulled away. 'As soon as they saw me, they ran, it was weird.'

'Yeah,' said Jay, his voice shaky. 'Like they didn't want any witnesses.'

'He's staying at mine tonight,' said Lizzie. 'It's not safe there.'

'No,' said Ella. 'You can't do that.'

'But, Mum,' she replied, evidently ready for an argument. 'He's not even got a proper door on yet.'

'It's OK, I get it,' said Jay. 'She doesn't want me around you.'

'No, it's not that,' Ella lied. 'You can stay in my room. It'll be safer for both of you.'

Lizzie softened. 'What about you?'

'I'll stay in the van.'

'Me too.' She grabbed her mother's arm and held it with both hands. 'I don't want to be alone tonight.'

They started to walk back across the open space to the hotel.

'It doesn't make sense,' said Jay. 'They were like military.'

'Yeah,' Lizzie agreed. 'All in the same gear.'

'They kept asking: "Where is it?"'

'Where's what?' asked Ella.

He shrugged. 'That's just it, I don't know.'

Lizzie gave his back a reassuring rub. 'Don't think about it tonight.'

'They must've thought you had something,' said Ella, falling into cross-examination mode. 'The people that set you up, did they think you had something of theirs?'

'No,' Jay replied, his frustration showing. 'You read the file, I just got them access, that was it.'

She stopped and faced him. 'What about anyone else you've dealt with? Think.'

He looked away for a moment, then, suddenly distracted, he dropped the bag off his shoulder and stared intently at the ground as if working something out. His expression became more intense. 'Maybe it wasn't about me.' He stared at Ella. 'Maybe it was about you?'

Her head went back in surprise. 'Me?'

Lizzie turned towards her. 'Mum?'

Ella was silent now, her expression troubled.

'Please tell me this isn't down to you?'

Ella couldn't get her head around it. She tried to think it through. 'The memory stick? No, it can't be...' Ella stuttered. 'It doesn't make any sense.' She tried to take hold of Lizzie's arm but she pulled away. Ella walked a few yards, then turned back, running a hand over her hair. 'One thing is for sure, I'm way out of my depth here.' She paced some more, 'Let's go back, I need to talk to McDonald.' She started walking towards the station.

Lizzie followed.

'No,' said Jay, firmly, stopping them in their tracks. 'Have you managed to open the file?'

Ella turned around. 'No, why?'

He took a few steps towards her. 'Let me try, I think I've earned the right.'

Ella found herself considering it.

'If you tell McDonald,' said Jay, 'he'll take the stick, and chances are there's something really important on it.'

She thought about this. Her instincts told her it was wrong to involve Jay any further, especially if he was right about the attack.

Jay continued, 'I know why you're in Cambridge.'

'How?' But she'd already guessed.

He looked at Lizzie. 'She told me.'

Lizzie mumbled a sheepish, 'Sorry.'

Ella stifled a desire to tick her off. She began pacing again. 'You said it could take weeks?'

'That's brute-forcing, with software.' His voice lowered. 'There's another way.'

She stopped. 'What?'

'Human engineering. I can always figure out the password if you tell me enough information – whose stick it is, what you know about them…'

'Tell you more? I've already put you in serious—' She stopped herself and looked at Lizzie. 'It doesn't bear thinking about.'

'I think I've earned the right to have a go,' said Jay. 'To know what this is all about, and so has Lizzie.'

'Too right,' said Lizzie, moving closer to Jay's side. 'Typical of you to have me running errands about Aristotle, managing what you tell me, never the full picture.'

Ella backed away. 'That's not fair.' She needed to think. 'No, we all need to get out of town for a bit until I know what's going on.'

'What?' Lizzie's voice rose. 'Have you heard yourself? Always running away.'

Hurt, Ella didn't reply.

'If you're worried about my safety,' said Jay, in a more conciliatory tone, 'then I should be on board. I was only vulnerable when they thought I was some young criminal nobody gave a shit about.'

Ella thought through what he was saying.

'If you make me part of this, they'll think twice about doing anything. It would draw too much attention.'

She let out a sigh of resignation. 'OK.' She held her eyes closed for a few seconds to help her focus. 'Let's go back to the room.' She walked off with the others falling into step behind her.

'Who was the American?' Jay called after her.

In disbelief at the events of the last few hours, Ella replied, 'He says he's a cop.'

Chapter Thirty-Four

Harris' colleague was waiting for her at the end of the corridor by the double doors. Her footsteps echoed off the polished parquet. He gave her a scornful head shake before ceremoniously opening the door. 'Not going very well, is it,' he whispered with a smirk.

Ignoring him, she brushed the front of her trouser suit, took a breath, then entered, her colleague in tow. She was still perspiring from the dash from the car park.

'You're late,' said Combover, jowls oscillating.

She didn't make excuses. 'Sorry, sir.' She took her usual seat.

Many of the same people as before were seated around the table, with a few additions. There was a plate of biscuits, a teapot and some half empty cups scattered around. Male body odour hung in the air.

'Well, what the hell's going on?' Combover took a hanky out of his breast pocket and wiped some of the stress off his face. 'I'm told all hell's broken loose?'

Harris remained calm. 'The American, Broady, has made contact with Ella Blake and is now—'

'I'm talking about the bloody robbery,' he said impatiently.

'Yes, three of them broke into Jason Pitois' flat and attacked him.'

'The computer kid?' He glanced around the table. 'How do we know it was them?'

We don't, but it's got his MO all over it and he's getting more reckless every day. He clearly thinks Blake's onto something.'

'Police involved?'

'Yes, McDonald. He won't be a problem.'

A conspiratorial nod. He took his glasses off and threw them on the table. He fiddled with his silver cufflinks, sighed and rubbed the bridge of his nose.

Harris said, 'Sir, I don't think Blake's got any idea of the danger she's in.'

'There's no evidence she's at risk,' barked one of the other men. There was a murmured agreement from around the room.

'I was wondering,' she said tentatively, despite the opposition to her previous comment. 'Whether we were duty-bound give her a danger-to-life warning?'

Her colleague shot her a withering look.

The others shifted in their seats. No one was making a note now.

'And blow the whole thing wide open?' said Combover in a raised voice, putting his glasses back on. He tapped the end of his pen on the table.

'She's smart,' Harris persisted. 'She could lead us to Matthew. That must be why they broke into Pitois' flat. Blake must know something.'

Combover's cheeks turned even ruddier than before. 'You want an amateur to find Shepherd for you? Because you can't?' He banged his fist on the table causing a few teacups to clatter on their saucers. 'Coming in here shooting your mouth off about Osman warnings.' He pointed at her across the table. 'This is your bloody mess, Harris.'

She didn't respond.

'Covert monitoring for now.' He shot her a look. 'Understood?'

'Yes, sir,' she replied.

He put the pen in an inside pocket. 'I'm sure this whole inquiry will hit the buffers in a couple of days,' he offered, recovering his composure. 'It's a sideshow.'

There was mumbled agreement around the table.

Harris got up to leave and pushed the chair carefully back in position.

'Wait,' Combover ordered. 'Have you got anything to hold him on yet?'

Harris stopped and exhaled. ''Fraid not sir, you know how clever he is and he surrounds himself with the right people.'

'All right, you can bring him in for interview, give him a shot across the bows.'

'Yes,' said one of the other suits. 'A shakedown, I think the Americans call it.'

'Yes, sir,' Harris replied. 'Thank you, sir.'

'But Harris,' Combover said gravely as the agent was almost at the door. 'Don't mention the target.'

'Of course not, sir.'

Chapter Thirty-Five

Greg was standing at the entrance to the Gonville, illuminated by the porchlight. He rushed out onto the forecourt as they approached. 'Lizzie...'

She ran to him.

After a hug, he bent down and inspected her face. 'You hurt?'

'No,' she said. 'Just a bit freaked out.'

He acknowledged Ella, then rested his eyes on Jay.

'This is Jay,' said Lizzie. 'Jay, Greg.'

They shook hands. There was an awkward silence as they measured each other up.

'Lizzie says you're starting at Cambridge in September?'

'Yeah, and you're at Wolfson, right?'

'For my sins,' Greg replied. 'Look, I heard what happened, mate,' he said. 'You need a place to crash?'

'No thanks,' Jay replied, nervously glancing away. 'I'm sorted.'

'OK, well the offer's there,' Greg replied, then turned to the others. 'Have they caught the bastards that did it?'

'I reckon that'll take a while,' Ella cut in. 'These guys need to get some rest, Greg.'

'Right, of course,' he replied.

Lizzie shot her mum daggers, then stood on tiptoes and kissed Greg's cheek. 'I'm going to stay with Mum tonight.'

He gave her another hug.

'I'll tell you all about it tomorrow, promise.'

'OK.' He nodded over at Ella and Jay, put his hands in his pockets and sauntered off, a picture of dejection.

Ella wasted no time heading inside and up to the room.

Lizzie had to skip to keep up. 'Why couldn't you invite him?'

Ella stared straight ahead. 'I hardly know him.'

Lizzie tried to get alongside her mother on the corridor. '*I* know him.'

This time she turned her head and looked Lizzie in the eye. 'Did he know you were going to Jay's?'

Lizzie gasped. 'I can't believe you asked that.'

The three of them stopped outside the room while Ella went through her pockets for her key card.

'Look,' said Ella, taking a breath. 'This is supposed to be a confidential inquiry. I've already involved too many people.'

Seeing the logic, Lizzie's anger subsided. 'He didn't know the address. He's just a student.'

'I know,' Ella agreed, realising her judgement was all over the place. 'I'm sorry.'

As soon as they were in the room, Ella sat down at the desk against the wall under the flat-screen TV. She started scribbling on a pad.

Jay sat on a chair in the corner. He took a laptop and charger out of his bag and set up on the coffee table. 'What's the Wi-Fi code?'

Ella tossed him the card and caught her reflection on the wall mirror in front of her, then Lizzie's anxious face, sitting on the edge of the bed, behind her. Their eyes met, then away. Ella wasn't used to being so in tune with her daughter.

She ripped the page off the pad, grabbed her wallet and went over to Jay. 'Do you want a job?' she asked, abruptly.

Jay shifted uneasily in his chair, as if wondering how to answer. 'You don't have to pay me.'

'Oh, I do.' She took a hundred pounds in notes out of her wallet and thrust it towards him. 'Take it.'

He looked at Lizzie, who nodded, then accepted the money.

Ella put the paper on the table. 'And sign that.'

'What is it?' he asked, leaning forward to read it.

'An employment contract with a confidentiality clause. I'm employing you on this inquiry – one hundred pounds to open that stick.'

He looked skywards, then back. 'I get it.'

'Good,' she said, staring him out. 'This is my insurance. You breach this contract, I will sue your arse and I will make sure there's no way Cambridge will ever take you.'

Lizzie tutted. 'All right, Mum, steady on.'

Jay raised a hand. 'It's fine. I won't tell a soul.'

She took the USB stick out of her jeans and was about to hand it to Jay when there was a knock at the door.

They all froze.

Chapter Thirty-Six

Lizzie was the first to move. 'It's probably Greg, don't worry, I'll talk to him.'

'Hang on,' said Ella, going over. 'Stand back.' She tentatively moved her head towards the spyhole and squinted through. A sigh of relief. 'It's OK.'

It was Broady. She opened the door. He walked in with a finger held to his lips.

Nobody spoke.

They watched as he turned on the TV and ran his fingers behind it, then under the dressing table. He did the same around the bed and coffee table. He stopped, then stood up straight, carefully surveying the room. He rummaged around on the breakfast tray and picked up a teaspoon, then pulled out a chair and stood on it.

The others watched in silence, mesmerized.

He used the end of the spoon to unscrew the air-con vent in the ceiling. Once he had the cover off, he felt around in the void with his free hand.

There was something there. He pulled it out, got down off the chair and held it between finger and thumb.

The others crowded in.

It was a tiny blob of black foam covering a piece of metal.

Ella gasped – was it a microphone?

He walked over to the bedside table and dropped it in a glass of water. 'I take it that robbery was to do with you?' he said, pointing at Ella.

She immediately looked at Jay but didn't reply.

'How do you know?' Jay asked.

'Gut.' He patted his stomach. 'Lady, you are involved in some heavy shit.'

'We don't know for sure,' she protested, without conviction, then looked from face to face, searching for reassurance. All but Broady's expression reflected her own – fear. 'Who would want to bug my room?'

'Who knows,' said Broady. 'Could be anyone, maybe more than one entity.'

'Entity?' she asked, wondering why he knew the jargon.

'A government agency from here, or overseas, or maybe a commercial operation.'

She tried to think quickly, logically, use her advocacy skills. 'How do I know you're not one of them?' Her mind began to race. 'Using the Phoenix Police as a cover?'

'Hold on…' he said, putting up his hands.

'Maybe you had something to do with Cameron's death?'

All eyes were on Broady now.

'You've got it wrong,' he protested.

'Google him, Jay,' she ordered. 'Detective Hank Broady, Phoenix Police Department.'

They all watched Jay's fingers dance over the keys. Within seconds he was reading off the screen. 'Nothing about personnel on the police site, which makes sense.' He kept typing away. 'Hang on, I've got something.' He glanced up at Broady. 'There's a lot actually. Deputy Chairman of the Phoenix Astronomical Society?'

Ella felt her body release some of its tension.

'Does a lot of stuff for a charity too, underprivileged kids. Look,' he said, swivelling the screen around. 'Detective from the Phoenix Police Department. That's him, getting an award from the mayor.'

Ella bent down and looked at the picture, then at Jay. 'What do you think?'

'There's just too much stuff here – he's who he says he is.'

'Thank you,' Broady said, giving Jay a nod.

Ella wasn't finished. 'How come you know about bugs and things? That's not everyday stuff for a cop.'

'I served in the military, did tours of Iraq, Afghanistan, got quite high up, 'cos I know about the desert. Did some counter-surveillance stuff.'

She was satisfied. 'OK.'

Broady picked up the remote and turned up the volume on the TV. He motioned for them to sit on the floor around the coffee table. 'McDonald gave me some intel.'

Ella was starting to see him differently. 'How did you manage that?'

'He likes having his ass kissed,' he said, directing his observation at Ella. 'It's an underrated technique.'

'Go on,' she said, ignoring the dig.

'They've investigated his cell phone number.' He looked at the faces of the others, drawing them in. 'The account was still active, but he stopped making calls a few weeks before he disappeared. Same with the email account, and all old emails deleted.'

'He knew his devices were being intercepted,' said Jay.

'I reckon,' Broady agreed. 'He didn't want them to know what he was doing.'

Jay shot Ella a look. 'So, he couldn't use his phone or email account?'

'Or even the internet,' added Broady. 'So, I recommend

we do the same – radio silence about anything to do with this investigation.'

Ella was still trying to take it all in.

'There's something else,' said Broady. 'He made a mistake.'

'Who?' asked Ella.

'Matthew. He got a few calls which went to voicemail.'

'Who was it?'

'They don't know, he deleted them, could be anyone that didn't know he wasn't using the phone, dry cleaning, IRS, doesn't matter.'

Ella immediately saw the point. 'Because they gave away his location.'

'That's right. If you get a call, even if you don't take it, it connects to a cell-site. Matthew hadn't figured that out yet.'

'Cell-site?' asked Lizzie.

'Masts with antennas, all over the place,' said Ella. 'In petrol stations, on top of tower blocks. When a mobile phone makes or receives a call, it sends a signal to the nearest mast – a cell-site.'

She glanced at Jay, then back at her mum. 'I've never noticed them.'

'The police swear by them, to catch drug dealers. There aren't many sites in rural areas,' Ella continued, 'but they're all over the place in cities, to deal with the volume of phone traffic.'

'McDonald's going to give me a map tomorrow, with the sites marked, but he says most of the hits are in Cambridge, probably sitting in his room, but one of the pings was in London, and another was in Oxford.'

'Well, at least we've got something to go on.' She gave Broady an encouraging smile. 'Whatever Matthew was working on…' she said, her voice trailing off.

'Everybody wants,' said Broady.

'Or somebody wants to stop us from finding out?' said Ella.

'Why go to such extremes to hide it?' asked Lizzie.

'He must've been scared,' said Jay, 'about what would happen if it got into the wrong hands.'

'Then why not share it with Cambridge, with De Jure?'

'Maybe he wasn't ready,' said Ella. 'Didn't know what he had? Or couldn't tell anyone until his work was finished, to make sure no one got there first?'

They all fell silent, deep in contemplation. They made a ridiculous spectacle, huddled around the tiny table.

Broady was the first to speak. 'Is there anything else you guys want to tell me?'

Ella had already decided that she wasn't ready. 'Like what?'

'Like how he fits into all this,' said Broady, gesturing towards Jay.

Jay waited for Ella to take the lead.

'He's Lizzie's friend and—'

'And you got him off a hacking charge, I know, McDonald told me.' His frustration was showing. 'But why did three dudes break into his apartment and put a knife to his throat?'

Ella took a while to reply. She wasn't going to lie. 'I'm sorry, detective.'

'Hank.'

'Hank.' She could see the dubious look on his face. 'I can't take this to the next level, not yet. I need to think about it?'

He looked affronted. 'I got to say, you ain't much of a team player.' Then, with more sympathy, he added, 'Sometimes you got to let people in, take a chance.'

The observation struck a chord with Lizzie. 'He's got a point, Mum.'

'It's not that simple,' Ella snapped. 'Look, I've been thinking about Cameron's death. He knew something, or had something, that's why he's dead.' She took a deep breath, then exhaled 'I'm probably only alive because they think I don't know anything.'

Broady seemed to get it. 'You're worried that after that, there's no going back?'

'Yes, for you it's a job, even me, it's these two I'm concerned about.'

'I thought we'd already decided this,' said Jay.

Ella reached over and touched Lizzie's cheek. 'You're just kids.'

Lizzie's brow furrowed. 'We're already involved.'

'Yeah,' Jay agreed. 'I'll take my chances. Knowledge is power, right?'

'How about you give me twenty-four hours? Let me think things through?'

Broady nodded.

'It would have to be done right. I'd need to speak to Desmond at De Jure, introduce Hank, formally.' She was already working things through in her head. 'Lizzie and Jay still have to make their statements about the robbery. Lizzie, when you've done that, take my credit card, get a load of cash out. Take Jay to get a laptop, second-hand, buy it in cash, nothing to link any of us to the device.' She was thinking like a criminal lawyer now. 'And some phones, pay-as-you-go, not contract. I'll sort new accommodation for all of us, so pack a bag.'

'Gees, that'll cost,' said Broady

'Don't worry about it, I'm on two thousand a day.'

Broady looked shocked. 'Euros or dollars?'

With a wry smile, Ella said, 'Pounds.'

'Wow! You must be one hell of a lawyer?'

Ella appreciated Broady's knack for releasing the tension.

'She is,' said Lizzie.

Chapter Thirty-Seven

'Hey, blue eyes,' said Broady as he sat down at the breakfast table.

'Blue eyes?' Ella repeated with disdain.

'Yeah,' he replied, helping himself to the breadbasket. 'Your eyes, they're blue.' He inspected a pain au chocolat.

'Save the flattery,' she said. 'I've been around a long time and besides, you can't say that shit anymore. Me too, remember?'

'Abso-god-damn-lutely,' he replied, totally deadpan. 'It will not happen again. Count on it.'

She couldn't tell if he was still flirting with her. He took a bite of his pastry. She waited for him to swallow. 'Aren't you scared, nervous about everything?' she asked.

He wiped a few loose flakes off his lip. 'You can't change the future.'

He seemed so matter-of-fact. Was that his military training, she wondered. She watched him pour himself some coffee from the pot. 'Don't you mean the past?'

Their eyes met, just for a moment. She'd hit a nerve. They both had a past.

It was a long time since she'd wanted to know more about someone other than Lizzie. 'Thanks for letting Jay stay in your room last night.'

'No sweat, I've got a twin, anyhow. He's a good kid, real bright.' He gave her a lazy smile. 'And your daughter, she's something' else.'

Ella couldn't help but like the guy. 'Thanks.'

He winked. 'Like her mom.'

She could feel the colour rushing to her cheeks. She didn't know how to take him. 'Do you have kids?'

He stiffened. 'I had a son. He died.'

'I'm so sorry.' Ella could see the pain in his eyes.

'Few years ago, serving in Afghanistan.' He sighed. 'Wanted to be just like his dad. Stood on an IED.'

She hated herself for it, but for a split second it crossed her mind that he was lying, trying to ingratiate himself. She was finding it hard to be sure of anything, or anyone, except Lizzie. 'How do you cope with something like that?'

'You don't.' He fidgeted with a fork on the table.

She hadn't seen him so unsure of himself.

'You've just got to carry on.'

She wanted to believe him. Everything she'd ever learned from dealing with murderers and every kind of criminal told her that he was a good man. She'd made a career out of trusting her instincts.

She made a decision to follow them now.

Once they'd finished breakfast, they set off on foot across town to see Desmond.

Ella kept checking behind her to see if they were being followed.

Broady told her not to bother, not until it mattered.

They'd never be able to tell, anyway. Whoever they were, they knew what they were doing.

After a while, Ella almost forgot the pressure she was under, riveted by the expressions on Broady's face as they walked up King's Parade.

She had to wait for him outside De Jure whilst he took a load of photos with his phone. She could see Bartlett in the lodge, who nodded hello as she approached.

'Mr Bartlett,' she asked, going over to the hatch, 'Do you have CCTV cameras on the entrance?'

'Of course, state-of-the-art here,' he said, nodding at a monitor with a split screen on a chipped Formica table. 'Records everything.'

Ella's eyes widened. 'How far back do they go?'

'Two weeks,' he replied, leaning on the hatch shelf. 'After that it deletes, storage can't handle more, I'm told.'

Her enthusiasm dipped. 'Did a police officer ask to see the footage after Mr Shepherd went missing?'

He puffed out his cheeks and scratched his head. 'Yeah, but it had been deleted,' he replied, eyes wandering over to the spectacle of Broady coming up the steps.

'A young guy, Officer McDonald?' she asked, trying to regain his attention.

'No,' he said, still focused on the stranger. 'It was a woman, ginger hair.'

'I never saw buildings this old,' Broady gushed as he joined Ella, still holding his phone. 'So beautiful.' His face was contorted in wonder. When he walked under the arch into De Jure and saw the immaculate, lawned courtyard, Ella thought he was going to have a coronary.

Bartlett came out of his lodge as if to make sure he was all right.

'It's fine,' Ella explained. 'He's from Arizona.'

'Ah,' said Bartlett. 'I don't suppose you get anything like this in the desert?'

'Only in Vegas, my friend,' Broady replied. 'Only in Vegas.'

'Of course, sir,' said Bartlett as he led them to Desmond's office. 'I hear they even have pyramids, better than the real thing?'

'I wouldn't go quite that far,' Broady replied, winking at Ella.

She grinned. All the panic of last night suddenly seemed so far away. Had she been paranoid about the whole thing? Maybe those robbers were nothing to do with her? Then she remembered the hidden microphone. That was proof. Or was it? Her thoughts and fears churned over. Broady could easily have put it there, to make her trust him. She watched him joking with Bartlett. Had she been taken in by the green eyes, the appealing rolling contours of his dune-like, weathered face? Her head was ready to burst. Think like a lawyer, she told herself, be cool and detached, study the evidence.

Or was Lizzie right – that she had to learn to trust? It was hard, she'd always done everything alone, even when Tom was around.

One thing was for sure, she needed to keep her wits about her.

Chapter Thirty-Eight

'Master Desmond,' Ella began, trying to sound as formal and as professional as possible. 'The primary reason for coming to see you was to introduce Detective Hank Broady from the Phoenix Police Department.'

'Pleased to meet you, sir,' said Broady stiffly. Ella could tell he was doing his best to keep his ebullient personality in check. More proof, she noted, that he knew how to play people.

'He's here investigating the death of Cameron Shepherd.'

'We think it may be connected to Matthew's disappearance,' added Broady with hands clasped behind his back in a formal pose that Ella could tell was just for show.

'I see,' Desmond replied, as Ella and Broady sat down opposite him.

'I've got some leads which I'm following up,' said Ella, thinking carefully how to couch her request. 'We feel it would be beneficial to all parties if Detective Broady and I worked together where there's overlap.'

'I see.' Desmond repeated, studying Broady, who was preoccupied with the historic oils adorning the walls.

Ella could see the alarm bells were ringing, that Desmond was worried the whole thing was getting out of hand. Was he going to pull the plug, hand the whole thing back to the police? To her surprise, she realised for the first time that it was the last thing she wanted. She had to see it through.

Despite his apparent inattention, Broady threw in, 'And of course, we've already had a meeting with DC McDonald and are sharing intelligence.'

Desmond gave an appreciative nod.

'I hope that's OK, but Miss Blake already told me you believe in co-operation and transparency?'

'Absolutely, thank you, detective.' He was persuaded. 'Always a pleasure to work with our brothers across the pond.'

Broady smiled politely.

'Anything else I should know?' Desmond inquired.

'I'll be moving accommodation, at my own expense of course.' She hesitated, but knew she had to tell him. 'A listening device was found in my room, by Detective Broady in fact.'

'What?' He lost his composure. 'You were being bugged?'

'It looks like industrial espionage to me,' explained Broady in a tone that conveyed it was no big deal.

'We think Matthew was working on something of extreme economic value,' added Ella.

Seemingly placated by the calmness of their responses, Desmond looked from one to the other, his expression now a picture of curiosity. 'Economic value?'

'Phoenix are only interested in any crimes that might have been committed in Arizona,' Broady continued. 'But where interests merge, we will assist Miss Blake in whatever way we can to try and find out what happened to Matthew Shepherd, and recover his work.'

Desmond nodded vigorously.

Broady added, 'Before anybody else does.'

Ella was impressed. 'We'll let you get on, Master,' she said, bringing the meeting to a close.

Desmond gave her his warmest smile. 'It's about time you called me John.'

'*John.*' She got up. 'I know how busy you are.'

Broady did the same.

'There's nothing else I should know?'

She cursed herself inwardly for being too eager to leave. Desmond had sensed it. 'One small matter,' she said, trying to sound nonchalant. 'There was an attempted robbery at a flat in King's Hedges, probably has nothing to do with the inquiry—'

Desmond pondered for a moment. 'So why are you telling me?'

'It's a rather convoluted story…' She was struggling. 'Err, it's probably best you don't know the details, save to say, the homeowner is assisting me on the inquiry.'

Panic broke out on Desmond's usually ordered face. 'What? Who? Why didn't you run this past me?'

Ella hadn't seen him this emotional.

'Were they injured? Is the college liable?'

She saw a way out, 'Absolutely not. He has signed a contract of employment, as my employee. I pay for his services. He is in no way connected to De Jure.' It was just enough to make Desmond settle down. 'He has certain technological skills that are essential to the inquiry.'

Puzzled, Desmond opened his mouth to speak, then closed it again.

Ella saw her opportunity. 'Thank you, John. Keep you posted.' She shot through the door.

Broady was right behind her. 'Great to meet you, sir.'

Chapter Thirty-Nine

The police station was a hive of activity. Lizzie and Jay sat patiently at McDonald's desk, watching him rushing around the open-plan office, answering calls and shouting orders at colleagues. He briefly left what he was doing to give Lizzie and Jay *pro-forma* documents on which to write out their witness statements.

'The most important thing to remember,' he said in a stern voice, 'is those lines at the top.' He put a finger on the page, then began reading: '*This statement is true to the best of my knowledge and belief and I make it knowing that, if it is tendered in evidence, I shall be liable to prosecution if I have wilfully stated anything in it, which I know to be false, or do not believe to be true.*' He glowered at them, gave Jay a long hard look, then left them to it.

'What was all that about?' Lizzie whispered even though her voice was lost in the hum of other conversations and phones ringing.

'Don't know,' Jay replied. 'Just don't lie, we've got nothing to hide.'

McDonald came back periodically to check on their progress. Then, once they were done, he sat down, put his feet on the desk, legs crossed, and read through what they had written. Jay's statement seemed to give him more cause for concern. McDonald stopped reading and peered over the top of the document. 'What do you think they were after?'

'What do you mean?' stuttered Jay.

'One of these masked men said: "Where is it?"' His eyes bore into Jay. 'Where's *what*?'

Lizzie looked at her friend.

McDonald noticed.

'I don't know, officer.' Jay stared down at his shoes avoiding McDonald's glare. 'That's why I didn't give them anything.'

There was a painful silence, then, apparently satisfied, he waved them away. 'Give your mother my regards.'

'I will, officer,' Lizzie replied in her most obsequious voice.

McDonald put his legs down. 'One more thing.'

Almost out the door, they stopped and turned around.

He stood up. 'Where can I reach you?'

'On my mobile?' Jay offered.

'Address?'

'Not sure yet,' he said, patting the sports bag. 'A bit reluctant to go home at the moment.'

'And I'm finishing for Easter,' said Lizzie, hoping to divert the conversation. 'But we'll both make sure my mother has contact details.'

McDonald grunted. Another plain clothes guy knocked and put his head around the door. 'She's 'ere, guv.'

Seizing the opportunity whilst McDonald was distracted, Lizzie made her way out through the gap, followed swiftly by Jay. They wasted no time exiting the building and then crossed over onto the Piece.

'Does he know something?' asked Lizzie. 'That freaked me right out.'

They stopped in the middle of the Green.

'He's a copper,' said Jay. 'It's their job to make you paranoid. You haven't done anything wrong.'

'So why do I feel guilty?' Then, thinking out loud, she asked, 'Is this a mistake?'

'Is what a mistake?'

'Getting involved in all this, with my mum?' She ran her fingers through her hair. She waited for reassurance. 'I mean, aren't you scared?'

Jay took his time. 'I think we're already involved; besides, I owe her.'

'You owe her nothing,' she snapped. 'You're nineteen.'

He huffed. 'All right, I like her.'

She tossed her head back in frustration. 'People seem to, God knows why.'

'The way I see it,' he said. 'Those people that came to my flat, you saw them, there's money behind them, proper organisation.'

She knew he was right about that.

'I reckon it's the same people that hounded that polymath out of Cambridge.' Jay became more animated. 'I'm sick of huge corporations and governments doing what they want, blind to the consequences. Did you know there's a garbage patch full of plastic waste in the Pacific Ocean?'

'What?' she said realigning her thoughts to the sudden change of topic. There was a fire behind Jay's eyes that Lizzie hadn't seen before.

He took hold of her arms. 'It's the size of France.'

'But, Jay,' she asked timidly, 'what's it got to do with my mum?'

He released his grip and exhaled. 'People still buy plastic bags every day – just to hold a bottle a milk and some bread. I don't want to be another zombie. I want to swim against the tide.'

She found his rant both endearing and alarming, in equal measure.

His eyes were still blazing. 'Isn't that why you came to Cambridge – to stand on the shoulders of those who came before?'

Now she understood.

'The great historians, scientists and writers, they were never about the money or the power.'

Her phone rang. It was Greg. She answered it.

Jay kicked out at a couple of empty bottles of ale that had been left on the grass.

'OK, Greg, yes, I will.' She avoided looking at Jay. 'OK… see you soon.' The call ended. 'I'm sorry, I've got to go.'

The break seemed to have given Jay time to reflect. 'I'm sorry for going on.'

'Don't be, you're entitled to your beliefs.' She took the wad of cash out of her bag that she'd withdrawn on Ella's card. 'Here, take this.'

His brow furrowed. 'Aren't you going to come with me?'

'I can't, I've got to meet Greg back at mine.'

He gave her a disapproving look.

'I'll pack some things and meet you all later. You get the laptop and stuff.'

He put the money in his pocket.

'See you in a bit,' she said, setting off across the Green.

'Hang on Lizzie,' Jay shouted after her.

She turned. 'What?'

He paused. 'You know you can't tell him anything.'

'I know,' she shouted back. 'But you didn't have to say it.'

Chapter Forty

M cDonald and Harris strode down the white-washed corridor, two abreast. 'If you're conducting the interview in my station, don't you think I should be allowed to sit in?' whined McDonald.

'I'm sorry but you don't have that level of clearance, officer,' Harris replied, holding open the file and giving her notes a once-over.

'Can you tell me anything?' he asked sulkily.

She tapped his arm with the folder. 'I'll see what I can do.' She entered the room where the suspect was already sitting at the table, next to a young woman dressed like a lawyer in a two-piece, but without a briefcase.

Harris took a mini-recorder out of her pocket and pressed play. 'This interview is being conducted at Cambridge Police Station, my name is Jane Harris and other persons present are?' She held the recorder out towards the lawyer.

David Kline pushed it away from her mouth. 'Shouldn't you be using the machine that's already here? He gave her a fox-like smile. 'If you're going to go to the trouble of doing it properly.' He ran a hand over his beard.

Harris didn't flinch. 'There is someone calling herself a lawyer in the room who won't give her name.'

The lawyer put a hand out over the table. 'For the tape, please state your rank and what agency you're from?' She followed up with a squinting smile. 'In accordance with the Codes of Practice under The Police and Criminal Evidence Act.'

Ignoring the hotshot, Harris ploughed on. 'And the suspect is—'

'Suspect?' said the brief. 'Mr Kline is here voluntarily. He is not under arrest. If there is evidence to suspect him of a crime you must caution him before asking any questions.'

David Kline winked then sat back in the chair with his arms folded and legs stretched out under the desk.

Harris huffed. Beaten, she turned off the recorder and put it down.

Kline laughed. 'Your neck is very red, Jane? Has it done that since you were a kid? When you were embarrassed? Happens a lot to people with very white skin.'

Remaining impassive, Harris opened the file. 'Your last tax return says you're a pig farmer?'

Kline stared at her as if mildly entertained.

'So how come when I got a production order for your bank accounts there was millions in there.'

'Charitable donations,' the lawyer replied.

Harris shot her a look. 'I wasn't asking you.'

Kline leaned forward. 'People want to do something; can't you understand that?'

Harris dithered for a split second then said: 'I'll ask the questions.'

Kline let his head drop down between his shoulders, then up again. 'The world is dying out there, Jane.' His eyes seemed to be imploring some kind of understanding. 'And you're asking me about pig farming.'

She rifled through her notes. 'All right, then, why don't you tell me about Genesis?' Harris shifted in her seat as if getting comfortable in readiness for the story.

Kline scoffed 'I really don't think your mind is open to it Jane.' He gave her a patronising smile. 'And even if it was, I don't think you have the intellect.'

This time Harris leaned forward into Kline's face. 'Humour me.'

He kept schtum.

Harris persisted: 'So, you're going to save it for all those kids you're brainwashing?'

Kline got to his feet. 'Interview's over.'

Harris did the same but stood between Kline and the door. 'Sit down.'

The lawyer got up too. 'He's not under arrest, you can't keep—'

Harris stepped forward. Her face was inches from Kline's. 'I said, sit down.'

After a tense stand-off Kline sat down again, sitting side-ways on and an arm draped over the back of the chair.

The women retook their seats. Harris shuffled her papers again. 'What do you know about the disappearance of Matthew Shepherd?'

Kline sniggered. 'I knew you'd get there in the end.'

Harris looked perplexed. 'What's so funny?'

'You people,' said Kline, crossing his arms. 'I despair.'

'That's not an answer,' said Harris robotically.

'I. Don't. Know,' Kline replied, stressing every word.

'What do you know about a robbery at an address in King's Hedges?'

Kline gave his lawyer a bemused look, then back at Harris. 'News to me.'

Harris stared at Kline. 'We know you're planning something.'

An ambivalent shrug. 'Can I go now?' He didn't wait for an answer.

Harris followed him out of the door.

McDonald and another officer were leaning against the wall just outside. They stood to attention on seeing the door open.

Kline and his lawyer swaggered off down the corridor without waiting for the escort.

'One more thing, Mr Kline…' Harris called after him.

He stopped and turned, eyebrows half-raised. 'What?'

'Your beard,' she said, rubbing her own chin. 'I noticed how well trimmed it is. Great grooming.' She took out a pen and held it on the front of the file. 'I'd love to know who you use?'

He didn't respond to the jibe, any reaction stayed behind the eyes.

McDonald smirked.

Chapter Forty-One

'Hey.' Greg held out his arms.

'Hey.' Lizzie fell into his embrace.

Neither moved, nor spoke. She felt safe. So much had happened since he last held her.

'Back to London already?' he enquired, seeing the half-packed holdall on the bed.

'You're not getting rid of me that easily,' she joked, detaching herself from his chest. 'I'm going to stay with my mum for a bit.'

'That's great. At the Gonville?' His face broke into a smile. 'So, you're not going home for Easter?'

She didn't want to lie to him. 'Not much point if she's here and I don't fancy being on my own, so she's going to rent somewhere for us.'

'Makes sense,' he said, moving a strand of hair away from her face and kissing her forehead. 'And does that mean I will get to see you too?'

A coy smile. 'I think that could be arranged.'

He kissed her lips. 'I've missed you.'

'Me too.'

'I've been so worried.' He stroked her hair then kissed her again. 'What actually happened?'

She ended the embrace. 'Do you mind if we don't talk about it?' She could see he was crushed but trying to hide it. 'It's just that I've been at the police station all morning and—'

He put his finger on her lips. 'I get it.'

She pushed him back onto the bed, narrowly missing the bag. 'I suppose you're not all bad,' she teased.

He reached up and pulled her onto him. 'Just be careful of that Jay guy.'

She raised her head so she could see his face. 'Where did that come from?'

His expression was suddenly grave. 'I've been asking around about him.'

She got off him and sat on the side of the bed. 'Why?'

He put a hand on her thigh. 'I was concerned.'

She studied him. 'Jealous, more like.'

'That's not fair.' He sat up. 'You told me people with knives broke into his apartment.'

Maybe she was being unfair. The last twenty-four hours had been so confusing.

'I'm told he's got a nasty temper.'

'Really?' She remembered the way he gripped her arms on the Piece.

In a more conciliatory tone, he said, 'I don't like telling tales, that's not normally my style.'

She had to know the rest. 'But?'

He touched her arm. 'But I care about you, a lot.'

She felt reassured. 'What else did you find out?'

He sighed. 'That he's the go-to guy for cocaine.'

'What?' Lizzie jumped off the bed. 'A drug dealer? Who told you that?'

'A few of the politics lot, it was pretty much common knowledge.'

She put a hand on her forehead. 'I don't believe it.'

Greg remained cool. 'He's not Pablo Escobar or anything, just fifty pound wraps to undergrads.'

She still wasn't convinced. 'How come you knew his surname to ask around?'

'I didn't, still don't. Everyone knows him as Jay, the gardener at Gonville – or was, he's left apparently.'

She sat back down. She felt like she'd been hit by a truck.

'I wondered whether that had something to do with the robbery?' he floated. 'Maybe he owed money to someone up the chain?'

Had Jay really lied about everything? The implications began to sink in – she had to tell her mother. Her head fell into her hands.

Chapter Forty-Two

B roady was the first to arrive. 'Not bad,' he said, putting down his stuff and checking out the living area.

Ella had rented a penthouse in an aparthotel by the station. 'It's got three bedrooms,' she said, 'Jay can have the sofa bed in here.'

'They may already know about this place,' he said.

Ella sighed. 'I know, but it might buy us a bit of time.'

Broady agreed.

'You and baby are in there,' she said, deadpan, pointing to one of the bedrooms.

'Very funny.' he said. 'You cooking something?'

'Chilli,' she explained, switching her attention to the pan on the hob.

He breathed in. 'Smells good.'

Strangely, she felt slightly embarrassed to be doing something so domestic. 'How did it go with McDonald?'

'Good,' he replied, taking some folded sheets of paper out of his jacket pocket. He spread them out on the dining table in the centre of the living area.

The buzzer went. Ella opened the door. It was Lizzie.

'You all right?' she asked, reading the stress in her daughter's face. 'Jay not with you?'

'No, I had to go and see Greg.'

Ella gave her a closer inspection. 'Everything OK?'

She frowned. 'Yeah, I didn't tell him anything, if that's what you're asking.'

'No, I just wondered if you got the laptop?'

'No, I left that to Jay,' came the sheepish reply.

Ella made a face. 'Did you give him the money?'

'Yeah, why? Don't you trust him?' she snapped.

'Of course I do.' Something wasn't right. 'What's wrong, Lizzie?'

Her daughter's shoulders dropped as if the air was being let out of her. 'There's something I've got to tell you...'

The buzzer went again. 'Hang on,' said Ella.

It was Jay. He came through the door and clocked everyone. 'Am I late?' he said, dropping his bag and opening the zip. He pulled out two laptops and handed them to Ella, then reached back in and pulled out four pay-as-you-go phones, still in the packaging. 'I was thinking,' he said. 'Best not to go online in the apartment, they could be monitoring anything that comes from the IP address.'

'That's sensible,' Broady replied.

'Jay, can I have a word, please,' Lizzie ordered, going into one of the bedrooms.

Jay looked at the others, then followed her in.

The door shut.

'What's all that about?' Broady asked.

'No idea.' Ella replied.

Lizzie pointed a finger in Jay's face. 'I know.'

'Know what?'

She analysed every contour, in readiness for the reaction. 'You deal drugs.'

'Eh?' He took a step back. 'What are you talking about?'

'You heard,' she said, firmly.

He moved towards her. 'I don't know where you got that from, but it's bollocks.'

She tried to read him, see behind the eyes. 'Was that what the robbery was about?'

He threw his arms up in the air. 'I don't believe this.'

She continued to examine every gesture.

He gave her one of his intense stares. 'You know me, Lizzie.'

'Do I?' Her eyes welled up. 'That's just it, I don't. All I really know is that you were up on charges.'

'I was innocent,' he protested. 'Who told you this? McDonald?'

'It doesn't matter who?'

He couldn't stand still. 'It does to me,' he shouted. He stopped. He seemed to be studying her now. 'Wait a minute. Was it Greg?'

She glanced off, unable to hold eye-contact.

His eyes narrowed. 'It was, wasn't it?'

She didn't respond at first. 'No,' was the best she could do.

He scoffed. 'Bullshit. Don't tell me, he's the jealous type?' He sneered. 'Won't be long before he's knocking you about.'

'Hey!' She didn't know what to think. 'I've got to tell my mother.'

He gripped her arm. 'No.'

'I have to.' She pulled herself free.

He sat down heavily on the bed. 'But it's lies,' he protested. 'You know she'll kick me off the job?'

'She might believe you,' Lizzie replied, a morsel of sympathy showing through.

'No,' replied firmly. 'She wouldn't take the risk.'

Lizzie knew he was right.

He gazed up at her, pleading. 'This is the first interesting thing I've done in a long time, ever. I want to be part of a team, belong to something.' He suddenly looked like a lost child. Much younger than his nineteen years. 'You saved my life last night,' he said with great sincerity. 'Risked your own. I would never lie to you.'

Exasperated, she looked skywards and said, 'Fucking hell, Jay.' She bent down and stared into his eyes, searching for the truth. She sighed. 'All right.'

Jay's face lost some of its tension. 'Thank you.'

'Don't make me regret this,' she said in her sternest voice.

He stood up. 'You won't.'

She had a horrible feeling that she would.

Chapter Forty-Three

Broady beckoned them over as he spread some maps out on the table. 'Come and check this out.'

Ella scrutinised her daughter. 'What were you going to tell me?'

Lizzie glanced at Jay. 'Oh, I can't remember, nothing important.'

Ella wasn't convinced.

'So, this is the map of King's Parade,' said Broady. 'And that's the cell-site,' he said, sticking his finger on the page. 'It covers a few colleges but also De Jure, which is probably where he was when his phone rang.'

All four crowded around the table.

He pulled out another map, half covered by the first. 'This is the location of the London cell-site, right next to St Pancras Station. Not much help – I figure he'd just come in on the train from Cambridge.'

'No,' said Ella. 'He'd come in at either Liverpool Street or King's Cross, which is a bit further away.' She put her finger on the map. 'Here.'

'OK,' he replied. 'Let's come back to that.' He pointed to

another map. 'The third site is here, in Oxford.' He tapped a finger on the spot. 'The mast is on top of a theatre called The Sheldonian.'

'It's a huge concert hall,' said Ella. 'Part of the university.' She peered closer at the map. 'It's right next to the Bodleian.'

'Bodleian?' asked Broady.

'The Bodleian Library. One of the most important libraries in England, second only to—' she stopped. 'Show me the London map again.'

Broady slid it across the table.

Ella took a closer look. Her eyes widened. 'It's not St Pancras.' She put her finger on the other side of the Euston Road. 'It's the British Library.'

'Coincidence?' asked Broady.

'Mathematically,' Jay replied, 'I say it's not. Of all the thousands of cell-sites in England, our two are next to the two biggest libraries in Britain.'

'I agree,' said Ella.

'So, what was he looking for?' asked Broady.

'We're just going to have to figure it out,' said Lizzie.

Ella nodded. She wanted to build up some momentum. 'Jay, let's just go over what you bought.'

'Sure,' he replied, picking up one of the phones. 'We have one each. You'll need to save each other's numbers.' He handed them out. 'We should try and use these from now on and keep our smart phones turned off whenever possible.' He picked up one of the laptops. 'This is the decoy. I will go online in the apartment and do some dummy searches. If anyone's eavesdropping, hopefully they will follow my misdirects.'

Ella was impressed.

'This is for real work,' Jay continued, pointing to the other laptop. 'But we only search away from the apartment, to avoid the IP address.'

'He knows his shit,' said Broady.

Lizzie shot Jay an anxious glance.

His face gave nothing away.

'OK,' said Ella, taking a deep breath. 'That brings us to this.' She held up the memory stick.' She turned towards Broady. 'Matthew's brother, Cameron Shepherd, sent me a note just before he died with a riddle about Darrell Duppa.'

Broady's brow furrowed. 'What? The guy who built the Duppa house in Phoenix?'

'Yes,' Ella replied, handing him the stick. 'Then I found that hidden inside a book about Duppa in Matthew's room.'

Broady rolled it over on his palm. 'Hell, I knew there was something.'

Ella wasn't so buoyant. 'But we need to work out the password.'

'Oh,' Broady replied, sounding less excited. 'How are we going to do that?

'Jay reckons he can do it. Let's see?' She handed him the stick.

He inserted it in the side of one of the laptops. 'Let's start by going through all the contact you had with Cameron.'

'Just a single phone call,' Ella replied. 'Then, after he's dead, I get this in the post.' She pulled the envelope out of her handbag. 'A short clip on a CD of Matthew as a kid and this note.' She read it aloud, finishing with, 'Just in case, Cam.'

'He was expecting trouble,' observed Broady. 'Let's watch the footage,'

They all huddled around the laptop.

'Nervous looking kid,' Broady remarked. 'Didn't look like he'd amount to much.'

'Have you got to be the quarterback to amount to anything in the States?' Jay retorted.

'Gees, you English are so touchy.'

'All right, that's enough,' said Ella. 'Anyone got any ideas?'

'He wanted you to have it,' said Jay. 'Which means you have the password.'

Ella hadn't thought of it like that.

'He wouldn't send you directions to something you couldn't open.'

'Maybe he thought he'd open it when he got here?' suggested Lizzie.

'No, it was *just in case* he didn't make it,' said Jay, dismissing her argument. 'Let's go through the conversation you had.'

'Ok.' Ella sat down on one of the chairs and cast her mind back. 'It was a very short call. He complained about De Jure. Said they hadn't taken Matthew's disappearance seriously. Said he would've called him.' She tried to remember more detail. 'He said Matthew's room kept getting broken into. Desmond didn't take it seriously as everyone thought Matthew was paranoid. I think he used the word nuts.'

Throughout Ella's monologue, Jay put in possible passwords. 'Keep going.'

'I said that people had labelled him autistic or aspergic but he said that labels didn't apply to a mind like his.' She recalled some more. 'Discussed getting the red eye from Phoenix, that was about it.'

Jay kept trying different words.

'Oh, there was something else.'

They were all listening intently.

'He told me Matthew once rang him, said he'd found a new way of looking at things. Something to do with Peter Sutcliffe.'

'Peter who?' asked Broady.

'Sutcliffe,' said Ella. 'He was a serial murderer in the eighties. Killed women, mainly prostitutes.'

'He was known as the Yorkshire Ripper,' said Lizzie.

'Yeah,' said Ella. 'Because the murders were around Leeds and Bradford.'

Broady scratched his head. 'Why would a guy from Arizona be interested in English murders that happened before he was born?'

Nobody had an answer.

Jay kept trying combinations of the words being thrown up, but still the folder wouldn't open.

The process helped Ella to remember more. 'He said Matthew kept repeating: "Elementary, my dear Watson".'

'Hey, that's from Sherlock Holmes,' said Broady.

'Yeah, Cameron said to him "no shit Sherlock" and Matthew found that funny.'

'Oh shit!' Jay sat back in his chair and put his hands behind his head. 'It's saying we've got three more tries before the folder corrupts itself.'

'You're kidding?' said Ella, getting up to pace around the room.

'I've tried everything I can think of related to what you've said. There's no way Cameron created the password.'

'How do you know?' Ella asked, stopping to stare at the screen.

'It's a sophisticated block. Matthew sent the letter to his brother. It's Matthew who set the password.'

Ella grimaced.

'Let's just put on the brakes for a minute,' Broady suggested. 'What has Peter Sutcliffe got to do with Sherlock Holmes?'

No one had an answer.

'Holmes,' Jay whispered to himself. Then louder: 'Holmes. The Holmes computer?'

'Of course,' Ella replied, 'which was introduced after the Sutcliffe case. It's got to be. Well done.'

Jay's face broke into a beaming smile.

'You're going to have to fill me in,' said Broady.

'It was the last big murder investigation before computers were used in crime detection.' Ella couldn't get her words out fast enough. 'The police investigation went on for years and everything was recorded on individual cards — millions of them. They had rooms full of the bloody things.'

'Wait a minute,' said Broady. 'I think I read about this in some training manual.' He frowned. 'Didn't they interview the suspect a few times?'

'That's right, nine times,' said Ella. 'But they didn't realise. Each time he got nicked they thought it was the first time, they didn't realise they already had the answers.'

'Jesus,' said Broady.

'So, they invented the Holmes computer system,' said Jay, proudly, 'so they could cross-reference huge amounts of information.'

'Desmond said something about Matthew…' said Ella. 'To him it was all about joining the dots, seeing the bigger picture.'

'You think Matthew learned from that case?' asked Lizzie. 'How to approach what he was doing?'

'I reckon,' said Ella.

'You want to try those – dots, picture?' asked Jay.

'No,' interrupted Broady. 'They're too obscure, don't risk it.'

'I agree,' said Ella.

'What about "Holmes"?' suggested Lizzie.

'OK,' Ella replied. 'But that's it.'

Broady nodded.

Jay tapped it in. 'Shit' He closed his eyes in frustration. 'Two tries left.'

'Let's stop,' said Ella. 'No more tonight. Come on, let's eat.'

Broady sighed. 'That chilli smells mighty fine.'

'Can someone clear those maps away,' Ella asked, walking over to the kitchenette and taking some bowls out of a cupboard.

'You cooked it?' Lizzie put her hands on her hips. 'You never cook.'

Ella ignored the observation and handed her the bowls and some forks. 'You can lay the table.'

Broady went into his room and came back with a bottle of red wine. 'I got this in duty free,' he said. 'It's a Bordeaux.'

'Good call,' said Lizzie. 'I'll get some glasses.'

Ella handed him a corkscrew and went back into the kitchenette. She brought out a French stick on a board and some butter, handing them to Jay to put on the table.

When she came back again carrying the pot between a pair of oven gloves, everyone cheered and raised their glasses.

She felt choked up.

For the first time in years, she realised she was happy.

Chapter Forty-Four

Ella sat bolt upright, sweating, her heart pounding. The same nightmare. It always took a few minutes to realise it was a dream, before she remembered that it had really happened.

She got out of bed, pulled on a pair of joggers and went into the kitchenette to get a drink. It had become a familiar routine over the years.

She waited while the kettle boiled, then noticed the door to the balcony was ajar. She moved closer. She peeked through the gap in the curtains. It was Broady.

'Hi there,' he said. 'Come and join me.'

She pushed open the door and walked out into the cold air.

'It's a clear night, take a look,' he said, patting the telescope which was sitting on a tripod.

She bent down and put an eye to the lens. She instinctively pulled away at the sight, then back again. 'Wow! I've never seen this kind of detail before... the colour. Is it Mars?'

'Full marks,' said Broady. 'The Red Planet. It's in a great position tonight.'

'Orbits,' she said, remembering what Desmond had said about Newton. She stood up straight.

'Yeah,' said Broady. 'It's busy up there.'

Ella laughed. She liked the easy way he used words.

'We never think that everything's moving all the time,' he said.

She looked up at the night sky. 'Like the heavens are breathing.'

Neither spoke, sharing the spectacle.

'You've got goose bumps,' he said gently brushing her arm. 'Put this on,' he said, unzipping his fleece.

It was a long time since anyone had looked after her, shown her any tenderness. She always felt so neglected, battle-weary.

He stood behind her and put the top around her shoulders, letting his hands rest there a moment. 'So, what's next?' he asked, almost in a whisper.

She turned around. 'What do you mean?'

'The inquiry, what are we going to do tomorrow?'

'Oh, I think we should check out the libraries, see if anyone remembers Matthew.' She could see he wasn't hopeful it would bear fruit. 'I know they have thousands of visitors, but—'

'But we've got nothing else to go on?'

'Yeah.' The wind blew a few strands of hair across her face. She swept it back. 'And I don't think we're going to be able to open that file.'

Broady bent down and looked through the lens. 'That may not be a bad thing.'

She waited for him to take his eye off. 'Why?'

He smiled without humour. 'Because if we did get in, we'd actually know something.'

She mulled it over, realising Broady was ahead of her.

'Like Jay said, knowledge is power.' He tilted his head. 'And powerful people usually become more of a target.'

His words made her shiver.

Chapter Forty-Five

E lla and Broady got the train down to King's Cross. They had decided it was safer if Lizzie and Jay stayed in Cambridge. They'd reluctantly promised not to stray far from the apartment, and only then for the purposes of internet searches.

The short walk to the British Library was another revelation for Broady. He marvelled at the beautiful old buildings, so much so that it made Ella see her own city with a fresh eye. As they joined the hordes of people queuing outside the library, Ella could see how hopeless their task was.

'Come on,' said Broady, pushing past the masses waiting for a bag check and flashing his badge to a guard.

His positive energy gave her a lift.

They were in.

'Impressive,' observed Ella, as she was engulfed in a tour group filing past in pursuit of a haughty-looking guide, holding up what looked like a selfie stick. 'There are over twenty-five million books in this library,' the guide announced to his party. 'And millions more manuscripts.'

Ella and Broady exchanged a glance.

'Just a minute, madam,' said an officious looking man just past the bag check tables. 'No one bypasses security.'

'I'm a cop,' Broady explained, showing his badge again.

'Doesn't mean you can push in,' replied the security guy.

'I'm sorry, sir,' Ella offered, in the hope of avoiding having to go to the back of the line. 'Do you want to have a look?' she said holding open her bag.

'Thank you,' he said, having a cursory rummage. 'But next time,' he said, turning to Broady, 'you can wait in line like everyone else.'

'Yes, sir,' Broady replied, clearly trying not to laugh. He whispered to Ella after the man had gone, 'What is it with Brits and queueing?'

'Nothing wrong with manners,' she replied with a smirk, then led him up to the registration desk.

'I'll handle this,' said Broady leaning onto the counter and showing his badge again, this time to a studious librarian in a tank top and thick-rimmed spectacles. 'Detective Broady, Phoenix Police.'

The librarian looked up from his computer terminal.

'We need a list of all the books borrowed by a man called Matthew Shepherd.'

The librarian half-raised an eyebrow and replied, 'Firstly, in this country we can't just hand over information without a court order. It's called the Data Protection Act.' With an almost imperceptible shake of the head, he added, 'And secondly, this is a reference library, no one can *borrow* books.'

Broady opened his mouth as if about to reply but closed it again.

'Sorry about my friend,' said Ella, fighting the urge to laugh. 'Ella Blake, I'm a lawyer.'

'I know, I recognise you,' replied the librarian in a more convivial tone. 'I've seen you on the telly. Didn't you get that woman off on appeal a few years ago? Wrongly convicted of murdering her husband?'

'That's right, Michelle Waters.' Ella couldn't help but enjoy Broady witnessing the adulation.

'Is this about another appeal?' the young man asked, lowering his voice.

Ella nodded. 'Total miscarriage of justice. It's an American death row case. Wish I could say more.' She could see that the man was intrigued. 'I have to confess we were just trying to cut corners – running out of time.' She gave him a forlorn smile. 'Come on, detective,' she said, turning away from the young man.

'What did you say his name was again?'

She turned back. 'Matthew Shepherd, De Jure College, Cambridge.'

The librarian gave her a sympathetic nod. 'There should be a record of what texts he accessed if he was here this year.' The man glanced surreptitiously at his co-workers, then began typing. 'There it is… It's printing off now.'

Ella felt a pang of excitement.

He handed her a sheet of A4.

'Thank you for your humanity,' she said in a sincere voice, usually reserved for jury speeches. She took Broady's arm and ushered him away from the desk. 'Damn,' she said, as they stared at the list. 'He looked at loads of sources, all ancient manuscripts.' She ran a finger down the page. 'Mainly written by early Christian monks.' She glanced at Broady.

He pointed to one of the names. 'Bede, I've heard of him.'

'Yeah, he was made a saint. A monk born in the seventh century. He wrote *The Ecclesiastical History of the English People*.'

'I guess we're going to have to read them all,' said Broady.

'It would take months,' Ella replied. 'Besides, the originals will be in Latin or Old English – I'm guessing that's not your forte?'

'Ah, I see,' he replied with a sheepish smile.

'There are translations but it would be a waste of time unless we knew roughly what we were looking for.' Ella tried to think of another approach. 'Hang on,' she announced suddenly. 'The cell-sites show he was only here a few days, right?'

Broady nodded. 'Three.'

'So, he couldn't have read every page, he must have been searching for something specific in these manuscripts.' Her mind began to focus in a way it hadn't for years. 'How many days was he at the Bodleian?'

'Just one,' Broady replied. 'And that was after he'd been here.'

'So, when he was here, he narrowed down the search. We need to go to Oxford.'

Broady nodded. 'Brilliant.' He was already setting off towards the exit.

'Hang on,' said Ella. 'There's something you have to see while you're here.' She led him through some reading rooms. There were rows of hundreds of people, sitting at desks, all silently beavering away on some important task.

She stopped at a glass case containing an ancient manuscript. 'It's the Lindisfarne Gospels, written by a monk called Eadrith in the seventh century on a little island off the northeast coast in the Kingdom of Northumbria.'

Broady tilted his head and gave her a lingering stare. 'Maybe you can show it to me one day?'

She met his gaze for a moment, then looked away. Broady turned towards the case and she watched him take in the beautiful swirling illustrations and the detail, betraying the love bestowed on the pages by its author. 'The colours are amazing,' he marvelled.

'The jewelled cover was replaced centuries later. The Vikings stole the original bindings when they invaded in 793 and discarded the actual manuscript because they worshipped Norse gods like Odin.'

'You didn't study law?' asked Broady, bringing her back.

'Not at first,' Ella replied, ruefully. 'I always wanted to be a historian.'

'So, what happened?'

'It's complicated,' she said. 'Let's go.'

Broady stayed put. 'You do that a lot.'

'Do what?' she pretended she didn't know what he meant, but she felt her cheeks flushing.

'Shut people down.'

She hovered awkwardly for a second, wanting to say more. Something stopped her.

'So, is this whole Shepherd thing about Christianity?' asked Broady.

'Maybe,' Ella replied, grateful for the change of subject. She gazed at the ancient writings again, then at the sheet. 'Or history, or both,' said Ella, thinking aloud. 'The monks were chroniclers, recording events.'

She could feel Broady studying her.

'You've got an amazing mind,' he said softly.

She laughed to break the intimacy and set off towards the exit.

They walked out onto the piazza, squinting momentarily as the sun hit their eyes.

'Sir Isaac Newton,' said Ella, pointing to a statue of a man, bending over, holding a pair of compasses, as if working something out.

'Doesn't look anything like him,' Broady observed.

'You'd know, I suppose,' she scoffed.

'Actually,' said Broady, puffing out his chest, 'he's a bit of a hero of mine.'

'Really?' Ella didn't know if it was another of his jokes.

'Yeah.' He took out his iPhone and swiped through his photos. 'This is my favourite picture of him.'

Ella looked at the screen at an image of an austere man in a flowing white wig. He seemed to be looking through her, as if contemplating some great theory.

'It was painted by Godfrey Kneller in 1744.'

Ella looked at Broady in wonder.

'Check out the bottom left corner,' he told her.

She looked closer. 'A telescope!'

They broke into laughter.

'You're full of surprises, detective.'

'The guy was one hell of an astronomer,' said Broady, his voice full of passion. 'What I like best is the two women in the circle below.' He used his little finger to point at the image.

'I see them,' Ella replied. 'She's pulling something off the other woman's face.'

'It's a blindfold, as if she's seeing something for the first time.'

'Yes,' Ella agreed. 'She's finally seeing the truth.'

'That's what I think too,' said Broady.

Ella looked at the American. She felt something. She had the acute feeling that Broady's eyes pierced deep inside her soul.

His face was serious. 'A truth that Newton already knew.'

She looked at the picture again, then back at Broady, somehow lost for words.

Broady put the phone back in his pocket and flagged down a black cab.

The driver pulled over and wound down his window, resting an elbow on the frame. 'Where to?'

Broady turned to Ella. 'Which station for Oxford?'

'Paddington,' Ella replied so the cabby could hear.

Broady opened the door and climbed in after her.

They plonked themselves on the rear seat.

Ella had been putting it off long enough but knew there was one stop she had to make. 'Can we go via my place? I need to collect a couple of things while we're here.'

'Sure,' Broady replied.

'Bourne Street, SW1,' she said, leaning forwards. 'And can you go up Horse Guards, so the tourist can see the Palace?' she added.

'No problem,' he replied, chewing his gum.

The cab headed off down the Euston Road.

Ella had a chance to consider things while Broady gazed out of the window at the sights. They spun around Trafalgar Square and up past Buckingham Palace. She found herself thinking about her life, reflecting on her mistakes. They skirted around Victoria Station and past the embassies onto Eaton Square. She watched Broady, transfixed by the plush white houses with their matching porticos.

'Here's perfect,' she said, pointing to a formal fronted, terraced house. The taxi drew up outside. She looked up at the house with a sinking feeling.

'What a great place to live,' said Broady, stepping out of the taxi.

Ella fumbled in her bag for the keys and then proceeded to work through the locks. She was sweating. She had thought the time away might have lessened the reaction. Hands shaking, she managed to open the door.

'Wow!' exclaimed Broady, entering the hall and seeing the modern artwork that adorned the walls. 'Love the chandelier.' He turned right into a huge study with books floor-to-ceiling on white, fitted shelves. 'It looks smaller from the outside,' he called back to Ella who was robotically picking the post up off the mat. 'Didn't figure you for the messy type though?'

'What do you mean?' she said, following him through.

There were papers strewn all over the floor.

She walked around the desk; all the drawers had been pulled out. 'I've been burgled.'

'What?' said Broady. 'Oh, Ella, I'm sorry.'

'I really don't need this,' she said, covering her face with her hands.

'Hey, it's going to be OK,' comforted Broady, sliding a gentle arm around her. 'We'll take care of it.' He gave her a squeeze. 'What is it you Brits say, we'll sort it?'

She forced a smile, sniffed a couple of times and wiped her eyes. 'Sorry about that, I'm fine,' she said pulling herself together and putting the guard back up.

'Hey, nothing to apologise for.'

She took a moment. 'Thanks, Hank.' She walked through to the kitchen and tugged at the metal security gates that blocked the back door – padlocks all in place. 'How did they get in?'

'Let's check out upstairs,' said Broady.

Ella followed him up the winding staircase past all the books empanelled on the walls. Most rooms seemed untouched, though in her bedroom a few drawers were open, but all the windows were locked and secure. 'It had to be the front door,' said Ella, checking a bedside drawer. Her jewellery, a couple of rolls of cash and her and Lizzie's passports were still there.

'Then they had to have keys,' said Broady.

'And it doesn't look like they've taken anything.'

'I hate to say it,' said Broady, 'but this doesn't look like a regular break-in.'

Ella agreed. 'You think it's got something to do with the inquiry?'

Broady tilted his head forwards in affirmation.

'Bastards,' said Ella, under her breath.

'You going to call the cops?'

'What's the point?' she replied, pulling out a holdall from under the bed and pouring in the contents of the drawer.

Broady didn't disagree.

Her phone rang. She reached into her bag and pulled out the Jay phone, then realised it was her iPhone that was ringing. She huffed and fished it out. Simon Carter's name was on the screen.

'Hi Simon,' she said walking over to the window and gazing out at an old woman in a fur coat on the pavement below.

'Hi Ella, how are things?'

'Not great, my house has been burgled, I'm here now.' She could see that the woman outside was waiting for her dog to take a shit. Ella put her face up against the window to see if she took out a poobag. She didn't.

'Oh Ella, I'm sorry, that's all you need.' Simon stopped.

Ella sensed he was deciding whether to say more. 'All OK with you, Simon?' She watched the woman continue on her way, leaving the steaming turd behind.

'Fine.' Another pause. 'I know this is a bad time, but I thought you should know...'

'Know what?' She heard him take a deep breath.

'Some members of the committee have been giving Desmond a hard time about his choice of Inquiry Chair.'

'Go on,' she said, suspecting what was coming.

'They say you should've made some progress by now.'

'It's not been easy, Simon,' she replied, realising that her voice had gone up a few decibels.

'You don't have to convince me, Ella,' he replied, sounding slightly wounded.

She winced. 'I'm sorry, I know what you did to get me this.' She could see Broady studying her as she did her usual pacing up and down.

'The committee is meeting at six tonight,' said Simon. 'At De Jure.'

'And they are going to sack me?'

'I don't see how I can stop it,' Simon replied.

'They're going to replace me?'

'Yes, with another silk, John Newport-Hartley.'

Ella glanced over at Broady. 'What? Not that pompous arse?'

'They're going to give him a week or two before pulling the plug on the whole thing. Now that Cameron Shepherd is dead…'

'Because there's no one to kick off anymore?' She sat down in a chair, resigned to her fate. 'Is there anything I can do?'

'Have you made any headway at all?'

'Not really,' she sighed.

'They need proof of progress. You can go to the meeting and try and persuade them, but they'll want to see something concrete.'

Ella thanked him for the heads up and ended the call. 'I take it you heard that?'

'Pretty much,' Broady replied, sitting down on the side of the bed.

'There's a meeting at six. I need to be there to stop them sacking me.'

'So, we go to Oxford first?'

She checked her watch. 'No time.' It was another blow. 'There's no direct train from Oxford to Cambridge, we'd have to come back via London.'

Broady got up and stared out of the window.

They were running out of time.

Chapter Forty-Six

Neither said much on the journey back.

Ella watched the fields and suburbs fly past as the train rolled on, beating out its rhythm on the tracks. She dreaded its arrival in Cambridge. What she would give for just a few more days.

Like two defeated soldiers, they alighted the train and began a slow trudge across town. By the time they turned up Trumpington Street towards De Jure it was 5.30 p.m.

Ella mulled over everything they knew so far as they passed the ancient colleges on either side. 'You know the Cambridge cell-site they found on Matthew's phone records?' she said to Broady. 'I suppose it would cover all of these buildings – this whole area?'

'I guess,' Broady replied.

Was she missing something? Her mind started to race. 'We've just assumed he was sitting in his room at De Jure.' She stopped outside Corpus Christi, admiring the golden yellow colour of the stone that takes a building half a millennium to earn. She stared at the great, ribbed arch. 'He could have been at any of these colleges,' she said, waving an arm in an arc.

Broady watched her. 'What're you thinking?'

She took out the list they'd got from the British Library and read it again. 'Just a hunch.' Her eyes refocused on the entrance to Corpus. 'We need to go to the Parker Library,'

'Parker Library?' he replied. 'Where's that?'

She pointed at the arch. 'In there, Corpus Christi.' She ran up the steps and showed her pass to a man standing at the entrance, with Broady following.

The full splendour of New Court opened up in their line of sight, framed by the archway with its ridged ceiling. They turned right along the path that ran alongside the lawn, then left towards the far corner. Inside the doorway, they went up the staircase and into the library. They stood for a moment, catching their breath. It wasn't a large chamber, but long and thin with a curved, high, panelled ceiling. They walked the length of the room, past wooden cabinets with glass fronts, displaying ancient scraps of paper with writing in some forgotten script.

'Can I help you?' An elderly lady in green tights and a tartan skirt appeared from behind a bookcase. Her glasses were on a piece of cord around her neck.

'Yes.' Ella showed her pass. 'I'm here on behalf of De Jure. We've got some questions about this man,' she said, handing her a photograph of Matthew. 'I don't suppose you recognise him?'

She put her glasses on the end of her nose and studied the picture. 'It's Mr Shepherd.'

Ella and Broady exchanged glances.

'You know him?' Ella said, a little too loudly. An academic with greasy hair and beige cords who was pouring over a manuscript with a magnifying glass looked up and scowled at her.

'Not really,' whispered the librarian. 'He came in occasionally. Very quiet and very polite.'

'So why do you remember him?' She could feel the blood rushing to her face.

'He could read Old English,' she replied, as if the answer was obvious.

Ella's heart skipped a beat.

'Do you remember what he'd look at here?'

'Of course,' she replied, sounding irritated that there might be any doubt. 'The A Manuscript.'

Ella could've kissed her.

'Interesting name,' observed Broady.

'It's also known as the Winchester Chronicle,' Ella explained, 'or the Parker Chronicle.'

'Must be important to have so many names.'

The librarian shot him a disparaging look. 'It's part of The Anglo-Saxon Chronicle.' She refocussed on Ella with a kindlier expression and asked in a conspiratorial voice, 'Would you like to see it?'

Ella gasped. 'Could I?' She'd only ever seen translations.

'Wait there.' The old lady shuffled off.

'It was the brainchild of King Alfred.' Ella was in her element.

'Alfred The Great, right?'

'That's him, he unified the tribes of Wessex and Mercia to fight against the Vikings.'

The man with the magnifying glass gave them another dirty look.

'When was this?' whispered Broady.

'Ninth century. He was a visionary, realised the value of education,' she enthused. 'He saw the need to create a national identity, to make us see ourselves as English, and fight as one, so he commissioned scribes to write the Anglo-

Saxon Chronicle, so that we could have a record of our own uniquely English, history.'

The librarian came back wearing a pair of white gloves, holding a leather binder with some leaves inside. She placed it carefully on the table and opened up the pages.

Ella marvelled at the sight. 'There are nine manuscripts. Parts of the Chronicle, written in different hands, added to over time, even as late as...' She looked to the librarian for assistance.

'1154,' she replied.

'So, it's a historical diary?' asked Broady.

'Exactly,' said the old lady, evidently warming to the American. 'It's invaluable. This manuscript refers to events going as far back as the first-century AD.'

'So, if this is the A, they go up to letter I, right?' asked Broady.

'Yes, the E is in the Bodleian,' said Ella, with a glint in her eye.

His eyebrows raised. 'And the others?'

Ella grinned. 'In the British Library.'

'But this one is the oldest,' the librarian replied, oblivious to the breakthrough that had just been made.

'Ella,' said Broady, 'You're a one-off.'

She smiled.

Broady gave a slow head shake. 'Matthew was focussing in on the Anglo-Saxon Chronicle. But why?'

'That's what we've got to work out,' Ella replied, full of renewed vigour. She checked her watch. 'It's six o'clock, we've got to go.' She turned to the librarian. 'Thank you so much.'

The librarian looked completely baffled as Broady took her hand and kissed it before he and Ella made for the stairs.

Chapter Forty-Seven

E lla pushed open the door of De Jure's committee room.
The last of the sun's rays penetrated the high sash windows, putting the antiquated books lining the opposite wall in the spotlight.

Breathing hard, Ella managed to say, 'I'm sorry,' between gulps of air.

'Ella,' said Simon Carter, standing up and staring at Broady beside her.

Desmond was at the head of the table. 'Miss Blake?'

'I'm sorry to barge in like this,' she said, taking in the people around the room. The dozen or so ageing academics and fellows from De Jure around the long table had turned towards them as they entered, craning to see the cause of the commotion.

'Actually,' Desmond said, in the calculating tone Ella had learned to read. 'There's something—'

'Stop.' She raised her arm. 'We've had a breakthrough.'

'Really?' said Carter. 'Come and sit down,' he offered, before Desmond had a chance to say more. 'Take my seat,' he said, patting the back of his chair.

'Thanks, but I'm better on my feet. It's a barrister thing.'

Nobody laughed.

'If you don't know already, this is Detective Broady from the Phoenix Police in Arizona. He's been working with me.'

No one raised an eyebrow; all had obviously been briefed by Desmond.

'We know that in the weeks leading up to his disappearance, Matthew was interested in the Anglo-Saxon Chronicle. He spent time reading the Parker Manuscript and we think he looked at the others at the Bodleian and the British Library.'

'How do you know this?' asked an elderly gentleman in a threadbare suit at the other end of the table.

'Mainly phone data,' said Broady.

'Perhaps he was trying to find the missing manuscripts?' suggested a younger man in a tweed jacket with patches on the elbows. 'So much has been lost over the years.'

'Or do you think he was trying to locate some lost Viking hoard?' said a woman with long, grey, frizzy hair in a red woolly scarf, wrapped several times around her neck.

A few of the others rolled their eyes.

'They are both possibilities,' Ella conceded. 'We know he was interested in the writings of Christian monks from Britain as far back as the seventh century.' She paused. 'But I don't think he was interested in material things, however valuable or important.' She glanced at Broady. 'I think he was working on something much bigger.'

'What makes you say that?' asked Simon.

'Matthew wasn't paranoid or mad. He was being watched, hounded. We don't know who by. He went to huge lengths to keep his work secret.'

'That's it?' asked another woman, sounding distinctly underwhelmed.

'And a lawyer's instinct,' she added, then regretted.

There were a few scoffs from around the table.

'And mine too, for what it's worth,' said Broady, taking a step forward.

'I…' She glanced over at Broady. '*We* need more time.'

'To do what exactly?' asked a bemused-looking man.

'For now, that's confidential.'

'Confidential?' repeated Desmond.

The committee needed more but Ella wasn't prepared to reveal the existence of the memory stick to a bunch of people she didn't know. 'Master Desmond, you know the importance of discretion in such a sensitive matter.' She searched the impassive faces for a connection. 'I'm sure whatever Matthew Shepherd was doing is vital to the reputation of this great university,' she said, clenching her hand into a fist. Her voice cracked. 'I can solve this.'

The room fell silent.

'Perhaps,' suggested Desmond, finally, 'you'd like to wait outside for a moment?'

Ella gave a nod. Sensing her job hung in the balance, she made a parting shot, 'I'd hate to see Oxford beat us to it.'

Desmond's face twitched.

Simon showed them to the door, then closed it behind them.

'You did good in there,' said Broady, leaning against the wall.

Ella paced up and down along the row of portraits of famous benefactors that lined the corridor. 'This job has become like an itch I can't scratch.'

'Tell me about it, and totally out of my comfort zone,' said Broady. 'Historical documents over a thousand years old…'

Eventually the door opened. Simon Carter beckoned them back in.

'Miss Blake,' Desmond began, with the top of his fingers touching in a pyramid. 'I think I can say that the committee is singularly unimpressed. You still have absolutely no idea where Matthew is or why he disappeared and—'

'Master Desmond, please—' Ella cut in.

He held up his hand. 'Let me finish.'

Ella fell silent.

'And you know next to nothing about what he was working on.' He took a breath. 'But, against our better judgement, we have decided to give you another forty-eight hours.'

'Forty-eight hours?' Ella protested, but inside she was relieved.

'To demonstrate some real progress.' He paused. 'Take it or leave it.'

She looked at Broady, who shrugged.

'I'll take it, but I need a commitment from you.'

Desmond's eyebrows shot up and then dropped into a frown. 'And what's that?'

She moved forward and scanned every face. 'That what we've discussed doesn't leave this room.'

The committee members exchanged glances, then all dipped their heads.

'Agreed,' confirmed Desmond.

Chapter Forty-Eight

'Hope you've had more fun than me?' Lizzie asked Jay, as he came back into the flat. 'Got these from the library,' she said, lifting a book off the pile on the table. 'I've been immersed in Plato.'

'I found something on Matthew,' he replied, putting the laptop on the table. 'But there's something I need to talk to you about.'

She walked over to him, seeing the apprehension in his eyes. 'You're going to tell me you lied?' If that was the case, she felt ready to explode.

Jay took a deep breath. 'No, someone else did.'

She was relieved. 'What do you mean?'

'I'm not trying to hurt you,' he said, moving closer.

His careful build up was irritating her. 'Just say it, Jay.'

'OK, OK,' he said, taking her hand. 'Sit down.'

They sat on the sofa facing each other.

'What Greg said about me,' he began.

It sounded as if he was laying the groundwork for an excuse. 'Yes?' she replied, becoming more impatient.

'It's an outright lie.'

'I never said it was Greg,' she replied, without any real conviction.

Jay tilted his head. 'Come on Lizzie…?'

She'd never been a good liar. 'He only said what he'd been told.'

Jay scoffed. 'I'm sorry but I don't believe that.'

She leaned back in a more defensive stance. 'So, what's your point?'

'I checked him out.'

'Not this again,' she replied, getting up. 'You're as bad as each other.'

'Lizzie,' he said, getting up to face her. 'You know who I am, you've seen everything about me – in court papers.' He paused. 'What do you really know about this guy?'

'What are you talking about?'

'Is that his real name? Have you ever seen where he lives, met his family?'

'I've only just met him, Jay. You're sounding a bit pathetic if I'm honest.' Once her bluster had subsided, Lizzie questioned herself, but only fleetingly. In a tone of commiseration, she said, 'You're so like my mum.' Hoping there was nothing else, she got up and walked over to the table and sat down, picking up the book she had been reading.

But Jay wasn't finished. 'I hacked Wolfson's database.'

She looked up.

He didn't need to say it.

She closed her eyes. 'And?' She opened them again.

'Greg Brooks is his name, right?'

She gave a reluctant nod, afraid of the answer.

'He's not a student there.'

'There could be some mistake?' Her eyes began to water. 'It's possible, right?'

'It's possible,' he replied, softly.

She had a sick feeling. 'I need to see him,' she said, wiping her eyes and standing up again.

Jay came over to the table. 'Is that wise?'

She shot him a look. 'I need to hear him out,' she said, going over to the door. She pulled on her coat and picked up one of her trainers.

'Hold on,' he said. 'I'll come with you.'

'No,' she said, her voice full of defiance. 'Stay out of it.' She pulled on the shoe and picked up the other. 'I gave you the same chance, didn't I?'

Jay didn't argue.

Before she had a chance to leave, the buzzer sounded.

Chapter Forty-Nine

They came back through the car park below the apartment. Ella stopped at her van to collect a few history books, throwing one at Broady. 'Some light reading for you.'

He caught it. '*The Anglo-Saxon Chronicles*, translated by Michael Swanton? You read this stuff for fun?'

'For that,' she said, 'you're doing dinner tonight.'

'You're kidding, my cooking sucks,' he laughed.

'Don't worry, you can do hot dogs. Sorry, wieners.'

They bickered about the difference between tomatoes and tom*a*toes on the way up in the lift and then Lizzie buzzed them in.

'You two look happy,' she said, as they walked in.

'You don't,' Ella observed, noticing the redness around Lizzie's eyes. 'Going somewhere?'

Lizzie took off her coat. 'No, I was but… I'm fine,' she said, glancing over at Jay. 'What's the news?'

'Desmond's given us another forty-eight hours,' said Ella.

Broady shrugged. 'And we only got that because your

incredible mom figured out what Matthew had been working on.'

Ella dumped the books on the sofa and they all joined Jay, who was sitting at the table in front of a laptop. 'The Anglo-Saxon Chronicle,' she said, directing the revelation at her daughter. 'The Cambridge cell-site covered the Parker Library.'

'Of course,' Lizzie exclaimed. 'The three libraries holding parts of the Chronicle. Why didn't I think of that?' She stared at Ella as if seeing her for the first time. 'I'm really impressed, Mum.'

Ella felt overwhelmed; her daughter's approval meant everything. 'Well, it's something to go on, at least,' Ella said, playing it down. 'He seems to have been looking at all the ancient Christian manuscripts and then focussed in on the Anglo-Saxon Chronicle, I just can't think why – and why it might have led to him disappearing.'

'Jay's got something, too,' said Lizzie, remembering they'd never actually discussed it.

'Really, that's great,' Ella replied, still riding the wave.

Jay looked nervous. His apprehension over what he was about to divulge was obvious. 'Matthew was ill.'

'Ill?' Ella repeated. 'How do you know?' She noticed he was avoiding eye-contact.

'Hospital records.'

'What, you worked out how to hack them?' she asked, anger rising up. 'That's illegal.'

'Strictly speaking, I already knew how.' Jay's eyes settled on Lizzie, as if searching for support.

'From when his mum was sick,' said Lizzie. 'The doctors wouldn't tell him anything because of his age.'

Jay's hands fiddled with the laptop screen. 'So, I found out for myself.'

Ella softened.

'Let's give the kid a break,' said Broady.

Jay looked relieved. His hands stopped moving. 'I just thought I'd check; I couldn't believe his name came up as a patient.'

Ella was silent. Then she asked, 'What was wrong with him?'

'Brain tumour – terminal.'

'That's tough,' said Broady.

'The notes say he only had months to live, and that was back in November, so he may already be—' Jay stopped.

He didn't need to spell it out.

'Why would he leave Cambridge when he was being treated at the hospital?' said Lizzie.

'He was running out of time,' said Ella. 'And he knew it.'

'But he doesn't go home either?' said Broady. 'Doesn't spend it with his brother, the only family he's got?'

'Something must have been more important,' said Jay. His observation made Ella's stomach tighten but there was something about what Broady had said that stuck in Ella's mind. 'What did you say about his family?'

Broady sat down at the table and pushed a pile of books away from him. 'About not going to see his brother?'

'Yes.' Ella tried to recall the phrase Cameron had used. She closed her eyes and scrunched up her face. 'There was something Cameron said...' She rubbed her forehead as if the motion would produce the answer. 'Little bro!'

The others stared at her blankly.

'That's what he called Matthew – little bro.'

'You think that's the password?' asked Jay, sitting up.

'It's got to be worth a try.' said Ella, reaching for her handbag to retrieve the stick.

'I agree,' said Broady, 'let's give it a go.'

She poked around in the bag, then stopped – the side pocket where she was sure she'd zipped the memory stick was empty. She patted her trouser pockets, front and back. Then searched the bag again. 'It's not here.' She tipped the contents onto the table and went through each item. 'I know I put it in this side pocket,' she said, turning the bag inside out. She was fighting a rising tide of panic.

The others joined the search.

'Check your coat,' said Broady.

'I wouldn't have put it there,' she replied, checking anyway. 'Someone must have stolen it.'

'Who?' asked Lizzie. 'Maybe you've just lost it.'

Ella began to pace the room. 'No way.'

'Oh shit,' exclaimed Broady. He got up and faced Ella. 'The security guy.'

Ella looked at him. 'At the British Library? No?'

'Was he even security? He wasn't behind the desk where they did the bag checks.'

'He had a uniform on...' Ella replied, trying to remember.

'Or was it just a suit?' asked Broady. He flopped onto one of the chairs. 'I honestly can't remember.'

It suddenly seemed obvious. Ella was furious with herself. 'Oh my god. He was nothing to do with the library.'

Broady's head dropped. 'We got played.'

Defeated, Ella sat on the chair next to him. 'Who the hell are these people?'

Broady didn't answer.

The room was silent.

'Don't freak,' said Jay, his tone faltering, 'but...' He took a deep breath. 'I made a copy.'

'What?' Ella got back up, her eyes boring into him. 'When?' She could see Jay's Adam's apple bobbing as he gulped.

'When?' she demanded again.

'Yesterday,' he replied tentatively.

She stood over him. 'Without telling me?'

'I'm sorry, couldn't help it.' His eyes were pleading. 'I back up everything.'

'Did you know about this?' she said, turning to Lizzie, who looked down. Ella turned to Jay and gave him an uncertain stare.

Ella didn't know what to think. 'How can I trust you?'

'Hold on,' said Broady. 'If he was planning to do something with it, he wouldn't have told us.'

Still feeling deceived, she snapped, 'Where is it?'

'On the laptop,' he replied, waving a finger at the screen.

'So,' Broady said to Ella. 'Are we good?'

She was still thinking. 'Pull another stunt like that,' she said, 'and you're out.'

'But luckily for you,' observed Broady, 'it was the right move.'

Jay looked like a dog that had been told off by its master. 'I'm sorry, Ella.'

Unable to deny he had actually rescued the situation, she finally let it go, giving him a weary smile.

Jay said, 'So shall I try it?' He looked to Ella for a response. 'Little bro – no spaces?'

She glanced at the others. No one had an objection.

'Do it,' she ordered.

Jay typed it in.

They waited. Ella held her breath.

'I don't believe it,' shouted Jay. 'I'm in!'

The excitement was electric.

They all leaned in around the screen. Ella rested her hands on Jay's shoulders to steady herself.

'It's a file,' said Jay, 'called Genesis.' His finger hovered over the keys. 'Here we go,' he said. 'Open.'

The document came up on the screen.

Ella stared at it, at a loss to understand.

'Dots?' said Lizzie.

Jay scrolled down. There were sheets of dots, seemingly random, on each page.

'You know what it looks like,' Lizzie suggested. 'A book where someone has deleted all the lines, leaving only the full stops.'

'Or maybe it's some kind of code?' said Jay. 'Like Morse?'

None of them could take their eyes off the screen. 'It's weird, I feel like I should know this pattern,' said Lizzie.

Ella kind of understood. There was something strangely familiar about it.

'Maybe it's a star map?' said Broady. 'A constellation.'

Ella stood up and pulled herself away. 'We're all saying what it could mean to us, coming from our own perspectives. We need to take a step back, look at it objectively.'

The others nodded.

'And work out how it could be connected to our only other clue.'

'The Anglo-Saxon Chronicle?' said Lizzie. 'It's got to be about history, not science.' She rubbed her chin. '*Genesis*, that's so weird.'

'What is?' said Ella, unable to take her eyes off the screen.

'Some climate change guy I met keeps talking about Genesis.'

'Do you mean David Kline?' asked Jay.

'Yeah,' Lizzie replied. 'You know him?'

'No, but he says some cool stuff. Supposed to have some mind-blowing central theory, apparently. You get to learn in stages if you support his organisation. It's all about reaching enlightenment.'

'Bet all the students love that,' said Ella.

'Sounds a bit like Scientology,' said Broady.

'I think it's more fact-based than that,' said Lizzie. 'I've heard him speak.'

'Thinking about it,' said Jay. 'He had a position at De Jure.'

Ella stared at him.

'Yeah,' he continued. 'The establishment didn't like his politics so he got sacked. 'It was in the local paper. Totally unfair, if you ask me.'

'Too many coincidences,' said Ella, putting on her coat. 'Come on, we're going to De Jure.'

Chapter Fifty

A light drizzle had all but cleared the streets. A few people in raincoats, their collars pulled up around their necks, scurried along under the streetlamps to their destinations. Ella marched, head down, across town to De Jure, oblivious to the weather.

'I need to make sure I'm not going mad,' she said when Broady asked what they were going to do.

Broady muttered his usual complaint about her not being a team player as Ella strode on down the shadowy streets.

'Evening,' she called out to Bartlett as they passed his office. 'Just checking something in Matthew's room.'

Bartlett looked up from his copy of *The Sun* and doffed his cap. 'Brought the whole family?' he said in a dry voice, as the others appeared at the window.

Ella looked around and laughed, then realised they were one short. 'Where's Lizzie?'

'Gone to see Greg,' Jay replied.

Ella remembered her puffy eyes. 'Lover's tiff?'

'Something like that,' Jay replied, without looking at her. 'I'm sure she won't be long.'

She wondered why he'd felt the need to reassure her, but then dismissed it. 'Mr Bartlett, is Master Desmond still here?'

'Course he is,' he replied, closing his paper.

Ella sensed he didn't have much affection for the man. 'Can you do me a favour and show Detective Broady and Jay, my assistant, to Matthew's rooms? I'll catch you up when I've seen the Master.'

'Right you are,' he replied, pulling himself up off his chair and wheezing into action.

Ella handed Broady the keys. 'Two silver at the top and brown at the bottom.'

Ella knocked on Desmond's door and waited. She couldn't stop thinking about Genesis and all its possible connotations.

'Come.'

The room was in semi-darkness apart from a desk light illuminating Desmond's head and some papers on his desk. 'Miss Blake?' Caught without his jacket, he stood up and pulled it bashfully off the back of his chair, quickly dressing himself. 'How can I help you?'

Ella suddenly felt underdressed in her jeans. 'What can you tell me about David Kline?'

Desmond groaned. 'Had the pleasure, have you?' He walked over to the door and switched on the main light.

'No, his name cropped up, that's all. Another academic from De Jure?'

'The bane of my life,' said Desmond wistfully. 'My own fault, we put his brilliance before everything else. He's still coming into Cambridge you know, to recruit undergraduates for whatever it is he does. We're not happy about it, but what can we do? They're all adults.'

The sound of the weather outside drew them to the

window. They stood side by side watching the rain batter the glass.

Ella broke the silence. 'I heard you had to let him go a couple of years ago?'

The mention of this made his face contort. 'We couldn't have someone with his profile getting involved in pitched battles at police cordons.' He put his chin into his chest. 'No, that just wouldn't do.' He faced Ella now. 'God knows I'm the first to acknowledge the need to put climate change higher up on the agenda. And I know how crucial the issue is to young people, particularly those at De Jure, but…' His voice trailed off.

'But you didn't approve of his methods?'

'How could we?' He went over to his desk and rummaged around in a drawer, pulling out a few sheets. He came back to the window and presented them to Ella. 'A petition signed by half of our students demanding his reinstatement.'

She perused the list of names and signatures. She could see this was still very much an open wound for Desmond.

'You see, the undergraduates loved him. He's handsome, charismatic – very different from Matthew, polar opposites.'

She handed back the petition. 'Did they know each other?'

He dropped the sheet of paper on the desk. 'Oh yes, they've known each other for years. They're the same age, competing child prodigies, I suppose you could say. They collaborated once I think, but sadly, never published what they were working on.'

'Were they friends?' She wondered why she hadn't been told any of this before.

'God no, chalk and cheese. Rivals.' Desmond reflected. 'Both great polymaths but Matthew was always a step ahead.'

'Was Kline spoken to when Matthew disappeared?'

'I assume so,' he replied. 'I told McDonald about him. You don't think…?'

Ella didn't reply. She was too busy trying to work out why McDonald had never given her this lead. 'You'd better email me everything you've got on Kline.'

Desmond gave her an anxious nod.

'I've got a feeling I'm going to need it.'

Ella found Broady working his way along the bookshelves in Matthew's room calling out obscure titles.

Jay was perched on a pile of books with his laptop open. 'I've got some software I'm running, to try and work out if there's some kind a pattern here.'

Ella stood over him, staring at the dots on the screen. '*Genesis*. Why Genesis?'

Broady stopped what he was doing and put his hands on his hips. 'What are we actually looking for?'

Ella began pacing, then suddenly stopped. 'It's all about joining the dots…' Her mind was racing.

'You've lost me,' said Broady.

'Something Desmond said…' She stood in the middle of the room, taking in her surroundings. Her expression changed. She put a hand on her head then and fixed the others with an intense stare. Then she went over to Jay and checked the dots on the screen, then looked around the room. 'Remind you of anything?' she asked.

Broady came over and joined Jay in studying the pattern, then turned to look at the walls.

'Look,' she said, sweeping an arm around the room. 'The wallpaper?'

Their eyes followed her hand. The pattern was of swirling

lines and arcs, connecting dots, from floor to ceiling. 'This,' she said, 'is Genesis.'

The position of the dots on the wall matched the pattern on the screen.

Broady was the first to speak, 'Why have it on the walls?' He went over and ran a finger over the pattern. 'Look at the seam – it's actual wallpaper.'

'So that he could look at it all day,' said Jay, unable to take his eyes off the curves. 'Without anyone suspecting this was what he was working on.'

'Ingenious,' said Ella. She felt a shiver down her spine.

Broady moved his finger along one of the lines. 'What the hell does it mean?'

Chapter Fifty-One

Lizzie fought her way through the bar, jam-packed with drinkers. Greg was sitting on the end of one of the tables with two glasses of Sancerre at the ready.

'You OK?' he asked above the din.

She gave nothing away.

'What was so urgent?' He handed her a glass as she sat down.

She noticed his eyes anxiously searching her face for clues. She took a sip and gathered herself. She'd decided not to mess about. 'Greg,' she asked, praying Jay was wrong. 'Are you really at Wolfson?'

His body stiffened. 'Where's this come from? Jay, I bet?'

'Are you really a student?' she asked more forcefully.

'What?' he replied with a laugh that sounded forced.

'I'm going to give you one more chance to tell me the truth.' She looked into his eyes, more with sorrow, than anger.

He opened his mouth as if about to protest, then his eyebrows dropped, his face falling out of character. 'Not in here.' He scanned the room, full of customers, then stood up. 'Come on.'

Her heart sank. She followed him outside and they found shelter under the old coachmen's entrance. She glanced over at a couple of students further down the lane under an umbrella, smoking a spliff and giggling. The sickly-sweet smell of marijuana wafted over.

Moving closer, Greg said, 'There's a lot you don't know.'

Water streamed down off the roof, making it hard to hear what he was saying. Unsure she'd heard right, Lizzie replied, 'About you?'

'I'm sorry,' he said, gently running a finger down her cheek. 'I've been trying to protect you.'

She swatted his hand away. 'In other words, you lied?'

'Before I tell you,' he said, his voice trembling with emotion. 'I want you to know my feelings for you are genuine.'

She felt nauseous.

'I work for the government.'

She stepped back. 'What are you saying?'

'You have to understand,' he implored. 'This is way bigger than both of us.'

She screwed her face up, irritated by the platitudes. 'So, this is about the inquiry?'

He didn't reply immediately.

'Is it?' she demanded.

'Yes.' He moved forward and held her arm. 'But—'

'So, how we met?' Tears beginning to flow. 'The bike crash?' Anger turned to sadness. 'It was all…'

He grimaced. 'You don't understand.'

She pulled her arm away. 'Is your name even Greg?'

He didn't answer.

'I slept with you.'

He didn't react.

The dope smokers looked over, sniggered, then refocussed on the reefer that was passing between them.

'You bastard,' she shrieked in his face, before running off into the rain.

He followed, grabbing at her arm again. 'Lizzie, please, just listen.'

She yanked it away. 'Leave me alone.'

'Don't you get it?' he shouted after her. 'We need you.'

She turned, curiosity overcoming the betrayal. 'Why?'

He walked towards her. 'They made me come to you and not your mother for a reason.'

Still backing away, she was listening.

'They need someone sensible, someone they can trust...' he said.

'Who's they?'

He lunged forward and pulled her into a shop doorway. Droplets were still rolling down his face. 'We have to find Matthew Shepherd's work before anyone else.'

She'd never seen him look so grave.

'I hated lying to you but...' He choked up. 'The British Government have to find it first.'

Lizzie was struggling to take in what he was saying.

'Your mother's great, but she's too flaky for this.'

'Why's it so important?' She brushed the water off her face. 'Tell me what you know?'

He glanced at the road. There was no one around.

'We think it's a weapon.'

'A weapon?' She didn't know what to believe. 'How do you know?'

'That's all they've told me.' He studied her face, as if deciding whether to disclose more. 'I'm a field intelligence operative. My job was to keep tabs on what Ella knows.'

Lizzie thought it through, then stepped back. 'This is bullshit, you could've just asked her.'

'We don't trust her, we trust you.' He sighed. 'I was supposed to just observe, check she didn't know anything.

Then we found out about the USB drive. By then she was too close to Jay and the American. We don't know who they are.'

Lizzie couldn't tell if she was being hoodwinked. She remembered what had happened to Jay. 'Are you from MI6?'

'No.'

She could see the tension in his face. He was a man under immense pressure.

'I'm part of a government team set up just for this. Doesn't even have a name.' Seeming to realise what he'd said, he added, 'We don't believe any of that Jay stuff about being duped, we just haven't been able to find out who he's working for.'

'I don't believe you,' she replied, her tone curt. 'He's certainly no coke dealer, is he?'

His head dropped. 'No,' he said, sounding contrite. 'It was all I could think of on the spot, I had orders to protect my cover.' Still looking strained, he shuddered. 'Lizzie, you have to understand, this is the most important thing you or I will ever do.'

The interrogation was nearly over. She got to the final question. 'So, what do you need from me?'

Greg looked deep into her eyes. 'The password.'

Chapter Fifty-Two

E lla and the others stood in the archway, patiently waiting for a lull in what had now become a full-blown rainstorm.

Jay had persuaded Ella that they should go via the Mitre on their way back to pick up Lizzie, even though it was in the opposite direction.

At last, the downpour began to ease off. They darted down the steps and turned right up King's Parade towards the pub, hugging the sides of the buildings for shelter.

Just as they crossed the road to turn onto Bridge Street, Ella turned to see Jay, who was bringing up the rear, watching two motorbikes which seemed to be bearing down on them, only metres away. The rain had muffled any warning.

'Look out!' he yelled.

Both bikes had two riders, in dark leathers and full-face helmets. The lead motorcycle slowed as it passed, allowing the pillion rider to thrust out an arm and grab at Jay's laptop bag.

The force yanked him off his feet and he landed splayed out on the wet pavement. The strap was diagonally across his body and the bag had stayed in place. The second bike came towards him, spray flying up on either side. Jay had got himself up onto all fours. Broady rushed across the bike's path and, in one movement, rolled Jay up onto the pavement.

The bike sped on, turned in a loop, and came to a stop.

Broady pulled Jay to his feet and looked over at Ella, whose expression was one of utter disbelief.

'Come on,' Broady said, pulling Jay back in the direction from which they'd come.

'Down here,' Ella shouted, taking a right down an alley towards St John's. She could hear the revving of engines behind them as they ran, splashing through the puddles. To her horror there was no way out. 'Dead end!' she shouted, desperately looking around her.

Jay had a confused expression as if trying to get his bearings. 'This way,' he said, leading them through a door and into Chapel Court. They ran across the open space and into the Master's Garden, coming out by the Cam.

Relying on Jay's knowledge of the gardens, they fell in behind as he weaved his way alongside the river, climbing over a wall and using cut-throughs to get across the lawns and past the Bridge of Sighs until they reached Kitchen Bridge.

Panting, they stopped to catch their breath.

Ella held her head up, gulping in air, whilst Broady hunched over, resting his hands on his knees.

'We need to keep going,' Jay shouted to be heard above the deafening splashing of water pouring off the gargoyles above.

They moved out onto the bridge, squinting for a view of the other side, the sheets of rain hampering visibility.

As they got halfway across, Ella heard the dreaded sound of revving engines again then suddenly a headlight illuminated their path – one of the motorcycles, waiting on the other side.

Ella was the first to double-back, only to be met by another bike blocking their way.

The pillion passenger dismounted and took several steps forward, positioning himself in front of the beam. His gait was male but the helmet made it impossible to be sure.

He pulled out a handgun and pointed it straight at Ella.

Before she had time to take in the full horror of what was happening, Broady dived in front of her and stuck out an arm. 'Wait!'

The man fired.

It took a moment for Ella to realise. It hardly made a sound, there was only the dull thud of the silencer. The force of it jerked Broady's body back. He staggered backwards into Ella, but managed to regain his balance, keeping his body in front of hers.

Ella screamed, 'No!'

The gunman lined up another shot, this time using his left arm to steady himself.

'You want this?' Jay shouted.

The shooter didn't move.

Ella turned around to see Jay dangling the laptop bag over the side of the bridge.

'Fire again and this is gone forever,' he snarled.

The man lowered his arm slightly, as if unsure of the right course.

On seeing his indecision, Ella took out her phone and dialled McDonald. 'I'm ringing the police,' she yelled at him.

The man raised his arm again, then stopped, as his companion said something to him that Ella couldn't make out. He got back on the motorbike and they accelerated past them, over the bridge, joining their companions. They disappeared off into the night.

'It's Ella Blake,' Ella said as her call was picked up, her voice shaking. 'We're on Kitchen Bridge, Broady has been shot.' Nothing seemed real anymore. 'Just get an ambulance.' Turning to Broady, Ella tried to process what just happened. His legs began to wobble. Ella grabbed at his torso before he fell, managing to support him as he dropped to the ground and helping him to sit, propped against the stone balustrades.

A patch of blood was forming on his jacket.

She pulled it back off his shoulder, trying to locate the wound. 'Why do you wear so many fucking layers?'

'English weather,' he mumbled. His eyelids were losing the battle to stay open.

She found the hole on the side of his gut. Blood was oozing out. She untucked her blouse and tore off a strip then pushed it hard onto the lesion. 'Stay with me, Hank,' she demanded. 'Stay with me.'

With no fight left, his eyes closed.

She slapped his cheek. 'Hank?' And again, 'Hank?'

The sound of police sirens drew closer.

Jay ran to the edge of the bridge and frantically waved his arms.

The rain had stopped.

Chapter Fifty-Three

Ella and Jay sat in silence, side by side, outside McDonald's office. Ella was numb, unable to process the evening's events.

A couple of young detectives ogled the bedraggled pair as they passed them on the corridor. Ella knew her smudged eyeliner, ripped shirt and the way her hair had dried made her look like someone out of *A Clockwork Orange*. Her phone pinged. 'Thank God,' she said, reading the message. 'Lizzie's at the hospital.'

'Wonder where she was all night?' Jay muttered.

The door opened and McDonald appeared, standing in the doorway with a disdainful expression. 'Come in,' he said like a headmaster beckoning in two unruly pupils.

Ella got up first. 'Can we make this quick? I want to get back to the hospital.'

'All in good time,' McDonald replied. 'Let's see if you can't help us catch whoever did this.' He gave Jay a contemptuous look. 'Don't you think that's the priority here?'

A smartly-dressed woman with a ginger bob and opaque

skin was standing behind McDonald's desk. The trouser creases on her two-piece were razor sharp.

McDonald shut the door behind them, then held out an arm in the stranger's direction. 'This is Jane Harris. She's from MI6.' The smugness on McDonald's face dissipated on seeing that Ella and Jay seemed unsurprised.

Ella spoke up. 'I'm Ella Blake, and this—'

'I know who you are,' Harris said, pointing to the two empty chairs in front of the desk. McDonald used an elbow to lean on a battered filing cabinet in the corner.

Ella and Jay sat down, while Harris remained standing, immediately giving it the feel of an interrogation. She bent over the desk. 'Do you have any idea who shot your colleague?'

Ella gave her an icy stare. 'Could I see your ID?'

Harris straightened up. After a brief vacillation, she produced it from her jacket pocket and held it open.

Ella reached across the desk and took it out of her hand. She studied it, then gave it to Jay, whilst she got out her phone and took a picture of it.

Harris watched with pursed lips.

'That's enough games,' said McDonald, snatching it back and handing it to Harris with a subservient bow.

Ignoring him, Ella replied in a tone devoid of emotion, 'No, I don't know who shot him, but I bet you do?'

Harris didn't blink. 'You seem angry, Miss Blake.'

Ella shot back, 'Wouldn't you be?'

Harris looked over at McDonald who didn't seem to understand the signal. 'Would you give us a minute please, detective?'

His mouth fell open and his face turned red. He shot Harris a look of disbelief and then glared with resentment at Ella before leaving the room, slamming the door behind him. A Snoopy cartoon on the wall vibrated then went lopsided.

Harris' posture lost some of its stiffness. She sat down in McDonald's chair. 'We're on the same side, Miss Blake.'

'Are we?' Ella uncrossed her legs and leaned forward. 'I'm not into spy games, I'm just a lawyer, instructed to do a job by a university.'

Harris leaned forward too. 'But first and foremost, you're British?'

Ella let out a scornful laugh. 'Cambridge are paying my bill.'

'How about,' said Jay, pointing at Harris, 'you tell us what the hell is going on?'

Harris looked as if she was about to rebuke him for his impudence, but then reclined and seemed to be reassessing her approach. 'Could you ask Mr Pitois to leave us for a moment?'

'He stays,' Ella shot back. 'He saved my life tonight.' Spitting out her words, she added: 'And I didn't see your arse anywhere.'

Harris gave a knowing nod then took a breath. 'We've been involved for some time.' She pressed her palms together. 'We know there are people interested in Matthew Shepherd.'

'Is he alive?'

'I don't know,' she replied, seemingly unperturbed by the directness of the question.

'You said *people*?' asked Jay.

'A group,' she replied, directing her answer to Ella. 'We think a group with Chinese links shot Detective Broady.'

'Government?' asked Ella.

'It's unlikely, not really their style. The bullet came from a Chinese pistol called a Type 67, it's got an integral silencer.' Harris tilted her head. 'Just a bit too old-fashioned for their top people. Easy to get on the black market.'

Ella wanted to mull it over but knew there were more

pressing questions. 'Do you know who killed Cameron Shepherd?'

Harris glanced over at Jay, clearly uncomfortable about his presence. 'The evidence points to suicide.'

Ella could tell Harris didn't believe that. 'You know what an Osman warning is, don't you?' said Ella. 'As a government agency, if a civilian's life is in danger, you have a duty to warn them?'

Harris' neck started to go red. 'I know the law, Miss Blake.'

'Then why didn't you warn us?' Ella slammed her hand down on the desk. 'You broke the law.'

'I'm telling you now,' she replied, remaining calm. 'If you work with us,' she said with an earnest expression, 'come under our protection, we can take you out of the field until it's all over.'

'Out of the field?' Ella let out a laugh. 'I'm a lawyer for Christ's sake.' She glanced over at Jay. 'He's a student.'

'Look,' Harris said with more force. 'Everyone's getting very jumpy about what Matthew Shepherd might've discovered.'

'And what's that?' Ella fired back.

Harris separated her hands. 'I hoped you might be able to answer that.'

Jay laughed. 'What, you mean you've got no idea?'

Harris didn't reply.

Ella thought it through. 'So how do you know it's important if you don't know anything?'

Harris put her hands on the desk. 'Because of the way other people are behaving, particularly those who know more than us.'

Ella didn't buy it. 'All this is happening here, on English soil, and you say you don't know anything? If you're not going to trust us, why should we trust you?' She began to get up. 'You're offering protection with conditions?'

'Not offering.' Harris gave her a cold stare. 'I'm insisting.'

Ella was on her feet now. 'Under what law?' She waited for a reply.

None came.

She made to leave. Jay stood up too.

'Hang on.' Harris held out an arm. 'I'll get McDonald to arrange some protection for twenty-four hours, while you think about it.' She got up and stared Ella down. 'But if you decide not to play ball, you realise you're on your own?'

Ella searched the agent's face for some hint of warmth, a connection. She saw only cold detachment.

Jay opened the door.

'One more thing,' said Harris, handing her a card with a phone number on. 'I'd keep your daughter away from Greg Brooks.'

Ella's face dropped. 'Why?'

Harris squinted, looking uncomfortable. 'He's not who he says he is.'

Ella's eyes narrowed. 'What does that mean?'

Harris shrugged. 'Classified.'

Ella could hardly bear to look at her. 'How long have you known that?'

Harris glanced at the door. 'I'll arrange for a police car to take you back to the hospital.'

Ella sneered. 'That's what I thought.' She looked pointedly at Jay and they walked out.

'Wait!'

Ella turned and saw the indecision on Harris' face.

The agent appeared to waver for a moment then ushered them back in, checking the corridor both ways, and shutting the door. 'You didn't hear it from me, OK?' She stared intently at the barrister.

Ella dipped her head. Jay did the same.

'We think he works for Kline,' Harris confided like a rush of air leaving a punctured tyre. 'One of his followers.'

'So Kline's not a climate change protester,' said Ella, glancing at Jay.

Harris perched on the edge of the desk and let out more air. 'That's the hook but he's a very dangerous individual. Got followers all over the world.'

'Genesis.' Ella let out a sardonic laugh. 'Were he and Matthew working on the same theory?'

'We think so,' Harris replied, her expression sombre. 'We've intercepted some chat online, Kline's planning something big.'

'What, some kind of protest?' asked Jay.

'I don't think so.' Harris' worry lines became more pronounced. 'Something impactful.' She sighed.

'This sounds like bullshit,' said Jay. 'He's not a terrorist, he's just a green activist.'

Ella wasn't so sure. Years at the Bar had taught her when to trust information. 'Are you saying his people shot Broady?'

'We've got nothing on him in relation to any crime, just snippets of intelligence.' Harris clasped her hands together. 'He's got all these brainwashed young techies working for him. Loads of different skill sets, all totally devoted.' She opened her hands in a gesture of exasperation.

'But why Broady, why me?'

'Maybe you've got something they need. Or they think you might know what they've got planned.' She shrugged. 'Everything seems to be linked to this Genesis thing.'

'And what is it?' Ella asked, already reading the answer in her face.

'Haven't got a clue.' Their eyes met properly. 'My people think it's a sideshow but I know it's important. It's the key.'

Ella felt a certain kinship with Harris despite everything.

'Key to what?' It was obvious to Ella that Harris was holding something back. 'What's the main show?'

'That's all I can say.' Harris was saved by a knock on the door. McDonald came in. 'Car's ready.'

Harris gave him a nod and stood up. 'Remember what I said, Miss Blake. 'Twenty-four hours.' She made another attempt at giving Ella her card.

This time Ella took it. Her head was spinning.

Chapter Fifty-Four

The car pulled up outside the Accident and Emergency Department at Addenbrooke's Hospital. Flanked on either side by firearms officers, Ella and Jay climbed out of the back seat and into the bright sunshine. It was already mid-morning. Members of staff stopped and stared as they were taken in and escorted past the queues of patients, waiting to be seen. The walls were magnolia and bare apart from a few whiteboards with work shifts written on in marker pen. Ella could smell the disinfectant.

They turned a corner on to a long corridor, blocked in the middle by people milling around outside a room with an armed police officer by the door.

'Mum,' shouted Lizzie, rushing towards her out of the crowd, followed by Simon Carter.

'Thank God you're all right,' Simon said.

Ella threw her arms around her daughter. 'I'm OK,' she replied, looking over Lizzie's shoulder at Desmond who was approaching. 'How's Broady?'

'He's going to be OK,' Desmond replied with a reassuring

nod. 'The doctors said he's very lucky.' He glanced at Jay. 'Have we met before?'

'My assistant,' she explained. 'Jason Pitois.'

Jay gave him an awkward smile.

'This is Mike Stone,' said Desmond, ushering a man in a trench coat into the huddle. 'From the US Embassy.'

He reached out to shake her hand.

Pleasantries over, Ella could see that Desmond was about to erupt.

'Ella Blake?' said a tall man in a white coat above the heads of those around her.

'Yes,' she replied, pushing her way over to him.

Desmond's eyes followed her.

The doctor rested a hand against the wall. 'He's been asking for you.'

Ella's eyes widened. 'He's awake?'

'Yes, he's had a blood transfusion.' The doctor steered her into a space by the door. 'The bullet imbedded itself in fatty tissue at the side of his waist. He's lucky.'

Ella let out a deep sigh.

'The recovery should be quick.' He smiled. 'It's when it hits bone or an artery that things get trickier.'

'Thank you, doctor,' she replied, trying to get a view through the panel. 'Can I see him?'

'Of course.' He pushed open the door to let her through. 'But keep it brief.'

Broady was in an apron, his head and torso in a slightly raised position, with a drip connected to his left arm.

'Hey,' Ella whispered, on reaching the side of the bed.

'Hey,' he replied with a tired smile.

She touched his arm and gave it a gentle stroke. 'You saved me.' Her eyes welled up.

His eyelids were still heavy. 'Someone has to.'

She couldn't find the words.

'What's happening?' he asked weakly.

She sat down on a metal chair, painted white. 'Someone from MI6 has told me it's like the wild west in Cambridge right now.'

He chuckled then grimaced.

She felt his pain shoot through her. 'They've offered protection for twenty-fours while I decide if I want to go into some kind of custody.'

He gave her a look.

She read it. 'I've got to think of Lizzie.' She paused. 'And Jay.'

'I've got to get out of here,' he said, trying in vain to sit up. He gritted his teeth and tried again.

She gently pushed him back on the pillow. 'Hank, you need rest, then you're going home.'

His eyes followed her. 'No.'

'They reckon that climate change guy Lizzie was talking about is involved in all this somehow.' Now that she said it aloud it sounded even more far-fetched. 'There's nothing more you can do.' She gave his arm another stroke.

He lifted his hand off the bed. She held it.

He squeezed. 'I need this.'

She gazed into his green eyes. 'Why?'

A slow blink. 'Don't do anything without me.'

She didn't know what to say.

What strength he'd got back appeared to be leaving him. 'Promise me?'

She glanced around at the door.

The embassy guy was staring through the glass panel, but too far away to hear.

'OK,' she said, squeezing back. 'I promise.'

Broady's eyes closed. He was asleep.

It reminded her of the bridge. She shuddered.

As soon as Ella went back out onto the corridor, she saw Desmond and Simon cross-examining an anxious-looking Jay.

Lizzie waved her over, causing Desmond to switch his attention to Ella. 'Are you going to tell us what the hell's going on?'

'Not here,' she replied, marching off.

The others followed.

She saw a sign for the canteen and led them past an old man in a dressing gown, leaning on a zimmer frame. She skirted around a lady in a wheelchair with a leg sticking out in a new cast and found an empty table in the corner.

Jay stacked some dirty plates and put them on the next table.

The others sat down, Desmond facing her. 'Well?' he asked, sticking out his chin.

Ella could see the blood rushing to his face. She was determined to remain calm. She quickly scanned the other tables, then said quietly, 'Whatever Matthew was doing, other people want to know.'

'That much is obvious,' he seethed. 'What did you find out?'

'Do you think that's a good idea?' she asked, failing to mirror his emotion. 'You'd have to tell the committee, right? That's a dozen or so people who would then be in danger.' She leaned forward. 'And I bet it leaks like a sieve.'

Desmond's eyebrows shot up. 'You are working for me, not the other way around,' he hissed. Foam was forming in the corners of his mouth. 'I've just had the third degree from some woman called Harris telling me to close the whole inquiry down.' He gulped in some air. 'I've got McDonald breathing down my neck and—'

Simon put a hand on Desmond's arm and gently pulled him back. 'Let's all calm down.'

Desmond exhaled. 'Nothing like this…' He rubbed his forehead.

Simon gave Desmond's shoulder a couple of light pats. 'Everyone's under a lot of pressure.'

'No one at De Jure has been shot at,' she said, her voice only just above a whisper. 'I…' She paused to glance at Jay and Lizzie. 'We, have been through hell for this inquiry, for you, and all I've had in return is ultimatums.'

Desmond flopped back in his chair. He lifted his hands, palms up. 'Tell me, what am I supposed to do?'

'Help her,' said Jay. 'Let Ella do her job.'

Desmond looked at him like he was from another planet, then at Ella. 'And what if something were to happen to you?' He looked Jay up and down. 'Or this young man?'

Simon looked at her gravely. 'Or Lizzie?'

Lizzie scoffed. 'Living in the shadow of death.' She glowered at Simon. 'I've been doing that for too long.' She turned to her mum. 'This is too important.'

Ella understood her daughter in a way no one else ever could. She gave Lizzie a knowing smile then pulled a serviette out of a metal holder on the table. 'Give me a pen.'

Desmond took a silver ball-point from inside his jacket and handed it to her.

Ella unfolded the tissue and began to write.

The others watched.

A sympathetic nurse helped a crying couple to a table and lingered for a moment before leaving them with their grief.

Desmond's patience was the first to wear out. 'What are you doing?'

She carried on writing. 'It's a waiver.' She looked up at the Master. 'Absolving you and De Jure of all responsibility.' She signed it at the bottom, causing a small tear, then slid it across the table to Jay.

He took the pen and signed.

Lizzie did the same.

'Ella?' said Simon. 'Are you sure about this?'

She looked at Lizzie, then at Simon. 'Never more so.' She carefully picked up the fragile document and handed it to Desmond.

He held it with two fingers. 'You think this solves everything?'

'No' said Ella with great sincerity. 'But if you let others dictate what happens it may turn out to be your greatest regret.'

He flinched.

'One thing we've learned,' said Jay, 'is that Matthew didn't trust anyone with what he knew.'

Ella nodded. 'Don't hand this over to McDonald, or some other government agency. I don't trust them. Cambridge is above politics.'

Desmond studied her, as if searching her face for an answer.

Ella could see he was still unpersuaded. She sighed. How was she going to get through to Desmond? Then, slowly and deliberately, she began to recite: '*Hinc lucem et pocula sacra.*'

Jay looked bemused. 'What does that mean?'

'It's Latin,' said Simon. 'The Cambridge motto.'

Desmond gave Ella a solemn nod. '*From this place, we gain enlightenment and precious knowledge.*' He carefully folded up the waiver and put it in his breast pocket. 'Bring us enlightenment, Miss Blake.'

Chapter Fifty-Five

I t was a relief to be back in the flat, but unnerving to have an armed police officer outside the door.

Ella stood in the shower, desperately trying to wash away the previous night. She noticed some of Broady's blood still on her hands and cleaned it off. She couldn't stop thinking about Lizzie's safety, questioning her bravado with Desmond. She'd never forgive herself if… And how would Lizzie take the news about Greg? She got out of the cubicle and rubbed her hair with a towel, craving a drink and a cigarette.

By the time she was dressed, Jay already had dinner underway. 'Thought I'd do a Mauritian curry,' he said on seeing her come into the living area.

Ella envied him the resilience of youth as she watched him slide some grated ginger into a pot.

Lizzie looked like she couldn't keep still, walking around the flat, making half-hearted attempts at tidying up.

Ella remembered the behaviour of old when she had something to confide or confess.

Jay added the chicken breasts and turned up the heat.

Lizzie stopped moving around. 'There's something I need to tell you.'

'Me too,' said Ella dreading what was to come.

'You first,' said Lizzie, fiddling with her hands.

Ella sat at the table. 'Sit down,' she said, using her foot to pull out the chair next to her. The aroma of garlic and frying meat wafted over.

Lizzie obeyed. 'Go on?'

Ella took Lizzie's hand and cupped it in hers. 'That MI6 woman I told you about, Harris…' She didn't know how to break the news.

'What about her?' Lizzie replied impatiently.

Ella patted Lizzie's hand. 'She says Greg is working for David Kline.'

Lizzie stared at her, without attempting a response. She pulled her hand away. 'Kline?' She took a deep breath, then exhaled. 'Since when? They don't know each other.'

It was torture watching her daughter process the revelation. A tear rolled down Lizzie's cheek.

Ella attempted to hug her but Lizzie got up and stood in the middle of the room, playing with her hands. 'He told me he works for the government.'

'What?' said Ella. 'When?'

'Last night.' Lizzie walked over to the balcony door and stared out over Cambridge. 'He said he had no choice.' She gave a humourless laugh. 'He targeted me to get to you. Did it for Britain.'

Ella went over and stood behind her, placing her hands on her shoulders. 'I'm so sorry, darling.'

Lizzie turned around and wiped her eyes on her sleeve. 'Yeah, well, I should've known it was all about you.'

Ella felt wretched. She pulled Lizzie to her and held her in a tight embrace.

This time, silently weeping, Lizzie didn't pull back. 'I feel so embarrassed. Dirty.'

Jay turned off the hob and came over, placing a hand on her back, but said nothing.

'He arranged the robbery at yours,' she said between sniffles.

Teeth gritted, Jay's whole body stiffened.

'Said he thought I'd already left because of the text I sent him.' Lizzie untangled herself. 'That bastard.' Her brow furrowed. 'Why hasn't he been arrested?'

Yeah,' said Jay. 'It's like nobody wants to rock the boat.'

Lizzie went over to the sofa and sat down. 'There's something else.'

Ella joined her.

'He said he thinks it's all about a weapon.'

Ella didn't respond at first, then said, 'It's always about power.' She glanced over at Jay who had his hands on his head.

'What kind of weapon?' he asked.

'That's all he said.' She ran her hands over her head. 'That could've been a lie too.'

Jay went over to the table and turned on the laptop. He opened up Genesis and stared at the dots on the screen, as if the new information would somehow help him decipher it.

'Why did he tell you all this?' Ella asked, thinking out loud. 'He must've wanted something.' She got up and began to pace.

'He did,' Lizzie replied. 'The password.'

Ella stopped. 'They've got the stick?'

'Must have.' Lizzie put her elbows on her knees, with her hands on her forehead.

Jay looked over at her but it was Ella who asked the question. 'Did you give it to him?'

Lizzie's hands parted. 'No.' Her eyes welled up. 'But I

239

nearly did.' She rubbed her face. 'If you hadn't texted me about Broady…'

Ella's mind was racing. 'So, he knows about that?'

'Not from me.' She became stronger. 'I just told him I needed time to think about it.'

It was Ella's turn to stare out of the window. She felt like she'd let everyone down, made the wrong decisions. She needed to take control, attack it like she was defending a case.

Sideways rain drummed softly on the glass door, then grew into a pounding beat, providing a backdrop to Ella's swirling thoughts. After a minute, it eased off. Something made her shut the curtains, even though it was daylight. She watched Jay go back to the hob and tip a tin of chopped tomatoes into the pot and then heap in some spoonfuls of curry powder, before mixing it in. A plan of sorts began to form in her mind. 'We need to get out of Cambridge.'

Jay stopped stirring and gave her a quizzical look. 'And go where?'

'It doesn't matter, just out of this goldfish bowl.' She went over to the table and started writing a list. 'How do we get a vehicle without using our names?'

'How quickly? Jay asked, leaving the pot to simmer.

Ella looked at him gravely. 'By first light, that's when we're on our own.'

Jay took out his phone and scrolled down. 'I may know somebody.' He didn't seem convinced. 'He's got an old ambulance, converted it to go around the festivals.' Uncertainly he added, 'It's a right shed.'

'Sounds perfect,' said Ella. 'Tell him to leave it in the underground car park, right next to my van. And to leave the keys on the rear tyre.'

Jay put the number in the pay-as-you go and texted. It didn't take long for the phone to ping. 'Says he wants two grand?'

Ella gave him one of her thinking stares. 'Tell him there's a diamond ring in the glove of my camper, worth more. There's a spare key taped behind the petrol cap. But, he keeps the whole thing to himself, and no logbooks filled out. I want it in situ by 3 a.m.'

'Mum,' said Lizzie. 'Your engagement ring from Dad?'

Jay waited for further orders.

Ella shrugged. 'I'm glad to have found a use for it,' she said, sounding matter of fact.

Lizzie didn't press her.

Jay sent another text. After a minute, his phone bleeped. 'Done.' He looked at Ella. 'What about Broady?'

She ignored the question at first. Then, without making eye-contact, she said, 'He comes with us.'

Jay glanced over at Lizzie but didn't question the decision.

'How?' Lizzie asked. 'There's cameras everywhere.'

Ella pondered for a moment. 'He's going to have to get out of Addenbrooke's and meet us somewhere.'

'In his condition?' she queried.

Ella wasn't interested in problems. She shot her daughter a look.

'All right,' said Lizzie. 'Tell him to get to the recreation ground on Nightingale Avenue, there are some trees by the side of the road.'

'Thanks.' Ella knew it was a big ask of the others, but she wasn't going to break her promise.

Chapter Fifty-Six

It was 4 a.m. Simon Carter looked ashen. 'Are you all OK?' he asked, checking the faces around the room.

'We're fine,' said Ella, giving him a hug. 'Thanks for coming.'

His eyes rested on the bags piled up in the middle of the room. 'Going somewhere?'

There was no easy way for Ella to say it. 'We're leaving Cambridge.'

He grimaced. 'Is that wise?' He glanced over at Lizzie.

Her face tense, she said nothing.

After a moment, seemingly resigned, he said, 'OK, where are you going?'

Ella shrugged. 'We need your help.' She looked straight into his eyes. 'To drive my van, as a decoy.'

Simon looked skywards and closed his eyes, then at Ella. 'Tell me you're joking?' He grabbed her shoulders as if trying to shake some sense into her. 'You know there's a police car out the front, and what about the guy outside the door?'

'I've thought of that,' Ella replied, trying to sound measured. 'Will you do it?'

He gave her a lingering stare, as if weighing up his options. Eventually, a reluctant dip of the head.

She handed him a piece of paper with a number on. 'Text me on this if you need to talk and I'll call you back.'

He put it in his pocket.

She hugged him again. 'Thank you.' She turned her attention to the others. 'Put the bags behind the door.' She watched Lizzie and Jay pick them up. 'Where's Broady's?'

Jay held it up.

She scanned the other holdalls. 'Where's his telescope?'

Jay cast an eye over the bags then went into Broady's room and brought out the case. 'Sorry,' he said, putting it with the others.

They all stood, adrenalin pumping, waiting for Ella's next orders.

'Right, let's do it,' she said, opening the front door.

The uniformed officer outside in a stab vest looked up, grateful for a break in the monotony. 'All right?'

'Quick, I think someone's been on our balcony,' she shouted.

An alarmed expression swept across his face as he followed Ella into the flat. She pulled back the curtain to allow room for the policeman to creep outside. She quickly shut the door behind him and locked it, pulling the curtain closed. On cue, the others picked up the bags and filed out through the door.

Ella could hear him rattling the balcony door as she locked up.

Their feet clattered down the stairwell, echoing off the walls, as they ran down to the car park in the basement.

A battered old white ambulance was parked next to Ella's van. She groaned inwardly at the huge flowers and a large CND sign painted on the bonnet. The grille had been made to look like a shark's mouth.

Jay swiped the key from under the wheel arch.

'Wait,' said Ella. 'CCTV. Everyone into mine first.'

Ella handed her key to Simon who got into the driver's side.

The others got in the passenger side and crept towards the back doors.

Jay and Lizzie got out of the back and hovered impatiently as

Ella pulled a cardboard box out from under the table and began taking books from the shelves, at first placing them inside and then just throwing them in.

'Hurry up, Mum,' hissed Lizzie.

'We might need them,' she snapped back, managing to lift the box and pass it to Jay before climbing out.

'Where am I going?' said Simon, turning on the ignition.

'Anywhere,' she replied as she shut the boot behind her.

Ella discreetly opened the back of the ambulance and they crept in, gently pulling the door shut behind them. They could hear Ella's van begin to move off, the clutch grinding as Simon tried to grapple with the gears. It stalled. Ella winced. It started again, this time slowly pulling away.

Ella took a moment to take in their new surroundings. The vehicle was basic. Two seats at the front with a central, narrow galley at the back with two thin metal bunkbeds, screwed in on either side.

The three of them crouched down between the bunks, hearts in their mouths, listening for the slightest noise.

Waiting.

They heard a sound getting louder – footsteps running across the concrete floor. It stopped, then whoever it was began running again, up the ramp and away.

Ella gave it five minutes, then slipped into the driver's seat and started the engine.

Lizzie climbed into the passenger seat. 'Out of the car park, then left.'

They set off, fully aware that they couldn't have chosen a more conspicuous mode of transport. As the vehicle got up to the road, Ella nudged the nose out, checking all around. It looked clear. The ground was still wet from the last downpour. She turned left and off towards Addenbrooke's Hospital.

They made their way to Nightingale Avenue in no time. There was nothing on the roads at that time of night. Jay crouched behind the seats, swaying with the movement of the vehicle, holding the seats to steady himself. Ella slowed as they went past the recreation ground, straining to see anything in the darkness.

Lizzie scanned the shadows under the treeline. 'Nothing.'

'He's not here,' said Jay as they reached the end of the road.

Ella swung the van into a three-point turn. 'Let's go back.'

'Mum?' Lizzie gave her an anxious glance, then took up position as they went back up along the road. She leaned forward, squinting out through the widescreen. 'What's that?' A silhouette, stepping out onto the pavement. 'It's him,' she yelled.

Jay opened up a door at the back as Ella came to a stop.

Broady staggered up the step and into the galley.

Ella looked over her shoulder.

Their eyes met in a brief, intense moment. Within seconds they were on their way.

Jay helped Broady carefully onto one of the lower bunks so that he was lying flat on his back.

'Where now?' asked Lizzie, taking a road atlas off the parcel shelf.

'Anywhere,' said Ella. 'East, Norfolk. We need to avoid the motorways – ANPR.'

Lizzie's nose crumpled up. 'What's that?'

'Automatic Number Plate Recognition.' Ella knew better than anyone how criminals got caught. 'Roadside cameras will send them a signal if we pass.'

'But they don't know what we're driving?'

She shot her daughter a pensive look. 'They'll work it out soon enough.'

Chapter Fifty-Seven

Ella pulled into a layby not far from King's Lynn. She was exhausted. 'We'll rest here for a bit.' She rubbed her bloodshot eyes and extricated herself from the seat, stretching out her back.

Jay was lying on his side on one of the bottom bunks, typing away on his laptop.

Ella squatted down to check on Broady who was waking up. 'How are you?' she asked.

He lifted his sweatshirt to reveal a bandage, worn around his waist like a sash. 'Is it bleeding?' he asked in a groggy voice.

'No,' she replied. 'It's clean.'

He let out a satisfied grunt and re-covered it.

'Did anyone see you leave – the copper on the door?'

Broady slowly moved his head from side to side. 'Pass me one of those pills,' he said, gesturing towards his jacket.

Ella picked up the coat at the bottom of the bunk and started going through the pockets. She took out a box of penicillin and handed it to him.

He took out a packet and pressed one of the tablets out of the blister.

'Where did you get those?' she asked, helping him put the pack back in the box.

Broady ignored her.

She had a sinking feeling. 'I asked you where you got them?'

'The hospital,' Broady murmured.

Ella stood up straight, still looking down at the patient. 'That's bullshit.' She turned the box in her hand. 'There's no prescription on this. The NHS don't hand out boxes of antibiotics. 'If you'd sneaked out you wouldn't have any meds?'

Lizzie and Jay had stopped what they were doing.

Broady eased his legs off the bed onto the floor, pushing up his body so that he was perched on the edge of the bunk. His breathing was laboured. 'I was going to tell you.'

Ella's head dropped. 'Tell me what?'

'I first got to thinking about it when I came to England.' He put an arm across his stomach and adjusted his posture. 'My boss is a mean old son-of-a-bitch.' He looked up at Ella. 'But he had no problem me coming over on some wild goose chase. He was all for it.'

'He wanted you to come?'

'I think someone wanted me to – someone high up.'

Ella couldn't work out where this was going.

'You got any water?' Broady asked, holding the top bunk to support himself.

Lizzie took a bottle out of the holder and went back with it.

Broady unscrewed the top and took a swig, then handed it back. 'That guy Stone, from the US Embassy. He gave me the pills. Told me to stick to you guys like glue.'

'You're saying he helped you sneak off?' Ella barked, sceptical about the whole thing – about Broady.

A slow nod. 'He wanted eyes on the ground. That's the truth, and I ain't no liar.'

'I don't get it, why would he care what we're doing?' Ella looked up and puffed out her cheeks. She fixed on Broady again. 'We've just risked everything to get away from bloody politics.'

He turned to her with child-like eyes. 'You kicking me out?'

She looked around at the others.

'I believe you,' said Jay, sitting up. 'I think you're being straight, but that doesn't solve the problem.'

Ella could see what he was driving at.

'We're all here for Cambridge, for knowledge.' Jay slid off the bunk so that he was sitting face-to-face with Broady. 'Who are *you* here for?'

Broady took in a laboured breath. 'I ain't going to lie, I love my country.' There was emotion in his voice. 'I fought for it, my boy died for it.' He paused. 'But maybe the Broadys have given enough.'

'If you want to stay,' said Ella, 'I need your word nothing goes back to your people. Nothing?'

Broady bowed his head. 'You have it.' He manoeuvred his upper body back down onto the bed, growling at the pain.

Ella lifted his legs off the floor and slid them onto the bunk.

'I don't know about Cambridge,' he said. 'But I'm a hundred percent for you guys.' A faint trace of his old grin showed up in the corners of his mouth.

Chapter Fifty-Eight

E lla woke with a start and banged her head on the roof of the van. It wasn't the dream, she hadn't had it for a couple of days now.

Jay was saying something. 'Sorry, didn't mean to startle you.'

She could see the sun was still up. 'What is it?' she said, getting her bearings. She peered over the bunk to see Jay and Lizzie on the laptop.

'We might have something,' Jay said with a trace of excitement.

Ella climbed down backwards, finding her footing on Broady's bunk, then stepped carefully down to the floor. Broady was awake. 'You've got more colour in your cheeks,' she observed.

'Feeling better,' he replied, rolling onto his good side so he could see Jay and Lizzie.

'Jay's a genius, Mum,' said Lizzie, turning the screen towards her. 'He's made a grid.'

'I've overlaid horizontal and vertical lines onto the file,' Jay explained. 'So that every dot is in its own box.'

Ella stared at the screen.

Jay pointed to the top of the page. 'When you look at the vertical lines you can see that there are only twelve columns.'

Ella was still trying to understand.

'There are only twelve set positions across the page that the dots sit,' he said in a louder voice.

'We think,' said Lizzie, 'that the horizontal axis could represent the twelve months of the year.'

The penny dropped. Ella's eyes widened. 'And the vertical would be—'

Lizzie couldn't contain her excitement. 'The year.'

Ella marvelled at their ingenuity. 'It's a timeline?'

'We reckon,' said Jay, failing to hide his pride at their discovery. 'Every dot pinpoints a month and year in time.'

'So how do we work out what dot represents which year?'

'That's the problem,' said Jay. 'We need to know what date one dot represents to calculate the others.'

Ella sat on Broady's bunk and contemplated the dilemma.

'What about your chronicle?' offered Broady.

They all stared at him.

'Of course,' said Ella. 'We know he was studying that period for a reason.' Her mind was clicking into gear. 'What's the most important date in the Chronicle?'

'1066?' suggested Lizzie. 'The Norman invasion?'

'Yes,' Ella replied. 'That was the end of the Anglo-Saxons.' She looked at Jay. 'Can you go through and see if 1066 is there?'

'I could run a programme,' he replied. 'Run every dot as 1066, but how would I know if I got it right?'

'You wouldn't,' said Ella. 'Unless the other dates seemed familiar, you know, important dates.'

'OK,' he said, sounding unsure. 'That could work.'

He started banging away at the keys, then stopped. 'Please don't watch me work,' he chided, glancing up at Ella.

'Sorry. I'll drive on a bit, try and find somewhere to eat.'

She got into the driver's seat, feeling energised.

Ella pulled into a truck stop that had a makeshift café in a portacabin to avoid any cameras. Broady, who was moving more freely, was able to get up the steps unaided.

The place was deserted. A sullen, twenty-something girl in stonewashed jeans, chewing on gum, ambled over and took a pad and pen out of her back pocket. 'Nice motor,' she said, ogling the motley group.

'Thanks,' Ella replied. 'I'll have a coffee and the full English.'

Jay and Ella opted for the same.

'Me too, I guess,' said Broady.

Still chewing, the waitress made a note. 'Eggs fried or scrambled?'

'Fried,' said Ella, checking the others agreed.

'Over easy,' said Broady.

'She gave him a blank stare.

'Sorry,' said Ella, coming to the rescue. 'Fried both sides.'

After the woman had mooched off, Jay got the laptop out and carried on working. Every time he ran the programme using a particular dot as the year 1066, Lizzie studied the dates the other dots would represent, each time shaking her head.

The waitress came back with a tray and plonked the drinks on the table, causing them to spill so that each cup sat in a saucer of coffee.

After what seemed like an age, she came back with the breakfasts, shoving them nonchalantly onto the table, saving Broady's until last. 'Eggs, over easy,' she said with a pointed expression.

Ella noticed he didn't have the strength for a witty retort.

Once they'd eaten, Jay got back to work, going through the dots, glancing at Lizzie each time, then, on seeing a shake of the head, moving on. The process continued for some time, until, about to move on to the next one, Lizzie suddenly shouted, 'Stop.' She ran a finger down the screen. '1812, Napoleonic Wars.'

'And what about the other war of 1812, between America and the UK?' added Broady.

'Yeah, big year,' Lizzie agreed.

'1222?' Jay asked, glancing up from the screen.

'Genghis Khan,' exclaimed Lizzie. 'He went west, conquering most of Europe?' She looked across at Ella, who bowed her head in confirmation.

'They go right back,' said Jay. '451?'

'The defeat of Attila the Hun by the Romans,' suggested Ella.

'Yeah,' Lizzie replied, leaning back for a moment to take it all in. 'After he crossed the Rhine.'

'AD 66?' said Jay.

No one had an answer, then Lizzie suggested: 'The Great Jewish Revolt against the Romans?' She looked at the others. 'Led to the destruction of Jerusalem.'

Ella held her breath, in awe of their discovery. The others seemed shocked into silence.

'Any other dates from the Chronicle?' asked Ella, half-turning the screen towards her.

Lizzie tracked back up. She stopped. 'Mum, 793 is on there.'

'Had to be!' Ella shouted, then realised what she'd done and scanned the portacabin, checking no one was listening in. In a whisper she said, 'Of all the dates in the Anglo-Saxon Chronicle, Matthew has picked the two most important – the first Viking invasion, then the Normans in 1066.'

'They're all invasions,' said Broady.

'Genesis,' said Lizzie. 'It's a chronicle of humanity.'

Jay stared at the screen. 'Of man's inhumanity to man, more like.'

A hush descended.

'But what are the curves on the wallpaper,' said Ella, 'that join the dots?' She picked up her phone and scrolled through the photos she'd taken. 'And why would they form a pattern – there has to be a link between these dates?'

No one had an answer.

'And why *these* invasions?' said Lizzie. Not every conflict in history is recorded here.'

The waitress came back over. 'Anything else?' she asked, staring into the middle distance.

'Just the bill,' said Ella.

The woman wandered off again.

'So, what now?' asked Broady.

Ella's head was still spinning from the discovery. 'We go north, to Lindisfarne.' She gave a firm nod, trying to convince herself. 'We need to work out why Matthew chose 793.' She stared out of the window. 'Why that invasion?' She could feel Genesis drawing her further in. The same pull she'd always felt towards Lindisfarne, towards history itself. Was it really possible that there was some great explanation? An answer that linked everything? She felt as if there was just a thin curtain shrouding her mind from a great revelation. Ella muttered to herself, 'We need to see the bigger picture.'

Chapter Fifty-Nine

Harris kicked in the front door. Half-empty cups of coffee and dirty plates were scattered around the lounge. She went upstairs and checked the other rooms. She walked into one of the bedrooms. Makeshift mattresses were packed into every bit of floorspace. On seeing a line of mobile phones plugged in and switched on, she swore.

She walked back downstairs and out into the yard under a cloudy sky. A damp, charred smell from an old bonfire hung in the air. The source was a round incinerator sitting on the wet cobbles. Harris walked over to it, almost losing her footing as her heels caught between the stones. She leaned in and rummaged through the cold remains of some documents. Nothing legible had survived.

She looked up as a car approached, bumping its way up the lane, throwing up a spray as it squelched through the puddles. The blacked-out windows blocked any view of its occupants. Harris brushed off some dead embers that had landed on her jacket.

The black saloon pulled into the courtyard and stopped. The electric window at the rear passenger seat opened.

Combover was sitting in the back. The lines on his forehead were deeper than before. 'Well?' he asked.

'Not a trace, they've all gone, sir.'

Combover clenched his eyes shut, then opened them. 'How the hell did this happen?'

'We were monitoring the phones' cell-site signals, which they deliberately left behind, so we assumed they were still here.'

'Assumed?' Combover shouted, opening the door and shifting his rotund frame out of the vehicle. 'So where are they now?' His polished shoes looked out of place in the muddy courtyard.

Harris shifted nervously. 'We don't know, sir.'

'What?' He hitched up the legs of his pinstripe and tiptoed clumsily through a few puddles towards the farm-house. 'I thought we had eyes on the place?'

'They dodged them somehow,' she replied. 'Their counter-surveillance is the best I've ever seen.'

'God knows how we're going to explain this to the Americans,' he said, glancing back over at the car as the other rear door opened. A man climbed out the other side. He had a noticeable scar on one side of his neck and deep concern etched on his face. 'Seems like he's always one step ahead,' he said. Harris recognised a Washington accent. 'There has to be a leak.'

Combover bristled at the suggestion. 'Not from our end, I can assure you.'

The American cast an eye over the small-holding. 'How long have we got?'

Harris looked to Combover for clearance. He nodded. 'Meet Mike Grant, Security Services. Agent Harris.'

She acknowledged him. 'If the intercepts are to be believed, three days.'

Grant looked to the heavens and let out a sigh. 'Three fucking days and not a clue.'

Combover glared at Harris. 'Anything more on what he's got planned?'

Harris looked at him gravely. 'No, sir.'

He took a packet of cigarettes out of his jacket and sparked up. The others waited for him take a drag and exhale. 'Shepherd?

'Flatline,' replied Harris.

Grant took a few paces across the cobbles towards the house. 'We've got to crack Genesis.'

'I agree,' said Harris, her voice sounding enthused by the suggestion. 'Blake is our best chance.'

Grant stopped and scanned the surrounding fields. 'I thought she was AWOL?'

'She is,' said Harris giving him her full attention. 'She was scared, she didn't know what was going on.'

'Then for Christ's sake find her,' Combover shouted between puffs. 'Tell her what you have to.' His head went still. 'What's that noise?'

It was coming from the barn.

Grant drew his firearm and moved silently across the courtyard to the doorway. He poked his head inside then dropped his arm and signalled to the others to join him.

A lone pig was grunting and shuffling its nose around in some straw as if searching for something. Three dead piglets were hanging above the pen on hooks.

Chapter Sixty

The van chugged northwards along the minor roads that skirted the east coast. Constant stops to put water in the over-heating radiator added considerably to the journey time, but they had at last made it to Northumbria.

Jay and Lizzie spent much of the drive on one of the bunks shouting out dates which Ella managed to match with some or other clash of cultures. It soon became clear that there were some dates that seemed to have no major event. They began to question their earlier hypothesis.

'I can't find anything for 1888,' said Lizzie, becoming more frustrated. 'Or 1769.'

Dozing in and out of sleep for most of the journey, Broady had missed much of the discussion. He rolled onto his side and put an elbow on the bed to prop up his head. He popped another pill and took a swig of water from the bottle. 'What's the earliest date he's got on there?'

'9500 BC,' said Jay. 'Then nothing for thousands of years.'

Broady scrunched up his face. 'But we would've been hunter gatherers back then, right?'

Ella agreed. 'Definitely no big invasions.'

Broady pulled his elbow away and let his head fall back onto the bed. 'Beats me.'

Ella turned off onto a country lane. It was getting dark. 'There's a campsite at West Kyloe.' Rain was drilling down on the windscreen, making it hard to see out, but she knew the road well. 'We'll have to wait for the morning tide before we can get across to the island.' She turned right and drove through the gate, stopping at the farm buildings on her left. She handed a twenty pound note to Lizzie. 'You remember?'

Lizzie smiled. She pulled her jacket over her head and got out, running into the stone hut around the side. Once she was back in the van, Ella drove down the path onto the field and parked up in her usual spot by the dry-stone wall. 'See if there's something we can use to hook up.'

Lizzie rummaged through the junk under the bunks, pulling out a hose and a foot pump. At the back, she found an old cable with a socket at both ends.

Jay took one end and dashed out of the back and into the storm, connecting it to another cable sticking out of the power box by the wall. 'Check this out,' said Lizzie, pulling out a rusty electric camp stove with two rings.

Before long they were boiling a pan of water, with four Pot Noodles in readiness on the shelf.

Ella's brain was aching from running the dates over and over in her mind. 'All these invasions,' she said gloomily. 'Was Greg telling the truth?' She swivelled around in her seat to face the others. 'Is all this about killing?'

The mood changed.

Lizzie turned off the ring and carefully poured the water into the plastic pots.

'Most things end up that way,' said Broady.

'No,' said Jay, in a voice full of defiance. 'It's got to be more than that.'

'I hope so,' said Ella. 'I really hope so.'

No one disagreed.

Lizzie opened a drawer, took out some spoons and dropped them in the containers.

Broady stirred his pot and slurped in some noodles. 'I've got to say,' he announced, immediately lifting the melancholy. 'You British know how to live it up.'

The others broke into laughter.

Ella was the last to wake, her face tickled by a ray of sun that had found its way through a gap in the fraying curtains hanging from a piece of drooping elastic over the side window. She opened her eyes. No nightmares, she realised, then wondered why she slept better when she was under pressure.

Jay opened up the back and helped Broady down the step and across the field towards the shower block. Ella pulled back the curtain so she could see them staggering over the boggy ground, towels slung over their shoulders. She could hear Lizzie yawning in the bunk underneath hers. Ella couldn't believe how much her life had changed in the short time since she'd last been here. Despite the craziness and the danger, she felt strangely at peace.

She slid open her window and watched Broady stop and take in his surroundings. The wind had dropped right off and there wasn't a cloud in the sky. He turned and waved back at Ella in an unspoken appreciation of the rolling green hills dotted with sheep and cows. The morning chorus of bleating and mooing echoed around the site.

Ella smiled and fell back onto her bunk, breathing in the beautiful jumble of smells that wafted in.

Broady held up his top while Ella dressed his wound. She used some plasters to keep the gauze in place. The injury appeared to be healing well. The night's rest had given them all renewed strength.

Jay unplugged the cable and left it under the bunk. Ella got in the driver's seat and had to pull down the visor to keep the sun out of her eyes. The van did a couple of wheel spins to gain traction before they were able to set off back across the field.

'So, what are we looking for?' Broady asked from his bunk during the drive down to the causeway.

'I wish I knew,' Ella replied, without taking her eyes off the road. 'A common denominator?'

They weaved their way down the country lanes towards the coast, past the patchwork of fields with young crops springing up in readiness for the new cycle. The unmistake-able smell of sea air filled their nostrils as the van reached the beginning of the causeway. A couple of cars were already queueing to get across, waiting for the final sheets of seawater to drain off the road.

Broady and Jay stood up in the galley to get a better view of Holy Island. 'I've never been anywhere,' confessed Jay, as the cars began the drive across, flanked by the North Sea on either side. 'Never been abroad.'

Lizzie turned around from the passenger seat and caught his rueful expression.

'Not even out of Cambridge since we moved there,' he said.

'Jay, you've got a lifetime to change that,' Lizzie replied.

Broady put a hand on Jay's shoulder, steadying himself against the movement of the van. 'Sure have.'

Once they were across, they left the ambulance in a space

amongst the dunes and headed off on foot along the path towards the castle, keeping the pace slow for Broady. The squawking of sea gulls seemed to announce their arrival on the island.

Ella felt the familiar soaring of her spirit as the castle came into view. On seeing the battlements rising precariously out of the rock, they stopped.

'It's like something out of King Arthur,' said Broady.

'It's actually sixteenth century,' said Ella. 'They used stones from the Priory to build it. I remember seeing it for the first time.'

'Me too,' said Lizzie, catching her mother's eye. 'Good times.'

Ella nodded, then stared wistfully off to her right over the small inlet. 'That's the Old Priory,' she said pointing to the roofless stone buildings, silhouetted against the sky. 'Built in the twelfth century, but there's been a monastery there since AD 635.'

'Hard to imagine,' said Broady in a voice full of wonder.

Ella watched a flock of gulls circle above the ruins, then land on one of the great arches that were still intact.

As they reached the castle, she saw Rob who was beginning his first tour of the day. A group of four in bright-coloured cagoules were hanging on his every word. 'The Anglo-Saxon Chronicle records that in 793,' he announced, pointing across the harbour at the Priory. '*The raiding of heathen men miserably devastated God's church at Lindisfarne Island by looting and slaughter.*'

'At least he's quoting from the E Manuscript,' said Ella under her breath. 'But he's missed the best bit.'

Rob noticed her, then, flustered, forgot his lines.

Ella gave him a self-satisfied grin, to which Rob responded by trying to shepherd his audience away.

'*Here, terrible portents came about over the land of Northumbria,*'

Ella shouted raising her arms in an exaggerated gesture.

Lizzie and the others found it hilarious. The tour group stopped to listen.

'And miserably frightened the people: these were immense flashes of lightning.' She lowered her voice into a ghostly monotone. *'And fiery dragons were seen flying in the air.'*

Everyone applauded.

Ella took a bow. She couldn't believe how different she felt to the last time she was on the island. She gave Lizzie a spontaneous hug.

The morning passed quickly. They wandered around the island and the ruins of the Priory, before heading to the Inn for lunch.

Ella translated the menu for Broady who settled on bangers and mash. Seduced by the roaring fire and the cosiness of the low-beamed ceiling, for brief moments they forgot why they had come, but every conversation always came back to Genesis.

Ella took a final mouthful then pushed her plate aside. 'I can't stop thinking about the link between what happened here and the Battle of Hastings.'

Lizzie's head tilted. 'Maybe it's just the fact they were both invasions?'

'No, it must be more,' Ella replied. 'There were so many other battles between those dates.' She glanced out of the window at the ruined Priory. 'Something else happened here when the Vikings invaded, something I'm missing.'

They paid and made their way back to the van.

Broady spent the afternoon sleeping while the others examined Genesis, linking more dots with invasion events. By the time Broady woke up, it was evening.

Ella felt a fondness for him as she watched him stir then pull back the curtain to reveal a clear night sky, full of stars.

Broady pulled himself up off the bunk. 'Time for a bit of

star-gazing,' he said. 'Can someone bring my baby?'

Ella smiled and took the telescope case from under the bunk, following Broady out into the still night.

Broady sat on the back step giving her directions on how to set it on the tripod.

Forgetting their place in time, they took turns to peek through the lens, marvelling at the constellations. Then they sat next to each other on the step drinking the tea Lizzie had brewed up.

'This is the life,' said Broady in a mock English accent, gazing up.

Ella watched him sipping at his mug. 'I suppose it's like this every night in Arizona?'

'It's strange,' he said, looking back up. 'The sky dominates everything back home.' He sighed. 'So clear.' He looked at Ella. 'That's what Matthew must've seen every night growing up. There wasn't much else for him out in the desert.'

'Yeah, I suppose so.' Ella hadn't thought of it like that.

'Look!' said Broady, pointing into the distance. 'A comet.'

Lizzie and Jay came to the back of the van. 'How can you tell?' asked Lizzie, gazing at the distant shape.

'You can see the tail.'

'Comets,' whispered Ella. She put down her cup. Her mind was racing. 'Of course.' She stood up and stared at the others. She brushed a hand over the top of her head, then shouted, 'comets…' She held out her arms. 'It's bloody comets.' She began to pace up and down.

The others stared at her.

'*Fiery dragons in the sky* – it's in the E Manuscript. That's what the monks saw in the sky when the Vikings invaded. That's how they saw comets back in 793.'

Lizzie's face dropped. 'Of course, and Halley's Comet in 1066. William the Conqueror said it was an omen.'

Ella gave a vigorous nod. 'The Normans saw it as

predicting victory at the Battle of Hastings.' She rushed into the van and rifled through a bag of books under one of the bunks, took one and came back outside. She flicked through then put her finger on a page. 'There, it's in the Bayeux Tapestry.'

'A tapestry?' said Broady squinting in the darkness at the image.

'It's embroidery,' said Lizzie. 'A seventy-metre-long depiction of the Norman Conquest.'

The others crowded in, transfixed by the picture of men in medieval dress, pointing up at the tailed comet, alongside the words: *ISTI MIRANT STELLA*.

'Is that Latin?' asked Broady, touching the writing.

'Yes,' Ella replied. 'It means: *these men wonder at the star.*'

Jay pulled away. 'And the other dates?'

Lizzie was already on it. '1222,' she almost shouted. 'Genghis Khan saw Halley's Comet, it inspired him to go west and conquer half the world.' She stopped, shivering at the thought. 'Killing millions.'

Ella felt overwhelmed. '451,' she said. 'Attila's first great defeat at the Catalaunian Plains by the Romans and the appearance of Halley's Comet.'

'Of course,' said Lizzie. 'And isn't there something in Tacitus about Nero's fear of comets?' asked Lizzie

'That rings a bell.' Ella strained to recall. 'There's a volume under the bunk.'

Lizzie used Jay's torch to search for the book.

'You're not going to believe this,' said Jay. 'I've just googled the Jewish War; Halley's Comet appeared over Jerusalem in the spring of AD 66. Writers from the time saw it as a portent of victory.' He stared at them, then back at the screen. 'They fought for thirteen years. It's like people become inspired to fight.'

'Here it is,' said Lizzie, poring over a book. 'Tacitus was

writing about AD 60, that's another dot.' She shone the light on the page. '*A comet blazed into view – in the opinion of the crowd, an apparition boding change to monarchies.*'

Ella looked at the others, then repeated, '...*boding change of monarchies.*'

Lizzie read on, '*Hence, as though Nero were already dethroned, men began to inquire on whom the next choice would fall.*' Lizzie moved her finger. 'It goes on to say Nero listened to his astrologers and *killed off his challengers on their advice.*' She gazed up at Ella.

'It's as if the Romans understood the power of comets,' said Jay.

'Maybe they did,' said Lizzie. 'They defeated Boudica in AD 60.'

'Boudica?' asked Broady.

'She was the Queen of the Iceni,' said Ella. 'She led the final revolt against the Romans who invaded Britain in AD 43. Burnt Colchester, St Albans and London to the ground.'

'Yeah,' said Lizzie. 'She very nearly pushed them off the island but got defeated in one final battle. Tens of thousands died. She was captured, topped herself after they raped her daughters.'

They were all silent.

'Do comets change history? Jay asked, turning to Ella.

Ella didn't know how to answer. She tried to remain objective, then, staring at Lizzie, said, 'It's so weird. Napoleon's Comet of 1812.'

Lizzie shook her head and laughed. 'Seen by him and everyone else as a portent for his invasion of Russia.'

They fell silent again, trying to comprehend.

Broady took a few steps and stared up at the heavens. 'Tecumseh,' he said to himself, barely audible. Then, his voice louder, he said, 'Can't believe I didn't see it.'

'What's that?' Ella asked, trying to hear.

'Tecumseh.' He turned to face her. 'A great Indian warrior chief. He united the tribes to fight against the United States with the British in the War of 1812. His name, it's Shawnee, it means shooting star.'

The others stared at him, at a loss what to make of it.

Broady looked back up. 'Because he was born in the year of the Great Comet of 1769.'

Jay looked at the laptop. 'That's one of the dates – one that we couldn't fit with an invasion.'

'We should go.' Broady started to dismantle the telescope in the darkness.

Ella watched him for a moment. 'Shouldn't we wait until morning?'

Broady zipped up the case. 'We've got what we came for, right?' He climbed up into the van, grimacing as he bent down to put it under the bunk. 'It's not safe to stay in one place so long.'

Ella knew he was right. She'd come to see the island of Lindisfarne as a sanctuary, a bubble, immune from danger. The revelations had brought them all back. She suddenly realised she'd stopped checking the tides. She looked at her watch, then cursed. 'The sea will be over the causeway in a few minutes.'

'Then let's go,' said Broady, his voice conveying a sense of urgency.

'We're cutting it fine,' she said, squeezing past him and getting into the driver's seat.

Lizzie poured the remnants of the tea onto the sand and walked through to the passenger seat as Jay secured the back doors.

They were ready to leave.

Suddenly there was a tapping on the passenger door window.

Everyone jumped.

Chapter Sixty-One

E lla looked over.

Glare from a torch obscured the face at the window.

Her heart was pounding.

Lizzie, who was closest, squinted to get a better look. 'It's Greg.'

'Just drive,' Jay said.

'No,' said Broady. 'We don't know who else is out there.'

Ella glanced at Lizzie for a reaction. She nodded.

Broady opened a door at the back.

Greg appeared, then, as Broady stepped aside, climbed in. He had a small knapsack on his back.

'What are you doing here? How did you find us?' said Ella, who had swivelled around in her seat.

'It wasn't hard,' he replied, switching his attention to Lizzie. 'I never had a chance to explain.'

Her brow furrowed. 'Explain the lies, you mean?'

He winced. 'I'm so sorry, I—'

Ella cut across him. 'You bastard.' She got up and punched him in the face.

Broady and Jay, who were standing behind him, exchanged glances.

Greg steadied himself. 'I deserved that.'

'What do you want?' Ella asked, still seething.

He held up his arms. 'To help.'

Jay put a hand on Greg's shoulder and turned him around. 'We don't need your help.'

Greg turned back to the women. 'Just hear me out.'

'Who do work for?' Ella demanded.

He kept eye-contact. 'David Kline.'

Lizzie's eyes moistened.

'I'm sorry.'

Ella checked her watch again. 'You've got two minutes to make your case.'

Greg took off his pack and perched on the edge of one of the bunks. 'I'm sorry I lied.' He took a deep breath. 'You're not safe, there's no balance.'

'Balance?' Ella repeated.

'All British and American.' He gestured at Broady. 'The only nation to have used a nuclear bomb in anger.'

'Watch your mouth,' Broady growled.

Greg ignored him. 'We don't want anything to get in the way of our mission.'

'What mission?' Ella was still weighing him up. 'Tell us what you know?'

Greg looked around at the others, his eyes finally settling back on Ella. 'I don't know, I'm only a level five. I know Matthew Shepherd is a dangerous man. He used history to study the optimum time for change.' He paused. 'He was working with the Chinese, planning something. Only Kline can stop him.'

Ella couldn't believe what she was hearing. 'Planning what?'

'I don't know,' Greg replied.

This didn't sound like the Matthew she knew about. 'What's your evidence?'

'We know he was in communication with another polymath at UCL, a Chinese national called Ying-Kwong Chan.' He reached into the side pocket of his bag, took out a photograph and handed it to Ella who looked at the picture of an old man, then passed it around. 'We've been looking for him. He disappeared at the same time – we think they're working together in China.'

Broady reached up and grabbed the frame of the top bunk, pulling himself to his feet. 'This is bullshit.'

Ella didn't know what to think. 'What else do you know?'

'That's pretty much it.' Greg shrugged. 'My people have been watching Shepherd for years, bugging his room, but he never spoke to anyone so all they got was him talking to himself – nonsensical mutterings.'

'Stop lying,' said Lizzie. 'This is about Kline and Genesis. You actually believe that rubbish?' There was a hint of pity in her voice. 'Do you even know what Kline's *mission* really is?'

For the first time, Greg looked like a confused kid. He reminded Ella of young gang members she'd defended during her career. Young assassins, so indoctrinated, they'd serve life in jail for a boss they hardly knew.

She looked over at Lizzie, who was clearly uncomfortable with Greg's presence. Her daughter gave an imperceptible sideways movement of her head.

That was enough for Ella. 'I'm sorry, we don't trust you.' Her tone was cold. 'You can go now.'

Greg's head dropped. 'I don't think you understand.' He stood up and took a couple of paces towards the front and pointed out of Ella's window. 'Kline's got people out there, on this island.' He lost his composure. 'They're waiting to see if you let me join the team, find out what you know and who you've told.'

Ella instinctively looked out into the blackness, then back at Greg.

'If you kick me out, then…' His voice trailed off.

Ella studied his face. 'Then, what?'

His tone lowered. 'Then, you'll be eliminated.'

Ella looked at him in disgust. 'Wake up, you know they'll kill us anyway.'

'Is that what you want?' Lizzie fumed, jumping out of her seat. 'To get us all killed? I thought Kline was supposed to be about climate change?'

'He is, but these are desperate times.' His voice cracked.

'It should be about *preserving* life, you idiot.' Lizzie looked him up and down, her face full of contempt. 'You can't think for yourself.' Dismissing him with a shake of the head. 'You're just a robot.'

'I'm not,' he protested, the stress showing for the first time. 'I want to help you.'

Ella knew how painful this was for Lizzie.

'You really want to help?' demanded Broady.

Greg spun around to face him. 'Yes.'

'Then you stay onboard until we get across.' Broady glanced over at Ella for approval. 'We'll drop you somewhere, when we know there's no one following.'

'But I need to go back and tell them you've let me join up,' Greg replied, looking over at Ella.

'Forget it,' Lizzie cut in. 'We don't trust you.'

Greg's eyes moved from face to face as if searching for a weakness. Eventually, he replied, 'OK.'

Full of apprehension, Ella checked her watch, concerned that they might've missed the tide. She got back in the seat, turned on the ignition and skidded off the sand for the causeway.

Greg stood in the galley, a hand on either bunk, looking through the rear window panels, watched by Broady and Jay.

Ella sped along the road with the sea on her left, only the immediate patch of road in front illuminated. As she reached the causeway, she slowed. Waves were already lapping over the road. 'We're too late.'

Light suddenly poured through the back.

Broady squinted, putting a hand above his eyes to shield the glare. 'We've got company.'

Ella could see headlights in her mirrors – two dark four by fours. Her mouth went dry.

'Go,' shouted Broady. 'We've got no choice.'

Ella hesitated.

'Go,' he shouted again.

She released the clutch and put her foot down. As she hit the causeway, spray shot up on either side, getting thicker as they moved further across towards the mainland. The van juddered, straining to push on through the sea water.

'Faster,' shouted Jay. 'They're gaining on us.'

'It won't go any faster,' came Ella's panicked response.

In the rear-view mirror she saw a figure put his head and an arm out of the passenger window. There was the sound of a bullet ricocheting off metal.

Broady ducked down. 'Your friends are firing at us.'

'Everyone get down,' said Greg, reaching for the rear doors.

'What the hell are you doing?' shouted Broady, lunging for the handle.

'Telling them to stop,' Greg replied, pushing them open and waving at his pursuers. Suddenly, his head jerked back – a bullet in the forehead. His frame crumpled in an instant, rolling out into the road, his body forming an island in the shallow water.

Jay stood frozen to the spot, blankly staring out as the car following them drove over Greg's lifeless body. The open door swung out, banging against the back of the ambulance, leaving Jay exposed in the line of fire.

Broady yanked him out of the way. 'Pass me the stove,' he yelled, causing Jay to come to his senses. He pulled it out from under the bunk and handed it to the American.

More gunfire hit the back of their vehicle.

Broady stood up, his face contorted under the weight of the cooker, then moved into the open doorway. Straining, he launched it at the chasing vehicle. It landed on the bonnet and bounced up, shattering the windscreen.

The car lurched from side to side, then skidded, coming to a stop, broadside in the road. The car behind it slowed, then screeched to a halt behind.

The ambulance struggled on, putting more water between them and their pursuers. Ella could hear the sound of repeated attempts to start the engine receding into the distance. She pressed on, the spray gradually reducing as they made it to the other side.

Finally across, the ambulance inched its way up the incline and off into the Northumbrian night.

Lizzie twisted around from the passenger seat, terror still in her eyes. 'Where's Greg,' she asked, staring at Jay.

In shock, he stood mute.

Broady reached around the outside and pulled the flapping door closed. 'He didn't make it.'

Her face twisted in pain.

Chapter Sixty-Two

The van pressed on up the lane and away from the coast, the engine gurgling. Ella glanced back to see Broady rummaging through Greg's bag. He pulled out a small bugging device, just like the one he'd found at the Gonville. He held it between finger and thumb. 'Looks like they weren't sure they could trust him.' He handed it to Ella who gave it a cursory inspection then threw it out the window.

Nobody spoke, all in their own private worlds, trying to process what had just happened.

The spluttering sounds from the engine became more acute. 'It's not going to make it much further,' Ella said in an anxious undertone.

Broady moved to the front and placed a hand on her shoulder. 'We need to dump it, anyway.'

A few hundred metres further on, she took a left turn up a gravel track and stopped in some woodland. 'I know a path we can take from here.'

'OK,' said Broady, turning to Jay, whose pupils were still dilated from the shock. 'Take only what you can carry.'

Ella pulled her daughter to her and kissed her head. 'I'm so sorry.' She squeezed her tight. 'For everything.'

'We need to go,' urged Broady.

Numb, acting on some kind of autopilot, they put some essentials in holdalls and got out.

'You forgot this,' said Ella, holding up the telescope carrier.

'Leave it,' he said, in military mode. 'And no torches, our eyes will adjust.'

'And turn off your phones,' added Ella. 'They can track us.'

Ella took one last look back at the ambulance, then they set off down the path, using the treeline to keep their bearings.

They made their way west, occasionally stumbling in the darkness and tripping over exposed tree-roots. Skirting open fields, then resting, they hiked throughout the night. Ella felt fear and confusion in every part of her, centred in the pit of her stomach. How she wished she hadn't taken the job, hadn't put her only child's life at risk. She wanted to scream but was too afraid to make a sound. As soon as they had the chance, she resolved to contact Harris and get them out.

After hours of walking, they saw some lights. As they drew closer, they could see a main road and a Shell sign, illuminated in the distance. They sat down behind some shrubbery to take stock.

Broady put a hand on his wound and grimaced.

'There's only one thing to do now,' said Ella, only just able to make out their shattered faces. 'This is way out of control.' Her voice was tense. 'Not that it wasn't already.' She puffed out her cheeks. 'I'm calling Harris to come and get us.'

She could see Lizzie's head drop. Ella looked to Broady for support. 'Hank?'

He sighed. 'It's not my call.'

Jay hadn't spoken since the van. 'That's up to you, but I'm not coming.'

Ella could make out the determination on his face.

'I have to know what this is all about. I have to.'

'Me too,' said Lizzie. 'I'm not coming either.'

Ella grabbed Lizzie's shoulder and shook it. 'Don't be so stupid – we nearly got killed.'

Lizzie's body didn't push back. 'You need to stop trying to control people.' Her voice trembled. 'You're always giving up.'

'Where did that come from?' Ella snapped back. 'What do you mean?'

'You *know* what I mean,' Lizzie replied, getting up.

Now that she'd broken cover, Broady checked the road.

Ella stood up too. 'No, I don't.'

'You do, Mum,' she said, oozing condemnation. 'The Bar?' Tears began to flow. 'Me?'

Ella could see her daughter's face more clearly now that dawn was breaking. 'I've never given up on you.'

'I was sixteen years old,' Lizzie replied, the strain and exhaustion audible in every word. 'My father had just hanged himself in our hallway. You sent me away to boarding school.' She began to shudder. 'When I needed you most.'

'No,' said Ella, reaching out an arm. 'I wanted to save you.'

Lizzie took a step back. 'From what?' she hissed.

Ella's shoulders dropped. 'From me. I was ashamed.' She broke down. 'I thought it was my fault.'

'Your fault?'

'I was a cold, selfish bitch.' Her chest convulsed with the admission. 'Too wrapped up in my career.'

Lizzie watched her mother, dumbfounded. 'That's not true, you were the glue that held us all together. He wasn't well.'

Ella saw car headlights in the distance. Broady reached up and yanked them back down.

The car drove on by.

Crouching in front of her mother, Lizzie said, 'I thought you blamed me?'

An expression of horror spread across Ella's face. 'You?'

'That's why you sent me away.' Then, in a whisper, 'Because Dad didn't love me enough?'

'No. No. You were his world.' She took Lizzie in her arms and hugged her. 'And mine. You have always been everything to me.' Tears streamed down her face. 'I love you so much.'

Her face pressed into Ella's shoulder, Lizzie said, 'I love you too, Mum.'

They remained tight in the embrace, grief and conflict gently ebbing away.

Broady put his arms around them.

After a moment's hesitation, Jay did the same.

Chapter Sixty-Three

B roady stood up. 'It's getting light. We need to make a decision.'

Ella and Lizzie wiped their faces and composed themselves.

Broady's face was stern. 'If they're not going with you,' he said to Ella. 'I'll stay with them.'

Ella could see the answer on the young peoples' faces. She was resigned. 'We stick together.'

Broady managed a smile. 'OK.' He bent down and opened his holdall, getting out a small kitchen knife he'd taken from the van. He began cutting open the canvas at the base until it exposed the metal piping that gave the bag its shape. He pulled out the metal wire. 'Wait here,' he said, moving gingerly across the road. He stopped at an old VW Polo, parked with two wheels on a section of pavement outside a row of houses. He loitered for a moment, peeking through the driver's window. After checking both ways, he started to push the wire through a gap.

'He's stealing it,' Lizzie said, glancing at Ella. 'Couldn't you get struck off for this?'

'Duress of circumstance,' Ella replied, seeing the irony. 'It's a defence to a crime if you're fleeing for your life.'

Lizzie gazed at her, speechless.

Broady was inside now, bending down under the dash. In a matter of seconds, the engine started. He did a big U-turn across the road and pulled up alongside them. 'Get in.'

They grabbed the bags and jumped in, pushing the luggage over the back seat into the boot once they were moving.

'I don't know where I'm headed,' he said as he sped off up the carriageway.

Ella saw a signpost. 'Newcastle. We can get a train anywhere from there.'

Broady put his foot down.

Their relief grew with each mile they put between them and their pursuers. Ella's thoughts kept returning to what had happened on the causeway. The others were lost in thought too, the silence broken eventually by Broady. 'Hey, Jay,' he said, glancing up at Jay's reflection in the rear-view mirror. 'Did you get a look at the shooter's face?'

'Fleeting,' he replied. 'He looked Chinese, East Asian, anyway.'

Broady refocused on the road ahead. 'Thought so too.'

Ella glanced over at him. 'Do you think Greg was telling the truth?'

'Not a chance,' said Broady. 'But I reckon he believed it, poor kid.'

They carried on in silence.

Ella turned to see Lizzie nodding off on Jay's shoulder, the car's movement repeatedly jolting her awake. Jay had his laptop open. 'I've been thinking about that Shawnee warrior,' he said.

Broady looked in the rear-view again. 'Tecumseh?'

'Yeah, Tecumseh.' He paused as if deciding whether he

was going to say something stupid. 'He was born in 1769, right?'

'Yup,' Broady replied.

'Maybe the comet of 1769 made him a great warrior?'

Ella scoffed. 'He might've been told it was his destiny to be great, and he fulfilled it.' She rotated her body so she could see over the seat. 'It must be about believing in something.'

'You're saying the comets don't have a physical effect on people?'

'That's impossible,' she replied. 'It's about people believing in the power of the comet and then making a choice to behave in a certain way.'

'Why is it impossible?' queried Broady. 'We all get energy from the sun.' He gestured up at the sky. 'Gives us vitamin D, skin colour.' He glanced over at Ella. 'Look at plants, they all need the sun to live, and if it's in the right spot, with just the right amount of light, it will thrive above its neighbours.'

'That's different, you're talking about weather,' Ella said, trying to find an opposing position.

'Isn't that what we're talking about?' he said, giving her one of his intense stares. 'Space weather?'

She struggled for a counter-argument. 'There's a correlation between events and comets, that much is proved by the pattern in Genesis,' she conceded. 'But I'm a lawyer, I need concrete evidence that there is something more than humanity's reaction to seeing a comet.'

'It's weird though,' said Jay, 'that Matthew put 1769 in there, you know, when nothing happened except Tecumseh's birth and a great comet.'

Broady nodded. 'Give me some of the other dates when nothing happened?'

Jay scrolled down. '1888 is one,' he said. 'I checked it out last night, Comet Barnard was over Europe.'

Lizzie, who had been half-dozing during the conversation, opened her eyes. 'When was Hitler born?'

Ella felt the hairs stand up on the back of her neck. '1888.'

There was a tangible hush.

'What about the year zero,' asked Broady.

'I know what you're thinking,' Jay asked, 'but it's not here.'

Ella was trying to resist being drawn in but couldn't resist saying: 'The experts now agree Jesus was born in 4 BC.'

'That's there,' Jay exclaimed. Then, more quietly. 'But I couldn't find a comet sighting for that year.'

'Are you nuts?' said Broady. 'You forgot the Bible?'

Jay looked blank.

Broady tutted. 'The Star of Bethlehem.'

Jay's mouth fell open.

Ella tried to rationalise the coincidence. 'So, you're comparing Jesus Christ to Adolf Hitler?'

Broady flicked his head. 'Course not.' He seemed to be brooding for a moment. 'But you've got to say, one was as good as the other was bad, haven't you?'

'But you are saying,' said Jay, 'That maybe Jesus wasn't the son of God?'

Broady scoffed. 'I ain't saying nothing.' He adjusted the sun visor. 'Maybe God sent the comet?'

Ella was too tired to smirk.

Jay wasn't laughing. 'What, to give Jesus the word of God?'

Broady shrugged. 'I don't know what I'm saying, it's just weird, 'tis all.' He shut up.

'Don't you think it's strange?' said Jay, leaning forward between the front seats. 'That no one seems to have noticed this link between comets and all these historical events.'

'We did notice,' said Lizzie. 'For thousands of years.'

Jay looked around at her.

'It's in so many ancient writings. We just forgot, unlearned it somehow.'

'She's right,' said Broady. 'Clouds got in the way. Or maybe we just stopped looking up. Too busy with our phones and all the shit going down on the ground.'

Broady's analogy had a chilling resonance.

'The answers are already out there,' Ella muttered to herself.

Chapter Sixty-Four

They dumped the car down by the quayside and walked up the hill towards Newcastle Station, stopping at a café under the Tyne Bridge to take stock.

Broady bought four Americanos in paper cups and splashed milk into three of them.

Jay was already making the use of the Wi-Fi. 'This Chinese guy,' he said, looking at the screen.

'Who, Chan?' said Ella, savouring a gulp of coffee.

'Yeah, Ying-Kwong Chan. He's an expert on ancient Chinese scrolls.'

'I've never heard of him,' said Ella.

'I'm reading here how a comet in AD 35 was seen as an indicator of the forthcoming defeat of Gongshan Shu, the Emperor of Chengdu.'

'Maybe Chan helped Matthew to compile one definitive document,' said Broady. 'Genesis.'

'Let's just think this through for a minute,' said Lizzie 'So, Matthew puts together a list of comets that link to historical events.'

Ella nodded.

Lizzie continued to think aloud, 'He's interested in the relationship between the two.' She paused. 'So why does he have to disappear, he's got all the stuff he needs?'

Jay and Ella were now scrolling through the dots on Genesis. Ella tapped the screen. 'Maybe not the first one.' She turned the computer around. '9500 BC. It's pre-history. There couldn't be any written record of a comet, or of any kind of invasion. This is even before the invention of the wheel, pre-pottery.'

'So, where did Matthew get the dot from?' asked Broady

'I wish I knew.' She shrugged. 'This date must be the key to everything.' She leaned forward. 'It's the beginning of the pattern, the first event.'

'Hang on,' said Jay. 'I thought this was all about what Kline was planning, based on whatever Genesis is? The future?'

Ella stirred the milk around her cup in swirls. 'Cycles.'

The others stared at her, waiting for more.

'Didn't you say Kline said it's all about cycles?' She looked at Lizzie and took out the plastic stirrer and dropped it on the table. 'Every cycle has a beginning and an end.' Ella tried to develop her line of thought but she was too exhausted.

'OK, when's the most recent dot?' Lizzie asked.

Jay peered back at the screen. 'March, now. We're on the 29th so it's happened or will in the next two days.'

'Of course,' said Broady, slapping his head. 'The comet we saw at Lindisfarne.' He pulled the laptop towards him and typed in to google.

Ella watched him read.

'Yeah, it's closest to the earth on the last night of March.' He showed the others the screen. 'You'll be able to see it from pretty much anywhere in the northern hemisphere. It says here it will be closest over the Middle East, Turkey or Syria.'

Lizzie's eyes widened. 'I bet whatever Kline is planning is connected to that date,' she said.

'And I'll wager Matthew worked out what that was,' said Ella, feeling a chill run down her spine. 'Let's go.'

Jay finished off his drink. 'We'll never be able to work that out in time.'

'We *can*,' said Broady. 'That's why people are trying to kill us.'

Ella tried to put that observation out of her mind. 'First, we have to work out that first dot in 9500 BC.'

'Yeah,' said Lizzie. 'I bet that explains everything.'

They decided to stick with the plan to take the first train south, which was to York. Ella pulled one of Broady's baseball caps low over her head and went to the ticket office, paying cash for four tickets. They headed for the platform where the train was waiting. They got four seats around a table in a half-empty carriage and stared anxiously out of the window, scouring the platform for any signs of people searching for them. They were beginning to look bedraggled, having spent the last few days on the road, and Ella could tell Broady was in no condition to keep going at such a frenetic pace. She fiddled nervously with her pay-as-you-go phone, in two minds about calling Jim, her clerk. They needed hotel rooms and it was too risky to book anything on her own card.

The train pulled out of the station. Ella breathed a sigh of relief as they crossed over the Tyne. The familiar sound of Jay gently tapping on the keys of his laptop over the hum of the train beating out its rhythm on the tracks soon brought sleep.

Ella was woken by the sound of Lizzie shouting, 'Aristotle!'

A couple of lads drinking tins of lager looked over from the other side of the aisle.

Jay stopped typing.

'What if Aristotle believed?' she said.

'Believed what?' asked Jay.

'In the power of comets.' They were all listening now. 'Socrates taught Plato. Plato taught Aristotle and he taught Alexander.' Lizzie took the laptop. 'They were passing on the knowledge. Look at all the stuff Aristotle wrote about comets, he was obsessed. He understood something about them. Is that what made Alexander believe in his invincibility, what gave Alexander the edge?'

'But what's your evidence?' said Ella.

Lizzie scoffed. 'The first man to write books about comets, to properly study them is the tutor of the greatest war leader of all time. Coincidence?'

Even Ella found it hard to dismiss out of hand. She asked, 'And who did Alexander pass the knowledge to?'

'Maybe he didn't,' Lizzie replied. 'He died young. Maybe he didn't even care about the next generation. He was a warlord, not an academic.'

Broady scratched his head. 'You know what, I've been thinking about Isaac Newton.' His brow furrowed. 'It's kind of weird, but he also spent his last years working on comets.'

'All right,' said Ella in a cynical tone. 'Even assuming some past polymaths saw comets as important—'

'And present,' Jay interrupted, 'if you include Matthew.'

'OK.' She paused. 'But if they knew more than we do today, then why don't they tell us about the first dot in 9500 BC?'

Nobody had an answer.

'Wait a minute,' said Ella, her eyes darting around. 'Maybe they did.' She stared at Lizzie. 'Plato – *Timaeus and Critias*.'

'Oh my God,' said Lizzie. 'How did we miss it?'

'Miss what?' asked Broady.

'Atlantis,' said Ella, her voice sounding almost reverent. 'The more we widen the lens, the more everything in history seems to be linked.'

'I don't get it,' said Jay.

'In his book *Timaeus and Critias*, written around 360 BC,' Lizzie replied, 'Plato wrote about a huge lost island called Atlantis, an advanced civilization – a kind of utopia. He said it was the size of Libya and Asia Minor combined. All destroyed by fire and earthquakes in one night, lost underwater.'

'But it's just a myth, right?' Jay said, sounding uncertain. 'Is there any evidence the place ever existed?'

'None,' said Ella. 'Just incredibly detailed accounts about it from Plato.'

'Yeah,' said Lizzie. 'From the type of building materials they used, metals, even the layout of the city and who their enemies were.'

'That's right, Plato even wrote about their conquests,' said Ella. 'Their wars, and ultimately their downfall due to avarice and greed.'

'The story was passed down from Socrates and before him a man called Solon,' said Lizzie. 'The night when Atlantis sunk without trace was calculated by Plato to be about 9500 BC.'

'The date of the first dot,' observed Jay.

'So, where did he say this island was?' asked Broady.

'All we know is west of the Pillars of Hercules,' Lizzie replied. 'People think that's the Straits of Gibraltar, the gateway to the Med.'

'So, west could be pretty much anywhere in the Atlantic?' said Jay.

Lizzie nodded.

The train pulled into York Station.

'But I thought we didn't have cities or any kind of organi-sation back then,' said Jay. 'Farming hadn't begun.'

Broady got up and pulled the bags off the rack. 'So, Plato was bullshitting, right?'

Ella swung her bag over her shoulder. 'Nothing would surprise me anymore.' She led the way down the aisle towards the doors.

Chapter Sixty-Five

As they got out of the train, Ella's eyes darted from left to right, checking for anything untoward on the platform.

'Let's just get away from here,' she said.

The others followed her out of the station and around the corner along the old city walls. Ella could feel the sun on her face.

Jay put a hand on Ella's shoulder, which slowed her down. 'Are you saying it was a comet that destroyed Atlantis?'

She shrugged. 'It's just a myth but—'

Broady cut in, 'But the whole thing is nuts.'

Ella was beginning to rethink everything she'd learned about history. She took them to the open space around the Law Courts and found a place to sit across the road on the grass hill of Clifford's Tower, a ruined castle built after the Norman invasion.

They lay back on the steep bank, taking a moment to digest their latest conversation.

'We're drifting,' said Ella, unable to relax for long. She sat up and fiddled with the strap on her holdall. 'We need a plan.'

Broady suddenly sat up, then grimaced, putting a hand to his wound.

'What is it?' Ella asked, sensing the urgency.

'Show me the photos of the wallpaper again.'

As soon as she'd got them up on her phone, Broady grabbed it from her. He swiped the pictures across the screen, backwards and forwards. Then he looked at Ella and said, 'Newton.'

'What about him?' Ella demanded.

'You know I said he was obsessed with comets – that's all he was working on when he died?'

'Yes?'

Broady became more animated. 'It's accepted by astronomers that it was the great comet of 1680 that he used to confirm his theory of gravity. It's the comet that inspired him.'

'How?' asked Jay.

Broady's eyes widened. 'By calculating the trajectory!'

The others stared at him, nonplussed.

'The curves on Matthew's walls – it's the trajectories of the comets – their relationship to the earth.'

Ella was open-mouthed, in awe of Broady's brilliance. 'But…' she ventured, trying to process this information. 'But there's a pattern.'

Broady nodded. 'It's crazy, like there's a link between them.'

'Is that so surprising?' offered Jay. 'There's maths, patterns and cycles in all nature, why not comets?'

'And check this out,' Broady said, pointing to the picture. 'That's the first dot, right?'

Jay confirmed it.

'How come Matthew knew the trajectory? He's got a curve there.'

'He worked it out. He knew the rest of the pattern,' said Jay.

Before anyone had time to reflect, the phone Jay had given Ella pinged. She read the message.

It's Harris, we need to talk – you're in a great deal of danger.

Ella showed the others.

'Bit late for that,' said Lizzie.

Jay rubbed his head. 'How did she get that number?' He examined the text again.

Ella's phone pinged again. She read out the text.

Come back to the train station.

'What the hell?' said Broady, getting up.

'I don't trust her,' said Jay. 'Your inquiry is over if we do what she says.'

Ella was in two minds.

Lizzie stared at her, eyes imploring.

Ella stood up, took a deep breath then dropped her phone on the ground and stamped on it. 'If they've traced us, so have others.' She swivelled her foot to pulverise the handset.

'Let's go,' she said, heading off towards the shopping precinct.

The others followed, checking about them as they went. They hurried past a man dressed as a Viking, leading a group of school children holding plastic shields up the street.

'In here,' said Ella, darting into a clothes shop and then sauntering along a rail, pulling out a few items while she tried to think.

'Just visiting?' said a young shop assistant, noticing the holdalls. 'Looking for a dress?'

'Just browsing, thanks,' said Ella in a tone that sent the girl off to the other side of the store.

'We've got to keep moving,' said Broady, flicking his head up towards the CCTV cameras on the ceiling. 'Get off the streets.'

Still without any real plan, they filed out onto the pedestrianised area.

The shop assistant followed them to the doorway and watched them disappear into the crowds.

'There,' said Ella, spotting a taxi rank. She marched over and opened the passenger door. 'We want to go to Leeds,' she said, climbing in and resting her bag on her knees. The others climbed in the back.

Ella could see the elderly cabby eyeing them suspiciously in the rear-view mirror. 'Do you want to put those int' boot?' he asked in a broad Yorkshire accent.

'No thanks,' said Ella. 'We're in a hurry.'

'Happen train's quicker,' he suggested.

She opened her bag and took out a roll of notes, pulled off two fifties and held them out. 'Hundred quid all right?'

He took the money and started the engine. 'That'll do just fine.'

The taxi skirted the city walls as it headed away from the town centre. Ella glanced across to the drop-off outside the station. A blacked-out Range Rover was parked up. Half-down, the passenger window revealed the top of someone's head, talking into a mobile. A ginger bob – it was Harris.

Ella's chest tightened. She turned to see the others in the back seat – oblivious. She chose to say nothing in front of the driver.

Ella kept turning around to check on Broady. He managed half-smiles but she could tell he was in some discomfort. They couldn't keep moving from place to place with no real destination. She turned in her seat to face the others. 'We need to make a decision.'

'What about trying to find this Chan guy?' suggested Jay. 'He's listed on the UCL website as a professor. What if Greg was wrong or lying?' Jay persisted. 'Maybe he's still there?'

Ella glanced at Broady. 'Or Greg wanted us to lead them to him.'

He shrugged. 'What else have we got?'

Jay leaned forward. 'Even if he's not there, London is a good place to lose ourselves.'

Ella felt sure it was a bad idea, but she knew Broady was right, they had no other leads.

'You can get lost in London, all right,' said the cabby. 'I went down Shaftesbury Avenue once,' he said, oblivious to the importance of their discussion. 'Theatreland they call it, just off Piccadilly,' he added with a supercilious sniff. 'Oh yeah, I've been to London before.'

Ella looked away from him in the hope it would put a stop to his reminiscing.

'Took the missus on one o' them theatre breaks,' he continued. 'Miss Saigon, I think it were.' He glanced over at Ella as if she was interested. 'Tell you what, them singers can't half belt out a tune, bloody marvellous.' He stared at Ella as if waiting for some kind of response.

'How much to go to London?'

Paying no attention, he broke into song, 'I dreamed a dream—'

'That's from Les Misérables,' Ella snapped.

'That's the one!' he exclaimed. 'Les Misérables!' He chuckled to himself. 'The wife called it Les Mis-er-ables. Funny old word.'

'How much to go to central London?' she said again, louder this time.

He stopped wittering and gave her a double take. 'Are you mad? There are trains all the time from Leeds.'

'How much?' she repeated, taking a wad of notes out of her pocket.

He glanced over at the bundle. 'Three hundred will do it.'

'Done.' She counted out the notes and handed it to him.

The man sighed. 'Should've said three-fifty.' He indicated to come off for the M1 then touched his mobile, sitting in a cradle attached to the windscreen. 'Better ring the missus to say I won't be home for tea.'

Ella put her hand over the screen. 'The price includes no phone calls.'

He gave her a sideways stare. There followed an awkward silence. Finally, he took his hand away. 'No calls costs another hundred.'

Ella handed him two fifties.

Chapter Sixty-Six

The taxi hit standing traffic as they got close to the centre of London, so they decided to get out at Euston Station and walk along Euston Road towards the university, hoping to be inconspicuous amongst the crowds of commuters and travellers. They wiped the dust from their eyes, blown up by the buses going by.

Ella could see Jay's focus was gone as he took in the sights and sounds of the capital. As they reached the left turning into Gower Street, Ella told them to wait on the corner while she went to make the enquiries.

She walked down Gower a little way then left past the two little gatehouses and into the quadrangle, an enclosed courtyard surrounded by a grand nineteenth-century building – and a sanctuary from the frenetic pace of the London streets. She scanned the benches scattered around the perimeter and scrutinised the faces of students lost in books or eating sandwiches. Facing her was the Octagon Building, with its imposing triangular pediment resting on ten great pillars. Students wearing headphones, engrossed in their mobiles, sitting in ones and twos, littered the great stone steps in front.

Ella gazed up at the dome that sat atop the structure, wondering where to start.

She decided to follow a steady stream of students coming in and out of a door to her right that had a sign saying Wilkins Building. She came out into a cloister and then went through a glass revolving door into a refectory area with rows of students on computers. On seeing a reception desk, she was about to go over when a woman caught her eye, chatting to a couple of scruffy students. She seemed familiar but Ella couldn't place her. Then she remembered. She approached. 'Claire?'

The woman turned, taking a few moments to recognise her. 'Oh my god! Ella Blake?'

Ella forced a smile. 'I thought it was you.' She moved closer, wondering whether a hug was appropriate, but decided against it. 'You haven't changed a bit.'

'Yeah, right,' Claire said with a flick of the head. 'Three kids have taken their toll.' She laughed. 'You're a barrister now, I've often seen stuff about you and your cases on telly.'

The students smiled at Ella then left them to it.

'You stuck with history?' Ella asked. Her old friend had the relaxed manner of someone who'd stayed in academia.

'Yeah, I'm a lecturer here, part-time. My husband works in London so it's perfect.' She was still taking Ella in. 'You married that rascal, Tom, right?' she said affectionately. 'How is he?'

Ella always dreaded that question. 'He died a few years ago.'

All levity was lost.

'I didn't know, I'm so sorry.' She gave Ella a hug with three pitiful pats on the back.

Once released, Ella saw an opportunity to move the conversation on, knowing how difficult people found it to dwell too long on other people's bereavement. 'I'm looking for the History Department actually, a work thing – Professor Chan?'

'Ah,' she said, 'Lovely man but he's not been here for a few weeks.'

Ella could tell she was assessing her unkempt appearance more closely now, assuming it to be related to Tom's death.

'He took some time off, without warning. I suspect it's to do with his health.' Claire lowered her voice. 'He's getting on a bit and I know he had a heart problem.'

'Don't suppose you've got a number for him?'

'No, I didn't really know him, but I can give you his work email?'

'Thanks,' Ella replied, remembering that her own email account was probably being monitored. 'That would be great.'

Claire picked up a flyer for a karaoke night off a pile on the reception desk and began to jot it down. 'They're all the same in our department, you just put the surname in front.' She gave Ella another sympathetic smile. 'I'll put my mobile on here too. Got to dash but let's catch up properly?'

'We must,' Ella replied, doing her best to sound upbeat.

Claire gave her a final hug. 'Hope you get hold of him.' She adjusted her shoulder bag and hurried off through the electric doors onto a side street.

Disorientated from the encounter, Ella stood for a moment, staring at the piece of paper, disconnected from all the chatter and activity around her. She glanced over at the computers then went over to an empty terminal and sat down.

A young man in ripped jeans and a lumberjack shirt was sitting on the table talking to a girl at the next computer. On seeing Ella, he slid off and budged the girl up so they could share the chair.

Ella went through the process of registering a new

account then wrote an email to Chan. She decided only to give her name, the fact that she was chairing the De Jure Inquiry into Matthew's disappearance and that if she didn't get a reply immediately, she wouldn't be able to check her emails for some time. Her finger hovered over the send button. Something made her do a final scan of the faces in the busy lobby. She pressed send then sat staring at the screen, arguing with herself about whether she should get back to check on the others.

Her attention was drawn to two girls by a vending machine laughing hysterically then whispering into cupped hands. Ella found herself wondering what was so funny. She'd never really had a friendship like that, it had always been Tom, even since freshers' week. She envied the young women their connection.

Her inbox pinged. An email from a Yahoo address. There was no text in the email, just the subject heading: *Wong Kei*. She knew the place immediately.

Chapter Sixty-Seven

E lla led the way down Charing Cross Road, taking the opportunity to fill the others in on what had happened without being overheard.

'Let's hang back for a while,' suggested Broady. 'Keep an eye on the corner for any activity.'

Ella agreed. They took a right at Cambridge Circus and along Shaftesbury Avenue. They stopped in a doorway over the road from Wardour Street, checking for anything untoward. All they could see were tourists and people of Chinese origin going in and out of Gerard Street, the entrance to Chinatown.

'We can't stay here forever, Mum,' said Lizzie after half an hour of watching the corner and searching the hundreds of faces for some unknown clue.

Ella took a deep breath. 'OK, let's go in.'

They waited for a gap in the traffic and ran across Shaftsbury Avenue and stopped outside the restaurant, peering through the window. Delicious aromas filled their nostrils.

'Wong Kei is the strangest Chinese in London, you have to share a table,' Lizzie explained to Jay. 'My parents used to bring me here when I was a kid. It's on five floors – the waiters are famous for being rude to customers.'

With some trepidation Ella led them inside.

A waiter in a black t-shirt pointed to the back of the restaurant and ordered, 'Upstair.'

They obeyed, going up a couple of flights to a room half-full of diners.

Another waiter held up four fingers.

Ella nodded.

He waved at a round table off to the side, covered with a white, paper tablecloth with eight chairs around it. A Japanese couple were tucking into some won ton soup, camera placed proudly on the table by the male customer. They looked up briefly as Ella and the others sat down.

The waiter plonked some cups and menus on the table then came back with some soy and chilli sauce. He shot off and then appeared again with a metal pot of tea.

'What you want?' he said, hands on hips.

Broady reached for a menu and began to read as the waiter hovered impatiently. 'I'll take the chicken chow mein.'

'Noodle soft or crispy?' he asked, snatching the menu.

'Crispy.'

The waiter swept up the other menus as each of them told him their choices then he swanned off.

'What do we do now?' asked Jay.

'We wait,' said Ella, checking out the diners around the tables.

The food arrived within minutes on plastic plates and the four of them scoffed it down, enjoying their first proper hot meal for some time. Ella kept watching the door, analysing each new diner being bossed to a seat.

Two male thirty-something Brits in suits without ties were ushered over.

Ella felt uneasy as she watched them order. She quickly

looked away as one of the men was obviously conscious of the strangers staring at him.

The meal was over in minutes despite Broady struggling with the chopsticks. They sat back in their chairs to let the food go down. As if on cue, the waiter appeared, 'Finish?' Without waiting for a reply, he piled up the plates and returned, moments later, with the bill.

Ella put some cash down, shrugged at the others and said, 'Let's go.'

They stood in a huddle outside, catching glimpses of faces in the hordes of passers-by and wondering what to do next.

Ella noticed a young woman of Chinese appearance on the other side of the street. Her clothes were nondescript, blending into her surroundings. They made eye-contact. The woman gave an imperceptible nod, walked a few steps, then turned left into Gerard Street.

Ella's heart began to race. 'This way,' she said, pulling Lizzie's bag. Just able to keep her in sight, Ella followed the woman under the Chinese arch with the others in tow. Rows of glazed ducks on hooks in the windows of the restaurants on either side lined the route.

Ella saw the woman stop at some steps off the pedestrianised street, descending to a small door below a restaurant. She walked down and entered, the others following. Jay closed the door behind him. They followed the woman along a dimly-lit passage with exposed brick walls and a broken tiled floor, through another door into some kind of stock room with cardboard boxes full of tins and vegetables piled up.

The woman turned and gave a slight bow then opened another door.

Ella went in first.

Chapter Sixty-Eight

The room was small and square with a light bulb inside a torn paper shade in the centre, hanging on a cord. The walls were covered with pieces of paper of all sizes, stuck on with Sellotape. Ella saw at once that the pictures were all depictions of comets. An elderly Chinese man with hollow cheeks and a sallow complexion was standing on a wicker mat which took up most of the floor space.

He had grey stubble and wore grey, suit-style trousers and a white, short-sleeved shirt. His forearms were wizened, his hands knobbled at the joints.

Ella saw that he had black socks but no shoes on his feet. She put down her bag, bent over to take hers off but the man shook his head, and said, 'No time.' Moving with the sluggishness of age, he sat down cross-legged on the mat and gestured with an arm for them to do the same.

They formed a semi-circle in front of him.

'I knew you'd come,' he said, his accent Chinese but his English, perfect. 'Tea?' He reached for a pot beside a stack of Chinese cups.

The young woman hurried over and gently chastised him

before taking over the task, expertly using a delicate finger to keep the lid in place as she poured.

Recognising the need to be courteous, Ella fought off her natural instinct to launch into a barrage of questions. Waiting for their host to begin the dialogue, she noticed a huge picture of rows of rudimentary drawings of comets, circles, but all with different shaped tails, some broom-like, some much thinner and some with two or three prongs. Chinese characters ran underneath the sketches.

'It's from the *Book of Silk*,' the man explained, seeing Ella staring. 'It was found in a cave forty years ago, written on a silk manuscript. It annotates the shapes of comets over hundreds of years, all recorded thousands of years ago.'

'And the writing?'

The man looked at the picture even though he obviously knew every inch of it. 'Important disasters that happened when the comets were overhead.' He looked back at Ella. 'Emperors and military generals saw them as important omens in warfare.'

'You're Ying-Kwong Chan?' asked Ella, adjusting her legs to the unfamiliar posture.

'I am,' he replied with a gentle smile. There was something innately calming about his presence.

'We were told you were in China?'

He scoffed but didn't bother with an answer. 'You work well together,' he said looking from one to the other. 'All bring something different.' He paused and seemed to reflect. 'As it should be.'

The woman finished handing round the tea, then stood by the door, as if on guard.

Clearly noticing their anxiety at her positioning, Chan said, 'They will be here soon, too many of them.'

'Who are they?' said Ella.

'Kline's *disciples*,' he replied with irony. There was no malice in his voice, only pity.

'Disciples?' asked Ella.

'That's what he calls them,' Chan replied, picking up his cup with both hands and taking a sip of tea. 'They are misguided.' He re-focussed on Ella. A knowing smile broke out on his face. 'David Kline has gone quite mad. The trouble is, even mad people can create a following if they are a genius.' He glanced over at Jay and Lizzie. 'And young people are desperate for solutions.'

'Is he after you? Is that why you're in hiding?' asked Ella. She couldn't get her questions out quick enough.

'Anyone trying to understand Genesis is in danger.'

'Why come here?' she said, glancing around the storeroom.

Chan smiled. 'I have friends here and it's the busiest place in London.' He picked up a smartphone from the mat. 'So, it's much harder for them to track this. Too many phones.'

'There's so much we don't know,' blurted Lizzie.

He nodded and put down his cup. 'You've learned a lot in a short time.'

'Did the ancient Greeks know about the comets?' she asked. 'Is that what Aristotle taught Alexander, passed down from other people like Socrates and Plato?'

'That is what history tells us,' Chan replied. 'But unlike the teachers that came before him, Alexander used the knowledge only to gain power, just like David Kline.' He made eye-contact with Ella. 'Knowledge worth having does not bring power, Miss Blake.'

Ella thought for a moment, sensing it was a test. 'No,' she replied. 'It brings enlightenment.'

'Exactly.' He gave a tired smile. 'Power never lasts and brings only pain and death.'

'But what did Aristotle teach Alexander?' Lizzie persisted.

He clasped his hands together, accentuating their bony appearance, then looked at Ella which she took as a request for an answer.

'To understand that we are always in the hands of the comets?' she replied.

Chan nodded. 'I don't know why we forgot. Part of learning is forgetting, I suppose.' Chan's brow furrowed as if he was troubled. He pointed to a large picture of Matthew's Genesis pattern on the wall off to his right. 'Try to see beyond power, war and destruction. Man has free will. We don't know what makes each individual choose a path. We have forged the wrong road for too long.' He glanced over at the *Book of Silk* again. 'Unfortunately, it is the rhythm of this cycle.'

'This cycle?' repeated Broady, leaning in.

'Comets have always brought change.' Chan took a breath as if getting ready for a long explanation. 'Even as far back as the dinosaurs. Life has evolved in tandem, driven by the comet cycles.' He looked from one to the other. 'They are of different durations, but they always come and go.'

'The bigger picture,' said Ella, truly seeing its meaning for the first time.

Chan took another breath. 'The earth warmed for thousands of years and then it suddenly reversed about twelve thousand eight hundred years ago, returning to glacial conditions.'

'Yes,' said Ella. 'The beginning of the Younger Dryas period.'

'Yes,' Chan replied, as if talking to a pupil, but there was nothing patronising in his tone. 'Scientists have found nanodiamonds from over fifty sites from this period, an indication of great comet impacts around the world. There were mass extinctions, lost species of animals, plants, and even humans like the Clovis people in North America.'

'Of course!' exclaimed Ella. 'The Younger Dryas lasted

one thousand three hundred years and then there was another dip in temperature.'

'Yes.' Chan smiled. 'Another comet strike, possibly remnants of the old shower. Some people call them the Taurids.'

'So that cycle ended about eleven thousand five hundred years ago?' asked Jay.

'Yes.' The old man took another sip of tea.

'And our cycle began,' said Ella, studying Chan. 'The Holocene. The beginning of which matches the first dot on Genesis.'

'You are on the road to enlightenment, Miss Blake.' He didn't say more, as if sensing the next question.

'All these people from history that correspond with great events,' she said her voice trailing off. 'Why are they all men?'

'Perhaps women aren't driven by power as men are,' Chan replied.

'So, they are not predisposed to the power of the comets in the same way?'

Chan shrugged. 'So much we don't yet understand.'

Ella looked deep into the old man's watery eyes. 'Did you work with Matthew?'

Chan gave an affirming blink. 'We corresponded, exchanged ideas. But I didn't like David Kline. They worked together on the Genesis theory in the early days.' He let out a sigh. 'They were very different people. Matthew was in search of enlightenment, Kline was only interested in what power knowledge could bring. He was seduced by it, he began to believe the comets brought some kind of strength, just like so many great leaders in history. It blinded him.'

Conscious of the urgency, Ella decided to move straight to the biggest question. 'And *does* a comet bring some kind of strength?'

'It's possible.' Chan replied matter-of-factly. 'Certainly, the belief that it does seems to be enough for some people. A self-fulfilling prophecy.'

Ella thought again about the great invasions in history and their single-minded leaders, then back to the present. 'But what about when people are still in the womb, like Tacumseh? They don't have the belief?'

Chan scratched his nose. 'Maybe they were told by others that they were chosen.'

Jay's brow furrowed. 'But the pattern of important historical events correlates so exactly with the comets?'

Chan opened up his hands. 'All I can say is that as a scientist or as a historian, I must have evidence.'

'Or as a lawyer,' Ella replied.

'There might be some kind of energy in the comets that can affect some people,' Chan said with a shrug. 'We know the sun and the wind can be turned into energy. There's nothing new there. We are constantly understanding new energies and how to harness them.'

Ella glanced over at Broady, remembering what he'd said in the car. She wouldn't make the mistake of underestimating him again.

'But I have no proof,' Chan continued. 'There is just, as you say, a correlation. And even if it were true, man has free will, choice. It is always what we do with knowledge that changes history.'

Lizzie and Jay stared at him, as if hypnotised.

Ella focussed on the task in hand. 'Do you know where Matthew is?'

He closed his eyes again, this time holding them shut. On opening them, he said quietly, 'I fear he's dead.'

'How?'

Chan shook his head. 'He was very ill, he couldn't keep moving, searching.'

Silence descended around the room. Ella felt her eyes

welling up, mourning the death of a man she'd never met. 'Where do you think he was?'

Chan shrugged. 'I don't know, maybe Turkey.'

'Turkey?' Ella looked at Broady again.

The woman said something in Chinese to Chan then left the room.

The others watched her leave then turned back to Chan who continued with his lesson. 'He was searching for the Genesis.'

'Genesis of what?' asked Lizzie.

'The Holocene,' Ella replied. 'Civilization, our cycle.'

Chan's smile conveyed an obvious affection for his new pupil. 'Yes, the source of our river.'

The pieces were falling into place. 'So Matthew believed we can only find enlightenment if we can retrace our steps, go back to the beginning, the birth of who we are.'

Chan nodded.

'So what is the beginning?' asked Ella.

Chan gave her a look that seemed to pierce her soul. 'You already know.'

Frustrated by the cryptic reply Ella huffed. Then, realisation dawned. 'Genesis.' She felt the blood rushing to her face. 'The Great Flood.'

The old man raised an arm and pointed at her. 'Yes.'

'Atlantis? It was destroyed in a flood at the exact time of the last impact.' She squinted trying to remember the exact date. 'Plato first wrote about Atlantis in 360 BC and said it was lost more than nine thousand years before, sunk beneath the sea.'

'Yes.' Chan elaborated. 'There is plenty of geological evidence that the comet melted huge glaciers in North America. The heat generated on impact would have been immense.'

'So, sea levels rose,' said Jay.

'The new cycle must have started after the flood waters receded,' said Lizzie, turning to Ella, as they said in unison, 'Noah!'

'You are your mother's daughter,' said Chan, beaming.

Ella and Lizzie's eyes locked and Ella was overwhelmed by a sense of connection with her daughter, an exchange of infinite love and respect.

Still choked, Ella refocussed on Chan. 'Matthew was looking for evidence of Noah, his ark.'

'Yes. Noah came from a sophisticated world, the old cycle. Plato called it Atlantis. Matthew was convinced there must be some proof, something to mark the birth of our civilisation.'

'Isaac Newton,' said Broady, slapping his thigh. 'He knew all this?' Broady stared excitedly at the others. 'He said in one of his last pieces of work that Noah's flood must have been caused by a comet.'

'That's right,' replied Chan. 'I think he came close to enlightenment before his death.'

The woman came rushing back into the room and locked the door, shouting something urgently to the old man.

'They have found us,' he said, getting up. 'We must go.' The woman rushed over to him and slipped some laceless plimsolls onto his feet as if dressing a child.

The others got to their feet and watched as the woman rolled back the mat uncovering a circular man-hole cover with an indented handle in the middle. She hauled it up and slid it off, revealing a metal ladder attached to a vertical tunnel leading into darkness.

The old man began to climb down. The woman waved at Ella to do the same.

Ella was still absorbed in Genesis but a sudden hammering on the door jolted her into action.

Chapter Sixty-Nine

They made their way down into the pitch black, condensation on the walls giving off a rank, damp smell.

The young woman went last, pulling the lid back across and turning a handle to seal it in place.

Ella could see a light below. Chan had reached the bottom and switched on a small torch. She could make out tunnels, leading off in all directions.

'Follow the light,' he said calmly, leading them off down a narrow walkway. His tiny frame and hunched gait made it easier for him to hobble along. Jay and Broady had to bend over to get through. They came to a dingy crossroads with the sound of running water. The stench was overwhelming. There was a stream of sewage in a huge channel across their path. Lizzie retched and covered her mouth.

The old man shone his torch at something on the ground. 'Please, put that across,' he said without a hint of panic. Jay put down his bag, came forward and picked up the plank of wood that had clearly been left there in readiness for a quick getaway. He slid it across the river of waste until it was firmly resting on both sides.

The old man went first, arms out like a seasoned tight-rope walker. The others followed, careful not to let their holdalls unbalance them.

Chan's companion was the last to cross, then she pushed the plank into the water. They all watched for a moment as it floated off downstream.

They continued on, taking several turns, right then left into different tunnels, the old man seemingly confident of the route.

Eventually they came to a door at the end of their path. The woman came forward, undid a catch, opened it slightly, then waited. After a minute or so she pulled it open and they filed out into the light, squinting to see a large, tiled passageway with an escalator at the end. It took a moment to get their bearings. A sign on the wall read *Green Park*. They were in a tube station.

They went up the escalator, still trying to adjust their eyes. As they came up to the top Ella could see the ticket barriers, manned by a bloke in uniform. 'We haven't got tickets,' she said, suddenly feeling panicked.

The woman, who hadn't spoken since they left the room, took a bundle of tickets out of her pocket and distributed them, finishing with a little bow. 'Please.'

They went through the barriers and up the steps.

It was nearly dark. The old man was exhausted, his pace slower and his footing unsteady. 'This way,' he said, leading them down into the park itself. They crossed the grass to a patch under a tree where he flopped down.

Commuters heading home from work were walking along the paths in different directions, all lost in their own worlds.

Once Chan had caught his breath, he spoke again. 'You must go now.'

The woman remained standing, keeping watch.

'Go where?' said Ella.

'Find the place Matthew was searching for.' He took a gulp of air. 'Finish his work.'

'I don't understand,' Ella protested. 'Why is it so important?'

Chan nodded as if realising there was something he hadn't explained. 'War is always about differences between men. Beliefs.'

'I don't get it,' said Broady.

Ella answered, 'Religion.'

Chan nodded. 'Christians and Muslims, Catholics and Protestants, Sunnis and Shiites. Our differences are what stop us from working together even though we can see our future clearly.'

'Pollution?' asked Jay. 'The destruction of our home?'

Chan bestowed a gentle smile on the young man.

Ella exhaled in realisation. 'He wanted to find the common bond, where religion began?'

Chan touched Ella's arm. 'We were once the same, all of us.'

'We thought Genesis might be a code word for some kind of weapon,' said Broady.

'On the contrary.' Chan gave a resigned shake of the head. 'People see what they want to see.'

Ella instinctively checked about them in the half light at the gloomy silhouettes heading towards the Tube. She remembered the Bible in Matthew's room. 'Doesn't the Bible say the flood happened in about 2300 BC?'

Chan waved a finger. 'There is no date in the Bible. That is just a calculation people make based on other stories.' Chan's knowledge was effortless. 'There is no geological evidence of a comet strike at that time. But there is no doubt that the flood happened, it is recorded in every ancient text, every religion, the Bible, the Quran.' He was almost laughing as he spoke. 'It's in Hindu mythology – the Satapatha Brahmana, written in the sixth century. The Sumerians wrote about it centuries earlier on the Deluge Tablet. It is in Norse legends, ancient Chinese texts – the Gun-Yu flood – Maya and Aboriginal mythology.'

'It's in the Hohokam creation story too,' said Broady in a tone of wonder. 'An Arizona desert people.'

Chan grinned. 'It is a story that unites all peoples, because we all come from this event, this is when our epoch began.'

Ella glanced at the others in the dusky gloom. 'So, where do we start looking, Turkey?'

'Yes, Cizre.' He smiled. 'That is where many ancient texts say Noah landed.'

'Cizre,' said Broady, moving up onto his knees to stretch out his torso. 'It's on the Turkish–Syrian border, right? In the south?'

'Yes,' Chan replied.

'But the Bible says Noah landed on Mount Ararat. I remember from my army days, that's north-east Turkey, on the border with Iran.' Broady rested an arm on Jay's shoulder for support. 'That's got to be hundreds of kilometres away from Cizre?'

Chan smiled. 'The original Hebrew texts from the Bible actually say Noah landed in the *Kingdom* of Ararat, that is a vast area covering the whole of the fertile crescent.'

Jay cut in, 'So why Cizre?'

'Matthew was convinced the Quran was more accurate.' Chan's passion for the subject held them all spellbound. 'It records that Noah's ark came to rest on Mount Judi.' He wiped his brow with a handkerchief from his shirt pocket. 'The ancient Kurdish city at its base is now called Cizre.'

Ella took a moment to take it all in. 'There's a comet overhead now. It's closest point to the earth will be over Turkey in a couple of days. The last dot.'

Chan nodded.

Broady stared intently at him. 'What's going to happen?'

'How can we know?' he replied. 'History is not yet written.' Chan stroked his stubble. 'I fear David Kline wants to be the man to write it.'

The old man's friend was becoming more impatient. Evidently unable to control her anxiety, she said something in Chinese and put an arm under Chan's shoulder, pulling him to his feet.

'Go now,' he said, waving them away like stray dogs. 'And good luck.'

Ella jumped to her feet, desperate to keep him there a little longer. There was so much more to discuss. 'Why us?'

He gently touched her cheek. 'Perhaps *that* is written.'

She stared into his eyes, for once lost for something to say.

'Please, one more question,' said Jay, getting up. 'One of the most recent dots on Genesis is 1986, Halley's Comet. Why is that date important?'

Chan straightened up as much as his curved spine would allow, held out a palm and smiled. Instead of providing an answer, he said, 'Rain.' Cajoled by his companion, he shuffled off into the half-light.

'What about 1986?' Jay called after him.

In one serene motion, the old man half-turned and said, 'Matthew Shepherd was born.'

Chapter Seventy

Ella and the others picked up their stuff and headed across the park in the opposite direction, weaving their way through the stream of commuters.

'Are we going to Cizre?' stuttered Jay, as he moved alongside Ella.

She didn't respond, she needed to think through their next move.

'Are we, Mum?' said Lizzie.

She didn't reply. 'Let's just get out of here.'

Broady tapped Ella's arm. 'We can't risk hotels, not with the check-in.'

'I know,' Ella replied stern-faced. 'But you could do with some rest.' She glanced at the others. 'We all could.'

They came out near The Mall and stood under a streetlight, taking in each other's ghostly expressions. Ella flagged down a black cab. 'I know a place we can go,' she said to Broady. 'I'd trust him with my life.' Something made her say to him, 'As I would you.'

She opened the door to let Jay and Lizzie climb in. Broady stopped. 'You OK, Ella?'

She managed a weary smile.

'You're doing great.'

Canary Wharf was still bustling. The lights from the windows in the skyscrapers gave the whole area an aura of dynamism.

'Just here's fine,' Ella said to the driver, who pulled up outside a gigantic tower block.

'This way,' she signalled to the others, walking down the ramp into an underground car park. 'There's a back entrance,' she explained. 'Just to be safe.'

They had to wait at the electric shutter until a car came down the ramp and zapped it up, its occupant giving the odd-looking band of four with their holdalls a once over.

Ella realised they were starting to attract attention with their unkempt appearance.

They hurried across the car park, past the Lamborghinis and Bentleys that their owners used to sit in five-mile-an-hour traffic every day. They went through a door that had been left ajar and waited for the lift.

'You'll like him,' Ella said to Broady, as they got in and pressed the button for the 25th floor. 'I hope he's back from work.'

They came out onto a plush landing. Ella led them down the corridor and pressed the buzzer outside the apartment.

The door opened. 'Ella!' Jim's face turned from one of surprise to concern on seeing two strange men stood behind her. Then he noticed Ella's daughter. 'Lizzie!'

'She moved to the front and gave him a hug. 'Hello Jim.'

'Come in, come in,' he said, ushering them inside.

The apartment was immaculate, just like Jim's suit.

Broady and Jay went straight over to the floor-to-ceiling

windows to admire the view over the Thames and the lights of London.

'This is some crib, man,' Broady exclaimed.

'Not bad for an old, cockney queen,' Jim replied, camping up his voice.

'The clerks earn more than the barristers,' said Ella with a wry smile before making the introductions.

Jim shook hands with Jay and Broady. 'So, what's going on?'

'It's a long story,' said Ella, collapsing onto the huge, L-shaped, grey sofa.

Jim sat down beside her. 'I knew something was up, there were people hanging about outside chambers today. A couple of people came in asking after you.'

Ella sat up and said, 'Who?'

'Said they were government people, that they were having trouble contacting you?' He pulled Harris' card out of his pocket and handed it to her. 'I was worried you'd had a melt-down and walked off the job.'

'Did you tell them anything?'

Jim harrumphed. 'I didn't know anything, still don't.'

'Probably best that way,' she said, patting his knee.

'I don't think we should stay,' said Broady.

Ella exhaled. 'Yeah, he's right, sorry Jim, we shouldn't have come.'

Jim's eyebrows shot up. 'You think people will come here?'

Ella put a hand on his shoulder. 'It's possible. I'm sorry to have put you in this position. Maybe go out for the evening after we've gone, stay with friends?'

Jim agreed. 'At least tell me if this is about the Cambridge thing?'

Ella took a breath then nodded.

'Then it's my problem, too.' He got up and walked over to a white granite worktop and picked something off the surface.

'I'm watering the plants for a neighbour, he's away for a few weeks.' He came back and handed her a key. 'You can stay there, it's only one floor down.'

'Are you sure?' she stood up and rolled the key around in her hand. 'Won't he mind?'

Jim shrugged. 'Hopefully, he won't know. I'll get the place cleaned up after you've gone. Besides, think he fancies me.' He cast an eye at Broady.

Ella gave him a hug. 'Thank you.'

Jim's face became serious. 'Take my spare too. You know where I am if you need me.'

Ella welled up. She couldn't figure out why she'd cut so many people off over the last few years. If she got the chance, she was going to change all that.

Chapter Seventy-One

The other apartment was much like Jim's – the same layout, but even more flash.

Jay and Lizzie used the two bathrooms to take showers while Ella and Broady sat at a black, glass table eating the remnants of a Domino's they'd had delivered. No one had yet touched on Chan's revelations. Their brains needed a break and Ella needed time to think things through.

Broady helped himself to another slither of cold pizza out of the box, took a bite then left the rest of the slice on his plate.

Ella tried to read him. 'Not like the ones back home?'

'Not even ball-park,' Broady replied.

'You miss it?' Ella asked. 'Home... the desert?'

'Kind of.' He made eye-contact. 'But there's been something missing for quite a while.'

She held his gaze. 'Something or *someone?*'

His eyes glistened. 'You know.'

She blinked. 'Yeah, I know.'

Neither pushed the conversation on. It felt good just to sit. Ella leaned forward and said, just above a whisper, 'Do you think it's really true?' Her eyes scanned his face for an answer. 'About the comets, everything?'

'You're the historian.' He took a swig of Coke from a can. 'But my gut says yeah.'

'Me too.'

Broady clasped his hands and put them on his head, yawning, seemingly unfazed. 'But evidence of Noah's existence, from eleven thousand five hundred years ago?' He scoffed. 'That's a big ask.'

Ella nodded. 'I've always understood that the first organised civilisation was the Sumerians dating back to 3500 BC. They could write and do complex maths.'

'From Iraq, right?' asked Broady.

'Yes, the fertile crescent, between the Tigris and the Euphrates. This was the perfect place for civilisation to evolve and flourish, of all the routes the first humans took when they came out of Africa. I'm not aware of any physical evidence of a highly organised civilisation before that date.'

Broady puffed out his cheeks. 'And we're being asked to believe that Noah came from a civilisation that existed six thousand years earlier?'

'But—' Before Ella could finish, Lizzie came in wearing a pair of joggers and a vest. 'Great shower,' she said, rubbing her head with a towel.

Ella got up and wrapped her arms around her.

'Mum,' said Lizzie, her chin buried in Ella's shoulder. 'That's not like you.'

She kissed her daughter's forehead. 'From now on it is.'

'Did I miss something?' said Jay, similarly dressed.

'No,' said Lizzie with a grin. 'Just Mum being sentimental.'

'So, have we decided what we're doing yet?' he asked.

All eyes were on Ella.

Lizzie threw the towel on the back of the sofa as if getting ready for a fight. 'I heard what you were saying about Noah.' She took a breath. 'What's the *but*, Mum?'

Ella shrugged, still trying to convince herself. 'I was just going to say that time and again people have proved myths and legends have a basis in truth.'

'Such as?' asked Jay.

'The Ebu Gogo, for one,' she replied as if the answer was obvious.

'The what?' asked Broady.

'The people on an Indonesian island called Flores talk of a tribe of tiny people that would raid the village and steal their babies. Parents still tell bedtime stories about them, to make their kids behave. Horrible little creatures that ate raw flesh.'

'So, what's your point?' asked Jay.

Ella watched Lizzie flick her wet hair over her head. 'In 2004 archaeologists found what they thought were human remains in a cave there, one full skeleton and nine partials. The fully grown adult was only one metre tall.'

'I've read about this,' said Lizzie. 'The Flores Hobbit. A separate species of homo that became extinct.'

'Yes,' said Ella, using her hands for emphasis. 'According to the experts, they died out at least twelve thousand years ago.' Her arms became more animated. 'But the stories lived on just through word of mouth, folklore.'

'That's incredible,' said Jay. 'All those generations.'

'Many scientists believe the same thing about the Yeti,' she continued, picking up the towel and folding it. 'All the Sherpas in Tibet have the same Neanderthal piece of DNA, it's why they can survive at altitude.'

'Neanderthal?' Jay repeated.

'Yeah, the last of the species died out around thirty-seven thousand years ago, pushed out by humans.'

Jay clicked his finger. 'So, their last refuse was in the Himalayas, where their DNA gave them an advantage?'

'It makes sense,' Ella replied, putting the towel on the back of a chair. 'Maybe the Tibetan tales of Yetis is their historical memory of Neanderthals from generations past.'

'So,' Jay began tentatively, 'we're going to Cizre?'

Ella stared him down then started pacing the apartment. 'We probably haven't even all got our passports?'

Lizzie screwed her face up. 'Mine's at Bourne Street.'

Ella remembered pouring the contents of the drawer into her holdall after the burglary. 'It's in my bag.'

'Really?' said Lizzie.

'I got mine,' added Broady.

'Me too,' said Jay, taking a seat at the table and pulling the pizza box towards him. 'Goes everywhere with me.'

'But you never go anywhere,' said Lizzie with a giggle.

Ella could see how important Jay's friendship had become to Lizzie.

'There's always a first time,' Jay said, clearly excited at the prospect of going abroad. Then, in a more sombre tone, he added, 'But as soon as we book the flights, Harris or Kline's people will go to the airport.'

'Yeah,' said Ella. 'It's not doable.' She looked at Broady for confirmation.

Broady glanced out of the huge window at the lights of the capital, then turned to Jay. 'What if we could bury that information?'

Jay's head tilted to the side. 'What do you mean?'

'What if we booked a whole lot of flights to different places, from different airports?'

Jay rubbed his chin. 'But they'd know from the manifest which one we boarded; they'd be waiting for us at the other end.'

Ella began pacing again. 'Could you hack in, change the

manifest, make it look like we got on another flight?' She stopped. 'Even take us off the one we do board?'

Jay stared at her, his mouth falling open. 'Do you know how illegal that is?'

She stopped. 'Could you do it?'

He ran his hands through his hair and took a deep breath before replying. 'I can't see why not.' He paused. 'The misdirect would have to be a long haul, so we've already arrived before they realise we're not on the other flight.'

'Los Angeles?' suggested Lizzie.

'Not a good idea, too much co-operation with UK while we're in the air.'

Ella's eyes fixed on him. 'China?'

Broady dipped his head. 'Yeah, China, that could work.'

Ella pointed a finger at him. 'It's probably what they'd expect.'

Jay had already opened up the laptop.

'You going online?' asked Ella.

Jay looked up at her. 'Yeah, but I'll use the free Wi-Fi from Costa.'

She wasn't convinced.

'It's a couple of blocks away, the reception's so good up here.'

Realising time was of the essence, she agreed. 'How do we get there?'

Lizzie's eyes met Broady's, her eyes suddenly wide with excitement.

Broady winked at her.

'The airport is called Sirnak,' said Jay, tapping away on the keys. 'We'd have to change at Istanbul and get an internal flight.'

'Too risky,' said Broady, leaning over the table. 'Leaves a trail and they'd catch us on the internal.'

Ella agreed.

'We could take a bus from Istanbul?' Jay suggested, putting a finger on the screen. 'But look, it takes twenty-three hours.'

'Better bring a book,' said Broady, deadpan.

Ella let out a giggle, releasing some of the nervous tension.

'There's a flight from Gatwick at 8.40 a.m.,' said Jay. His fingers danced over the keys. 'There's an earlier flight to Beijing from Heathrow.'

'OK, book those after you've put us on a load of others, from different airports.'

'I don't want to sound negative,' said Jay. 'But won't Harris just put a block out on us travelling?'

'Yeah,' said Broady with a long face. 'It's called red-flagging.'

Ella's shoulders slumped a little. 'We just have to hope she'd rather follow us.'

'Right then,' Jay replied. 'Give me your passports. He scratched his head. 'I've also got to get visas for Turkey online, which might not come through in time.' His eyes narrowed into a squint. 'And you know you're going to have to pay for all the flights?'

'Just do it,' she replied, rolling her eyes towards the ceiling. She rummaged around in her bag, took out a card and dropped it on the table. 'There's a twenty-grand limit on that.'

'Think of the air miles,' said Broady.

This time she didn't laugh.

Chapter Seventy-Two

In Jim's flat, the door buzzer sounded, then twice more.

Jim already had his coat on and was brushing some fluff off his threads in the hall mirror. 'Hang on, hang on.' He turned the handle. 'Forgotten something?'

The door came flying open, knocking him back.

Two men in black marched in. One began searching the apartment, the second, larger man kicked the door shut behind him and pulled Jim into the lounge, throwing him onto the floor. 'Where are they?' he said in a Continental accent.

'Who?' Jim replied, lifting his torso up onto his elbows.

The searcher came back in and said something in a foreign language.

Acknowledging the signal, the big man kneeled down beside Jim and punched him hard in the face. 'Where are they?'

'Who?' Jim spluttered, his voice shaking with terror.

Another punch.

'We know they were here.'

Jim tried to get up.

The man punched him again, the force putting him on his back. Blood oozed from his mouth.

Where did they go?'

Jim moved his head from side to side in a panicked flurry. 'I don't know anything.'

The attacker took something from his pocket. It clicked – a flick knife coming out of its sheath. He held it under Jim's chin, piercing the skin.

The man sneered. 'One last chance.'

'OK, OK,' Jim replied. 'They said they were going north, Edinburgh.'

The man seemed unsure of the admission. 'Why?'

Jim could hardly get his words out, a mixture of fear and the blood filling his mouth. 'That's all they said, I swear blind.'

Jim's captor turned to his associate, who gave an order.

Slowly, the stranger pushed the point of the knife up through Jim's jaw.

His mouth opened wide, in a silent scream. The man pulled the knife back out and plunged it into Jim's neck. Blood spurted in an arc across the room, almost spraying the man in charge who said something indicating his displeasure at the carelessness.

There was one last gasp from the dying man.

His killer pulled out the blooded blade and wiped both sides clean on Jim's coat.

Chapter Seventy-Three

D awn was breaking.

'Time to go.' Ella gave Jay's shoulder a gentle shake. He'd fallen asleep at the table, his head nestled in folded arms. He raised his head then slowly sat up, sitting back in the chair and rubbing his eyes.

'All done?' asked Ella.

'Yeah,' came the groggy reply. 'Had to switch airlines for the China flight.' He yawned. 'Couldn't hack into the manifest with the bigger ones.'

Ella acknowledged the change of plan. 'The others are nearly ready; you'd better get your stuff together.'

Within minutes they were all packed and, after one final sweep, they left the apartment. 'Hang on,' said Ella, walking towards the stairwell. 'Just going to leave Jim's keys.'

'Wait,' said Broady, firmly. 'We stay together.'

They all followed her up the stairs.

Ella put her bag down and inserted the key in the lock while the others waited outside on the landing, taking in the view. It was a clear day and the remnants of a light mist was lifting off the Thames unveiling the bridges.

Ella walked through the hall towards the kitchen. She stopped when she saw the splashes of red in her path. Her heart beat faster. She looked right.

She screamed.

Broady came rushing in.

Ella's whole body shook as she stood rooted to the spot.

Broady held out his hand to stop the others coming in. He moved across to where Jim's body was lying, dried blood everywhere, and crouched down to take a pulse. It was pointless, he was long dead. He made the sign of the cross then turned towards Ella. She didn't need confirmation – Broady's face said it all.

Vivid flashbacks of finding her husband's body hanging from the chandelier… Ella let out a deep moan. 'No.'

Despite Broady's order, the others came in.

On seeing the corpse, Lizzie's mouth opened in horror, but no sound came out.

Jay grabbed hold of Ella, whose legs were giving way.

Broady stood up. 'We need to go. There's nothing we can do for him.'

No one responded.

Broady went back to Ella and held her face gently in both hands. 'I'm so sorry.'

Ella's eyes could hardly focus.

'We have to leave – now,' said Broady.

Ella stared off into the middle distance. 'My fault,' she gasped. 'Always my fault.'

'No,' said Broady, gripping her face even tighter.

She didn't register.

'Kline's people did this, not you.' For once Broady's anxiety was obvious.

Glimpsing the horror on Lizzie's face caused Ella to gather herself.

'Bring the bags in and shut the door,' he shouted at Jay who immediately obeyed.

Ella and Broady lowered Lizzie onto the sofa. He bent down in front of her, blocking the view of Jim's lifeless body. He called out to Jay, 'Get something to cover him up, will you.'

Ella looked up to see Jay wipe the tears from his eyes and head towards the bedroom. He came back with a sheet and carefully covered the body. Then he went over to Lizzie and wrapped his arms around her.

Ella shook her head in slow motion. 'Why did we come here?'

'He wanted to help,' Broady implored her, taking hold of her hand. 'He didn't give us away.' He squeezed it tighter. 'A real hero.'

Her mouth formed into a grimace. 'Bastards.'

'You said it,' Broady replied. 'Don't let this be for nothing.'

Ella felt her heart breaking all over again.

The sun was rising and found its way between the skyscrapers, casting incongruous shafts of light on the windows.

Motionless and without a sound, they remained huddled around the sofa. Suddenly, there was a noise – they all jumped.

Music – Vivaldi's *Four Seasons*.

It was coming from Jim.

They all stared at the figure under the sheet.

'What is it?' said Jay.

Broady went over and gently moved back the cover. 'Sounds like a ring tone.' He went through the coat pockets and pulled out a phone. 'No Caller ID,' he said, covering the body up again with his free hand.

Jay was the only one who showed any interest. 'Are you going to answer it?'

Broady held out the handset in Ella's direction.

With a listless arm she took the phone and swiped across.

'Hello?' said a woman. 'Hello, who's this?'

Ella recognised the voice. She pressed speaker. 'You're too late.'

A pause. 'Ella, is that you?'

'What do you want?' she replied, her voice devoid of emotion.

'It's Agent Harris, thank God you're OK. Stay where you are, we'll be with you in fifteen minutes.' Another pause. 'Stay on the phone, you're going to be OK.'

Ella didn't reply at first. Then, looking at Broady as she spoke. 'Meet us in Trafalgar Square in two hours, there's something we need to do first.'

Broady nodded at the misdirect.

'No, Ella, it's too dangerous, stay—'

She pressed *end call*.

Still in shock, they took the lift down and exited the building. Somehow the default tactic of keeping moving drove them on. The morning light glistened off the glass-covered buildings.

Ella walked to the front of a queue of taxis and tapped on the passenger window.

The driver closed his newspaper and wound it down. 'Where to, love?'

'My husband's a barrister, he forgot this,' she said, holding up Jim's phone. 'He's waiting outside the Old Bailey – needs it for work.'

The driver eyed the phone with disdain. 'I ain't a delivery service – could lose me licence.'

She took a wad of cash out so that he could see it. 'Two hundred?'

He raised an eyebrow. 'What if he ain't there?'

'Then keep it,' she said, putting the notes in the same hand as the phone and reaching across the inside of the cab.

He tutted. 'Go on then.' He took the money and the handset and put them in his shirt pocket.

They watched him leave then jumped in the cab behind. 'Victoria Station,' Ella said.

Chapter Seventy-Four

The train journey from Victoria to Gatwick passed without a word. Mother and daughter huddled up. Ella took comfort from the sensation of her daughter leaning against her shoulder as she tried to make sense of events. But even that and the rhythm of the train speeding along the tracks failed to soothe her nerves. She had no confidence that they would make it onto the flight without being pulled but Ella was now more determined than ever.

They got off the train and walked into the airport complex.

'Look out for earpieces,' Broady whispered as they walked through the departures hall.

The check-in queue was short; mainly lone travellers, businesspeople in suits, a few in traditional Islamic dress. One man, standing a few passengers in front, wearing a beige salwar kameez, gazed around aimlessly then smiled at Broady.

Ella noticed it. Was he just being friendly? It was impossible to tell.

'Passports?' asked the young lady behind the desk with a

scarf around her neck, the knot pushed off to one side. She only half looked up as Ella plonked them down.

'Any baggage to check-in?'

'Hand luggage only,' came Ella's flat reply.

The woman gave Ella a second glance.

Conscious that her face was drawn and her eyes puffed up, Ella forced a smile which seemed to placate the woman. She handed over the boarding cards. 'Have a nice flight.'

Stifling a sigh of relief, Ella took the cards and they followed the sign for departures. One more hurdle. They joined the queue for the security check.

Broady had taken off his bandage to lessen the chances of his injury being felt in the body search. Ella had made sure his t-shirt was tucked in and his top pulled down. 'I'll go last,' he murmured to the others.

Ella grabbed a tray and began emptying her pockets whilst her companions kept their heads down. Ella went through without a problem and waited for her tray to arrive. Lizzie and Jay did the same, slowly putting belts and shoes back while watching Broady.

A man holding an electric wand waved him to one side. 'Need to do a quick search.'

Without a flicker of emotion, Broady took a couple of paces towards him and held out his arms.

The security guy ran his hands along Broady's limbs and finished with a quick brush of his chest. 'That's fine, you can go.'

They were clear. Without celebration they went into the main hall and found a table outside Pret. Beginning to refocus on the task ahead, Ella handed Lizzie a wad of cash. 'Change this for Turkish Lira,' she said as the tannoy announced the last call for a flight.

'I'll grab some coffees,' said Broady, giving Ella an encouraging smile.

'Use cash,' she said, handing him some notes. 'Get some food as well.' She sat down next to Jay. 'Check if the visas have come through.'

'I daren't go online,' he replied. 'Could give away our position.'

Ella tutted to herself. 'Yeah, sorry, I'm still not with it.'

'That's understandable,' Jay replied, placing a hand on hers. He shifted in his seat. 'Do you think they found us because of me going on that Costa Wi-Fi?'

'What do you mean?' Ella replied, then seeing the anxiety on his face, said, 'Jim? I doubt it.' She put her free hand on his. 'I know all about blaming yourself for other people's actions.'

Jay opened his mouth to say something else but at that moment Broady came back with the coffees and he closed it again.

Lizzie joined them with the currency and announced, 'Gate's open.'

Ella took a breath. 'We won't know if the visas have come through until we land.' She looked at each of them in turn. 'Are we all sure we want to do this?'

There was no dissent.

'Right,' she said, picking up her coffee. 'Let's do it.'

They fell in behind the flow of travellers making their way towards the gates then chose a row of metal seats behind the main waiting area at their gate and scanned the other passengers for familiar faces. No one seemed to be paying them any attention; they were more interested in a toddler with a dummy in his mouth running up and down between the seats. Only the child was laughing.

Ella felt detached from the world. If only those people knew what they had been through, why they were making this journey.

A woman by the gate announced over the tannoy that the flight was ready for boarding.

They waited while the other passengers rushed to form a queue.

'Good morning, Ella.'

The voice came from behind them and made them all jump.

It was Harris with a couple of men in suits and some security people.

Ella's heart sank. There was nowhere to run. She noticed that her captor looked different, same razor-sharp creases in her trouser suit but dark circles around the eyes. She looked like someone under pressure.

Harris' expression betrayed a glimmer of satisfaction. 'I'm not as stupid as you think.'

The laughing child came running over and grabbed Harris' leg, then, after looking up and seeing Harris' frosty glare, thought better of it and waddled off to the sound of her mother gently chastising her.

'Bring them,' Harris barked at the security people, who proceeded to surround the fugitives, each taking one by the upper arm and pulling them off their seats.

Broady yanked his arm away. 'OK, OK. Where are we going to run?'

Harris nodded at the underling, who took it as a signal not to pursue physical contact. His colleagues released their grips as they marched them back towards the concourse. Travellers stopped as they passed, staring at the spectacle.

Ella tried to come up with a strategy, reminding herself she'd come through a thousand times in court when all had seemed lost. They were too close to fail now.

One of the suits entered a code on the door which led onto a corridor with interview rooms down one side.

Harris tapped a window with a wire mesh inside the glass. 'Put Blake in there.'

Ella suddenly felt clear on what to do. 'Don't tell them anything,' she shouted over her shoulder as she was shoved into the room, empty but for a small table and two chairs bolted to the floor. It was soundproof; she stood at the glass watching Harris' mouth shouting orders before she entered the room accompanied by one of the men. His chiselled features and muscular build gave Ella the impression he was military. He stood in front of the door with his arms folded and legs slightly apart.

'Sit down,' Harris said in a gruff voice, then used both hands to tuck her hair behind her ears, as if readying herself for a fight.

Ella watched her for a moment, then complied.

Harris couldn't keep still. Her eyes bored into her captive. 'Why Istanbul?'

Ella stared back at her. 'Am I under arrest?'

Harris slammed a hand down on the table. 'Just answer the question.'

'You do know about the Police and Criminal Evidence Act?' Ella replied, trying to remain cool. 'An interview must be tape recorded.' She gave a theatrical look around the room. 'I don't see any equipment?'

'We're not police,' said Harris.

'Makes no difference,' Ella replied, sounding matter of fact. 'All agencies are bound by the Act.' Seeing Harris' frustration, Ella continued. 'And I want to see my lawyer.'

'Where were you going?'

'No comment.'

A contemptuous scoff from Harris. 'Think you're pretty clever, don't you?'

Ella stared straight ahead. 'I'm not answering any questions until you to tell me the grounds for detention.'

'How about stupidity?' Harris replied. 'For getting James Hodges killed.'

The unexpected comment felt like a bullet shooting through her. Ella shot Harris a look. She wanted to scream. She had to fight to control her emotions. 'I know what you're doing.'

And what's that?' Harris replied.

Ella stared her down. 'You're trying to mess with my head, soften me up.'

Harris' tone became more assuaging. 'Why does this inquiry matter so much to you?'

Exhausted by the emotional roller-coaster of the last few days, Ella let her head drop.

Harris took a step closer. 'Why risk everything just to know?'

Ella let out a cynical laugh. She decided to just say what was in her heart, which in that moment seemed clear to her. 'Because I can never know the answer to the question that really matters to me.'

Harris took a seat. 'Which is?'

Ella looked up at her interviewer. A weary blink. 'Why did my husband kill himself?' Her eyes welled up.

Harris didn't react at first. She turned to the guard. 'Wait outside.'

His eyebrows raised. 'Ma'am?'

'Just do it.'

He hovered for a moment, then left the room, keeping a close eye through the glass.

'Look, Ella, why don't you tell us what you know.' Her tone had changed. 'Just come out of the field until this is over.' She took a pack of tissues out of her pocket and offered one.

Ella refused the offer and studied the woman sitting opposite. She could see the anxiety behind the façade. 'You have no power to stop this inquiry.'

'Your husband's death…' said Harris, tentatively.

Ella came back with a jolt.

'I can help. He had secrets,' Harris said softly.

Ella felt her heart begin to race. 'What are you talking about?'

Harris fiddled with her hands. 'He had an addiction.'

She could feel the blood rushing to her face. 'Addiction?'

Harris tilted her head sympathetically to one side. 'Yes, to opioids.'

Ella's mouth fell open. 'What, you mean heroin?'

'Yeah, and pills. There's a lot of addicts out there, hiding it from family for years, holding down jobs.'

'I do know that,' Ella snapped. 'I am a barrister.' She stopped. 'But that's impossible. I would've known.' She stood up. She went to the door and turned the handle – locked. She stood still, staring at the door. 'How do you know?'

Harris got up. 'It was by chance, investigating something else.' She came over and rested a hand on Ella's shoulder.

She brushed it off and turned around. 'Why are you telling me this?'

Harris held her gaze. 'We both need answers.'

Ella didn't respond, only moved back to the table and flopped back onto the chair. She ran a hand across the top of her head. 'I knew he dabbled at Cambridge,' she mumbled.

Harris stood next to her. 'It always leads to depression, over time.'

Ella grunted an acknowledgement. 'I would've known…' she repeated, but she knew it didn't sound convincing.

'Take a few minutes,' said Harris, sounding conciliatory. 'I'll be back.'

Ella didn't even notice her leave the room. She lost track of time, obsessing over Harris' disclosure. She'd always known there was something… just not that. It all made sense now. How could she not have seen the signs? A criminal lawyer.

Her own husband, the father of her child. She slapped her forehead. The horrible sordid truth had been staring her in the face and she'd never seen it – or maybe hadn't wanted to. Then she swung the other way. Was this just an interrogation technique? Was it even true about Tom?

Chapter Seventy-Five

Harris came back in but before she had a chance to sit down, she was distracted by someone being led past the window. Ella was just able to catch sight of one of the men in suits pushing someone along. She only caught the back of the man's head. There was something familiar about him.

Harris went back out and shouted something after them before coming back in.

'Who was that?' Ella asked.

'No one,' Harris replied, sounding agitated. 'Now, where were we?'

It was still niggling. Ella got up and moved towards the door, then stopped. 'Was that Simon Carter?'

Harris' neck went red.

'It was, wasn't it?'

No reply.

'Why've you got him?'

Ella could see Harris was avoiding eye-contact. Ella scratched her head, wheels turning. 'Has he been helping you?'

'No,' Harris replied emphatically.

Ella tried to read her face. 'You found out about Tom from Simon? He knew?'

Harris got up and went for the door handle.

Ella pulled her arm away. 'I need to know.'

Finally, a resigned dip of the head. 'They'd both been junkies since Cambridge.'

'Tom and Simon?' Ella's thoughts were whirring. It all made sense. That was the bond between them.

'Carter was being blackmailed by Kline, threatening to reveal his drug addiction. He was easy to manipulate.'

Ella felt a tide of anger rising up. 'He was leaking information about the inquiry?' She already knew the answer. 'I want to see him.'

'That won't be possible,' Harris replied, her voice cold again. 'Unless of course,' she said with a wry smile. 'You tell me what you know about Genesis.'

Ella sat back in her chair and slapped her forehead. 'You nearly got me.' She laughed. 'You *wanted* me to catch a glimpse of Carter. I've just been played. You'll have to do better than that.'

Harris' face twitched. 'It's up to you,' she replied in an obviously over-zealous attempt at sounding nonchalant.

But Ella needed answers. She was going to have to give Harris something. 'OK,' she said finally. 'It's not about power.'

Harris straightened up. 'But what about the comets?'

A wry smile crept across Ella's face. 'I thought you didn't know anything?'

Harris leaned forward. 'We know Kline believes they have an effect on some people.' She lowered her voice. 'Sometimes even before they're born.' She fell silent for a moment. 'We don't know how it's connected to what he's planning.'

341

Ella sniffed, then wiped her nose. 'Matthew was working on the same theory – Genesis.'

Harris was hanging on her every word.

'Matthew was trying to understand everything, the cycles of nature.'

Harris fidgeted in her seat, clearly impatient to hear more.

Ella sighed. 'He was trying to find the one place and point in time that unites us all.'

Harris' brow furrowed. 'And do you know what that is?'

Ella sat back. 'No.'

Harris stared at her captive. 'It's in Istanbul?'

'Maybe,' said Ella.

Harris was a picture of confusion. 'What do you mean by *unites us all*?'

Ella shrugged. 'I don't know.'

Harris put her elbows on the table. 'We need to understand this before others do.'

'No,' Ella replied, her voice firm now. 'Everyone needs to know. We are one people. Take a step back. We are stuck in cycles of conflict.'

'What do you mean?'

Ella sighed again. 'Don't you get it? We always have a choice – power or enlightenment.'

Harris looked blank.

'We need to evolve our thinking.'

Harris fired another question, 'How?'

It was Ella's turn to lean across the table, exasperated by her interviewer. 'By going back to the beginning.' It was only by explaining it to Harris that these thoughts had begun to crystallise in Ella's head, and it finally made sense.

Harris' eyes narrowed. 'How do I know you're telling the truth?'

Ella laughed. 'Then we're really not on the same page.'

She stood up. 'That's enough for now. We've helped each other, now I see Carter.'

Harris huffed. 'All right, five minutes, that's it.' She opened the door and led Ella down the corridor. Ella scanned the empty rooms for Lizzie and the others, but there was no sign. Harris stopped at the door to another interview room at the end of the corridor. Ella could see Simon sitting alone at the table, twitching. He looked so different.

'He's withdrawing,' said Harris.

Ella went in and shut the door.

Simon glanced at her then closed his eyes, his face scrunched up.

'I sometimes wondered if Tom was bisexual,' Ella began, ignoring Simon's discomfort.

He opened his eyes, then scoffed. 'We had a stronger connection.'

Ella could see the sweat on his forehead. 'Why didn't he tell me?'

Simon shrugged. 'He loved you.' He rubbed a shaky hand over his face. 'He was trying to get clean when he did it.' He moved his head up and down like a dog seeking approval. 'He was always trying to get clean.'

Ella regarded Simon so differently now. 'You risked our lives... Lizzie's.'

Simon winced. He looked broken.

'Did you put Greg on to Lizzie?'

He grimaced then manically rubbed his stomach. 'I had no choice.'

'There's always a choice,' she shouted. Her mind raced ahead. 'That's why you wanted me on the inquiry, someone you knew, so you could get the inside track?'

Simon rocked backwards and forwards in his chair.

'You knew I'd go to Jim for help?' Full realisation dawned. 'You told them?'

'I'm sorry,' he whined. 'I had no idea he was so dangerous.'

'I never liked you,' she said with an icy stare. 'I just never knew why.' She gave him a last lingering look of contempt, then left him swaying in his seat.

Chapter Seventy-Six

Harris was waiting for Ella outside the door. Ella nodded her appreciation as Harris led her back to the interview room.

They retook their seats, ready for the next round.

Harris went first. 'I didn't understand half of what you were saying but...' she paused. 'But we know from the chatter we've picked up online that something is happening very soon, something we need to stop.' Her eyes were almost pleading.

Ella scrutinized Harris' face. She could read her now. See the desperation. She decided it was time to make her trade. 'I can help you with that, but you'll have to tell me everything you know.'

Harris got up and walked around the table. Ella could feel her agonising over what to do. She decided not to press, let the witness get there on her own.

Harris retook her seat. 'OK.' she sighed. 'I went to see Matthew Shepherd before he disappeared. We wanted him to become a CHIS for MI6 – it stands for covert human intelligence source.'

'I know what it stands for,' said Ella. 'So, you wanted him to give you information about Kline?'

Harris nodded. 'He said he wouldn't get involved in politics.'

'Go on,' said Ella, at last feeling she was gaining the upper hand.

'We knew Kline was recruiting very intelligent young people, using the guise of climate change activism to attract them.' She rubbed an eye in a tired gesture. 'People are afraid of the future, they're easy targets. And like Shepherd, he was working on this amazing theory, Genesis, based on historical facts. Kline is using it to seduce people into following him.'

'I know this already,' Ella replied. It was time to play her trump card. 'I know when Kline is going to strike.'

'Really?' Harris' eyes widened. 'How do you know?'

'What I don't get,' Ella replied, 'is why it matters so much to you?'

Harris took a breath. 'One of his followers is the daughter of the President of the United States.'

'What?' Ella leaned forward.

'Sarah Hart.' Harris dipped her head. 'She came over as a student at Cambridge, Kline got his claws into her and, well, the US Government are pulling their hair out. There's nothing they can do to stop her.'

Ella almost laughed. 'Her dad doesn't even believe in climate change?'

'They're very embarrassed about the whole thing and it's coming to a head.'

Ella wanted to laugh. 'Can't they put her on a plane home?'

Harris scoffed. 'The leader of the free world kidnap his adult daughter?'

'Where is she now?'

'We think she took a flight to Syria with Kline and some of his cronies.'

Ella's eyebrows went up. 'Syria. Why?'

Harris shrugged. 'No idea, but it's not far from where you were planning to go. Coincidence?'

'No,' Ella replied. 'I'm very close to understanding everything. I'll give you the date,' she said. 'But in exchange, you'd have to let us go, so that we can find the exact location.'

Harris leaned back and put her hands on her head. 'This was your endgame all along.' She snorted. 'To get me to release you.'

There was no point replying.

'I'm the one who's been played.'

Ella remained impassive.

Harris glared at her. 'I'd never get the clearance.'

'What choice do you have?' Ella shrugged. 'Who else is going to work it out in time?'

Harris sat motionless for a moment. 'Wait here,' she said, getting up and leaving the room.

In complete control, Ella let her eyes wander, meandering along the walls of the sparse room. She felt strangely calm, nothing was going to stop her.

Harris came back in carrying Ella's bag and some paperwork. Her shoulders had lost some of their tension. 'OK, but there's a condition.'

Ella had already guessed.

'I'm coming with you and I have to bring Sarah's security detail, an agent called Grant.' She put her palms together. 'I don't have a choice.'

Ella regarded her for a moment. 'It's a free country.'

Harris' eyes lit up. 'Thank you.' She opened the door

'Let's go. The others are waiting for you on the plane.' She handed Ella the sheets of paper. 'Visas.'

Ella still didn't entirely trust Harris. 'You let me think I led them to Jim, that it was my fault?'

'I'm sorry,' Harris replied with no sincerity. 'We've both got jobs to do.' She fiddled with the buttons on her jacket. 'So when's it happening?'

Ella took her bag and walked out. 'The night of the 31st of March.'

'That's tomorrow night!'

Chapter Seventy-Seven

An air hostess led Ella down the aisle passed all the scowling passengers in their seats, who must have assumed she was the reason for the delayed departure.

She saw Lizzie first, in an aisle seat next to Jay.

'Mum!'

She bent down and hugged her daughter.

The stewardess stuffed Ella's bag into the overhead locker and guided her into a seat on the other side of the walkway, next to Broady. 'We've got company,' said Ella, causing the others to look down the aisle. Harris and Grant came past and headed to the back of the plane where they took their seats. Ella noticed Harris was now wearing a brand-new pair of black trainers that looked odd with the rest of her outfit. 'I did a deal,' said Ella.

'I don't know how you did it,' he whispered in her ear. 'But I'm impressed.'

Ella buckled up and gave Broady's arm an appreciative rub.

'Mum,' said Lizzie, leaning across the aisle. 'I've seen that guy before. He was at one of Kline's meetings, and watching the farm.'

'He's the bodyguard of Sarah Hart.'

'The President's daughter?' said Broady, making a face.

Ella nodded. 'She's gone to Syria with Kline.'

'Syria?' repeated Broady.

'She's at Cambridge,' said Lizzie, realisation spreading across her face. 'I knew I recognised her.'

'Jesus,' said Jay leaning into the conversation. 'Not her father's daughter then?'

Ella didn't have the energy for any more questions. She let her body fall back into the seat. The plane began to reverse off the stand and out onto the apron.

'You OK?' asked Lizzie, studying her mother.

'I'm fine, why?' she replied, without bothering to move.

'You seem different,' Lizzie replied, examining every inch of Ella's face. 'You seem… lighter, like a weight's been lifted.'

Ella reached across the open space and cupped Lizzie's face in her hand, then mouthed, 'I love you.' She sat back in her seat and closed her eyes; sleep came easily.

When she woke, the plane was in the air. She checked her watch and let out a yawn. 'How long was I out?' She rubbed her eyes.

'Couple of hours,' said Broady, glancing up from his pocket-sized book. 'Check him out,' he said, flicking his head towards Jay whose face was pressed against his window. He turned to share something with Lizzie, giggling like an excited school kid. 'He's been like that since we took off.'

Ella laughed. 'What are you reading?'

Broady closed the cover.

'The Bible?' Ella asked. 'Where did you get that?'

'It's mine,' Broady replied. He ran a hand across the cover. 'Helped me through some tough times.' He opened it up again. 'I've been reading Genesis,' he said. 'I guess I'm kind of seeing it for the first time.' He put a finger on the page and began to read aloud in his Arizona twang. '*Then the Lord saw the wickedness of man was great on the earth, and that every intent of the thoughts of his heart was only evil continually.*'

'Sends a shiver down the spine,' said Ella.

'Yeah,' Broady replied, glancing at her with a quizzical expression. 'God could have sent that comet, right? There's nothing in Matthew's theory that says he didn't?'

Ella's forehead wrinkled up. She could see her opinion mattered to him. 'I suppose Matthew would've said there could only be one god who sent the floods. 'She paused. 'Some call him *God*, some call him *Allah*. Some call him nature.' Her brow relaxed. 'I think his point might've been that there are too many ways of saying the same thing. Fighting over differences that will only divide us. That's why he wanted to find this single point from where it all began.'

At first, Broady appeared satisfied with the answer. 'But we know others must have survived the floods, right? Take the aborigines, they go back before Noah. And the tribes in the Himalayas must have survived that high up? And to pass on the Yeti story?'

'I agree,' said Ella letting her voice raise into a passionate whisper. 'But the fertile crescent is where farming began, we know that's where corn was first cultivated and where a worldwide religion eventually took hold. This is where modern civilisation begins.' She paused. 'Our cycle.' It felt strange saying that word, as if it implied an acceptance that she believed it. She gave Broady an awkward smile. 'Then the religion kept splitting. Chan would say forming new tributaries, wouldn't he?'

He held her gaze for a moment, then ran his finger down

the page. '*Make yourself an ark of gopher wood: you shall make the ark with rooms and shall cover it inside and out with pitch.*' He looked at her again. 'If that part is accurate it's got to be dust now.'

'Keep reading,' said Ella unsure if it was because she liked the sound of his voice.

'*The water prevailed upon the earth one hundred and fifty days.* Hey, check this out: *In the seventh month on the seventeenth day of the month, the ark rested on the mountains of Ararat.* Chan was right.' Broady tapped the verse with a digit. 'My dad gave me this bible when I was a kid. It's the only one I've ever read.' He rubbed his chin. 'Why do we all think Noah landed on Mount Ararat?'

'Don't beat yourself up,' Ella mocked. 'You're still a good Christian.'

Broady went to strike Ella with it in mock anger just as a stewardess came past and glowered at him.

'What about after the flood?' Ella asked. 'Did Noah build anything else?'

'No,' Broady turned over a couple of pages. 'Wait a minute,' he said, spotting another passage. 'After the waters have receded, Genesis 8, verse 20: *Then Noah built an altar to the Lord and took of every clean animal and of every clean bird and offered burnt offerings on the altar.*'

'An altar?' said Ella, leaning into Broady's shoulder to see the text for herself. 'Made of what?'

He read on. 'Doesn't say.' He seemed troubled. 'Beats me, but I never noticed that verse before.'

'We remember what's important to us at the time,' said Ella.

'Guess so,' he replied, half to himself, glancing out of the window at the cloud-bed below. 'The world's first altar.' He gave Ella a look, missing his customary mischievous humour. 'Is that what we're trying to find?'

That was one question that Ella didn't have the answer to.

Chapter Seventy-Eight

The guy on passport control hardly gave them a second glance. Within minutes they were in the arrivals hall, waiting for Harris. A large woman dressed in black, only her eyes visible through the slit in her Niqab, stopped and stared at a large flat-screen high up on a wall, pumping out news. She started to flick some beads around her hand, backwards and forwards. Ella met her anxious eyes, then followed them towards the screen. A moving band at the bottom in alternating Arabic and English read:

US President's daughter kidnapped.

Harris and Grant joined them and immediately turned on their phones which started pinging.

Kline appeared onscreen surrounded by microphones. He looked stressed, lacking his usual confidence. He began recounting how armed men had raided the house they were staying in and threatened them before taking Sarah.

More people of all nationalities and dress gathered in front of the television, speaking to each other in hushed tones.

'Did they say who they were?' asked one reporter.

Kline was trying to back away from the journalists, all jostling for position. 'I recognised the language as Farsi. They were Iranian. Kept saying death to the United States.'

'My god. This could start a war,' said Broady without taking his eyes off the screen.

The reporter battled to keep the mic under Kline's chin. 'Didn't you think it was dangerous to go somewhere as dangerous as Aleppo with someone of her profile?'

'We came here to talk about climate change,' he said with his more familiar pomposity. 'No region is outside that dialogue.' His supporters frantically tried to clear a path. 'Sarah was a very brave young woman.'

Harris and Grant had moved off to make phone calls.

Ella kept an eye on Harris, watching her neck go red as she protested into her phone. 'As I said, I think that's a mistake, sir.' She moved backwards and forwards, rubbing her forehead. 'We should stay with Blake.' There was another pause then a reluctant, 'But—' She glanced over at Ella. 'Yes, sir.' The call ended and, after a quick conflab with Grant who had finished his own call, she rejoined Ella.

A lone reporter was now doing an anxious piece to camera. 'Iran has denied responsibility but this could push the already fragile peace between Iran and the USA to breaking point.'

'We've been ordered to go to Aleppo to help look for Sarah,' said Harris through gritted teeth. 'This doesn't feel right.'

'What do you mean?' said Ella, leading them to some clear space in the hall. 'You think Kline is lying?'

Harris checked her phone again. 'Something's happening tomorrow night, that's what we should be focusing on.'

'And Kline is a snake,' said Grant.

'It talks,' said Broady with a grunt.

Grant shot his fellow countryman a look.

Harris faced Ella, her expression gravely serious. 'Kline wants you dead because he thinks you might know what's going to happen.' She put a hand on Ella's arm. 'Please tell me where you're going?' Then, more gently. 'In case something happens to you.'

Ella felt the hairs on her neck stand up. She glanced at Broady who blinked. 'Cizre, on the Syrian border.'

'That's where we should be going too,' said Harris. 'Why Cizre?'

Ella didn't reply at first, realising how crazy it would sound. 'We think it's got something to do with Noah.'

Harris wasn't laughing. 'Noah? From the Bible?'

Ella nodded.

Harris seemed to be studying Ella, as if in awe. 'Well, you've got my number?' She patted the barrister's arm and nodded at the others. 'Be careful.'

'Yeah,' said Grant 'If we know you're here, I reckon Kline does.'

Harris shot him a look.

Ella waited for an explanation.

Harris sighed. 'He thinks we've got a leak.'

Ella rolled her eyes. 'To Kline?'

Harris held up her arms. 'The reach of his network keeps surprising us.'

A swathe of noisy European teenagers wearing matching tracksuits and holding tennis rackets distracted them for a moment.

Ella waited for further explanation but all she got from Harris was an apologetic, 'Good luck,' before the agent and her companion left them standing in the hall.

Chapter Seventy-Nine

As soon as they stepped outside, the heat engulfed them. Ella took off her top layer, wishing Harris was still with them.

From nowhere, groups of men in leather sandals descended on them offering taxis. 'Come, come,' one man with a beer belly and moustache kept saying.

Another man butted in. 'Yes, yes, taxi, please, yes, come, where you go?' They decided to follow him and dropped the luggage into an open boot.

'Not this taxi,' shouted some men in sunglasses and short sleeved shirts. 'Over here.'

They ignored the requests and piled into the cab.

A van pulled into the drop off bay at speed. A load of young, Middle Eastern looking young men and women jumped out of the back, two at a time, then spread out.

'Kline's people?' said Broady, flicking his head towards them.

A young Arabic man got into the driver's seat of the cab. 'Where you go?' he said into the rear-view mirror.

'Esenler Otogari,' said Jay, in a bad Turkish accent.

'Eh?' the man replied.

They could see a few more people jump out of the van and march towards the taxi rank.

'Bus station,' said Jay with more urgency. 'Esenler Otogari.'

'Otogar!' the driver repeated, then laughed. He pulled out of the rank just as the searchers reached the line of parked taxis and bent down to peer inside.

'Looks like we got them on our tail already,' said Broady.

'Yeah,' Ella replied willing the traffic would move a little faster. The constant beeping of horns made it hard to think.

The taxi honked its way across Istanbul to the main bus station, where they forced their way through the crowds to what looked like a ticket office. The place was so rammed people were sitting on the floor, eating food off newspapers laid out neatly on the ground.

After some miming by Jay, they managed to get four return tickets to Cizre on a bus leaving in twenty minutes. They went in search of their coach amongst the hundreds that were parked up.

'This is it,' said Jay. 'Cizre?' he asked the driver, dressed in a clean white shirt through the open door.

He nodded. They climbed on and up the steps. Their seats were in front of each other, two and two.

'They've got sockets,' said Jay.

'Yeah, not the dust cart I was expecting,' said Broady.

'Might as well get comfortable,' said Ella. 'If it's a twenty-three-hour drive.'

Jay plugged in his laptop and hacked into the hotspot of an unsuspecting passenger's iPhone.

Ella leaned forward so that she could speak to Jay between the seats. 'It would be nice if we had somewhere to go other than just "Cizre".'

'I know, I know,' Jay replied going back online, scrolling

and searching everything on Noah and his Ark. 'There's loads,' he said to Lizzie, after clicking on a few links and speed-reading. 'Competing theories on places all over the Middle East.'

'But why Cizre?' she asked, looking at the screen.

The coach stopped and started, making its way down through the traffic towards the crossing. Skirting the coast, they could see the sun's rays sparkling on the Sea of Marmaris off to their right. The water was an inviting, deep blue. Serenaded by car horns, the coach made its way onto the long bridge over the Phosphorous towards the Asian side.

'Chan said Matthew was basing it on the ancient Islamic and old Hebrew texts which say Mount Judi was the landing site. The Turks call it Chudi Dagi.' He clicked on an article. 'But there are even arguments about which peak is Chudi Dagi.'

'So, it's like looking for a needle in a haystack?' said Lizzie.

Broady and Ella leaned forward to listen to the discussion. Their heads touched momentarily as they looked between the seats at the screen.

'We can rule out Mount Ararat though,' said Jay, as he read on. 'It's volcanic, the mountain is too new.'

'Some people seem to go for this place,' he said pointing to an image. 'It's called the Durunipar Site, about fifteen miles south of Ararat.'

'What's that?' asked Ella looking at the image.

A curious rock formation resembling the broken base of a huge ship protruded from the mountain top.

'It's weird, isn't it,' Jay observed. 'That's why some people say this is the place but I've just read a geological report that says it's just rocks, there are post volcanic formations like this one all over the mountain ranges.' He scrolled down. 'An

American called Ron Wyatt found it in the sixties. Reckoned it was the place. Found what he called drogue stones nearby. Massive rocks with holes in. Said they were for attaching rope to give the ark ballast or even moor the thing.'

Ella scoffed. 'Guesswork.'

'Yeah,' Jay agreed. 'People said he was wrong.'

'Anything else?'

'Lots of wood found on different mountains over the years but none of the carbon-dating goes further than about six thousand years.'

'Oh, great,' said Lizzie.

'So, Cizre sounds like as good a base as any,' said Broady. 'Matthew believed he was in the right ballpark – that's good enough for me.'

'Me too,' Jay replied. 'Most people say Mount Judi is a peak near Cizre, today people call it Qardu.'

'Hand me that laptop,' said Ella. 'I need to read everything.'

After hours of researching online, Ella spent the rest of the journey drifting in and out of sleep, worrying about everything. When her thoughts moved away from the inquiry, she found herself getting lost in the past, reconstructing her marriage. Why hadn't she seen the signs? Despite the revelation about Tom, she felt curiously liberated, somehow the guilt was lessened. She wondered whether to tell Lizzie, if she had a right to know? Whatever she decided, it could wait. She glanced over at Broady who was fast asleep. She took out her make up bag and applied some foundation then giggled at the irony. She put on some lipstick. She couldn't remember the last time she'd given a shit about how she looked.

'Guys,' said Jay gravely. 'I think I've got something.'

'Go on,' said Ella while the others began to stir.

'A twenty-five-year-old English man called Peter Walker was taken to the morgue in Cizre.'

'Dead, I assume?' Ella asked.

'Yeah but there's a bloke with exactly the same details at De Jure and he's alive. His bank account is active, buying shopping and stuff in Cambridge.'

'Could be a coincidence,' said Ella. 'What was the cause of death?'

Jay turned his body so he could see through the gap in the seats. 'Brain tumour.'

Ella shut her eyes and grimaced.

Lizzie's face screwed up. 'I don't get it.'

'Walker was in debt,' explained Jay, running a finger down a bank statement. 'Out of nowhere he paid in five grand when Matthew disappeared.'

'Matthew must've bought his passport off him,' said Broady, sitting up. 'That's how he got out the country.'

'Chan was right,' said Ella. 'Matthew's dead.' The sadness in her voice triggered a silence; Ella wondered if anyone else would ever mourn his passing. 'How did he get to the morgue?' she asked.

'It's in Turkish,' Jay replied, tapping the words into google translate. 'Someone called Azade Kamandi.'

'Kurdish,' said Broady. 'Surprised there are any left.'

'Yeah,' said Jay. 'They've been coming back since the violence ended.'

'That's the thing,' said Broady. 'People haven't been visiting Cizre for a long time.' Ella waited for him to expand. 'The war in Syria which was just over the border, and the fighting in Cizre itself between the Kurdish P.K.K. and the Turkish Government. The whole area was a war zone for a long time.'

Jay read off the screen. 'Yeah, it's only settled down in the last couple of years.'

'Is there an address for this man?' Ella asked.

Jay used the computer to translate the rest of the entry. 'Yes! Looks like it's in the Old Town. Some sort of pension.'

'Good work, Jay,' said Broady. 'We got ourselves a plan.'

Chapter Eighty

Cizre was a town in transition. Smart new office blocks next to piles of rubble left by the bombings that had plagued the ancient border town in recent years.

Grateful for fresh air after the long journey they walked across Cizre using the hand-drawn map Jay had copied from google maps. The sun was setting behind the buildings providing some protection from the heat. The smell of grilled meat made their stomachs growl.

As they walked, Ella was aware of men sitting outside in rundown cafes, smoking shisha pipes, stopping what they were doing to watch the strangers.

They found the pension half-way up a steep, cobbled alley with water trickling down a central gutter. The source was a young woman in a dust-weathered skirt and red flip-flops. She was tipping a plastic bowl full of washing. She stopped and stared at them, hypnotised for a moment, then hurried inside.

The exterior of the hostel had the feel of a low-grade option, even for budget travellers. A Turkish word in peeling black paint had been written over the old wooden door.

Broady knocked then turned to the others. 'Let's take this slowly, we don't want to scare the guy.'

Ella agreed.

The door opened. A small boy stood holding it semi-open. He couldn't have been more than nine or ten. His trousers were baggy, a variation on a salwar kameez. His traditional top was a dirty cream. His dark eyes viewed Broady with suspicion.

'You have rooms?' Broady asked touching his own chest and then waving towards the others. 'For tourists?'

'Tourist?' said the boy, as if cottoning on to a familiar word.

'Yeah, tourists,' Broady repeated, this time with a smile.

The boy closed the door leaving them in the alley to ponder their next move.

A few moments later the door opened again. This time a man stood in the boy's place. He said something in Turkish?

Broady tilted his head apologetically and held out his open palms.

The boy appeared from behind the man that had to be his father, judging by the piercing eyes they shared. 'He say we only have one room.' Watching Broady's face, the boy added, 'Four can sleep.'

'Thank you,' Broady replied.

They followed the pair into the dingy dwelling with damp rendered walls revealing patches of exposed brick. The man pushed open a makeshift, plywood door and stood at the entrance waiting for the visitors to accept the arrangement.

The room contained a single bed with a thin mattress and a small table with no chair under a window without glass, just an old wooden shutter.

'This will do just fine,' said Broady, signalling his appreciation with a smile.

The boy squeezed between the two men struggling under

363

the weight of a pile of blankets, which he placed lovingly on the bed.

'Thank you,' said Lizzie with her sweetest smile. 'What's your name?'

'Olan.' He blushed then ran out, only to return a couple of minutes later dragging another wafer-thin mattress.

Jay helped him arrange it against the opposite wall.

'We need to ask them about Matthew before tonight,' he said to Broady, who looked shattered from the journey. 'Time's running out.'

'Don't want to spook them,' Ella replied, arranging one of the blankets. 'Give it a few minutes then find out what we can and get going.'

The walls were covered in graffiti, all indecipherable. Marks left by travelling Turks.

Ella noticed a couple of brown cockroaches race across the floor.

There was a tap on the open door. Olan beckoned them. 'Come, come…'

They followed him down a dingy passage and out into a beautiful, tiny courtyard with fig trees growing between the paving. A table had been laid with four chairs, a gaslight in the centre providing the illumination. A woman in Kurdish dress, covered apart from her face, come out carrying two plates, each with a long, grilled kebab and a perfect half ball of rice. The man came out after her with the other two plates and set them down, bending in a gesture of humility.

Mouths watering at the sight of their first hot meal in days, they attacked the food.

Olan put a heap of flat breads in the centre of the table and remained next to his dad, who said something in Turkish. 'My father, he ask why you come here?'

Broady hesitated. 'The guidebook said this is the place to come.'

Olan translated. The man spoke again.

'Not in book. This place for worker, no for tourist.'

Ella stopped eating and eyeballed the man. 'Azade kamandi?'

Olan immediately looked at his father, who suddenly looked afraid: 'Yes.'

There was no point lying. 'Our friend came here.'

More translation. 'Friend?'

'Peter Walker?'

Olan's head dropped. 'Dead,' he said quietly.

'I know,' Ella replied softly.

The father gave him some kind of order, as a result of which the boy ran out of the courtyard.

The woman came out with four glasses of black tea on a wooden tray. She set them carefully on the table.

Olan came back with a knapsack over his shoulder. He put it down at Ella's feet.

Ella glanced at the others, wide-eyed. Could it be Matthew's? She bent down and opened the zip, then respect-fully went through the contents. Just clothes, and a wallet in a side pocket containing Turkish Lira.

The man blurted something to his son, sounding sharper than before.

Olan began to cry, then whispered, 'I take one hundred Lira.'

Lizzie reached out and took his hand. 'That's OK,' she said with a sympathetic smile.

'Did he have a phone or computer?' asked Jay.

Olan shook his head again and pointed to the rucksack.

'Just this?' Jay clarified.

He dipped his head.

'Do you know why he was here?' Ella asked Olan in her softest voice.

More discussion between father and son. 'Like all

foreigner – Noah.' Olan became more animated. 'He go mountain every day.' He pointed up towards the stars.

Ella glanced at Broady. 'Did he find what he was looking for?'

Olan gave a shake of the head. 'He sick. Want leave but no strong.'

Ella had to fight every instinct to turn it into a breakneck cross-examination. 'Did he say where he was going?'

Olan tilted his head, as if trying to recall. 'Urfa. He say go Urfa.'

'Go Urfa?' Ella repeated loudly, her voice failing to hide the importance of his reply.

Olan nodded then reached out for his father's hand, seemingly unsettled by Ella's strong reaction.

Lizzie took over, asking softly. 'What's Urfa?'

Azade smiled at the word. 'Sanliurfa.' He said something to his son who repeated in English, 'Ancient city. It mean: glorious Urfa.'

'How far?' asked Broady.

Olan spoke to his father again in Turkish. 'Three, four hundred kilometre.' He struggled with the next word. 'W – West.'

'He'd been looking in the wrong place,' exclaimed Ella. 'Everyone has.'

Jay was already getting up. 'We need a taxi, Azade.'

'Too far for taxi,' said Olan, translating for his father. 'You wait, my cousin have car.' He gave the boy an order who ran out.

'Let's grab our stuff,' said Broady, getting up. The sudden exertion caused another twinge. He touched his waist.

'You OK?' said Ella.

'I'm good,' he replied, giving her a quick, tense smile.

They went back into their room and Ella stuffed Matthew's meagre possessions into her bag.

Broady reached into his kit for his pills. He popped one out of the blister pack, then, about to swallow, stopped. He analysed it on his palm. 'What the hell?'

Jay and Lizzie crowded in.

He spilt the capsule. 'It's a god damn tracker.'

'What?' said Ella.

'Stone, the Embassy guy.' Broady's face turned paler. 'He's been keeping tabs on us.' He dropped it on the floor and lifted his foot to stamp.

'Stop!' shouted Jay. He looked at Aazde, then at the boy. 'They'll come here.'

Broady lowered his foot to the side.

Jay picked up the device and handed it to Broady. 'Let's not make this the last place it transmits.'

Broady stared at Jay, gratitude etched onto his face. 'Don't know what I was thinking.'

Within minutes there was the sound of a car horn outside in the alley.

Ella peaked around the shutter and saw Azade's son getting out of the passenger seat of an old Škoda.

Azade stood in the doorway. 'Come, come' he said ushering them towards the hallway.

Ella met Olan coming back inside and gave him a goodbye hug.

Olan turned red.

She pushed Matthew's wallet with the Lira into his little chest.

He instinctively took a step back.

'Please,' she said forcing it on him. 'He'd want you to have it.'

He looked up at his father who gave a solemn nod.

Olan's mouth hesitated, then the corners turned upwards.

'And besides,' said Ella. 'You never know, you might've just helped to change the course of history.'

His cherubic face conveyed no understanding of the observation.

A young man in his twenties was standing outside the front door, one hand planted proudly on the bonnet as if posing for a photograph. 'Hey guys, I'm Badil, my friends call me Bad because I'm a real bad-ass.' He started laughing but no one joined in.

Lizzie and Jay shared an amused glance.

Badil was wearing jeans and a short-sleeve shirt, undone almost to the navel revealing a large medallion, and had a pair of sunglasses on his forehead, despite the sun having set. 'Let's rock and roll,' he shouted excitedly at Broady with a strong Turkish accent. 'You want to go Sanliurfa, right?' He patted the bonnet. 'Me and this baby will take you anywhere.'

Broady ignored him and loaded the bags into the boot then got into the passenger seat.

Ella took out some cash. 'How much?'

He waved her away. 'You pay me later. You decide how much. You happy, you pay me well…'

Ella was already getting into the back.

'If you not happy…' he wittered on to no one in particular. He got into the driver's seat and said to Broady, 'What's your name, man?'

'Broady,' he replied without taking his eyes off the windscreen. 'Let's go.'

'OK, man,' he replied with a dumb grin. 'Let's get the hell out of here, yes.' He started the car, the exhaust spluttering into action as they pulled away, leaving Olan and his father standing in the alley looking totally confused by the whole episode.

'Slow down at these crossroads,' said Broady on the way out of town. As they passed the junction, he threw the rest of the antibiotics out of the window.

'I wonder if Harris and Grant know about Stone,' said

Ella who was squeezed in behind the driver's seat. 'Seems like everyone wants to know what we're doing.'

Badil gave Broady a double-take. 'You must be into some crazy shit, man?'

Broady gave him a withering stare.

'Talking of shit,' said Jay. 'Hope you had one recently – there might be another tracker still inside you.'

Broady rolled his eyes. 'I'm going to take the fifth on that but you don't need to worry.'

'Hey, take the fifth, man – you from the good old US of A?'

'Sure am,' Broady replied without matching his enthusiasm.

Badil took one hand off the wheel. 'High five, man.'

In a limp, reluctant motion, Broady slapped his palm.

Seemingly getting the message, Badil drove on in silence. The traffic thinned out as the night wore on until they were alone on the highway.

'Can't you go any faster?' said Ella, looking at her watch. 'What time will we get to Sanliurfa?'

He put his foot down. 'Before sunrise,' Badil replied, checking her out in the rear-view. 'You want see where Abraham born, yes?'

Her curiosity was peaked. 'What's that?'

'Yeah, man. It's a cave below the castle, right in the middle of the city.' he replied. 'He born there, man. Pilgrim come from all over to see.'

Broady made a careful rotation of his body. 'He was a descendant of Noah, it's in Genesis.' He took the bible out of his pocket and went straight to the passage. 'Yeah, Chapter Eleven. There's a whole list of descendants of Shem, one of Noah's sons. Then Verse Twenty-Six, *Terah begot Abraham*.'

Badil went in for another high five. 'Hey, you know your shit, man.'

This time Broady left him hanging.

Ella leaned in to see for herself. 'It's not far back enough, but I suppose it's something.'

'I can take you ancient places all over my country,' said Badil, sounding deflated from Broady's rejection. 'Many, many in Turkey.'

'Abraham's cave will do fine,' said Ella.

Chapter Eighty-One

B adil hadn't said anything for a while.

Ella watched him check the rear-view mirror again.
'What's up?'

'Car behind,' he replied. 'Been there long time.' His facial expression had changed from grinning fool to one of total seriousness. 'Maybe police.' He glanced over at Broady for a reaction. 'Often they stop driver at this time.'

They all looked through the back window at the head-lights in the distance. Ella glanced at her watch: 1 a.m. 'Pull over, see if it goes by.'

Badil slowed, veering onto the side of the road, the tyres crunching on the stoney verge.

They concentrated on the lights, waiting for the beam to get bigger.

'It's stopping,' said Broady. 'Go.'

Badil immediately put the car in first and skidded off the stones, moving expertly up the gears.

The car behind appeared to speed up.

'It's getting closer,' Lizzie shouted.

Badil put his foot down even further causing the steering wheel to shake.

The car was gaining all the time, until they were almost bumper to bumper. They could see the shape of the vehicle now, a large four by four.

Ella put a hand on Broady's shoulder. 'What do we do?'

The car pulled out suddenly and then eased alongside.

The windows were tinted, but they could make out the silhouettes of several people inside, maybe three. The vehicle edged in front at an angle, forcing them off to the side.

'It's pointless,' said Broady. 'Pull over before there's a crash.'

Badil eased up on the accelerator and started gentle braking. The passengers exchanged nervous glances. They came to a stop with what they could now see was a Range Rover coming to a halt at an angle, blocking their path.

They held their breath.

Two meat heads in civvies got out of the back and stood on guard.

'They look like Americans,' said Badil. 'Not Turkish.'

A third man in a suit climbed out of the passenger seat and walked around the front, his face illuminated in the Škoda's offside headlight.

'It's Stone,' said Broady. He opened the door and got out. 'I'll handle this.' He walked around to where Stone was standing.

Ella opened her door. 'Stay here,' she said to Lizzie and Jay.

Jay made to get out but Lizzie put a hand on his shoulder and pulled him back.

Ella stood a few feet behind Broady, checking out the sinister faces of Stone's henchmen. The road was deserted. She couldn't see lights from any buildings. Only the sound of cicadas clicking on the breeze.

'Get in Broady,' said Stone with a confidence that his order would not be questioned.

Broady hesitated, turned to look at Ella, then back at Stone. 'I'm going to stick with these guys.'

Ella felt a lump in her throat.

Stone's expression changed. 'It's not a request.'

Broady didn't reply at first. Then, 'Who are you anyway? You don't talk like no Embassy guy.'

Stone's posture stiffened. 'All you need to know is I'm here on behalf of the President. Consider it a direct order.'

No one spoke.

Finally, Broady said, 'I'm not coming.' He moved slowly back towards the Škoda.

'Stand down marine,' Stone barked.

Broady kept walking backwards. 'I ain't a marine no more.'

One of the goons pulled a side arm from out of his jacket and pointed it at Broady.

Stone had a rueful expression. 'You turned Indian on me?'

Broady stopped in his tracks.

Ella saw him wince at the racist insult but he didn't rise to it. 'We're just trying to find our history, maybe even find Hart's daughter.'

'Don't be so goddamn naïve,' said Stone. 'We know what you're doing.'

Ella's curiosity overrode her instinct to stay out of it. 'Naïve?'

Stone kept his eyes on Broady. 'People don't want to hear Shepherd's crazy theories.' He sniffed, then took a handkerchief out of his pocket and wiped the sweat off his forehead. 'The birth of civilisation?' He scoffed. 'How do you think middle America would take that?'

'Take what?' said Broady, his irritation showing.

Stone gestured around him. 'That it all started in this godforsaken country. By a bunch of Arabs.'

Broady moved forward, then stopped on hearing one of the men cock his gun. 'Jesus was from the Middle East.'

'Israel,' Stone yelled. 'There's a difference. Our people think of him as white. You want to tell folks that Noah is actually the guy – that he started the whole damn thing?' Stone signalled to the other subordinate who took out his gun too. 'That we all share the same goddamn religion?'

Ella was dumbfounded. 'Seriously? Is that so bad?' she said.

'We need something to fight for,' Stone replied. 'That's what makes us American, patriots.'

'That's bullshit,' said Broady. 'Things got twisted over time, 'tis all. Humanity lost its way.'

Stone let out a cynical laugh.

'What about Sarah?' asked Ella.

Stone gave her a cold shrug. 'Better a dead martyr than a nuisance.'

'You're the leak,' said Ella. 'You're working with Kline?'

Stone gave a nonchalant smile. 'Let's just say we have some shared goals.' He waved at Broady. 'Last chance, get in.'

'And what about my friends?'

No response. Stone's silence said enough.

Ella's mouth went dry. Instinct made her look to her daughter, Lizzie's childhood flashed before her eyes. 'You don't have to do this,' she pleaded. 'Please, we're British.'

Stone was unmoved.

Broady backed into Ella, shielding her from the inevitable.

The other man pointed a gun through the window at Jay and Lizzie.

'No,' Ella screamed.

'Don't do this,' begged Jay. He pushed Lizzie towards the nearside door. 'Run.'

Frozen with fear, she didn't move.

The first guard pointed his firearm at Broady's head.

Stone nodded to his men.

This was it.

In one swift movement, Badil pulled something out from under his seat. Within seconds an AK47 was resting on the open window, pointing directly at Stone's head. 'If anyone move, you die.'

Stone's arrogant expression disappeared in a flash, surprise and fear replacing it. He swallowed hard. Awaiting orders, his men remained still.

Broady pushed Ella into the back seat and ran around to the passenger side.

'Take the wheel,' Badil shouted at Broady as he got in.

Badil let his foot off the clutch. 'Everybody down.'

Ella pushed Jay and Lizzie's heads into their laps and did the same herself. Broady steered around the Range Rover as Badil fired at the tyres. A whooshing sound confirmed he'd hit his target.

'Don't be a fool, Broady,' Stone yelled after them.

Badil speeded up then pushed the machine gun onto Broady's lap so that he could take back the wheel. A few shots ricocheted off the boot as the Škoda pulled away.

Chapter Eighty-Two

Lizzie was visibly shaking. No one spoke at first – gripped by shock.

As the Range Rover disappeared from view, Broady checked on the others. 'Everyone OK?'

Ella nodded, her face ashen. She reached across Jay to wrap her arms around Lizzie.

'I'm ashamed,' said Broady. 'My own people. I don't get it.'

'It's happening all over the world,' said Lizzie. She stared out the window at the dark shapes of fields and mountains. 'Greg said something to me about the trees in Thetford Forest being planted after the First World War. Terrible events bringing new life.' She looked gravely at the others. 'Is Kline trying to start a war?'

'A new cycle,' said Jay ominously. 'He wouldn't be the first crazy who did.'

Broady leaned back in his seat and let out a deep sigh. He looked over at Badil. 'How come you had that firearm?'

'I'm from Cizre,' he replied, as if the answer was obvious.

'You're one bad-ass,' Broady said with a faraway smile. He raised his arm and said in a sombre voice, 'Gimme five.'

Badil slapped his palm and beamed.

Ella wound down the window to help her think. She lifted her head and let her face bathe in the cool night air. It took a while for things to become clear. 'Badil, can I use your phone?'

'Sure.' He took it off the dash and handed it to her.

She took out the card Harris had given her back in Cambridge. It felt like a lifetime ago. She dialled the number.

Harris answered. 'Hello?'

'It's Ella, can you get to a city called Sanliurfa?'

'I think so,' Harris replied, 'There's nothing happening here. You all OK?'

'Some Americans just tried to kill us on the road.'

'I see,' Harris replied, sounding unsurprised. 'Do you know who they were?'

'A guy from the US Embassy – Stone.'

Harris didn't reply at first. 'Go somewhere public and wait.'

'Abraham's cave. Can you be there before daybreak?'

'I reckon.' Harris paused. 'Is that where it's happening?'

'We still don't know where or what,' Ella replied. 'Just that it's in Sanliurfa.' She ended the call.

Nobody felt like talking, even Badil seemed to have plugged into the mood.

The Škoda pressed on through the night, heading West towards the ancient city of Sanliurfa.

As they reached the outskirts Ella began to see a few buildings dotted along the roadside.

'We have to stop for gas,' said Badil. 'Think they hit the tank,' he said, touching the gauge.

Ella looked out the back and saw a line of fluid illuminated by the rear lights leaving a trail on the road.

'What was that?' she said, turning away from her window towards Badil as they passed a tiny junction.

'What?' he replied.

'That little sign? Gob something.'

'Göbekli Tepe,' said Badil. 'Ancient stones, very old.'

'What does it mean, Göbekli Tepe?' she asked.

Badil smiled and patted his stomach. 'How you say, pot-belly hill. Mean like pregnant woman.'

Ella looked back down the road towards the turning. 'So, it's on a hill?'

'On a mountain,' Badil replied. 'Pot-belly is on the top. You can see very far, but tourist only start coming now because Syria war finish.'

'Birth,' Ella said to herself. 'It's odd how it starts with a G and an O,'

'Yeah, but he said: "go Urfa," not Gob,' said Broady.

Lizzie wasn't so quick to dismiss it. 'What else do you know about the place, Badil?'

Badil sat up straighter in the seat. 'German archaeologist discover in nineties. It so big they still find more all time. Many stone circle with great carving.'

'Carvings of what?'

Badil glanced at Lizzie in the mirror. 'Every kind of animal.'

Chapter Eighty-Three

Cizre, a few weeks before

Exhausted, Matthew Shepherd stumbled over the cobbles as he made his way along the alley, the shaded walls peppered with bullet holes from past conflict. The sound of Muslim prayer echoed above him from some distant tannoy.

He stopped and gulped in air. The illness had robbed him of his youth, of precious time. A memory of his Arizona childhood flitted through his mind – lifting his head out of a book to watch his brother shooting hoops in the sand covered yard.

He grimaced, then forced himself on. He tried to focus on the figure of an elder in a white salwar kameez and black waistcoat shuffling towards him down the alley.

The old man slowed and stared at him before continuing on down the hill. Matthew knew he stood out; his skin was dark enough, but anyone could see he had African blood flowing through his veins.

He reached the pension's battered wooden doorway and made his way through the dingy, concrete hall to his room.

Graffiti in Arabic was scrawled across the cracked plaster, and the decaying shutter on the glassless window thudded against the wall with each gust of wind that whirled down from the mountain.

He pulled out a piece of paper from the pocket of his jeans and, with shaking fingers, unfolded it on the table. He picked up a protractor with a pencil attached and began to add some markings, half-heartedly swatting away the flies that buzzed around his head as he did so. He looked at the drawing, nodded, then collapsed onto the bed, making the rusty springs squeal.

'Sir, Mister?' Matthew turned his head to see the boy, Olan at the door, holding a clay pitcher in one hand and a glass in the other. He tiptoed into the room, poured out some water and put the jug on the table.

Mouth dry as dust, Matthew tried to sit up but couldn't. 'Help me pack,' he said with a delirious wave at his rucksack. 'I know where...'

Olan held out the glass. But instead of taking it, Matthew grabbed the kid's shirt and mumbled, 'Don't you see, we've all been looking in the wrong place?'

The boy didn't seem to understand. 'You must go hospital.'

'No,' he replied. 'No hospitals.' His eyelids felt heavy. 'I need to get there.' The room became a blur. 'Need to rest first.'

Olan hovered by the bedside.

Matthew opened his eyes again. 'Oor-fa.'

Olan's eyes gave the impression he understood.

Matthew raised his head and fixed his stare on the child. In a croaked whisper he urged, 'G-go...' His head fell back onto the bed.

Olan shuffled backwards out of the room.

Matthew opened his eyes. The room was pitch black but for a shaft of moonlight falling through the open shutter onto the table. The wind cooled his face, drying the beads of sweat on his forehead.

He felt a presence in the room. He turned his head to the side, straining to see. There was a shadow, moving. It was above him now, illuminated in the starlight – the figure of a hooded man, in traditional dress, a beard and moustache covering most of his face. The man crouched down beside the bed.

'You?' said Matthew.

Kline gave a fox-like smile. 'We've been watching. You know where it is, don't you?'

Matthew tried to get up but his body wouldn't respond.

The intruder's mouth was at his ear. 'You're dying, don't waste that knowledge – tell me.'

Matthew turned his head away.

'Let me be the one to finish it,' Kline whispered.

'No,' Matthew hissed back. 'You'll never see its true value.'

Kline sneered. He stood up and swept a hand over the books and manuscripts on the table. He picked up the protractor, examining it in the half-light. And then he saw the piece of paper. He grinned. 'You wrote it down for me?' He picked it up, holding it in the light. 'Of course! Göbekli Tepe.' He pointed through the window and waved the scrap of paper in front of Matthew's face. 'I had a hunch it wasn't in Cizre.' He folded up the paper and put it in his pocket. 'Oh well, I don't need you anymore,' he said in a mock apology. 'Looks like destiny is mine.'

The man bent down towards Matthew, took a pillow off

the bed and placed it gently over Matthew's head. He pressed down harder, smothering his face.

Already close to death, Matthew's lungs made one last stand, allowing his mind a final dance.

And then, as he felt his life slipping away, he prayed for a messiah.

Chapter Eighty-Four

The Škoda limped into a petrol station with a dimly lit, dusty forecourt with one lone pump. Badil went straight to the back of the vehicle and inspected the damage.

Ella and Broady got out and stretched their legs. Lizzie and Jay followed, taking it in turns to swig from a bottle of water.

Two men were sitting at a table with rusty metal legs outside a small kiosk. The attendant in a dirty boiler suit got up and sauntered over, engaging Badil in conversation.

The other, a studious-looking young man with a leather briefcase on the ground beside him, was just visible under a naked light bulb with flies orbiting around it.

Broady pointed up at the sky. 'Can you see the comet?'

Ella looked up at the stars. It was beautiful, a crystal clear night, the comet above the horizon to the north, its tail in a wonderful cascade.

'It looks like a broom,' said Lizzie.

'They used to call them broom stars,' said Broady.

'A new broom sweeps clean,' said a voice from the direction of the table.

Ella wandered over, noticing a row of pens in his shirt pocket. 'Hello?'

'Ah,' he replied. 'English?'

'Yes.'

'Whereabouts?'

'Cambridge,' Ella answered.

The man seemed totally out of place in the dilapidated surroundings. 'Cambridge?' he repeated, eyes widening at the name.

'Yes, we're historians, just on our way home,' Ella lied, unsure why.

He gazed at the rest of the odd-looking party. 'Historians?'

'Yes,' Ella replied.

The young man was clearly impressed. 'I'm a student archaeologist from Istanbul, working at Göbekli Tepe. Just waiting for my lift.' He pointed across the road into the darkness. 'I say I like to work before the sun gets too hot, but the truth is I just can't stay away.' He gave her a coy smile. 'Please,' he said, waving at the three-legged chair on which the attendant had been sitting. 'What is your specialism, may I ask?'

'Ancient history, Stonehenge,' Ella replied.

'Ah!' the man exclaimed. 'Well, I'm afraid Göbekli Tepe is much older,' he said, puffing out his chest.

Lizzie and Jay shared a glance and came over, followed by Broady.

Ella noted their expressions which she took as a warning to be careful with strangers. 'Really?' she said to the student. 'How much older?'

'Seven thousand years,' he announced with pride and acknowledging the growing audience. 'This site has been dated to 9500 BC.'

Ella was thrown. 'How do you know?'

'Carbon dating,' he replied in a tone that verged on condescension.

Ella frowned. 'How come I've never heard of it?'

The man laughed. 'Maybe the world is not yet ready for a rewriting of history.'

'Yes, but…' Ella was tongue-tied by the revelation.

'What she means,' said Lizzie, 'is why isn't the world talking about this place?'

'It's not easy to change the way we've always thought about our history,' the man replied with a smile.

Ella understood. 'It changes everything.'

Chapter Eighty-Five

From the outside it looked just like any old lorry, with photos of foodstuffs and some Turkish livery on the side. Twelve men and women of all ethnicities were sitting cross-legged against the sides of the enclosed section at the back on a steel floor. All were in traditional Islamic dress and head-scarves like a group of ancient Mujahideen fighters. Some had machine guns in their laps and one was holding a digital camera.

Sarah Hart lay curled up in the corner with hands and legs tied together and a gag in her mouth. Her eyes were wide with terror.

Once the vehicle stopped, David Kline stood up and lifted his scarf away from his bearded face. He bestowed an intimate smile on each of his disciples, one by one, in the way only a leader can. 'You, the chosen ones,' he began, 'have shown great loyalty to me and to the cause. You had the courage to see things as they really are, the death of our planet. For decades world leaders had the chance to save us, but they stood by, watching while the Amazon burns, our oceans drown in plastic and our air chokes on carbon dioxide.

Tonight, we will finish this destructive cycle in the very place it all began. And we will begin anew.' He walked amongst them touching their covered heads. 'I promised you enlightenment. I promised you we would show our power – and now you shall see it with your own eyes.'

The fighters twitched with excitement, hanging on Kline's every word.

'As Plato tells us, the world was destroyed by a great event eleven thousand five hundred years ago. Atlantis was lost as the sea levels rose. A man called Noah knew the comet was coming and so he built an ark. He filled it with every animal he could find.' Kline screwed his hand into a fist. 'He wanted to preserve life, just as we do.' Kline scanned the expectant faces. 'The ark landed in the mountains of Ararat at a place called Göbekli Tepe. Using all his knowledge from the old world Noah built a temple to give thanks. Then, just as the Bible tells us: *Noah built an altar to the Lord and, taking some of the clean animals and clean birds, he sacrificed burnt offerings on it.*' Kline crouched down on one knee. 'But it was more than just a temple, it was an observatory, a warning through time, telling us when the cycle would end.'

'Have you found it, David?' asked a disciple unable to contain his excitement.

Kline smiled. 'They built more and more great stone circles to commemorate comets as they passed and then a thousand years after Noah had landed, they carefully buried the whole site under a million stones, perfectly preserving it for us tonight.' He banged his fist on the side of the lorry at the driver's end. 'Come, it is time.'

The driver, similarly dressed, got down from the cab, walked around the vehicle and unlocked the rear doors.

'Bring her,' said Kline stepping down into a small deserted mountain-top car park with an empty attendant's hut in the corner. The starry sky covered them like a great dome. The distant lights of Sanliurfa could be seen far below them. The disciples followed Kline towards the path to the summit, some holding torches. A large man carried Sarah in his arms. All seemed oblivious to her distress and muffled protests.

'Already it's about money,' said Kline waving an arm at a brand-new visitor's centre, illuminated by a few uplights in a flower bed. 'Thirty years they've been excavating this site.' He turned to his followers and walked backwards a few paces. 'They've even carbon-dated the first stone circle to eleven thousand five hundred years ago and still they don't know what they've got.' He laughed. 'Staring them in the face.'

They climbed over a row of turnstiles and carried on up a newly laid brick path to the top, passing a half-constructed roof over some excavations to their left until they reached the main site. A curved roof on stilts covered an open air, circular walkway at the top of a wooden, slatted stairway. The walkway surrounded a large, deep pit. 'Look,' said Kline leaning over the balustrade. His followers shone their torches into the pit lighting up a number of stone circles, each slab metres high but much thinner than the boulders at Stone-henge, and these slabs standing before them had beautiful, ornate carvings in relief of different animals. Each pillar had a wider cross-section on top giving them a T-shape. 'A lion,' shouted one of the disciples, pointing like an excited child at the three-dimensional figure protruding from the side of a monolith.

Kline led them around the walkway to the other end of the circle. 'The earliest and greatest enclosure of them all,' he announced pointing at the two huge flat pillars within a stone circle and in pride of place, an altar.

Two women flung a rope ladder over the rail, secured it and waited for the guru to be the first to climb down.

Chapter Eighty-Six

The young archaeologist gave Ella a knowing smile. 'We always thought that in 9500 BC we were hunter gatherers. Before farming, before the wheel.' He lifted his hands off his lap. 'But then, here we have people who must have come together in vast numbers to build this place. Such organisation. And use tools in the most intricate way.' He seemed to be studying Ella. He hesitated, then said, 'Would you like to see some pictures?' He was already opening his case.

'Yes please,' said Ella as they all crowded around the table.

He took out an A4-size album, gave the table a cursory wipe with his hand and opened it up. 'This is the main excavation site,' he said pointing to a photo of a circular pit containing several stone circles with a series of T-shaped stone pillars. The monoliths had the most extraordinary, three-dimensional stone carvings protruding from the side.

Ella stared in awe at the intricacy.

'That looks like a dodo,' said Jay pointing to the carving on one of the upstanding stones. 'But they've never existed outside Mauritius.'

The young Turk revelled in the wonder of his guests. 'There are many unanswered questions about Göbekli Tepe.'

Ella felt her heart beating faster. 'Everything is in perfect condition. I don't understand it.'

He gave her a knowing smile. 'The site was used for a thousand years then deliberately buried under a huge pile of stones. Protected all these years.'

'Like a marker in time,' said Broady. 'A time-capsule.'

The man nodded then turned the pages until he found a large photograph. 'The greatest mysteries are in the oldest enclosure, D. They even used plaster in 9500 BC. What we don't understand is why the older circles are more impressive than the newer ones. If you look at other circles, Stonehenge for example, the earliest evidence is of wooden post holes, and then they move on to more permanent structures, here it's the other way around.'

'They were forgetting the old cycle, their building skills,' said Ella, glancing excitedly at Broady.

'Old cycle?' the young man asked, regarding Ella with some confusion.

They could see that of all the rings, Enclosure D was the most impressive. Huge slabs in a perfect circle with two massive stones in the centre facing each other, each several metres high. Even the ground around the stones had a smooth floor like modern concrete.

'Foxes,' said Broady, pointing to the depictions on the central columns. 'Their tails have signified comets throughout history.'

'And check that out,' said Jay pointing to a monolith on the outer ring covered in more carvings than any other.

'Ah yes,' said the young archaeologist 'Pillar 43. The most intriguing of all the stones. People call it the Vulture Stone.'

The side of the T-shaped pillar was covered in ornate relief carvings, with various animals depicted in the central area. A scorpion was clearly visible on the lower section and a bird-like creature in the centre was indeed a vulture. Above its wing was what appeared to be a perfect circle.

'What does that represent?' said Lizzie pointing to the disc.

'We think it's a severed head,' he replied.

Broady looked mesmerised.

'There's something about their positions on the pillar,' said Ella. 'It's so deliberate, the way they relate to each other.'

'Totally,' said Jay. 'It's telling us something.'

'It's a date,' said Broady slowly tilting his head. 'The first dot.'

The young man looked puzzled.

'That's not a severed head,' suggested Broady. 'It's the sun's position in the sky in relation to the other carvings – the constellations.'

They all looked at the pillar anew.

'The scorpion is Scorpio.'

Lizzie stared at the scorpion. 'I didn't think people identified the constellations until about 3000 BC?'

'Nor did I,' said Broady.

'Maybe you are right,' gushed the young man. He pointed to another pillar with a small, round hole in its centre. 'That site hole would have pointed to Deneb in the constellation of Cygnus eleven thousand five hundred years ago, if one takes into account precession.'

'Precession?' said Jay.

'The position of the stars gradually moves over time,' said Broady, moving around the table for a better view of the photograph. 'Deneb is the head of the Northern Cross but some people call it the Swan because it looks like wings. Maybe they saw it as a vulture.

Ella had never seen Broady so enthused.

'Look at that!' he exclaimed pointing to one of the two

larger central columns. Along the longer sides of the pillar were three-dimensional arms clasping the rock, with the hands meeting on the thinner side. On the wedge end was what appeared to be a belt carved in relief with a fox-pelt hanging off it.

Ella peered closer at the detail on the belt. She could make out a cup shape with three prongs inside the semi-circle. 'It's a three-tailed comet, just like the ones in the *Book of Silk*.'

Everyone stared at the pattern.

'Look at the cup,' said Broady. 'That's the bowshock that you get at the front of a comet. They were worshipping comets.'

The young man stared at the historians, his mouth hanging open.

'Göbekli Tepe,' said Ella. 'It's a monument to the comet strike. Rebirth and the beginning of the Holocene.'

'And the animals,' asked Jay. 'From the ark?'

'Maybe,' said Ella, turning the page to find another photo of Enclosure D, taken from a different angle. To their astonishment, something else came into view.

Between two of the outer stones was a smooth, flat, stone altar.

Ella felt a shiver down her spine. 'This is the place.'

Broady nodded. 'We need to go.'

'Oh, I'm afraid it doesn't open until eight,' the man said, fingering the pens in his shirt pocket.

'No,' stuttered Ella, 'I meant the airport.'

'I see,' the man replied.

'Lovely to meet you,' said Ella before striding off towards the Škoda where Badil was putting the finishing touches to a tape job over the bullet holes whilst the attendant filled the tank.

She handed the petrol guy some lira and watched him wipe his free hand on his overalls before taking the notes.

They all piled back into the car and waited for Badil. Before he had even put the key in the ignition, Ella asked to use his phone again. He handed it over. As they pulled out, she said, 'You need to go back the other way.'

Badil gave her a look. 'Not Abraham Cave?'

'No,' she replied, typing the words into a text to Harris. 'Göbekli Tepe.'

Chapter Eighty-Seven

The last man came down into the pit with Sarah draped over one shoulder. He dumped her on the stone floor of Enclosure D whilst the others set up some free-standing torches. The pristine condition of the place belied its antiquity.

Kline ran his hand over the carving of the comet belt on the thinner edge of one of the two central T-shaped monoliths inside the stone circle. 'This is the spot,' he said in a kind of manic enthusiasm. 'The birth of religion, modern civilisation.' He swaggered over to the altar and sat on it. 'They all harnessed the power,' he said, facing his believers. 'Alexander, Atilla, Khan, William, Napoleon. Now it is my turn.' He got up again and walked across to the outer stone with a site hole. The view of the constellations was blocked by the rubble surrounding the pit. 'Deneb is in alignment with our comet.' He patted the defunct stone. 'It's time.'

Kline produced a flick knife from his pocket and opened the blade, then sauntered over to where Sarah was curled up on the floor. He bent down and took the gag out of her mouth. He moved his head to the side in a gesture of sympathy for his captive. 'This is a great thing you are doing – a tool for change.' He used the knife to cut through her bindings. 'Please, David, I don't understand,' she pleaded, the American accent incongruous with the surroundings. 'Please let me go.'

He gave an almost apologetic smile. He handed the knife to the nearest man. 'Strip her and place her on the altar.'

'No, please,' she whimpered.

After a brief hesitation, the disciple bent down and began to cut through her t-shirt.

Kline covered his face with his scarf and the others followed his lead. Then they busied themselves arranging placards in an Arabic script around the altar.

A woman fixed the camera to a tripod.

Chapter Eighty-Eight

B adil drove them back up the highway towards the sign then turned off up the road. In the distance Ella could just make out the looming shadows of hills and mountains. There were no lights anywhere.

Ten minutes later the headlights illuminated a left turn winding up a mountain with rocks and debris on either side.

Ella's mind was in overdrive, thinking through all the permutations of what might be waiting for them at the top. Her heart raced as they drove on up into the sky.

The road began to level out as they reached a car park with a small hut and a brand-new building off to the left. The complex seemed out of place after the emptiness of their journey up.

'What's that?' said Broady, pointing to a Turkish food lorry parked in one of the bays.

Ella gulped and turned around in her seat. 'I think it's best if you two stay here.'

Lizzie shot her a look. 'Too late for all that.' She opened the door and was the first to get out. Badil followed them, swinging his AK47 over his shoulder. Ella saw it, glanced at her daughter, then decided against saying anything. It was impossible not to be gripped by the sky above, their elevation providing a panoramic view of the constellations. The whole of the heavens was twinkling.

The place was quiet apart from the sound of cicadas and the distant barking of a dog.

They followed the path up towards another hut. 'There's the comet,' said Broady pointing up towards the summit. 'And there's Deneb, just behind. The tip of the Northern Cross.'

They reached the turnstiles and, after an anxious exchange of glances in the starlight, they climbed over. They could see lights moving, coming from the top of Pot-belly Hill.

'Torches,' Broady whispered.

Ella put a finger to her lips. Her heart was pounding as they crept up the newly laid path towards the source of the light. She could make out a roof, standing on girders. A stairway led up to an open walkway that circled a pit from where the beams of light were emanating. On all fours, they silently manoeuvred their way up the steps onto the wooden walkway then slithered on their bellies to the balustrade. The lights were coming from the furthest section.

They moved back from the rail and crawled their way around using their elbows to pull themselves along until a stone circle became visible, lit up like a beacon in a sea of darkness. The two pillars facing each other in the centre stood out. They could see the comet belt on the thin end, gripped by hands and arms, carved in relief along the longer sides of the pillar. It was Enclosure D.

As they peeked over the edge, a dozen or so people came into view, dressed like jihadis, all busily arranging placards around something. Ella squinted to see. Her heart pumped faster. The altar.

One man seemed to be in charge, barking orders in

English at someone adjusting a tripod. The whole thing looked like a film set.

'That's Kline's voice,' mouthed Lizzie, raising herself up on her elbows.

'It's a set up,' whispered Broady. He moved his head, straining to see one of the placards. 'It's in Farsi. They're trying to fit up the Iranians.'

'For what?' Ella whispered back, able to discern Broady's features now her eyes had adjusted. She caught a glimpse of the astonishment on Badil's face, glued to the spectacle unfolding.

Two of the jihadis bent down and lifted something heavy off the ground. A female voice, whimpering followed by a weak scream. 'Please,' the voice protested. A woman in her underwear was being laid down lengthways on the altar.

'Oh my God,' whispered Lizzie. 'It's Sarah Hart.'

Ella shuddered.

One of the masked men pulled a long knife out of its scabbard and handed it to Kline, who was now standing over Sarah's body, splayed out on the stone surface. 'Hold her tightly,' he ordered his subordinates.

The animal carvings took on a macabre essence, the expressions magnified by their shadowy illumination in the torchlight. The starlight around the sides of the roof added to the surrealness of what they were seeing.

Kline glanced over at the cameraman. 'Turn it on.'

Sarah's ribcage heaved up and down as she struggled in vain to break free. Her frantic pleas echoed off the stones.

Badil had moved back from the rail and crept along the walkway to get behind them.

I can't stand by and watch this,' said Broady, beginning to get up.

Jay put a hand on the middle of Broady's back and

pushed him back down. 'You haven't got a weapon, they'll kill you.'

'I have,' said Ella getting to her feet.

Broady gave her a quizzical look.

'My advocacy,' she said with supreme confidence. 'This is insane,' she shouted, her voice bouncing off the metal roof giving it an added resonance. 'You're not killers,' she said directing her observations at Kline's henchmen.

Kline flinched, then put his free hand above his forehead like a visor. 'Ella Blake?' He let out a demonic laugh. 'What a good student you are.'

Some of the disciples pointed their weapons at her.

'I thought you *understood* Genesis?' she shouted across the pit. 'You've studied the pattern. We need to break the cycle of violence, not perpetuate it. We should be seeking unity, dialogue.'

'But nobody listens,' shouted Kline dismissively from the pit.

'Or cares,' shouted one of his followers. 'The Amazon is burning.'

'Species are dying,' said a male voice.

Broady got up and stood side by side with Ella, as did Jay and then Lizzie. 'You want more division to divert us from the right course?' shouted Ella.

'Rebirth is the only way to effect change,' bellowed Kline. Holding the knife with both hands he raised it in front of his body with the tip pointing down towards Sarah's abdomen. 'Kill them,' he said.

'Like you killed Greg?' said Ella. She leaned over the balustrade. 'The trouble with cults is there is only ever one voice. Proper debate requires two people.' The attention of the armed disciples moved from the intruders to Kline and then back. 'This is how the last cycle ended,' Ella said. 'Plato said the people of Atlantis were consumed by war and greed.'

'God spoke to Noah, the man who built this place you're desecrating,' shouted Broady, his voice bouncing off the stones. 'Genesis, Chapter Six, Verse Thirteen: *Then God said to Noah, the end of all living creatures has come before me, because through them the earth is full of violence.*'

'Attila, Alexander, William the Conqueror, Napoleon,' said Ella, desperate to keep the dialogue going. 'None of them made a difference. They were driven by their egos, like him,' she said, pointing an accusing finger at the man stood at the altar. 'The people that brought the greatest change chose another path – they were against any form of violence.'

'Jesus Christ for one,' said Broady.

'I was chosen, destined to lead,' Kline roared. 'Born under the power of Halley's Comet in 1986.'

'No David, that's just wishful thinking,' Ella said in a controlled, patronising tone. 'If anyone was chosen it was Matthew Shepherd. He was born on the 11th April when the comet was nearest the earth.' She let out a scornful laugh. 'You were born on the 6th January. Halley's Comet wasn't even in our solar system until February.'

Kline's disciples looked to him as if waiting for a response.

He faltered. 'Kill them,' was his only answer.

Jay and Broady moved in front of Lizzie, trying to shield her.

'Don't do it,' shouted Ella. 'Man's greatest strength is free will. Our ability to choose, to change. Don't let Kline take that from you.'

The man nearest Kline hesitated then slowly lowered his weapon. Others quickly followed.

Kline sneered then raised the knife above his head, ready to plunge.

'Don't move or you die.' It was Badil. He had climbed down into the pit to the edge of the circle. The nozzle of his gun was pointing at Kline through the site hole, his body protected by the rest of the monolith.

Ella heard the sound of a gun being cocked immediately behind her.

'No, your friends die.' It was Stone, pushing a sidearm into the back of Ella's head. She turned her head a fraction to see that his goons were in similar positions behind the others on the walkway. 'Do it, Kline,' Stone commanded.

The great leader plunged the knife towards Sarah's abdomen.

A gun fired. Kline staggered backwards, a bullet through his stomach. His arms went limp.

Stone and his men twisted around. Behind them, Harris and Grant were standing, firearms drawn, smoke still coming off Harris' gun. Before Stone had time to take aim, Harris fired again. Stone dropped to the ground. At the same time, Grant took out the others, all hitting the floor like ragdolls.

Ella and the others stood frozen to the spot as they watched a troop of Turkish soldiers take orders from Harris and then file off in two lines around the walkway, pointing their weapons at the disciples, who dropped their guns and pulled off their scarves, revealing their faces. Ella was shocked to see that most were no older than Lizzie.

Badil dropped his weapon and walked across the stone floor of the circle towards the altar. He ripped a scarf from one of the men and placed it carefully over Sarah's bare flesh before lifting her off the slab and carrying her in his arms.

She wrapped her hands around his neck and sobbed into his chest.

Ella stepped over Stone's body, pulled Lizzie to her and gripped her with all her might.

Seemingly unperturbed by what had just unfolded, Harris came over to Ella, ran a hand along the rail and leaned over, taking in the stone circle of Enclosure D. 'Göbekli Tepe?' she asked, stumbling over the pronunciation. 'What the hell is this place?'

Ella followed her eyes down to the altar and the carved slabs, standing proudly in the torchlight. 'It's the world's first temple.'

Epilogue

Cambridge was at its glorious best. Spring was on the turn. The sun reflected off the silver and golden stone of the colleges, accentuating their timeless splendour.

Ella, Lizzie and Jay skipped up the steps into the arched entrance to De Jure.

Bartlett was leaning against the doorframe of the gate-house, munching on a piece of shortbread. 'Ah, the wanderers return,' he said, half-raising an eyebrow as he flicked a few stray crumbs off his shirt. 'You've caused quite a stir,' he said, tipping his head towards the quadrangle. 'So many journalists, we've had to put up a marquee.'

Ella looked at the enormous white tent that covered the lawned courtyard. It was full of TV crews and photographers, all jostling for position.

'Where's the Yank?' Bartlett asked.

Ella's cheery countenance wavered. 'He went home.'

'Nice fella,' Bartlett replied. 'Shall we?' He held out his elbow.

Ella laughed and put her arm through his.

Bartlett puffed out his chest, lifted his chin and in a regal walk, escorted her to the marquee's side entrance.

Master Desmond was waiting for her at the side of the stage like an excited puppy. 'Ella!' he gushed. 'Lizzie, Jay, can I call you that?' He didn't wait for a reply. 'This is a momentous day for De Jure.'

Ella smiled.

He calmed himself down, then said, deadly serious: 'Words are not enough.' He dipped his head to emphasise the point. 'De Jure is in your debt.'

'No,' she replied, totally at peace. 'I'm in yours.' She felt herself welling up.

Someone tapped Desmond on the shoulder. 'It's time.'

Desmond took a deep breath and readied himself for his great entrance.

'Hey, blue eyes…'

Ella would know that voice anywhere. She swung around. 'Hank!'

He gave her a sheepish grin.

'I thought you were in Arizona?'

'How could I miss the big reveal?' he said. 'And besides, I never got to see the Old Observatory.'

Ella flung her arms around his neck and planted a lingering kiss on his cheek, holding on to the embrace as if he were a raft in a stormy sea.

'Wow,' he said, winking at Lizzie over Ella's arm. 'This isn't the Ella Blake I know.'

She let go and held his gaze. 'She's gone. Thought it was about time I started a new cycle.'

Broady laughed. 'I was kind of thinking the same thing.'

'Ladies and gentlemen,' announced Master Desmond. 'Welcome to De Jure.' He looked down at his notes on the lectern. 'Thank you all for coming today for the announcement of the most important discovery of our time.'

The buzz around the room intensified. 'A theory that goes to the very core of our humanity. We are honoured to have someone very special here today to tell you more.'

'By the way,' said Broady with a mischievous grin. I've been meaning to ask; how come you knew all that stuff about Halley's Comet and Kline's birthday?'

Ella smiled. 'It's the first thing they teach you at Bar School.'

He looked confused. 'What is?'

'Please put your hands together for Ella Blake QC.'

'Know your opponent,' she replied before walking up onto the podium.

Ella waited for the applause to peter out. 'A great polymath, who you've probably never heard of, called Matthew Shepherd understood the difference between two of the greatest reasons for learning anything – knowledge and enlightenment.' She paused. 'He realised the pattern of the world, the ebbing and flowing of our inhumanity to man. He wanted to find a common denominator that unites us all… To help us find a new beginning so that we can work together to save this planet. I was never fortunate enough to meet him but I think he would have approved of the words of another former member of this great university, almost four hundred years ago.' She glanced at Broady, watching from the wings. 'Isaac Newton once said: *Truth is ever to be found in simplicity, and not in the multiplicity and confusion of things. If I have seen further than others, it is by standing on the shoulders of others. We build too many walls and not enough bridges.*'

She nodded to Desmond who, on cue, pressed a button causing dots and swirls to appear on a big screen behind the stage.

The audience was transfixed.

'This is the story of how we lost our way.' She waved an arm at the screen. 'This is the story of Genesis.'

Note from the Author

February 2019, 4 a.m. The alarm on my phone echoed off the rendered walls of my hotel room, jolting me awake. I wanted to see the stars from the top of the mountain before the sun came up, just as our ancestors had done. I'd heard about Göbekli Tepe but had to see it for myself. Eleven thousand, five hundred years old, some kind of temple that seemed to have been inexplicably and deliberately preserved in a mound of thousands of rocks ten millennia before. Monoliths with great carvings in relief – lions, scorpions and ducks that looked like dodos. It changed everything I thought I knew about prehistory.

Still groggy from the flights, the first to Istanbul, then a delayed internal to Sanliurfa, I set off from the hotel in my temperamental hire car and headed out of town through the checkpoint that had a system of cones to create a chicane. Was I really doing this? Why did it matter to me so much?

The car made it up to the top of the mountain and I stopped in an empty car park. There was no one around. I'd expected security guards, especially at night. Surely it couldn't be as important as some were saying?

Lost in time, I watched the constellations fade as morning began to break. At last, a few workers arrived to let me through to the site itself. I hurried up the path, past the new excavations off to my left and towards the circular walkway I'd heard so much about.

I'd finally made it. Leaning over the balustrade, I impatiently scanned the stone circles in the pit below until I saw what I was looking for. In all its mysterious splendour, Enclosure D. I moved around the walkway and fixed on the intricate, Pillar 43, the Vulture Stone. And off to the side, there it was, the altar.

A moment I shall never forget.

Why wasn't the world shouting about this place? Seven thousand years older than Stonehenge. It didn't make sense.

And then I realised. An inevitable part of learning is forgetting. This book is about remembering.

Olly Jarvis
June 2021

Acknowledgments

First and foremost, to Rebecca Collins and Adrian Hobart of Hobeck Books for all their tireless work in publishing this book. I thank them for seeing beyond the usual genres and for understanding so perfectly what I was trying to say with this novel.

My thanks to Victoria Blunden for an early edit and some straight talking. And to Vanessa O'Loughlin for some valuable advice.

Much gratitude to all my friends and family for their support and understanding whilst I was obsessively writing this novel. Special thanks to my daughter, Amber, and my son, Ben, for their inspiration and for sharing the optimism and enthusiasm of youth. Your breath is in these pages.

All the people I came across, whether in Cambridge or Sanliurfa, too many to name here, thank you for making my journey so memorable.

A humble acknowledgement to all the great thinkers and scholars through time, each sewing a stitch in the great tapestry of our shared history.

And finally, an acknowledgement to my wife, Kelly, not just for reading drafts along the way, but for always believing.

About the Author

Olly Jarvis is a thriller writer and practising criminal defence barrister.

His first book, *Death By Dangerous* was longlisted for the CWA Debut Dagger in 2016. He subsequently wrote *Cut-Throat Defence* and *Unconvicted*, a two book series featuring a young barrister, Jack Kowalski.

He wrote and presented a documentary short on location in Sumatra for BBC Radio 4 about tribal law and a crime drama, *Judgement*, exploring a barrister's thought processes when defending in a rape trial.

He is also the founder and presenter on thecrimehub.com. Launched in 2019, the site is about all things crime – both fact and fiction. He hosts interview podcasts with crime writers and people who work in the criminal justice system. He also produces solo voice monologues with leading writers and actors.

He tweets from @ollyjarviso and @crimehubsite.

Hobeck Advanced Reader Team

Hobeck Books has a team of dedicated advanced readers who read our books before publication (not all of them, they choose which they would like to read). Here is what a selection of them said about *The Genesis Inquiry*.

'I found myself having to read just one more chapter before I could go to sleep!'

'...will keep you hooked...'

'...fast moving and exciting.'

Hobeck Books - the home of great stories

Hobeck Books is an independent publisher of crime, thrillers and suspense fiction and we have one aim – to bring you the books you want to read.

For more details about our books, our authors, including Olly Jarvis, and our plans, and the chance to enter competitions, plus to download *Crime Bites*, a free compilation of novellas and short stories by our authors, please sign up for our newsletter at **www.hobeck.net**.

You can also find us on Twitter **@hobeckbooks** or on Facebook **www.facebook.com/hobeckbooks10**.

Hobeck Books also presents a weekly podcast, the Hobcast, where founders Adrian Hobart and Rebecca Collins discuss all things book related, key issues from each week, including the ups and downs of running a creative business. Each episode includes an interview with one of the people who make Hobeck possible: the editors, the authors, the cover designers. These are the people who help Hobeck bring great stories to life. Without them, Hobeck wouldn't exist. The Hobcast can be listened to from all the usual platforms but it can also be found on the Hobeck website: **www.hobeck.net/hobcast**.

Finally, if you enjoyed this book, please also leave a review on the site you bought it from and spread the word. Reviews are hugely important to writers and they help other readers also.

Other Hobeck Books to Explore

The Rock Crime Series by Robert Daws

The Rock

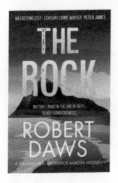

DS Tamara Sullivan, fighting to save her career is exiled to Gibraltar from London's Metropolitan Police after a lapse of judgement.

But this is no sleepy siesta of a posting on the Mediterranean. Paired with her new boss, DCI Gus Broderick, Sullivan will need all her skills to survive the most dangerous case of her career.

Poisoned Rock

As the bright lights of a Hollywood movie production shine into the dark recesses of Gibraltar, murky secrets emerge from the shadows of the Rock's past.

It seems the legacy of wartime spying, sabotage and treachery runs deep on the Rock.

Past and present collide plunging detectives Tamara Sullivan and Gus Broderick into a tangled web of intrigue and murder, and their skills and uneasy working relationship are about to be tested to the limit.

Killing Rock

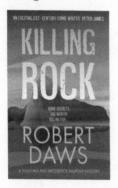

A wealthy household massacred in Spain. Unidentified mummified remains found at the foot of the Rock. A US Congressman's run for president hangs on events in Gibraltar. What's the connection?

Detectives Tamara Sullivan and Gus Broderick face the most dangerous and elusive murder investigation of their lives, and for Broderick, it's about to become all too personal, with his career in real peril as his past comes back to haunt him.

Will Sullivan and Broderick's partnership survive this latest case, as killers stalk the narrow streets of Gibraltar?

The Merseyside Crime Series by Malcolm Hollingdrake

Catch as Catch Can

A mutilated body apparently washed up on a windswept beach. A violent criminal gang preys on moped riders across the area. A teenage girl is desperate to escape sexual exploitation.

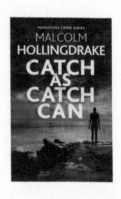

It's a tough introduction to Merseyside for Detective Inspector April Decent, who's just arrived from her native Yorkshire. Together with new colleague Skeeter Warlock, Decent quickly discovers there's a sinister link between them all, one that will bring them face-to-face with some uncomfortable home truths.

Syn

An everyday Friday night out. A few too many drinks. A few harsh words said. No one was hurt. All easily forgotten.

Except he didn't forget. Their threats. How they made him *feel*. They must pay – with their lives.

A young woman goes missing. She's done it before, but Detective Inspector April Decent senses this time it's serious. Can she convince her colleagues she's right before it's too late?

The Clifford-Mackenzie Crime Series by R.D. Nixon

Crossfire

Hogmanay 1987 and a prank robbery has fatal consequences. Five years later and the Highlands town Abergarry is shaken by the seemingly gratuitous murder of a local man. The case is unsolved.

Now in the present and ten-year-old Jamie, while on holiday in Abergarry with his mum Charis, overhears a conversation. To him, it is all part of a game. But this is no game and the consequences are far more serious than Jamie ever imagined.

Struggling PI team Maddy Clifford and Paul Mackenzie find themselves involved by a chance meeting. How deep into those wounds will they have to delve to unravel the mystery?

The Jane Haven Thriller Series by Antony Dunford

Hunted

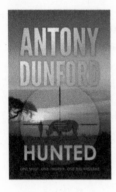

Once a member of the world's first all-female special forces unit, the Norwegian Hunter Troop, Jane Haven is now helping her brother Kennet protect some of the world's most endangered animals at his Kenyan Wildlife Conservancy.

Drawn away from her vigil protecting Douglas, the world's last remaining male Northern White rhino, Jane returns to find a scene of devastation and murder.

Everything and everyone Jane cares for is affected.

But before she can track down the killers, Jane finds that she's the one being hunted.

The Betancourt Crime Series by Mark Wightman

Waking the Tiger

Longlisted for the Bloody Scotland McIlvanney Crime Novel of 2021 and shortlisted for the Crime Debut of 2021, Mark Wightman's *Waking the Tiger* is historic crime fiction at its best.

Singapore, 1939 and a young Japanese woman is found dead on the dockside, her throat slashed. A distinctive tiger tattoo is the only clue to her identity.

Inspector Maximo Betancourt is working a new beat, one

he didn't ask for. Following the disappearance of his wife, his life and career have fallen apart.

Once a rising star of Singapore CID, Betancourt has been relegated to the Marine Division, with tedious dockyard disputes and goods inspections among his new duties.

But when a beautiful, unidentified Japanese woman is found murdered in the shadow of a warehouse owned by one of Singapore's most powerful families, Betancourt defies orders and pursues those responsible. What he discovers will bring him into conflict with powerful enemies, and force him to face his personal demons.